RANDY SINGER

A NOVEL

SELF INCRIMINATION

WATERBROOK
PRESS

SELF INCRIMINATION
PUBLISHED BY WATERBROOK PRESS
12265 Oracle Blvd., Suite 200
Colorado Springs, Colorado 80921
A division of Random House, Inc.

Scriptures quoted or paraphrased are taken from the *New King James Version.* Copyright © 1982 by Thomas Nelson Inc. Used by permission. All rights reserved.

ISBN 0-7394-6083-8

Printed in the United States of America

PROLOGUE

By 10:00 p.m., Trish Bannister was worried sick.

It was Friday, so she didn't expect him right after work. If he made it by seven or eight, the night would be tolerable. Nine o'clock would mean he had broken his promise and had been drinking. There would be shouting and cursing, but nothing physical. But it was now ten. It had been two months since James had been this late on a Friday. It would be ugly.

For a moment she pondered the irony of it. Her husband picks Good Friday to come home drunk. The day of the Crucifixion, the suffering of Christ. Why do they call it *Good* Friday anyway?

Dinner was beyond cold. She would pop it in the microwave as soon as she heard his car, but the steak would still be dry and the rolls would be too hot. Two months ago she had used the microwave, and he had backhanded the plate across their formal dining room table. She scrubbed the carpet for half an hour. He stood over her, pointing out spots she had missed.

The next day she almost left.

She stayed for the kids. And she stayed because she wanted to believe his promises. No more drinking. He would get counseling. Things would change as soon as he could pull the company out of its nosedive.

The company. She remembered the banquet a few weeks ago, how the booze had flowed like water but James had never touched a drop. She remembered how she felt when it was his turn at the mike. He paused, choked back the tears, then thanked her for being his strength.

She stayed because there were some things worth fighting for.

She paced the front foyer, nibbling at the fingernail on her right thumb, oblivious to the extravagance she called home. She stood in the midst of carved white pillars on a marble floor. From her position next to the front door, she could see most of the first floor, every spacious room flowing into every other room. The family room opened to a cut-stone patio and an Olympic-sized pool.

She glanced again out the front windows to the circular drive. No sign of James and his Town Car. No sign of sixteen-year-old Tara and her Explorer. She prayed that Tara would get home before James. After all, Tara was supposed to be grounded. But Tara had left earlier in a huff, after Trish had nagged her about her progress report. Trish couldn't stop the kid. She was sixteen years old and strong willed. Trish would deal with Tara tomorrow.

"Jamie, turn it down!" Trish yelled toward the general direction of her eleven-year-old's room. There was no chance he would hear. She glanced again out the front window, then hurried up the steps.

She pounded on his locked door. "C'mon, honey. Dad'll be home soon." No response. *"Turn it down! Now!"* The volume lowered to a softer roar. But the carpet in the hallway still vibrated with every beat of the bass. Trish rubbed her forehead. The pressure was building, the migraine forming.

Jamie's progress report had been the only bright spot this week. A fifth grader, he had been diagnosed with Tourette's syndrome and attention deficit disorder less than two years ago. At times, despite heavy doses of Ritalin, clonidine, and haloperidol, Jamie was hard to control. But his teacher was understanding, and his classmates were, for the most part, accepting of him. Unlike Tara, Jamie was at least trying.

Trish walked quickly to the master bathroom, listening for the sound of car engines. She opened the top drawer under her sink, found her migraine prescriptions, and popped two Fiorinal tablets and two Imitrex. She stopped and stared at her reflection. The lines on her face ran deep, creeping farther each day from the corners of hollow eyes.

Too late she heard the sound of wheels on asphalt. If it was James, she would not be at the door to greet him. There would be no time to slide his plate into the microwave before he entered.

She heard heavy footsteps on the front porch. A man's footsteps. James was home.

And dinner was stone cold.

She made it to the top of the foyer steps just as he entered. He closed the door and stood in the foyer, teetering back and forth, shifting from one leg to the other.

The red eyes, the storm that darkened his face. Even before the stench of stale liquor permeated the foyer, she knew.

"Hey honey," she said, trying to sound light and casual. She descended the steps and greeted him with a quick kiss. There were no fists, but she could sense the rage.

"Where's dinner?" The words came out thick and menacing. His shocks of wavy black hair, full of styling gel, were smeared haphazardly about his head. His tie hung loose around his neck, not even knotted. But for the custom suit, he looked like a homeless person, not the CEO of a cell phone company.

"In the kitchen," Trish said, taking one step back. "Let me go heat it up real quick."

"Where're Tara and Jamie?" he asked as he followed her toward the kitchen.

"Jamie's upstairs. Tara's out."

"I thought she was grounded," James mumbled. "Any calls today, Patricia?"

Trish froze. Denying it only made things worse. *Keep moving,* she told herself. *Act natural.* She put his plate in the microwave. He leaned against the island counter in the middle of the kitchen and stared at her, studied her…unnerved her.

"How was work?" Trish asked, trying to change the subject.

He snorted, as if the question didn't deserve an answer. "Same as always."

She pulled the plate from the microwave and placed it on the kitchen table. James threw his coat on the sofa in the living room and sat at the table. Trish dutifully took her spot at the other end, her mind racing with thoughts of Tara. If she came home now, with James acting this way, there would be war.

"Did you already eat?" he asked.

"I'm not hungry."

For a few moments James ate in stony silence. She watched warily, looking for signs of an eruption. Thankfully, he hadn't taken umbrage about the microwaved meal. At least that was something. Maybe she would survive the night with minimal damage. Each bite that he took, each minute that passed without further incident raised her hopes ever so slightly.

Why did she live like this? Why didn't she just leave? How many times could she watch him come home drunk one night, then beg forgiveness the next day, showering her with attention and gifts?

She sat there conflicted, torn between survival instincts—just make it through the night—and her desire to confront James for his own good, if nothing else. She took a deep breath and faced into her responsibilities. She was tired of playing the victim.

"What about your promises?" she asked, her voice quivering in the silence. "Is this how much you care about your family?"

James looked up from his food with disdain. She returned the look without flinching, proud of her stance but dreading the price she might pay. She relaxed ever so slightly as he lowered his defiant gaze to his plate and ate in silence.

Less than a minute later the phone rang. It startled Trish, and she rose quickly to get it.

"Sit down," James barked, glaring at her with dark, liquid eyes.

He rose slowly and checked the caller ID. Trish knew from the look on his face that it was another random calling card number.

He picked up the phone anyway. "Who is this?"

Trish sat there, not daring to breathe. She prayed for another phrase from her husband, anything to indicate the person on the other end had spoken. But her husband was silent, the phone to his ear, the blood rushing to his face. After an unbearable pause, he returned the phone to the cradle with exaggerated patience. Trish felt the wind leave her lungs. As usual, the caller had hung up without saying a word.

"Lover boy must have thought I'd be home a little late tonight," James whispered.

He stood by the phone, looking her over. "Oh, I know," he mocked. "It's just some prank caller. Probably dialed our number at random."

Trish stared at the table.

"Who is he?"

"I don't know! Honest, I don't."

"You're lying."

Trish put her hands against the table and slid her chair back, standing quickly and turning away from James. "I'm not talking to you when you're like this."

But he was on her in a flash, grabbing her arm and jerking her back toward him. He unleashed a violent backhand across her face. Then, perhaps stunned by the violence of his own blow, he let go of her arm.

Trish tasted the blood and slowly raised her hand to her mouth to rub the lip and assess the damage. This time she looked him in the eye.

"You disgust me," she said.

She turned to walk away, heading toward the family room and the back steps.

"*Don't* turn your back on me," he snapped.

But Trish kept walking.

She took only four steps before he grabbed her again, squeezing her slender bicep and twisting her toward him. He tossed her like a rag doll up against the wall, knocking over a floor lamp. The light bulb shattered on the carpet.

"Don't ever try to hide things from me," he said. "You think the old man's a fool?" He squeezed her arm with viselike force, and Trish raised up on her toes. "Who's making these calls? Who's sleeping with my wife?"

"Nobody... I d-don't know." It came out as a whimper. Then, out of the corner of her eye, Trish saw another flash. A backhanded slap blurred her vision. She fell to her knees, then James grabbed her by the arm and jerked her to her feet again.

"No...please...no..." She lifted her right arm to fend off the next blow. But this time there was no blow, only the iron grip of James's thumb and forefinger on her neck. He slammed her head back against the wall with a force that sent a picture crashing to the carpet. "Tell me!" he shouted. He moved up against her, shoving his thumb and forefinger harder against her throat.

Trish flailed her arms, trying to find some leverage, trying to force him away from her. But still he squeezed, using both hands now, choking the air out of her for five seconds, ten seconds, twenty. She tried to plead with him but couldn't speak. He pinned her neck hard against the wall, his face inches away, threatening, smiling, glaring with those hooded eyes. She felt the stale bursts of his putrid breath, his sweaty body sandwiching her against the wall. Things started spinning, going black. Her body went limp, and then, inexplicably, her husband backed away, removing his hands from her throat as she slumped down the wall, gasping for air.

James hovered over her for a moment, his rage riding on every labored breath. "You disgust *me*," he said, mocking her earlier statement. "Now get out of here." Then he turned and headed back toward the kitchen. He took his seat at the table and began calmly cutting his steak.

Trish squatted there on the floor, trembling, until the room stopped spinning. She ran her tongue against the inside of her left cheek, felt the swelling, and winced. She rose slowly and deliberately, glanced at her husband, then climbed the back steps to her bedroom.

"Patricia."

She froze on the top step, her hand trembling on the doorknob to her bedroom. James was still in the kitchen, but there was no mistaking the tone in his voice.

"Wear something nice."

Without answering, she went through the bedroom and into the master bathroom, where she gingerly washed her face. She sobbed as she put on her pajamas. She turned out the lights, crawled into bed, and waited in petrified silence with the covers pulled up to her chin. She stared at the ceiling, her vision blurred from the swelling and tears, the pain throbbing in her cheek, and her head splitting despite the medication she had taken earlier. She prayed that Tara would come home late. She prayed James would pass out watching television. Twice she thought she heard the stairs squeak, and her heart froze midbeat, the bile rising in her throat. This would be the most humiliating part of all, far worse than the beatings. Her bedroom was no safe place.

She waited, not daring to breathe. But James didn't come.

She listened for tires in the driveway as the minutes marched by slowly, ever so slowly, *ever* so slowly. Twenty minutes crept by, then thirty, with no sound but muffled noises from Jamie's bedroom and the faint echo of the television downstairs. Finally, she mustered the courage to sneak out to the catwalk that overlooked the family room. She saw James passed out in his leather recliner, remote in hand, television blaring. For the first time all night, she felt relief flood her body. She had survived. She would confront him with his behavior in the morning, after he sobered up. He would apologize and promise to change. She would beg him to get counseling. And this time she would leave if he didn't follow through.

She took ten milligrams of Ambien and headed back to bed. Tara was not home yet, but she would come in quietly. You don't make a big scene when you're supposed to be grounded.

Trish would later tell police that the Ambien took less than thirty minutes to work its magic, knocking her out cold. It always brought about a deep sleep, she said, chasing the world's troubles away until dawn.

So deep, in fact, that she never heard the gunshots.

CHAPTER ONE

Forty Days Later

I'm glad he's dead," says the sulking teenager as she slouches lower in the high-backed leather chair on the other side of the conference table. My business card lies untouched in front of her. *Leslie Connors, Attorney-at-Law.*

Those are not the words you want to hear from a new client. Especially when it's your first murder case.

Her name is Tara Bannister. And she comes with an attitude. Sixteen years old. Willowy thin. Short blond hair with platinum highlights. Four earrings on each side. Dark eye shadow surrounding narrow, brown, lifeless eyes. Even her clothes scream, "I don't care!" She wears a spaghetti-strap tank top and frayed jeans that ride low on her hips. She displays so much midriff that at first I can't help but lock my gaze on her pierced navel. With teenage boys, that's probably the whole idea. With a thirty-year-old female lawyer like me, who at the moment is feeling rather ancient, I'm sure Tara couldn't care less.

"I probably wouldn't tell that to a jury," I say.

She shrugs. Her favorite response.

"Tara, I'm just trying to help. But I can't help if you won't let me." I hate it when I sound so much like my mother. One of my goals in life is to avoid becoming her.

Tara shrugs again.

It's time for Tara to taste a dose of reality. I have already talked to her mom. The girl is in serious trouble.

"You're lucky to be out on bond," I say, narrowing my eyes. "This is a most serious charge—the murder of your stepfather." Even as I hear myself talk, it seems surreal. A few months ago, in February, I was studying for the bar exam. Now I'm advising a client charged with first-degree murder. I know her mom came to our firm hoping to hire my senior partner, Brad Carson. To alleviate her concerns, I promised her that Brad would be personally involved, that I was just an associate helping him out. But at this moment, as usual, Brad's in court. For the time being, Tara is my client.

"Your case is currently pending in juvenile and domestic relations court because of your age. But the commonwealth's attorney has requested a transfer to circuit court, where you will be tried as an adult. Because it's first-degree murder, all they have to do is show probable cause and the case gets transferred automatically." I lean forward, elbows on the table, and pause for effect. "If we lose in circuit court, you'll be looking at twenty years to life…not in some juvenile detention center but in the state pen. You might never see or taste freedom again, Tara."

This brings no visible reaction, not even the slightest change of expression. She just stares at me, looking contemptuous. I decide to wait her out.

Finally, she shakes her head and speaks. "I'm scared," she says sarcastically. "Ready to pee my pants. Is that what you want me to say? Is this some kind of scared-straight deal?"

That does it. My Irish temper and red hair go hand in hand. "Tara, this is not a game. You're sixteen years old. This is your life we're talking about. Do you know what those women would do to you in a maximum security joint?" To emphasize my point, I look her over and shake my head. "You'd be their toy." I notice a slight flinch, followed by the stone face. "If you want me to represent you, you've got to trust me. If you want to play games, get somebody else. Your mom's got lots of money; she can hire anyone you want."

I put my pen down on the table, sit back, and cross my arms.

"Why should I trust *you?*" Tara asks. "How many murder cases have *you* tried?"

A fair question. But one I have no intention of answering.

"You trust me because I'm your lawyer," I say. "I'm the only one who stands between you and life behind bars. And I can't represent you unless you're completely honest with me and tell me everything. And furthermore, everything you tell me—everything—is confidential and will stay that way. I will tell nobody, including your mom."

Tara looks back up at me, a devilish glint in her eyes. She smirks, then says, "It's your first one, isn't it?"

Busted.

I nod. Professionally. My eyes never leave hers.

"How did you do in law school?" she asks.

Great. Now I'm being put through a job interview by a sixteen-year-old murder suspect. "Second in my class," I reply with a scowl.

"Who finished first—a man or a woman?"

"A man."

"Then I want you."

I resist the urge to pump my fist or even smile. There is something humiliating about being interviewed by a teenager, even if you're hired. It's time to regain control.

"Will you be 100 percent honest with me?" I ask.

She nods her head.

"Yes?" I want to hear her say the word.

"Yes," she says grudgingly. I am unconvinced.

"And will you follow my instructions to the very letter?"

She nods again. I frown.

"Yes," she says through clenched teeth.

"Good." I pick up my pen and stare past her for a moment. I am about to do what my law school professors warned me against. If Brad were here, he too would dance around this issue. But that's never been my style. I want to know. If my client did the crime, I've got to find out up front. I'll deal with the repercussions later.

The textbook move would be to explain all the legal defenses available to this young girl. If I raise my voice in all the right places, give her a wink and a nod, she'll get the hint. Then I could ask her what happened, and she would tailor her story to fit the proper defense.

But like I said, that's not my style.

"Tell me what happened. Step by step. Starting at the beginning."

She hesitates a moment, looking around the room while she processes the question. It's a habit I'll have to break before she testifies at trial. "I came home from a party about six weeks ago on a Friday night around eleven. My stepdad was wasted." Her eyes lock on the wall behind me as she talks. Her voice is matter-of-fact, like she's describing the weather. "I was supposed to be grounded, so we got into a big argument in the front foyer. I gave him some lip and he hit me." She reaches up and touches her cheek. "Hard. He'd never hit me before, just my mom. I went stomping up to my room. I was scared, but I was also really pissed...um, sorry...ticked off. So then I, like, look at my face in the mirror, and it's already beginning to swell up a little right next to my eye. So I decide to go back down and get some ice to put on it. I took a towel down so I could put the ice in the towel, and I hid my gun under the towel."

"Your gun?" I ask. "Where'd you get the gun?"

She hesitates, looking down at the table. "My bedroom."

"You had a gun in your bedroom?"

"Uh-huh. Kept it under the mattress. Got it a few weeks before that night. You'd have one too if you lived with *him*."

"Where'd you get it?"

"A friend."

I lean forward a little. "Does your friend have a name?"

She pushes some imaginary specks of dust around on the table, trying to decide if she trusts me. "Can't say."

"Can't or won't?"

"Won't."

I decide not to push the point. Later, maybe. But not now. "Okay, what happened next?"

"On my way to the kitchen, I walked past James. I guess I could have waited until he went to bed or something, but I wanted to make a point." Now Tara looks up again—not at me but almost through me, as if she were seeing the events in her mind's eye. "I wasn't going to live in fear of him, tiptoe around him like my mom does. Anyway, when I walked by him, he's like, 'What do you think you're doing?' or something like that. I ignored him; he didn't deserve an answer. Then he, like, jumped up from his chair and grabbed my shoulder and jerked me around. I told him to let go of me and probably called him a bunch of names. He got all belligerent and he's like, 'Nobody talks to me that way.' Then he started choking me with both hands, going berserk on me. I mean, he's practically foaming at the mouth, his eyes are bugging out of his head…"

Tara is breathing hard now, her eyes wide as she relives the horror. "I can't breathe; he's choking the air out of me. I'm like, 'Let go of me,' but nothing's coming out 'cause I can hardly breathe. This whole time I've still got the gun in my hand, under the towel. He's jerking me around the living room, squeezing harder—"

She stops in midsentence, and her eyes refocus on me. It's as if she has finished her trance and snapped back to the present. She exhales deeply and leans back in her chair.

"Then what?" I prompt.

"I pulled the trigger. The first shot hit him in the chest. He let go and fell to one knee. Then he started to get up again, like a scene from one of those horror movies, and I freaked. I shot him again—right in the head. This time he crumpled to the floor and didn't get up. Didn't even move." She stares at me with the coldest brown eyes I have ever seen on a teenager. "And I'm glad."

Then she gives me a sardonic half smile, and the girl suddenly looks much older than sixteen. "But don't worry," she says. "I won't tell that to a jury."

I'm sorry I asked.

CHAPTER TWO

After Tara and her mother leave, I drop off my notes and a client intake sheet with Bella at the reception desk. Bella is the firm's no-nonsense receptionist, bookkeeper, and secretary. She is old, mean, paunchy, and loyal. She has been with Brad from day one. I am one of the few other people on the face of the earth she can stomach. For that, I am grateful.

Ours is a three-person shop. Brad has tried numerous times to hire a paralegal, but Bella always runs them off. His most recent hire, a fireball named Nikki Moreno, probably could have given Bella a run for her money but opted instead for law school. Nikki always thought she knew more than the lawyers anyway. In a few years, she'll have the chance to prove it.

Just to tweak Bella, Nikki will occasionally call and threaten to return as an attorney as soon as she graduates. This will put Bella in a foul mood for the rest of the day.

"Did you get a retainer?" asks Bella in her thick Brooklyn accent. She looks up at me over the top of her reading glasses.

"I was going to discuss that next time," I mumble.

The phone rings. I must be living right. Bella takes the call but holds up her hand and won't let me leave. Bella's tone turns sweet—it must be a plaintiff's case with some value—and she promises the caller that I will call back first thing tomorrow. She hangs up and takes off her specs.

"Let's try this again," she says. "You did get a retainer, didn't ya?"

I shrug my shoulders and give her a half grin. "I refuse to answer on the grounds that it might incriminate me?"

Bella shakes her head. "Do you know who you were meeting with?" she asks. "How much money she has?"

"I refuse to answer that on the basis of attorney-client privilege."

"Leslie," she scolds, "that's just my point. There ain't no attorney-client privilege until you've got a retainer and a signed agreement. Girl, what *were* you thinking?"

"Truthfully…that I was in over my head." I sense she can't resist this display of humility, and I see her expression soften. "What kind of retainer would we normally ask for on a case like that anyway?"

"Well," Bella says, warming to the subject, "considering that you are representing Ms. Tara Bannister on a case of first-degree murder, and considering that Ms. Tara Bannister is the daughter of Mrs. Patricia Bannister, heiress to her husband's estate and insurance policies, which I'm sure are worth several million dollars, and considering that you will be working your fingers to the bone at a time when you would much rather be making wedding plans…" The phone rings again. Bella punches a button and sends the caller who knows where. "I'd say at least seventy-five thousand."

I gulp. Bella chuckles. "You'd better practice asking for big retainers so you don't blush when you say the amount," she advises. "In criminal work, if you don't get it up front, honey, you don't get it."

"I'll remember that," I say. I start to head down the hall and then turn back to Bella's reception desk. I lower my voice to a conspiratorial whisper, even though we're the only ones in the office.

"How's Operation Steeple coming?" I ask. It's the code name we've given to our joint efforts to get Brad's agreement on a church wedding. This will be the second wedding for both Brad and me. Brad's first wife left when he was in law school. Bill, my first husband, died unmercifully young from cancer almost three years ago. Brad wants to keep the ceremony low key. For him that means a justice of the peace—a court wedding with no guests. He says it's only appropriate for two lawyers to be married in court.

But Bella has been working on him. At times she is more insistent than I that this wedding take place in a church. Bella has recently gone through a radical spiritual conversion. I've seen the change. From a chain-smoking cynic who was mad at the world to a chain-smoking born-againer (who swears she's trying to quit). Bella doesn't realize it, but I'm keeping my eye on her. So far, she's the best reason I've encountered to give religion another chance.

"I've been naggin' him all week," she says proudly. "Droppin' hints about what women like at their weddings." Then she winks. "Act surprised tonight."

I reach down and give her a hug. She pretends to be put off, but I notice a little smile. Bella doesn't fool me.

"Thanks," I say. "And would you mind calling Ms. Bannister and telling her about that retainer."

"Thought you'd never ask," says Bella. She's already punching numbers.

CHAPTER THREE

I check my watch again and glance around the food court. Brad, as usual, is late. I'm a stickler for being on time. I set my watch ahead five minutes and then try to fool myself into thinking it's not really fast. So why am I getting married to a man who's never been on time in his life? Brad seems to operate outside the strictures of normal time zones. "Bradley Standard Time," I call it. Whatever it is, it drives me crazy.

I skipped a workout at the gym to get here on time. Actually I was looking for a reason to avoid the StairMaster, and this was as good as any. My workouts have been a real struggle lately. I chalk it up to all the stress I'm under. I've been blessed with long legs and five feet eight inches of height. But I'm also a size 6 determined to wear a size 4 wedding dress. And I'm no natural athlete—I'd much rather read than sweat. Still, right now, I'm blaming Brad for making me miss my workout, as if I would have hit the gym with a passion if only I'd known he'd be so late.

When I first see Brad strolling across the food court in my direction, I instinctively smile before I remember that I'm supposed to be mad.

I frown as he approaches.

"Sorry I'm late," he says.

Where have I heard that before? I stand and give him a noncommittal hug.

Brad is tall, about six-two, with a wiry runner's build. I've been trying to fatten him up for the six months we've known each other. Nothing works. He has jet-black hair, a jaw that looks like it was chiseled from Mount Rushmore, and these deep-set and intense steel blue eyes that I absolutely love. If he never said another word, those eyes could convey every feeling he ever felt.

People say we make the perfect couple. I don't see it. I feel lucky just to have him.

But for now, he has earned a chilly reception.

"Let's grab something," I say. "I'm starving."

"Okay, but give me a minute." He takes both my arms and gently sits me down in the chair next to him. He then takes my hand, his charm working overtime.

"First, I really am sorry for being so late. I didn't get out of depositions today until five, then I had this witness to prepare for tomorrow who needed a lot of work, then the traffic—"

"I'm fine," I interrupt. "It's just that every time, there's something."

"I know. I know." He smiles. He knows I can't resist the smile. "But listen to this," he says as he leans forward. His enthusiasm overtakes me and my frown is gone. "I've been thinking about this issue of a church wedding. And I've got an idea."

Now he has my attention. I prepare to look surprised.

"I really want this wedding to be special for you," he continues. He's talking fast, unable to conceal his excitement. "And I know you've wanted to get married in a church. But you just moved down here to Virginia Beach a few months ago, and I don't really have a church, so I haven't been all that excited about getting married in some strange church that doesn't mean anything special."

I nod. I'm holding my breath.

"But this stuff I've been saying about getting married with a JP, that was just a smoke screen," he confesses. "I really wanted to do something special as well, and I've been working on it. I just didn't tell you because I didn't want you disappointed if it didn't work out." He pauses. This is why he's so great with jurors. He has a way of drawing people in, playing out the drama. "So, are you ready for this?" he asks.

"No, let's just get some Chinese; we can talk about it later," I tease. I start to stand, but he squeezes my hand and pulls me back down.

"For our wedding date, August 6, I've pulled some strings and rented Bruton Parish in Williamsburg!"

I generally pride myself on keeping my cool. But this time, he's done it! I'm stunned. Speechless. Bruton Parish is the beautifully restored historic church right in the middle of Colonial Williamsburg, the town where Brad and I met. I didn't even know they would rent it for weddings, much less on short notice. Much less for us.

It's perfect.

"You what?" I ask. I just want to hear it again.

"I've reserved and rented Bruton Parish for August 6," he repeats, grinning ear to ear.

"How?" I ask. Brad is thirty-five and has been practicing law for eleven years. Seems like everybody I meet owes him a favor.

"I just showed them the picture of my bride-to-be, and they said somebody as beautiful as you deserves to get married in the most beautiful church in Virginia."

I roll my eyes and then lean forward and give him a kiss. How can I stay mad at a guy like this?

CHAPTER
FOUR

As we finish dinner, the conversation turns to our new case.

"So you know who James Bannister is?" Brad asks.

"Was," I say as I chase the last bit of rice around my paper plate. "He *was* the CEO of TalkNet."

"Very good," Brad says. A pause, then, "How'd we get this case?"

I finish chewing my last bite and make a quick wipe with my napkin before I answer. "A family attorney represented them at the arraignment in J&DR a little over a month ago. He's not really much of a trial lawyer but apparently wanted to make a name for himself. Commonwealth's Attorney Harlan Fowler started putting some serious heat on the guy, and he withdrew. Seems that Fowler and Bannister were buds." This draws a raised eyebrow from Brad. "Mrs. Bannister came to the office looking for you, but I think Tara wants me to handle it. She thinks I'm more hip. Won't trust anybody over thirty." I smirk, knowing Brad hates it when I tweak him about his age. I also know he will take the lead on the case as soon as he can get untangled from the ridiculous federal court case that now commands his attention.

"Good," he says, "because it's yours. I've got a full plate right up through the wedding. Like you said, you'll have better rapport with her anyway."

"I was kidding, Brad. I can't handle this case alone. Trish Bannister came to the firm to hire you. I'm still trying to figure out why the judge carries that little hammer around with him. This girl's life is on the line, and I'm not willing to make her my own private guinea pig."

I tilt my head sideways and give him "the look." He can't resist my sad and downcast sky blue eyes, lips pursed nervously together. I only trot it out for the really serious requests. Overuse would destroy its effectiveness. *This* is such a request.

"Trish Bannister is not the client; her daughter is." *What? Is the look losing its magic?*

"I'll work with you every step of the way," my fiancé promises, "but you're going to be lead counsel." I start to protest but he holds up his hand. "You can do this, Leslie. I saw you in court when you clerked with me during law school and helped me try the Sarah Reed case. You were better as a law student than most lawyers who've been at it for years. And much better than you give yourself credit for."

Another skill of Brad the trial lawyer. He can talk you into anything. "I don't know," I say, but I'm already losing my conviction. Secretly, I would love to take on this challenge.

"Look," says Brad, "if you were a sixteen-year-old girl on trial for murder, and your defense was that your crazy old man was about to kill you, and you knew that somehow you had to win over all the women on the jury, would you rather have a beautiful and brilliant young female lawyer trying your case or some middle-aged man who will probably abuse his own wife as soon as he can find someone to marry him?"

Before I can answer, he's off and running with his own theme. "You've heard of playing the race card, Leslie. Well, we've got to play the sex card. Revenge of the abused woman's daughter. Even if I had the time, I'd still insist that you try it."

He's got a point. But I don't have to admit it. "If I were on trial for my life, I'd want someone who knew which counsel table to sit at," I say.

He rubs his chin and thinks, as if he doesn't know. I frown at his foolishness and he turns serious again.

"Anyway," he says, "the case will probably never even go to a jury trial. If Harlan Fowler has any sense, he'll hand this case off to one of his minions and have them plead it out right away. If he's a friend of the family, he won't drag them through the mud."

He stops speaking but I don't respond. I figure we'll find out soon enough what Fowler wants to do. I've had enough shoptalk. I'm still thinking about Bruton Parish.

"How'd you do it?" I ask again. "I mean, Bruton Parish."

I don't really expect a straight answer, and I don't get one. "One of my many old girlfriends owed me a favor."

For the next hour we walk around the mall, holding hands and talking. I find it hard to keep up with the long strides of the man who literally takes my breath away. Brad tries to buy me a few things and I refuse. We part company with a long kiss in the parking lot. As he does most every night, he asks me over. As I do almost every night, I politely decline. I get in my car and head to the small and ancient duplex I rent in the densely populated Green Run area of the city. Brad knows the landlord of the duplex, got a great deal on the rent, and convinced me that the location on an out-of-the-way side street would be safer and quieter than an apartment complex. Quiet? He apparently never met the family next door, including their two preschool children. Still, it's only a temporary way station until we get married, and I've got an open invitation to stay at Brad's large Colonial-style home on the Lynnhaven River if things get too loud.

So far I've only gone to his place during the day. We promised each other months ago that we would wait for our wedding night. It's a promise that somehow strengthens our love and demonstrates our commitment. It's why I avoid his house at night. It's not that I don't trust him. It's more like I don't trust me. Especially on a night like tonight. After all, the man just commandeered Bruton Parish for *our* wedding.

I am awake half the night. During the other half I dream of an old-fashioned wedding in Colonial Williamsburg at Bruton Parish and have nightmares of a pale blond-haired girl being hauled in leg irons down the street to the old colonial jail.

CHAPTER
FIVE

I t does not take long to find out where Harlan Fowler stands on this case. Two days later, on Thursday morning, I get a call from a secretary in his office asking if I can meet with him that afternoon. I arrange for a 5:30 start time so that Brad can attend after his depositions. The secretary is not happy. I get the impression that the commonwealth's attorney is usually on his way home by 5:00.

I park my aging Honda Accord in the nearly deserted parking lot of the municipal building and check myself out in the mirror before getting out. I have pinned my hair on top of my head. I also went sparse on the makeup, eye shadow, and lip liner. It's a look that says "serious professional." At least, that's what I want it to say.

People have a hard time believing I'm thirty, or so they say. And though I've never thought of myself as having cover-girl looks, I'm apparently too pretty to be taken seriously by any of the men I meet. Most seem more interested in how short my skirt is or in flirting with me than they are in what I have to say about the law. Accordingly, I have perfected the studious look, complete with black-frame reading glasses that I started wearing about two years before I really needed them. Today I'm wearing a plain gray pinstriped suit and looking every inch the counselor-at-law. Still, construction workers will hoot and whistle when I walk by, and older lawyers are bound to ask how long I've been out of law school.

When I get out of the car, the hot and muggy breeze is stifling. It's only the first week of May, but the Tidewater summer is starting early. Real ladies don't sweat, yet by the time I hit the building that houses the commonwealth's attorney's office, the combination of the humid weather and the tension of the upcoming meeting have my blouse sticking to my back. I'm out of breath, another unwelcome reminder that my workout routine lacks discipline. I wonder how the lawyers did it in the old days, before air conditioning, trying their cases in stuffy courthouses all summer long.

I take the stairs to the second floor, dragging my Carson & Associates briefcase. I'd feel more comfortable with a backpack, but that wouldn't exactly enhance the professional look. I always make Brad carry the new firm briefcase, and I carry his old one, partly for luck and partly to avoid advertising how new I am to the practice of law.

I wander around the hallways until I stumble on the commonwealth's attorney's office. I am a few minutes early and tell the receptionist that I am waiting for my partner to join me.

For nearly twenty minutes I cool my heels in the reception area. Brad Carson is now in serious trouble. This is the reason that everyone I know, except for Bella, is telling me it will never work to be married to your law partner. By 5:50 I am beginning to think they're right.

Brad's not answering his cell phone, and I finally give up waiting for him. The receptionist takes me down two hallways and back to a large corner office. I recognize the short, stocky man standing behind the desk in the far corner of the room as Harlan Fowler. He's my height and has a square build—broad shoulders, barrel chest, and squat neck. He has a flat and broad Roman nose and a jaw that juts out, like he's some distant cousin of Jay Leno. His most distinguishing characteristic is a shock of gray (almost white) hair that gives him an air of gravitas and maturity that is probably undeserved.

He starts around the desk to greet me. "Nice to meet you," he says on the way across the office. "I'm Harlan Fowler. Thanks for coming on such short notice."

"Leslie Connors," I say, looking at him eye to eye and shaking his hand. The fingers are short, strong, and squat, and to my surprise, the hand is a little sweaty. And I thought I would be the nervous one.

I turn and shake hands with the other man in the room. I vaguely recognize him but can't quite place him.

"Mitchell Taylor," he says. "Nice to meet you." His handshake is firm, like he's trying to impress.

It hits me. He's the young lawyer whose face was plastered all over television last year when he represented a surrogate mother in her quest to avoid having to abort an embryo that had been diagnosed with Down's syndrome. In the process he made quite a name for himself by exposing a high-level crime ring that was manipulating embryo research. He also endeared himself to the Religious Right, a faction that Fowler has a hard time mobilizing politically. It looks like the embryo case landed Mitchell a job with the commonwealth's attorney's office.

Mitchell stands ramrod straight, like a marine. He is average height with lean muscles that cannot be entirely hidden by his dark blue suit. He has close-cropped blond hair, close-knit eyebrows, and an angular and clean-shaven face—a young Spartacus in a business suit. He has law enforcement in his blood; I can sense it. He does not smile.

"Have a seat," Fowler says as he retreats behind his huge mahogany desk. The boys seem to be waiting for me to sit—true Southern gentlemen. I park myself in one of the client chairs in front of Fowler's desk and cross my legs. Fowler sits in his leather desk chair and leans back, trying to look relaxed. Mitchell Taylor takes the other client chair next to me.

"Want anything to drink?" asks Fowler. Before I can answer, he continues. "Thought Brad Carson was coming too. Bradley and I go back a long way."

Brad hates it when people call him Bradley. "I'll tell him you said hello. He's taking depositions. Must have gotten long-winded."

"I know how that goes," Fowler drawls, rubbing his face in distraction. "We really do appreciate your coming on short notice. This case will only get worse for everyone with time." He pauses to see if I will nod or give him some positive body language. I am wearing my poker face, so he continues. "I just want to make my role in this case perfectly clear, then I want to turn this meeting over to Mitchell."

"No thanks," I say.

"What?" asks Fowler.

"I don't care for anything to drink." Nobody smiles. I thought it was rather cute.

"Oh," says Fowler. "Sorry." He collects his thoughts and continues. "Listen, I want you to understand that I will not personally be handling this case. I've been somewhat involved in some peripheral issues, but as of today, this case will belong entirely to Mitchell. I have given him full authority to resolve the case as he sees fit. This is a family tragedy." He pauses, swallows hard, and seems to be on the verge of tears. But the eyes remain noticeably dry as he continues. "James Bannister was one of my closest friends." I take that to mean Bannister must have been a big campaign contributor. "I'm heartbroken for this entire family and personally involved to the point where I can't objectively manage this case. One of my best friends is dead, and all the evidence points to his daughter as being guilty of murder, or at least manslaughter."

There it is—he mentioned manslaughter, a lesser charge—the first concession that this case could be pled out. I make a mental note.

"There is no good resolution to this," Fowler continues, "but surely the worst resolution is for the case to drag on and on. I've asked Mitchell if there isn't some way this matter could be resolved as quickly and as painlessly as possible."

Fowler is not sounding to me like a man who is staying out of the case. But I'm not going to complain if it means a "quick and painless" resolution for my client.

"I don't mind telling you," Fowler continues, "that I'm taking all kinds of heat for this case. There are no winners here. The liberals are screaming because we charged her with murder. The law-and-order types are complaining because she's out on bail." Fowler shrugs his shoulders and holds out his hands, palms up. If he wants sympathy, he's looking in the wrong place.

Two days earlier, in my office, Trish Bannister had filled me in on the bond situation. The deputy commonwealth's attorney handling the original bond hearing had opposed bail because it was a murder case. Bail was denied. After the hearing, Trish asked for and was granted a private meeting with Fowler. In that meeting she begged Harlan to allow Tara to be released on bond. Trish told Harlan that she would never ask him for another thing this entire case, but that Tara could not survive in jail pending trial. Eventually, the two agreed on a creative bond proposal that Harlan sold to his staff and eventually to the judge.

Tara was released on a half-million-dollar bond into her mother's custody. Under the terms of the bond agreement, Tara could not leave her home unless her mother was with her. In essence, it was house arrest. Tara was allowed to finish the school year, but only if Trish took her to school and picked her up afterward. A court-appointed probation officer had the right to drop by the home and inspect for compliance with the agreement at any time. In the days that followed, Harlan had been subject to withering attacks in the newspaper for allegedly giving preferential treatment to a rich kid.

"It's your job to take the heat," I say unsympathetically. "It's your job to seek justice, not good press."

"Don't lecture me," he says sharply, leaning forward. There is no semblance of tears or sadness now. "I've been more than fair to your client and at considerable cost to my reputation. Tomorrow I will be announcing that the case has been turned over to Mitchell and that I will play no further role. And I'm not sure you'll find Mitchell as amenable to bail as I was."

It smells to me like the classic good cop–bad cop. I keep my eyes on the good cop—Fowler—since he appears to be my best chance of cutting a deal I can recommend.

"Tara is sixteen," I remind him in a softer tone than before. "We ought to be able to resolve this in J&DR without dragging it out and putting the family through more pain."

"I am hoping we can resolve this even before the preliminary hearing next week," confirms Fowler.

In my peripheral vision, I notice Mitchell Taylor bristle.

Immediately, I'm suspicious. Granted, I'm new at this. But Fowler is very anxious to plead this one out. Too anxious. I'm missing something, but I'm not sure what.

"What do you have in mind?" I ask.

Fowler nods at Mitchell. "She pleads to voluntary manslaughter," Mitchell says. "Tara Bannister gets sentenced as an adult, and the felony stays on her record. We'll agree to a range of two-to-five. You're free to argue for the minimum; we'll argue for five years. In addition, we won't file any additional charges relating to the gun offenses. The ATF trace showed the gun was stolen. The gun charges alone—possession of stolen property and possession of an unregistered firearm—could get her two-to-five."

I snort, which seems to be the appropriate response. "I liked his attitude better," I say, pointing to Fowler.

Mitchell does not flinch but simply bores in on me with his intense green eyes. "Two-to-five," he says. "That's the deal. Take it or leave it before the preliminary hearing. That's when we'll file an amended indictment."

This guy's a jerk. "You've made my life easy." I stand and grab my briefcase, looking down my nose at him. Mitchell shows no reaction, and now I'm getting frustrated. I turn to Fowler.

"With all due respect, sir, your friend was an abusive man who maliciously beat his wife and started in on his stepdaughter. Unfortunately for him, she wasn't as meek and accommodating as her mom. James Bannister assaulted my client as soon as she returned home that night. Later he tried to choke her to death. She protected herself in the only way possible, with deadly force. It's textbook self-defense, fellas. If you'll check your statutes, it means the defendant, who in this case is really the victim, gets to walk. And if you think a jury's going to nail her for a firearms charge after they hear all this abuse testimony...well, you need to start living in the real world."

I turn on my heels to leave. I will highlight my indignation by stalking out.

"Nice story," says Mitchell as I head to the door. "Only problem is, it's not true." I stop walking. "Not a word of it."

I turn. He's still seated. "Last I knew, you were not there," I say snidely. "Tara *was* there, and you have her statement. Classic self-defense. And of course James Bannister was there, in all his drunken glory, but he pushed one too many buttons and attacked one too many women that night to live to tell about it."

I am now upset and talking more than I should. But this whole thing stinks. Mitchell stands and waits for a moment. I can tell he's enjoying this little game and is ready to drop a bombshell.

"The science doesn't lie," he says, pointing with his chin to several folders and documents sitting on a round table in the corner of the office. "And the science says that your client committed murder."

I turn up my palms—*so what?*

"Want to look?" he asks.

I try to act indifferent. "How long will it take?"

"Just a few minutes."

I huff over to the table and sit down, crossing my arms and acting put out. But in my gut I've got this strange sense of foreboding as I remember the advice of my crim law professor at William and Mary: *Never take the word of your client at face value.*

CHAPTER SIX

F or ten minutes an animated Mitchell Taylor walks me through the commonwealth's file as Fowler looks on. There are grisly crime-scene photographs, ballistics reports, videotaped statements from the surviving family members, the gun, some bullets, the towel and a few other items in evidence bags, a crime-scene diagram, and an autopsy report with accompanying photographs. It's clear that Mitchell has been living with this file and directing this investigation for the last forty days. For my part, I try to nod in all the right places and make little guttural noises like I understand what in the world he's talking about. In truth, it takes everything within me just to keep lunch down.

I'm going to kill Brad Carson.

"So"—Mitchell is now summarizing and pointing to one photograph that shows an entry wound in James Bannister's chest, just above the heart, and another photo of Bannister's hairy back—"we know for a fact that this shot was fired first and is the shot that killed the victim. It punctured a lung and hit some arteries, causing massive bleeding. It was deflected by the back of Mr. Bannister's rib cage, causing the bullet to lodge in his body. Thus, no exit wound. "

I bend down and look closely at the photographs, as if my "expert" eyes can either confirm or deny any of this. There is no exit wound; I'll give him that much.

"We also know that this bullet was fired at a distance of greater than twelve feet. This blow-up of the entry wound and abrasion collar shows no smudging, stippling, or tattooing around the entry wound. This would be expected if the suspect had been closer than about twelve feet."

Mitchell looks up at me, apparently searching my face for questions. Finding none, he points to a photograph from the autopsy report that shows a metal rod inserted in the bullet hole. "As you can tell from the angle of this rod, it appears the gun was fired down at Mr. Bannister. Your client is several inches shorter than the victim. But this angle of entry indicates a shot fired from above the point of entry and at a distance of greater than twelve feet."

I can see he's got a point. I can also see it's time to brush up on my geometry. In my mind I'm trying to picture Tara holding this gun up in the air and pointing down at her father. Awkward, to say the least. Despite these growing doubts, I manage a halfhearted shrug. *So what?* Mitchell takes it as a cue to continue and points to a picture of Bannister lying on his side in a pool of blood on the living room floor. The towel that Tara had mentioned to me is covering Bannister's face. Tara must have placed it there after the shooting, while waiting for the police.

I'm getting queasier.

"Mr. Bannister was found here, next to this leather recliner chair in the living room," Mitchell explains. "Look at this picture." He points to a blow-up of the recliner. "We found a blood-spatter pattern on this leather recliner, but there was no blood in places that would be covered by a man of Mr. Bannister's size when sitting in the recliner." He pauses to let the impact of this sink in. It does. "In our view, the most likely scenario is that Mr. Bannister was shot, while sitting in this chair, from a distance of about twenty-five feet. After taking the first bullet, Bannister rose from the chair, either to defend himself or to reason with his attacker. But he was losing blood fast. He collapsed right next to the chair and died within seconds."

"Monday morning quarterbacking," I say. "There are a million reasons that can explain the angle of this bullet and the blood pattern." *Problem is, right now I can't think of one.* "Tara was there. She'd already been beat up by this man." I glance down at all the photos on the table. I'm starting to understand why they charged Tara with first-degree murder, which requires premeditation. With the facts turning against me, I decide to play the emotions. "I notice you don't have any photos of my client's bruised face or the face of Trish Bannister, beaten to a pulp." My voice turns raw. The thought of what Bannister did to these women is bad enough. The fact that the prosecutors are defending Bannister is that much worse.

Mitchell just gives me that cold stare, so I turn again to the commonwealth's attorney. "Pardon me, Mr. Fowler, but your friend was out of control. Nobody will dispute that. Tara was in fear for her life. She called 911 as soon as the shootings occurred. She may have been confused afterward about exactly who was standing where when the shots were fired, but the poor girl was probably in shock. She was forced to shoot her own stepfather in self-defense. And now you're charging her with first-degree murder, as if she were lying in wait for her stepfather and shot him in cold blood."

Though I wasn't speaking to him, Mitchell answers with amazing calm. "I'm not without sympathy for your client," he says. "But it doesn't justify a premeditated execution. She can't just take the law into her own hands, Leslie."

"Save your tears." I shuffle through a few of the photos, my mind racing with the possibilities. I make a mental note to pay Tara a visit tomorrow. For now, I'll just go with a bluff. "This is all you've got?" I ask. "Geometry, blood spatters, and this other stuff with the bullet wound—what do you call it?"

"Stippling and tattooing."

"Yeah, stippling and tattooing. That's all you're going on to put a sixteen-year-old abused child away for life? We both know that blood patterns can be highly irregular. And maybe she did fire the gun from farther away than she said. Maybe she wanted to stop him in his tracks before he got his hands on her a second time. She was still in fear for her life, Mr. Taylor. It's still self-defense." I raise my voice to show this is ridiculous nitpicking. "Twenty-five feet may sound impressive when you're dissecting this in the safety of your conference room. But when you're a sixteen-year-old girl with a crazed lunatic bearing down on you, you're in fear either way."

"There's also the problem of the second bullet," Mitchell explains, totally ignoring everything I just said. He clearly thrives on this forensic science. "The shot to Mr. Bannister's head." He points to one of the more grisly photographs. "This bullet entered the forehead of the victim just above his left eye." Mitchell puts his finger on an autopsy photograph showing the bullet track in the skull cavity. "In this photo, we see that the coroner has inserted another small rod, a probe, through the brain to show the track of this bullet. The bullet lodged here." Pointing again. "From the stippling around the entrance wound, those pinpoint areas where the burned powder and bullet fragments hit the flesh, and the absence of any tattooing from the muzzle of the gun, we know that this shot was fired at close range but not point-blank range."

"Just like Tara said," I add.

Again he ignores me. "About the same distance as somebody standing over a person who is lying on the floor. But most important, the absence of hemorrhaging around this wound makes it very clear that the victim was already clinically dead for some length of time before this bullet entered. Also, the bullet entered more from the side than straight on."

Mitchell pauses again and silence fills the room. He now looks straight at me.

"In other words," he says, "some substantial amount of time after the victim was dead, your client stands over this dead man and shoots him again in the face at close range. Then she covers his face with this towel."

I begin to taste my lunch again, but this time for reasons other than the grotesque nature of the photographs. Then a thought hits me. "The towel," I say. "She had wrapped her gun in the towel. That would explain why there were no burn marks from the gunpowder on Bannister's body."

Mitchell looks like he's already considered this. "But then of course," he says, "you would expect the towel to have a bullet hole in it and blood spattered on it. It has a bullet hole, but the only blood on the towel is from smudge stains consistent with being laid on top of the victim. We believe the towel was placed over the gun during the second shot, not the first, in order to help support the self-defense story your client told to the police. There are no spatter stains on the towel because the victim was dead by the time the second shot was fired."

I feel out of my league on this. I decide it's time to retreat and regroup. I sit in silence for a moment, just trying to process all this. "I'll want to see the towel," I say. "Have some experts look at it."

"Of course," says Mitchell. As I stand to leave he also hands me copies of the photos and a videotape. "Have a forensic expert come by and look at the towel. Go watch your client's confession and study these photos. The deal stays open until next week's preliminary hearing."

I manage one last act of bravado, a sarcastic "That's big of you." I shake hands with an overconfident Mitchell Taylor and a worried Harlan Fowler. I see my own growing doubts reflected in Fowler's eyes. Without saying a word, he pleads with me to take the deal.

CHAPTER SEVEN

My cell phone rings on the way back to my duplex. I check the number on the display. It's Brad.

"Where were you?" I ask.

There is a moment's pause. "Oh, I'm sorry," he says. "I must have the wrong number. I was trying to dial my sweet, loving fiancée."

"Very funny."

"Sorry, Leslie. They were deposing my client today and wouldn't quit. He made a fool of himself."

"He did that on national television too," I remind Brad. "At least he's consistent."

Brad doesn't chuckle. Maybe he's getting as repulsed by this case as I was the day the client walked in the door. Brad's client (I refuse to touch this case) is a workout freak named Brandon Matthews. Before his fifteen minutes of fame, Brandon was a trainer at Gold's Gym in Virginia Beach, the same gym where Brad and I occasionally work out. Brandon, a blond-haired Fabio clone, somehow finagled his way onto one of those reality dating shows named *Girl Next Door* and his life changed forever.

Like *Average Joe,* the premise of *Girl Next Door* is to see whether someone will choose inner beauty over outer beauty. On the first show a whole busload of average-looking girls, the "girls next door," were brought to a mansion in Maui where Brandon set up residence for the six weeks of filming. As he flirted with the girls, there was a lot of endearing footage of Brandon waxing eloquent about how much personality mattered to him and how beauty was more than skin deep. For the next several weeks, he dated and eliminated these sweet girls who all fell hopelessly in love with him. When there were three average girls left, all with incredible personalities and passable looks, the producers pulled their usual stunt and brought a bombshell into the mix—a woman named Jewel with a knockout figure and a mind that was missing in action.

Predictably, Brandon fell for Jewel, eliminating the remaining next-door girls one week at a time. On the last climactic show, Brandon nearly wept as he sent the final next-door girl packing, a sweetheart named Annie, and professed his love to Jewel.

But there was still fifteen minutes of television time to fill, and the shocking conclusion surprised Brandon most of all. I never watched the show during its airing, but Brad made me watch the tape of the finale when he first took the case.

Imagine the surprised look on Brandon's face when he learned that Jewel was a transvestite.

He retained Brad Carson to teach the show's producers a lesson. Brad immediately filed a thick lawsuit alleging fraudulent inducement. The tabloids loved it.

"I was hoping to settle," Brad mumbles. "We go in front of a mediator tomorrow to see if she can help resolve this thing. But after today the producers would be fools to offer me a penny."

Hearing the depression in his voice, I resist the urge to say, "I told you so." "I really could have used you there today," I say in a softer tone.

"I know. I really am sorry." A pause. He's probably waiting for me to tell him not to worry about it. I don't say a thing.

"Got dinner plans?" he asks.

"Yeah, dinner and a movie. I've got to watch a video of our client's confession."

"How bad is it?"

"I don't think the video's too bad, but they've got some strong forensic evidence."

"Like what?"

"Can we talk about it later?" I sound more perturbed than I intend. But if he's so curious about the case, he should have figured out a way to make our conference with Fowler.

"Sure," he replies.

There is silence on the phone.

"Want some company?" He sounds desperate.

"I'd love it, but let's take a rain check. I know you've got to get ready for the mediation tomorrow, and I'm beat. It's been a long day."

"Okay," he says, his voice flat. "But tomorrow night's Friday. And nothing stands in our way."

It's not like Brad to sound so down. The deposition must have been an absolute disaster. And tomorrow sounds like such a long way off. Much as I try, I can't resist.

"Tell you what," I say. "I'll meet you at the office in thirty minutes. You bring dinner; I'll bring the movie."

"It's a date," he says. I detect a hint of enthusiasm returning. "Pizza?"

"Just grab me a salad."

"Are you sure?"

"Yeah."

He'll know what to put in the salad and what kind of dressing to order. We know each other so well, it's scary.

"I love you," I say.

"I love you too," he replies. The enthusiasm is back.

CHAPTER
EIGHT

Brad has nearly devoured an entire medium Domino's pizza. Still, he won't gain a pound. The man is always moving, always burning calories, running in the morning, pacing and fidgeting the rest of the day, attacking life. I haven't touched any of the pizza. After our wedding—maybe. But I've still got to lose five pounds before then. I refuse to weigh more for this wedding than I did my first. I munch on my salad and endure the low-fat Italian dressing. I am drinking bottled water.

Out of deference to me, Brad is drinking a Coke. I know he'd rather have a beer, but he's aware of how much I depended on alcohol in the two years following Bill's death. Though I don't consider myself a recovering alcoholic, I'm all too familiar with where that first drink will lead. Alcohol deadened the pain. But two years of pretty heavy drinking could never make the pain disappear. One particularly tough morning, after I took a good look in the mirror and didn't like what I saw, I weaned myself from the booze and found other ways to cope.

"You ready?" Brad asks. He's holding the remote, finger on the Play button. We've been together for more than an hour, talking about anything and everything. We have put off watching the confession.

"Sure," I say. I slide back in my chair.

"Before we watch *your* tape," Brad says gingerly, "can I show you mine? It'll just take a minute. I want to get your opinion on something."

I look at him suspiciously. "This isn't about your *Girl Next Door* case, is it?"

He jams another bite in his mouth. "Maybe. But I really need your advice."

"I hate that case, Brad. I don't want anything to do with it."

"Exactly," he says, chasing the pizza with a gulp of soda. "That's why I need your input. You're totally unbiased, just like our mediator will be. Just take a second." He's already pushing the Play button.

I sigh and cup my chin in my hand. He shows me the scene where Jewel is initially brought on the show. The *Girl Next Door* candidates are all dressed up in beautiful evening gowns, enjoying a night with Brandon in the grand ballroom, when the show emcee gets their attention and announces one more contestant will be added to the mix. Jewel struts into the room, wearing a dress that would make Jennifer Lopez blush, and Brandon follows her every move. I think I detect a thin line of drool spilling down his jaw.

"What do you notice?" Brad asks.

"Your client—panting like a dog in heat?"

"Not that. Focus on the women. Look at their faces."

"They're blurry," I say.

"And smiling," he adds. He rewinds and runs it forward again in slow motion.

One of the *Girl Next Door* contestants has her hands over her mouth, but her raised cheeks and twinkling eyes can't hide her smile. Another is looking down and away, hiding her face from the camera. The third is just grinning stupidly as she watches Brandon ogle her new curvy competition.

"Okay, they're smiling," I admit. "So?"

"So I've studied similar tapes from when the new hunks come on the scene in the show *Average Joe*," Brad says excitedly. "The Average Joes are always shocked. They look stunned, or angry, anything but smiling." He says this like he's just discovered the cure for cancer. I do my best to look unimpressed.

"Don't you get it?" he asks. "I think all these other *Girl Next Door* contestants were in on this. I think this whole show was a setup...

including these other contestants." He's talking faster. "Now I know why they all changed their attitudes toward Brandon after this new babe came on the show. One of the girls next door turned all cold and frigid. Another was just plain nasty to poor Brandon. The third one, Annie, got all giddy on her next date…downright annoying."

Right now this case is downright annoying! "*Poor* Brandon?" I ask. "The poor boy who chose looks over personality and dissed the three sweet, ordinary girls who had been so nice to him all along. My heart bleeds."

But my sarcasm does not dim the enthusiasm in Brad's eyes. "I'm going to use this tape at the mediation tomorrow," he pledges. "And if we don't settle, I'll take the deposition of every contestant, subpoena documents, expose this whole nasty fraud."

I stand and give Brad my most rebuking look. "And I'm going to the bathroom," I say. "When I return, I hope we can look at the tape of Tara's confession. *Your client* got what he deserved." I head toward the door. There's no point in arguing with Brad when he's so focused on one of his cases. But I hate the thought of him making this stupid case any more high-profile than it already is. Brad is such a talented lawyer; why does he want to mess around with this dog?

"You can't leave now," he calls out. "This is our smoking gun, our glove that doesn't fit, our stained blue dress…"

I just keep walking. He knows how much this case aggravates me, but he thinks he's being cute, and truth be known, if I turn around I might be tempted to smile at his childish antics. I won't give him that satisfaction. "Maybe you're confusing me with someone who cares," I say over my shoulder, leaving my fiancé alone in the conference room with his annoying case and conspiracy theories.

When I return, the pizza is gone. Brad hits the Play button and the image of Tara Bannister comes into full view. She is seated at a metal table in a stark interview room. A thin detective with rounded shoulders sits with his back to us. He is wearing a plain white shirt and a tie. The image is a little grainy, the sound a little rough. He is informing Tara of her rights.

"That's Detective Lawrence Anderson," says Brad. "He's ruthless, slick, and slimy."

"Oughta be a lawyer."

The camera angle widens and takes in Trish Bannister, seated to Tara's left, at the end of the table. My eyes are immediately drawn to Trish. She looks awful. Her right eye is swollen nearly shut. There is a butterfly bandage just below the eyebrow near the outside of the socket. Her lip is swollen on the same side, giving her face a lopsided appearance. She looks like a losing prizefighter in a postfight interview.

Brad lets out a low whistle.

"He deserved to be shot," I hear myself say.

"You really think they're dumb enough to show this to a jury?" Brad asks.

I stare at the grainy image of Trish Bannister. She is docile and confused. I feel at once both sorry for her and mad because she did not leave this monster earlier.

The detective finishes his Miranda spiel.

"I think we ought to get an attorney," mumbles Trish. I make a note.

The detective stays focused on Tara, ignoring the comment from her mom.

"We can't help you if don't tell us what happened," he says.

Tara stays silent.

"Shouldn't we call Peter?" Trish suggests. Peter Dickson is the Bannister family lawyer who withdrew from the case.

"Is that what you want?" the detective asks Tara. "You want to get a lawyer involved, or you want to tell us what happened so we can help you?"

Tara just stares straight ahead.

"Serious Miranda issue," says Brad, as if he's doing color commentary. "Sixteen-year-old kid. Mom asks for an attorney. Cops keep on asking questions."

"Shh," I say.

Detective Anderson is talking again in an earnest tone. "Tara, your mom was asleep upstairs, knocked out cold from those sleeping pills. Jamie's already told us what happened. We just need someone to confirm…"

"He doesn't know," Tara blurts out. "How can Jamie know anything? He wasn't there."

"He says he was in his bedroom with headphones on when the shots were fired. Didn't hear anything. Says you came upstairs and told him exactly what happened." The detective's voice is reassuring but firm.

"Tara," Trish says, "we really need to talk with Peter. He can—"

"Shut up!" Tara snaps, turning on her mom. "Mom, just stop it."

Trish recoils at the rebuke. Then she leans toward her daughter. "Tara, we need legal help."

Tara rubs her forehead and is nearly hyperventilating. On the verge of tears, she turns and looks at the detective.

"I shot him," she says defiantly. "In self-defense. I don't care what Jamie or anybody else says. I shot him to save my life. And I killed him."

The detective leans forward. "Tell me exactly what happened."

"Tara," Trish pleads.

Tara cuts her mom off with a cold-blooded look, then turns back to the detective. Tara tells him, in a matter-of-fact tone, exactly what she told me earlier this week in my office.

"How far away from your father were you when you fired the first shot?" asks the detective. "The one that hit him in the chest, just above the heart?"

"Don't answer that," I advise the television screen.

"He was choking me," says Tara. "He was right up next to me."

"Less than three feet?" Anderson presses.

"I don't know," Tara shrugs. "I guess so."

"And how long was there between your first and second shot?"

"How long between?" asks Tara, wrinkling her forehead.

"Yeah."

"No time at all, really. I mean, he went to his knees, tried to get back up. Maybe, like, five seconds."

The detective nods. "Did you call 911 right after you shot your dad?"

"Yes."

"When did you wake up your mom?"

Tara sighs and rubs her forehead, the strain evident on her face. Trish is looking on with the concerned face of a parent watching her child run in front of a car, too far away to help. "I don't know," says Tara, "right after I called 911, I guess."

"Before or after you went and got Jamie."

"After."

Anderson jots a few notes and leans forward. "Now this is very important, Tara." He pauses, looking her right in the eye. She does not return his gaze. "At any time after you shot your dad, did you return to your own bedroom?"

Tara looks confused. She stares at the wall, thinking hard. Finally, she says, "No. After I shot him, I went to Jamie's room and told him what happened. Then we went and woke up my mom. Mom made Jamie stay upstairs. We went downstairs to wait."

Detective Anderson nods his head. I can tell he's just extracted a valuable admission, but I'm not sure what it is. He conceals the importance of his next question with a matter-of-fact delivery: "You did cut yourself at some time that night, right?"

Again, Tara thinks for a moment. I don't like the way she hesitates before answering each question. "I was barefoot," she says belligerently. "I cut my heel on some broken glass in the family room."

"So this would have been when you were struggling with your dad. When you shot him."

"I guess."

"Are you sure about that?" asks Anderson. "Are you sure you didn't cut yourself before you went up to your bedroom to get the gun?"

"Yeah. I'm sure," Tara replies. She is getting perturbed at all the questions. "I didn't even go into the family room before I went to get the gun. He hit me in the front foyer, then I got my gun, then I came back down, and he attacked me in the living room. That must be when I cut my foot."

"Okay," says Anderson, jotting a few more notes. "So there would be no reason for *your* blood from that cut on your heel to be in your bedroom, right?"

"Crap," I say. Now Tara really looks confused. *How will I explain this?* My cell phone rings. At first I don't notice. It rings again. Brad hits the Pause button on the videotape.

"Leslie Connors."

"Tara's gone." It's the anguished voice of Trish Bannister. "I thought she would be back by now. I don't know where she's at. What do I do?"

"Slow down," I advise. "What do you mean Tara's gone?"

"She left earlier tonight when I went to the store. I think she ran away." Trish is nearly hysterical.

"What time?"

"I don't know. An hour. Maybe two."

"Have you told anybody else?"

"I didn't know who else to call." Trish is crying now; I can hear it in her voice.

"Okay," I say. "Let's not panic." It occurs to me that she already has. "I want you to call her friends, see if they know anything."

I glance at my watch: eight forty-five. "Brad and I will cover the airports. Call me on my cell if you hear anything, okay?"

"Okay." Her voice seems to be a little steadier. At least we have a plan.

"Whatever you do," I say, "don't call the cops. This is a violation of bail. If we can find her soon, we'll be fine. If we don't find her in the next hour, we'll call the cops. If the authorities find out she's gone and they find her, she'll spend the next three months in jail waiting for trial."

"Okay," says Trish.

Brad shoots me a disapproving look.

I reassure Trish again, say good-bye, and hang up the phone.

"Tara's missing. You want the Newport News or the Norfolk airport?" I ask.

He shakes his head. "Just what I needed," he grumbles.

I work my cell phone all the way to the airport. I call every airline, then the bus companies, then the hotel chains. I might as well have been listening to the radio. Nobody knows anything about Tara Bannister.

If I could get my hands on this kid right now, I'd probably strangle her. There'd be no need for a trial. She's just determined to flout the authorities every step of the way and make things harder on herself. Maybe a few months in jail before her trial would straighten her out. She's been my client all of two days, and I'm already sick of her attitude. I can imagine how her mother feels.

I didn't go to law school to practice criminal law, and this is one of the reasons. You can't trust the clients. Plus crime and criminals do not punch a clock. The clients will call you at all hours of the day and night. Your life is not your own.

I was going to be an international business lawyer. I would travel the world and represent huge corporations in sophisticated deals at exotic locations. Then I fell in love with Brad and everything changed. Though I like the excitement of criminal law and plaintiff's cases, I could do without baby-sitting this sixteen-year-old right now.

I pull into the hourly parking lot in front of the airport. It has started to drizzle, so I jog toward the building. Brad and I decided together that we should call the authorities if we didn't find Tara at the airports. There are really no rules for something like this. You aren't forced to report that your client has skipped bond. But then again, the authorities will eventually find out, and you will look like an idiot if you try to hide it.

I enter through the automatic doors, already winded from jogging less than half a mile. I stop for a moment to catch a few deep breaths. I've got to get back on that treadmill! I get my wind back and immediately begin scanning the first-floor ticket counters. It's 9:15 p.m., so there is not much activity. Nobody looks remotely like Tara. I have no chance of getting past security to the gates, so I have to limit my search to nonsecure areas. I climb the escalator and then jog down a moving sidewalk to a down escalator that leads to baggage claim and the rental car counters. My lungs are again burning, and I feel like I'm going to collapse. This is what happens when I try to lose weight; I've got no fuel in my body, so the slightest exertion wipes me out. Still, I've only been jogging a few minutes. Can I be that out of shape?

Breathing hard, I go from rental counter to rental counter, flashing my license and bar card, as if being a lawyer somehow gives me extra privileges. I describe what Tara looks like, but nobody has seen her or rented a car to anybody who was with a sixteen-year-old blond.

For the next half hour I check every bathroom, hallway, gate, store, and restaurant at Norfolk International Airport. Twice. She is not here. No store clerks or waiters have seen her. It's time to face the music.

I call Brad first. His search of the Newport News airport was also futile. He suggests that I call Trish and then the cops. He suggests that we hang out at the airports for another hour or so until the last flights leave. Just in case.

I dial Trish's number. I now have it memorized. I've talked to her three times in the last half hour alone. She seems to have calmed down some.

"Anything new?" I ask.

"No. I've called all her friends. They're either lying or they haven't seen her."

"I've checked the Norfolk airport. Nobody's seen her here. Brad's at Newport News. Nothing there either."

There is silence on the phone. Trish knows what this means.

"We've got to call the authorities," I say.

"I know." Her voice is barely audible.

"I'll call the police. Then Brad and I will wait at the airports until the last flights go out. Then I'll stop by on my way home."

There is no answer. I think I can hear her sobbing.

"Are you okay, Trish?"

"Yeah, I'm fine," she says between sobs. I wait another minute, and then she seems to get control of herself.

"Leslie," she says, "would it be okay if I just called Harlan first, instead of calling the police. I feel like I owe him that much. He stuck his neck out so that Tara could get out on bond in the first place."

I think about that for a moment. Informing Fowler is certainly as good as telling the cops. He is, after all, the chief law enforcement officer for the city of Virginia Beach.

"That's fine. Just make sure he knows that you're calling him as the commonwealth's attorney, not as a friend of the family. I don't want anybody to say we failed to report this to the authorities."

"Okay," says Trish. Then the sobs start all over again. I can hear Jamie in the background. My heart goes out to her.

"I'll be over in a few minutes, Trish," I promise. "Call me back if you need anything."

There's a pause as she regains her composure. "Okay. Thanks, Leslie. You've been great."

I feel helpless as I hang up. There are some things they don't teach you in crim law class.

CHAPTER ELEVEN

Tara is home. I get the call from Trish a few minutes before eleven, just as the last plane is leaving the Norfolk airport. Trish said she heard a car horn in her driveway and the sound of squealing tires. When Trish ran to the front door, she found Tara lying on the front steps. According to Trish, Tara is stone drunk and can give no good reason for skipping out.

The good news, according to Trish, is that Harlan Fowler promised he would wait until about midnight or so before reporting Tara's disappearance to the police. And Trish called him back in time—before he involved the police. For that, I am both grateful and wary. It seems that Fowler is sticking his neck out a lot further than he should, and it makes me wonder why.

I immediately call Brad. He is frustrated with Tara and says that bond revocation probably would have served her right. He has hours of work to do before his mediation hearing tomorrow morning. I climb into my car and head to the Bannister home. I am dog-tired, but Trish begged me to come. She said I was the only one who might be able to make Tara understand the seriousness of her actions. I wonder if Tara can understand anything in her condition.

The Bannister house is impressive. It is on ten acres in an exclusive subdivision in the Bay Colony area of Virginia Beach. It sits on a gated lot, and I wind down a long elegant driveway for several hundred yards before I even see the house.

The front porch has imposing white columns the size of redwood trunks, with marble lions on each side. The place is huge. It's the kind of house that people build as a monument to their egos, not as a home for a family. It is nearly midnight. I ring the bell and half expect a butler to answer.

Instead, Trish opens the door. She looks haggard. Her eyes are red and swollen. Her entire face looks puffy. With her left hand she unconsciously brushes her hair back over her head. Then she gives me a quick hug.

"Thanks so much for coming," she sighs. "Tara's upstairs in her room."

Trish nods to the staircase just past her shoulder. I pause for a moment to take in my surroundings. The place is breathtaking.

I am standing on the polished marble floor of an immense foyer under the largest crystal chandelier I have ever seen outside a hotel lobby. The steps leading upstairs are elaborately decorated and wind to the left. They look like something from *Gone with the Wind*. To my right is a beautiful formal dining room with a wall full of mirrors and china cabinets. I make a mental note to make sure Trish gets a wedding invitation.

Past the stairs to my left I see the entrance to the sunken family room. The back wall of the room appears to be lined with picture windows and French doors.

"Would you mind if I took a look at the family room first?" I ask. The forensic evidence outlined by Mitchell Taylor is still fresh in my mind. I need to be able to put the photos and evidence in context.

"No problem," says Trish. She starts leading me across the foyer and down a short hallway. "Would you like some coffee or something?"

"No thanks." As we reach the entrance to the family room, Jamie is sitting on the couch, leaning forward, zoned in on the television. He is playing some kind of Xbox game, *Tomb Raider* or something like that. Whatever the game is called, it is dark and loud and the body count is escalating. Jamie mumbles as his character, a machine-gun toting knockout brunette in a tight outfit, fends off one bloody attacker after another.

Jamie is a little pudgy with a round baby face that makes him look younger than the eleven-year-old that Trish described to me in the office. He is wearing a baggy striped T-shirt and baggy Docker shorts that hang below his knees even as he sits. He also displays a fair amount of polka-dot boxer shorts between the bottom of his shirt and the top of his shorts. He is constantly jerking his head and flipping his shaggy brown bangs away from his eyes.

"We had this room totally remodeled a few weeks after the shooting." Trish is practically shouting as she walks toward Jamie to retrieve the remote control. I stand by the entrance to the room and nod.

"I wasn't even sure if we could keep living in this house," she continues as she points the remote and lowers the volume. "But I knew we had to at least do something with this room."

She now has Jamie's attention. He turns and grabs the remote.

"Jamie, this is Leslie Connors," Trish says, ignoring the fact that the kid has just commandeered the remote. "She is the lawyer representing Tara."

Jamie flicks his hair and stares at me. He is still sitting down.

"How are you doing, Jamie?"

"All right," he mumbles. "Tara's upstairs."

"I know. Thanks."

"Sure." He turns and resumes his game. Another flick of the hair. He grunts at the screen again and says a few indecipherable words. Then, without even looking and with one hand still on the Xbox joystick, he picks up the remote with the other and pumps the volume back up to an obnoxious level. The kid needs a good swift kick in the boxers. The images flash so quickly on the screen that my eyes have no time to focus. I feel old.

Trish ignores this show of disrespect. She looks so tired.

"Can you tell me where your husband's body was found?" I ask, loud enough to be heard above the tube.

"This is where they found his body," she says, raising her voice. "Right next to a recliner that was sitting right there." I notice that Trish has replaced the recliner with a big cushy easy chair and ottoman.

"Jamie, turn that down. *Please,*" Trish says sternly.

She walks close to the other side of the room. "This is where he choked me earlier that night."

The television is still blaring. Jamie is still playing the game. I'm getting a headache.

"What happened to the recliner and carpet?" I ask.

"As far as I know, the detectives cut out any carpet pieces with blood or other evidence on them. They took the recliner as evidence too. The rest of the furniture and the carpet were trashed when we had the crew in to remodel."

I frown and Trish apparently notices. "We should have kept it?" she asks.

"You never know what might become important."

I walk around the room and try to commit this picture to memory. It's hard to focus with the television so loud. I glance at Jamie again, which reminds me of a question I had been meaning to ask Trish.

"Did Jamie speak to the cops before you and Tara did?"

Trish scrunches her forehead and thinks for a minute. "You mean before Tara confessed to the detective?"

I nod.

"I don't think so."

She walks over to Jamie, grabs the remote, and turns down the volume. For the second time.

"Hey," he yells. "What're you *doing?*"

"Jamie," Trish says sharply, "Ms. Connors has a couple of questions for you."

"In a minute," he says. "Let me just finish this next—"

Trish hits some kind of Stop button on the controls. Jamie jumps to his feet.

"You ruined my game!" he yells. He is breathing in short, sharp bursts, nearly hyperventilating.

Trish speaks calmly in a tone that only mothers can master. "Jamie, you can finish your game as soon as you answer a few questions. This is really important."

"For who?! Important for who?" He twitches his head and tosses the hair out of his eyes. Twice. Three times. His eyes are accusatory, looking at Trish, then me, then back to Trish.

"You never let me finish. You always just make me do what *you* want." He is toe to toe with his mother now. I feel embarrassed that I have to watch this family fight.

"It's okay—" I start.

"Jamie, relax," says Trish. She reaches out to hold his arm, but this only seems to infuriate him more.

"Don't tell me what to do!" he shouts. Then he spits. I can't believe my eyes. The boy spits on the carpet of his own family room!

Trish is not fazed. She gently grabs both of his arms, but he jerks away. He starts talking, faster and faster. I can't understand what he's saying. I stand frozen, wanting to hide my eyes, not knowing what to do.

Then he does it again. He spits a second time. His head is jerking a little, and he is babbling. He pulls away from his mother and starts stalking from the room. As he's walking by me, he spits a third time. I twist away. Too late. The saliva lands on the top of my right arm.

"Ugh!" I resist the urge to slap the kid. Barely. I quickly wipe my arm on the back of my jeans. This is gross. I stare darts at him as he sulks from the room, babbling on the way.

Trish comes rushing over. "I'm so sorry, Leslie. This is the last thing we need tonight." The tears are starting to well up in her eyes. "I know there's no excuse for it, but there are times when the ADD and the Tourette's..." Her voice trails off.

Personally, I think the kid just needs a little discipline. I don't normally believe in spankings. But here I would definitely make an exception.

"I'm okay," I lie, as if I get spit on every day. "Don't worry about it. I just need to talk with Tara."

Trish holds back the tears a few more seconds. "Her room is the first door on the left, at the top of the stairs. I'm so sorry," she says again. "I'll go deal with Jamie while you talk to Tara."

"Works for me." I give her a quick, reassuring and phony smile. Then I head up the stairs to talk with the real problem child in the Bannister family.

CHAPTER
TWELVE

Tara's room is a disaster area that ought to be condemned by the health department. Clothes, shoes, papers, magazines, dishes, toiletries, and hair products litter the floor and any flat surface. It looks like somebody dumped the contents of her dresser, her bathroom, and half the kitchen cabinets into her room, then turned the room upside down and shook it. Hard.

Tara is lying in the middle of this mess, sprawled across her bed, eyes closed. She did not respond to my tapping on the door, so I just let myself in. She is wearing only her panties and the spaghetti-strap tank top that she presumably wore out tonight. She has on a set of earphones hooked up to her iPod mini. Her large flat-screen television, which hangs on the wall opposite her bed, is blaring.

I pick my way across the room toward her bed. I find a remote and turn down the television. Then I reach down and pull one of the earphones out of her ear. This gets her attention, so she opens her eyes and focuses on me. Or at least she tries.

The girl smells like brandy.

"Tara, we've got to talk." I say it loud and stern, like my mother used to.

She tries again to make her eyes focus on me, but I get the feeling I'm just a blur. "Tara, this is Leslie Connors, your lawyer. We've got to talk."

She smiles. It is the cockeyed, smart-aleck grin of the cat who feels the canary slithering down her esophagus. "I know you," she says loudly and with a thick tongue. "You're that Judge Judy woman…lawyer… Laura…" She points at me and snaps her fingers, trying to remember.

"Leslie," I say. "Leslie Connors." What a waste of time.

"Yeah, that's it. Lawyer Leslie!" She says it with an air of excitement and self-satisfaction, like she has just solved one of the world's great mysteries. "Lawyer Leslie," she exclaims again emphatically.

Suddenly her face goes from bright and cheery to a quizzical, worried look.

"Uh-oh," she says, "I don't feel good." She grabs her stomach and frowns.

My eyes dart around the room for a trash can. If there is one, it's camouflaged so well by all the junk, I can't find it.

She sits up and I grab her arm to steady her. "I gotta puke," she says.

Great. Just what I need to cap the perfect night.

She has her own large private bathroom attached to her room. To my surprise, she manages to stand and stagger into the bathroom, leaning heavily on my arm for support. I help her sit on the floor in front of the toilet.

"Thanks," she says. Tara is always pretty pale, but right now her face is ghastly white.

She puts her arms around the toilet seat, like she is hugging the thing, head hanging over the bowl. I decide she needs some privacy and step back into her bedroom, shutting the bathroom door. I was always the kid in grade school who would throw up just from watching someone else do it. My teachers would always get two for the price of one. I'm not about to watch Tara.

I hear her begin to hurl, the gut-wrenching sound of someone turning their intestines inside out. I hope she hit the toilet. It sounded like she did.

I decide not to stick around and find out.

On my way out, Trish has Jamie apologize to me. I assure him it's okay, though I keep my distance. As I leave the Bannister estate, driving past the stone pillars and the black iron gate, I am struck by the contrast between the exterior of the house and the interior of the home. Everything looks so perfect on the outside—a manicured lawn and the elegant brick-and-stone facade. But inside is a family torn apart by violence, substance abuse, and self-centeredness. I wonder how Trish survives from one day to the next.

I also wonder how it came to this. Brad and I will soon start our own home. A family of two. Someday we will add kids. Can we build a family that love will bond together, even through the tough times? Or will we travel our own separate paths, strangers and combatants just living under the same roof?

Brad is no James Bannister. Brad is everything I ever dreamed about. Fun. Handsome. Sensitive. Understanding. Successful. We've got enough love for ten marriages.

But I know that James and Trish didn't start out this way, either. Somewhere along the way, probably imperceptibly, the love faded and darker emotions took its place. Now fear, distrust, and selfishness rule the home, even after the abuser is dead. How could a marriage that starts with two people loving each other turn out so bad?

I look up at the stars and whisper my thanks for Brad. I assure myself that he will never change.

CHAPTER
THIRTEEN

It's Friday morning. Tonight is date night. I've got so much to get done today that I need to put tonight out of my mind, but Brad Carson dominates my every thought. And even though I've seen him every day this week, it seems as if we haven't had any time together in months. As with every case he handles, he has turned this *Girl Next Door* case into a holy war. The depositions and mediation are eating him alive. And now Tara's case is distracting me. Tonight we will put all that aside and focus on each other.

I can't wait until we get married. Every night will be Friday night. Funny thing is, I know it's not true. Much as I loved my first husband, Bill, I found that living together had a way of deadening the senses. Though you fight it, you learn to take for granted the very person you love more than life itself. You know you can't live without him, but you find yourself ignoring him and assuming that he will always be there.

Not this time, I promise myself. I will work on this marriage and never take Brad for granted.

"Hold my calls," I tell Bella as I head toward my office. I'm still thinking about Brad and don't take time to engage in the normal banter.

"Ex-cuse me," drawls Bella. "Aren't we testy today?"

"C'mon, Bella, you know I don't mean anything by it. It's just that if I don't get some research done on the Bannister case today—"

Bella gives me one of those holier-than-thou looks. "I know," she says, in one of her condescending motherly tones. "And I know you had a long night last night, so I've already fixed some coffee."

I stop dead in my tracks. Bella always seems to know everything. But it still amazes me how quickly she finds out.

"How'd you hear about that?"

"Your fiancé left me a voice mail this morning at about six o'clock." She rolls her eyes. "Said you had a long night last night and I should go easy on you today. As if I don't every day. Said you would probably need some time alone to get ready for the hearing next week. Probably left you a few messages too, maybe of a somewhat more personal nature."

Incredible. I am no longer amazed at Bella; now it is Brad. I keep the guy up late working on *my* case when he has a mediation hearing to get ready for. Then this morning, right in the midst of chaotic last-minute prep for the mediation, he has the thoughtfulness to call our secretary and make sure she's looking out for me. *Amazing.* What did I do to deserve this? What can I do to make sure it never ends?

"Thanks, Bella," I say, skipping the coffee and heading straight for the voice mail. Only ten hours stand between me and my date. He's lucky he's not in the office right now. I would probably attack him.

Throughout the morning I force myself to concentrate on the business at hand. I am glued to my computer for three hours, taking notes as I read case after case about the premeditation required for first-degree murder and the evidentiary issues in our case. The words are starting to blur, but I'm not complaining. I know this sounds geeky, but I love research. There is something pure and noble about it—hunting down and analyzing prior cases to help a real-life client with serious needs. There is something majestic and certain about it—black ink on white pages. We are a nation of laws that apply to all men and women equally, regardless of race, religion, or social status.

Maybe I won't feel this way in ten years, or even two. Maybe not next year. But right now I could sit in front of this computer all day and read these cases, looking for just the right opinion to set Tara free. I know I will lose my fair share of cases, but I will never lose them because I am outresearched. I owe it to my clients to know the law— every angle, every rule, every exception, every exception to every exception. I might get outlawyered, but I will not get outworked.

I stand up and walk around the office, stretching my arms and back. I walk down to the small kitchen for a bottled water. Then I return and begin my fourth hour. No phone calls, no breaks. Just me and ghosts from cases past. I turn my attention to the interrogation of my client.

The police tricked Tara into a confession by lying to her. They said her brother had told them everything, when in fact he had said nothing. Here is a sixteen-year-old kid, traumatized by her father's death, who confesses only because the police purposefully misled her. That can't be legal. It seems open and shut.

Not so fast, say the cases popping up on my screen.

Like the one involving sixteen-year-old Sean Novak. He was accused of killing two younger boys in his neighborhood. He confessed only after police lied to him about supposedly finding his fingerprints on the victims' clothing.

The Virginia Supreme Court was apparently unfazed by lying police officers, holding that the key issue was whether the confession was voluntary. "While a deliberate falsehood by a police officer may undermine the confidence of the public in law enforcement"—*duh*— "a lie by an interrogating officer, in and of itself, does not require a finding that a resulting confession was involuntary."

"Give me a break," I mutter to my computer. It will be hard to argue that Tara's confession was involuntary. Unfortunately for us, they've got it on videotape. And for the most part, Tara was calm, cool, and collected. An ice queen.

But there is still the issue of whether she should have been pro-

vided an attorney based on the comments made by Trish at the interrogation. I begin researching a new line of cases, hopeful as before,
sure that a request by a mother to talk with a lawyer ought to be worth
something. I am just digesting the first of those cases when the phone
rings. One quick ring, then another. The signal for an internal call.

"You've got a funny way of holding my calls," I tell Bella.

"I've got Tara on the other line," she counters. "Thought you
might want to take this one."

"Put her through."

A few seconds later I'm talking to Tara. She sounds hung over and
apathetic. She lets me know that her mom *made* her call.

"Sorry about last night," she says sullenly. It's as if her mom is listening in the background and forcing her to say the words.

"What do you remember about last night?" I ask coldly.

"Not much. But Mom told me what happened."

I take a few minutes to read her the riot act. "What you did was
stupid... You risked everything... Your mom stuck her neck out for
you and you let her down... You're lucky you're not stuck in jail until
the trial... Any more stunts like that and you can get a new lawyer..."
On and on I go, venting for several minutes.

I get no response from Tara, just maddening silence on the other
end of the phone.

"Do you understand what I'm saying? Do you even begin to
comprehend how serious this is?" I can feel my blood pressure rising.

A few seconds of silence, then, "Okay, Leslie. But what do you
want me to do? I said I'm sorry."

"Promise me it won't ever happen again."

"Okay."

"Okay, what?"

She lets out a loud sigh. "It won't happen again."

I take a deep breath and soften my tone. "Good. Now Tara, I've got an obligation to tell you about a deal the commonwealth has offered. I'm not recommending this, but it's my duty to tell you about it so you can consider it. Is that clear?"

"Yeah."

"The commonwealth's attorney is offering a plea bargain. They want you to plead guilty to voluntary manslaughter. You would get a minimum of two years and a maximum of five. That part would be up to the judge."

"Excuse me?" says Tara snidely. "They just want me to plead guilty like I don't even have a defense—just throw myself on the mercy of some nasty old judge I don't even know." She snorts. "I don't think so."

"Tara," I respond evenly, "they're not asking you to plead guilty to first-degree murder, which is the charge. They're asking you to plead to a lesser offense and agree to a sentence that would be a fraction of the time you would serve if you were convicted. If you get two years, with good behavior you could be out in less than one."

"Yeah, and be a convicted felon for the rest of my life."

Her attitude is making me nuts. I don't want her to take this deal, but the way she just dismisses it out of hand, like there's no chance she could ever be convicted—it just isn't right.

"Tara, you shot a man—your stepfather. And the commonwealth has some pretty strong scientific evidence of—"

"You don't believe me, do you?"

"Tara, whether I believe you is not the issue—"

"I knew it," she interrupts me again. "I could hear it in your voice." Her own voice is rising now. The words come tumbling out, mixed with short stabbing breaths. "Yes, I shot my stepdad. He was strangling me! He hit me earlier. He nearly killed my mom! You don't get it, do you?! What was I supposed to do? I killed him or he would have killed me." She pauses, collecting herself. "How can you even suggest I plead guilty?"

It's the first time I've heard any emotion in Tara's voice, and it somehow comforts me. I push the scientific evidence aside for a moment and focus on the fear and anger in my client's voice.

"I hear you," I say. "And I do believe you, Tara."

She says nothing, but her breathing evens out. I can sense her relaxing, coming back down from orbit. In my mind's eye, I can see her taut jaw relax, the fierce eyes soften.

"The only question is whether we can prove it."

Rules were made to be broken. So here I sit at 7:00 p.m. on Friday night, on Brad Carson's deck, my legs straddling a long lounge chair. He's finishing the shish kebabs on the grill. I'm reading and highlighting a few more cases that I had Bella copy just before she left the office. I'm wearing a pair of khaki shorts, a sleeveless white cotton top, and a pair of Oakley wraparound shades that Brad bought me a month ago when I met him for a Saturday morning run on the Virginia Beach boardwalk. I complained every minute of the run as the in-line skaters and bicyclists blew by us. Brad hasn't invited me back since, which is fine with me.

I'll stick to the elliptical trainer in the air-conditioned gym.

"So at about three o'clock, after we've both put on our two best witnesses, I decimate their case in fifteen minutes with a closing argument that ought to be required reading in every trial practice class in the country," Brad says in his running commentary about the mediation he finished earlier that day. It's not unusual for a mediator to have both sides put on their case—conduct a little minitrial—before trying to persuade them to settle at a fair number.

"Mmm," I offer. I'm knee deep in the nuances of Miranda warnings in a case that seems right on point for Tara. The words are getting a little blurry, both because I'm tired and because I'm wearing shades instead of reading glasses. I notice out of the corner of my eye a flame briefly engulf one of the kebabs before Brad squirts it with a water bottle.

"Did you say rare?" he asks.

"Yeah." In this case, just like the last ten, the judge seems determined to give lip service to Miranda but then do whatever it takes to allow the confession into evidence anyway.

"So the mediator waits a few minutes, clearly choking back tears, then looks over the top of her glasses at the defense lawyer and says just one word..." Brad pauses, turning the kebabs.

I highlight another phrase from the case that will gut my Miranda argument.

"*Settle.*"

"That's nice." I'm beginning to really dislike the judge who wrote this particular opinion. A father, outside the interrogation room, demands a lawyer for his fourteen-year-old daughter. But the judge says the girl was old enough to knowingly waive her right to a lawyer, and since she didn't ask for one herself...

"Yep. But the defense lawyer's got a problem. I've got the mediator absolutely eating out of my hand now and I know it. So I up my settlement demand in my own mind, and this drop-dead gorgeous mediator named Roxanna asks me what it will take to settle the case. I decide to go for seven figures, tell her a million bucks..."

Again Brad pauses, thinking I'm not listening. I decide to play along. Yesterday the case was worthless, now it's worth a million? "Uh-huh," I mumble absent-mindedly.

"And the defense lawyer says okay! So we settle for a million, and then Roxanna takes off her glasses, motions for me to slide down toward her end of the conference table, then whispers something in my ear that I couldn't believe, so I asked her to repeat it. 'Marry me,' she said. Can you believe it?"

I put my cases down on the chair in front of me—this man is desperate for attention—and pull my shades down to the end of my nose, looking up at my fiancé. "Nah," I say. "Too unbelievable. You could never give a closing argument in just fifteen minutes."

I pull the shades back up over my eyes and refocus on my case. Next thing I know, without another word, Brad Carson is standing behind me giving me a back rub. This is so unfair!

And *so* relaxing.

The case in front of me loses its luster—I never liked that judge anyway—and I lean back to enjoy the pleasure of the moment. For the first time that evening, I notice the sun starting its descent over the far bank of the lazy Lynnhaven River, spraying the horizon with a beautiful collage of oranges and reds. The marsh, the long wooden dock, and the large cypress tree in Brad's backyard have this incredible calming effect, making it impossible to do anything but relax and lean back into Brad. I take off my shades, close my eyes, and drink in the salty marsh air scented with the delicious smells from the grill.

"Did you really settle?" I ask. My voice sounds like I'm in a trance.

"Not a chance," he says. "They only offered fifty thousand. The only one crying was my client."

"A little lower," I say. "Perfect... Don't you dare stop."

The man knows how to rub out every ounce of anxiety. Strong fingers, penetrating hands. As good as this feels—I could let him do this all night—I can't resist turning toward him and leaning into a slow kiss. *This* is perfect—the kind of moment you want to freeze-frame forever. Every one of the senses perfectly engaged. A beautiful summer night, the rhythm and sounds of the river in the background, the feel of the salty air tingling your skin, kissing the man you love more than any other, and smelling deeply of his...*smoke?*

I pull back from Brad and quickly turn to the grill. The kebabs are burnt offerings. They flame brightly as Brad jumps up and grabs the water bottle, turns off the gas, and douses the fire.

He stares at the charred remains of peppers, tomatoes, onions, meat, and some other unidentifiable substance. "You did say medium well, didn't you?"

I jump up and give him a quick kiss. "Good thing I'm not marrying you for your cooking." He grabs me and smiles. "I've got other strong suits," he says.

"Let's go out," I counter. "The fire gods have sent us a sign."

He looks a little disappointed but instantly knows what I mean. Our vow to wait, made when cooler heads prevailed, has no chance of surviving the heat of this night. He knows it. I know it. It's why I've been so careful not to put us in these situations. I guess I'm old-fashioned. But I want that special sense of romance on my wedding night that comes only by waiting. The great thing is he wants it too.

"You win," Brad moans. "We'll go out." He traces my face with a finger and gives me a soft, romantic kiss. "But we're moving up the wedding to tomorrow morning."

Like I said. He wants to wait too. All of twenty-four hours.

Instead of getting married Saturday morning, I head to the gym. Finally. I do stomach crunches until my abs catch fire, thinking about how good I will look in my wedding dress. Next I head to the elliptical trainer for my cardio workout. I start my CD player and settle into my normal pace—about an eight-minute mile. I decide to stay on for thirty minutes, ten minutes longer than normal, as punishment for making excuses and not coming in earlier this week.

The guy on the stationary bike next to me keeps stealing sideways glances that I pretend not to notice. He's about fifty pounds overweight, balding, and sweating like a pig. I guess that's the price I pay for wearing my white Lycra top. Though it's more modest than what some women wear, it's still apparently tight enough to get noticed by Tubby. Tomorrow, if I come, I'll wear a baggy T-shirt.

But first I've got to survive today's workout, and by mile two I'm starting to wonder. I've slowed the pace twice, but my legs are getting heavy and my lungs are on fire. Eleven minutes. I feel like I'm sprinting uphill in combat boots. The machine printout says I've slowed to a nine-minute mile. That's almost a crawl.

I talk myself out of quitting. I've felt this bad before and always worked through it. I concentrate on the next stride. I tell myself to relax, but the burning in my chest is real. It feels like the machine is running away with me, my arms and legs locked into vicious cycles that suck every ounce of air out of my lungs. I reach and stab the display, slowing the machine, but the pain in my chest increases. This is ridiculous! I've only been running on this thing for twelve lousy minutes. *If* you can call this pace "running."

The guy next to me is staring now, and I realize that I'm huffing and puffing like a train. I mentally shorten my workout goal. Twenty minutes. Surely I can make twenty minutes! I drop my head and focus on the readout, hanging in there for ten seconds at a time. My eyes start playing tricks as heat waves distort the atmosphere. It's like my batteries are running out and somebody is playing the tape in slow motion. Things begin to blur, then spin. Though I'm not thinking clearly, I know I've got to get off this machine! My chest constricts as I reach for the Stop button. Pain sears my lungs and the world fades to black, my batteries completely discharged.

This has got to be a nightmare. When the world comes back into focus, I'm lying next to the elliptical machine, staring into the earnest square face of none other than Fabio! He helps me sit up and offers me a drink of bottled water. I blink hard and focus. As the heat waves stop their undulating, I realize that it's not Fabio sitting next to me; it's Brad's client Brandon, a trainer at the gym.

I take a sip of water and things start coming back to me. Brandon looks concerned. A few others have gathered around; some members are staring at me from other areas of the gym.

"You okay?" Brandon asks.

"Yeah. I think I just passed out for a second," I mumble.

"You did," says a voice from above me. I feel a drop of sweat hit my shoulder. I turn to see the chubby bike guy standing. He seems oblivious to the drops of sweat rolling off his double chin. I slide over a little as he continues. "One minute you're running like a champ, the next thing I know...bam! You're on the floor and out like a light bulb."

Brandon gives Chubby a look of frustration. "Why don't we all give her a little room?" he suggests. He stares at the pack of vultures circled around me until they start heading back to their workout stations. "I had someone call the paramedics," he says to me. "You want to hang out in the aerobics room until they get here? There's nobody in there now."

I nod my assent, grateful for the opportunity to retreat from the stares of the others. I feel like such an idiot. Brandon helps me up, and I walk slowly toward the secluded room. My chest feels better, but it's still hard to draw a deep breath. My legs feel like they weigh a thousand pounds each. What's wrong with me?

Brandon is surprisingly kind and reassuring as we wait for the paramedics. I've done such a great job avoiding his case that we've never even met at the office. I've exchanged a few grunted greetings at the gym, but that's about it. He asks me if I've been drinking any Gatorade, lectures me about keeping my electrolytes up, and assures me that people push themselves too hard all the time. "We usually have one or two people a month pass out," he says, eying me up and down the same way he did Jewel when he first laid eyes on her. "But most aren't in as good of shape as you are."

By the time the paramedics arrive, I am feeling much better physically. My main concern now is how I get out of this place without everyone gawking at me. I deny any chest pain, convincing myself that there is a major difference between burning lungs and heart attack symptoms. They take my blood pressure and other vital signs and quiz me endlessly about any family history of heart problems. Like Brandon, they don't act too concerned, and that helps me relax a little.

"Your vital signs look good, but you really need to go to the hospital and get this checked out," they say. Unfortunately for them, I know my rights, including the right to refuse medical treatment. I sign all the forms and promise I will see my doctor first thing Monday. They are not happy but eventually agree to leave after repeated assurances that I am fine and that I have no chest pain, numbness, or dizziness.

"You aren't planning on driving, are you?" asks one of the paramedics.

"I'm taking her home," says Brandon. I start to protest but quickly realize I have no choice. Instead, I just give everyone the sweetest little smile I can muster.

This whole thing has me spooked, and I would normally go to the hospital, but I've got another major problem arriving in town in just a few hours. My mom, a world-class worrier and control freak, is arriving at the Norfolk airport early this afternoon. She originally planned to stay a week or so, but with the Bannister hearing looming, I convinced her to fly back out Monday morning so I can focus on work. The thought of calling Brad so that he can pick up my mom and drive her from the airport to the hospital is all I need to convince myself that I really am okay. If my mom thought I was having physical problems, she'd never leave again. Spurred on by that thought, I thank Brandon for the offer and prepare to run the gauntlet of rubberneckers on my way through the gym with Brandon.

The ride home is pleasant enough. I don't talk much because my mind is still spinning with the events at the gym. Without realizing that I'm doing it, I find myself staring at Brandon's profile. He has an extraordinarily flat nose, like he spent too many rounds in the ring with Mike Tyson and didn't keep his guard up. This is how Fabio would look if he made a habit of chasing parked cars.

"Broke it for the first time in the ninth grade," Brandon says. "Playing football." He smiles, knowing he has read my mind. "Broke it about three times since."

"Broke what?"

This makes him chuckle. "Nice try," he says. "Anyway, I asked the

Girl Next Door producers not to shoot too many profile shots. You don't notice the nose as much head-on."

"Oh," I say. *Does he know I work with Brad?*

"Guess I should have mentioned for them to leave the transvestite models out of the show as well, huh?"

Where's this stuff coming from? "Uh...yeah, I guess so." I can't keep up with him. Maybe it's from passing out earlier, but my mind is having a hard time processing this conversation. Brandon is throwing me off guard, surprising me with his unassuming and easygoing manner.

"Maybe my next show should be an extreme makeover," he announces. "I could get the Michael Jackson nose job special."

This makes me smile. "You look fine just the way you are," I say. Then I turn to the window so he won't see me blush.

CHAPTER SIXTEEN

I think it makes your shoulders look a little broad," says Mom. Nobody but my mom has ever accused me of having broad shoulders. I suspect that the real reason she doesn't like this dress is because it's strapless and shows a little cleavage. It also has a hemline just above the knee. The only things that identify it as a wedding dress are its color, the layers of frill from top to bottom, and the eleven-hundred-dollar price tag.

"I kind of like it," I lie. "I love the way it draws in at the waist— makes my stomach look flat."

"I don't know," Mom hedges. "What's wrong with the dress back at David's Bridal?"

"Which one?" I spin in front of the mirror. The salesclerk tells me how beautiful I look.

"The second one you tried on," Mom says—which also happens to be the one she picked out. "You look so elegant in those traditional styles."

I take one long last look at this dress—who but a swimsuit model could ever wear this?—and start heading back to the changing room. "Mom, it's my second wedding," I say. "Think small wedding, informal…stylish…twenty-first century."

"At Bruton Parish?" Mom calls out. "Are you sure you don't want to even try on your grandmother's wedding dress?"

I grunt. This is not going well. Our tastes in clothes are so different I have no hope of finding a dress we both like. But I knew how much it would mean for my mom to be part of this. A few offhand comments about my physique is a small price to pay.

Though the incident at the gym weighs heavily on my mind, the last three hours with Mom have confirmed my decision not to say anything about it. I love my mom, don't get me wrong; it's just that she sometimes smothers me with love. And she *always* acts like I'm still eighteen. I tolerate it because I know I'm all she's got and because, well, sometimes it's nice to have somebody worry about you.

Before I take the dress off, I size it up in one of those little mirrors in the changing room. I square my shoulders; they do look just a little wider, maybe even stronger, than most women's. "That's ridiculous," I mumble to myself as I slip out of this stupid little sorority girl special.

For another hour and a half, Mom and I debate dresses as I worry about my health. I analyze every breath. Was that pain in my chest just now? Is my breathing constricted? Is my chest tight? No, I think that's the way it always feels. But suddenly I can't remember. Did I feel tingling in my arms or legs before I fainted? I don't think so, but it all happened so fast.

On the ride home from the gym, Brandon said that lots of people pass out from overexertion, especially if their electrolytes get low. "The blood sugar decreases, your blood pressure drops, less oxygen gets to the brain, and the room spins into blackness." I was amazed at how sensitive and intelligent Brandon sounded. He went to the trouble of having somebody follow us in his car so he could drive my car home and not leave it stranded at the gym parking lot.

I never found a chance to tell him I was Brad Carson's law partner. Or his fiancée.

I try to focus on Mom's comments about the dresses, but she can tell I'm distracted. She asks several times if I'm feeling okay.

"Sure," I say. "It's just so surreal, shopping for wedding dresses."

The afternoon passes and Brad joins us for dinner. He gives Mom a polite hug, tells her how great she looks, and pulls out a metal chair for her at this little outdoor café.

"Is the wedding still on?" he asks.

"For now," I answer. "I didn't have the heart to tell Mom we almost eloped last night."

I notice the twinkle in Brad's eyes as he catches my meaning immediately. One of the great things about being in love is knowing someone so well you can tell secrets in the middle of a crowd without anybody else knowing.

"Yeah," says Brad with a sigh. "If it were up to your daughter, we would have eloped a long time ago." I shoot him a sideways look. He pretends not to notice, leaning toward Mom and lowering his voice. "But I'm not going to let that happen. I'm holding out for one of those nice, big, formal weddings. You know, something befitting a queen like Leslie."

"That's what I'm talking about," says Mom. "Maybe you and I should just get married."

Brad smiles broadly. He has smitten both of us, and he knows it. I kick him under the table.

One thing leads to another and soon we're talking guest list. I know what's coming, and I have all my ammunition ready.

"It's going to be really small, Mom," I say as earnestly as I can. "Brad and I want to invite just a few friends and family."

My mom takes a bite of her salad—how she eats those things with no dressing, I'll never know—and looks concerned. "Is your father on the family list?"

This is the ironic thing about Mom. She's the first one to badmouth my dad, which he richly deserves, but she also wants him invited to everything. "Mom, he didn't come to my wedding with Bill. He hasn't called or written in three years." I pause and the silence is deafening. Brad looks like he's ready to excuse himself. "And what if he surprised us all and actually showed up? It would ruin it."

Mom swallows the bite and dabs at her mouth. "Leslie, he left us at a tough time—"

"For a younger woman he was already sleeping with," I add, as if Mom doesn't know.

She ignores the comment. "But he put you through college, and he made every child support and alimony payment on time. After you laid into his new wife at your college graduation, I think he could be forgiven for not hanging around more. I really think he's at least entitled to an invitation."

I stare at Mom and notice for the first time that day how dramatically she seems to have aged in the last few months. The lines on her face are deeper, longer, and more pronounced than I've seen before. I'd been so focused on myself all day that we hadn't even talked about how *she* was doing. She's been divorced for twelve years now and just never seemed to meet the right man. In moments like this, I feel sorry for her. And that doesn't make it any easier to forgive my dad.

"I've talked it over with Brad. We know how you feel about this. And we respect so much the way you stick up for Dad even after the way he treated you. But it's our wedding...and we don't think he should come."

Mom puts down her fork as she digests our final answer. It seems she has lost her appetite.

Brad reaches under the table and takes my hand. Thank God he's nothing like my dad, I tell myself for the hundred and tenth time.

CHAPTER
SEVENTEEN

Tuesday morning comes more quickly than I would have liked, so quickly that I am not close to being ready for the preliminary hearing. I spent half of Monday sitting in my doctor's office, waiting to be seen. He checked my vital signs, asked me a few questions, took some blood and urine samples, and told me that things looked okay to him. As a precaution he referred me to a cardiologist for a stress test and told me to avoid any exercise or stressful activity until my appointment on Wednesday.

So here I am on Tuesday morning, walking from the parking lot to the Juvenile and Domestic Relations Court Building, stressing out because I'm not adequately prepared for one of the most important hearings of my short professional career. If I survive this day, tomorrow's stroll on the treadmill will be a cakewalk.

I like to overprepare for things. If I had six months, I wouldn't feel quite ready for this hearing. A year might be about right. But the real world doesn't operate on my schedule. I am learning that in the harried lifestyle of criminal defense work you are almost never as ready as you would like to be, certainly never as ready as your client would like you to be.

Unless your client is like Tara. In a three-hour briefing on Monday afternoon, she continued to display her "I couldn't care less" attitude about this whole thing—as if the court might ground her for a month or two at the most. "Do you realize you could spend the rest of your life behind bars?" I asked her a half-dozen times. She answered with that infuriating shrug.

I hope we win, but I hope the judge chews her out good.

Contrary to his earlier promises to be with me every step of the way, Brad is stuck at a hearing in federal court that carried over from yesterday. So this hearing is entirely up to me. If I weren't so frustrated with Tara, I might feel sorry for her.

Juvenile court is nothing like the courtrooms you see on television. This one is small and dark, with just a few rows for spectators—I checked it out late Monday afternoon. As I arrive at 9:00 a.m. on Tuesday, there is an excited mob of reporters in the hallway that I push through with Tara and Trish. I look straight ahead with my meanest "no comment" look—that part I learned from the lawyers on *Law and Order*—and emerge into the relative silence of the courtroom.

Mitchell Taylor is already there. Of course. Harlan Fowler is jawboning with a small bevy of lawyers. Their conversation tones down a notch when I enter, never a good sign. I notice them staring at Tara. It's hard to blame them.

She is not a defendant who cleans up well. I insisted that she wear a dress but should have been more specific. She is wearing a skintight black leather miniskirt and a cropped top that leaves her wonderful little pierced navel exposed. Where was Trish when this kid got dressed?

My thoughts are interrupted when Judge Franklin Overstreet takes the bench, his black robes flying everywhere. The court clerk does a halfhearted version of the "Oyez, oyez" introduction, but Overstreet waves her off before she can finish. "Stay seated," he grunts. As far as I can tell, I am the only person who made an effort to stand.

"We are here today to determine whether there is probable cause to charge the defendant with first-degree murder," Overstreet begins. He has a pointed face, lots of wrinkles and creases, and little black reading glasses creeping down his nose. His thin black hair is combed straight back and looks a little out of place on a guy pushing sixty. Generous doses of Grecian Formula, I figure. He looks like a ferret, the type of guy who was probably nicknamed Weasel growing up.

"Because the defendant is older than fourteen, if I find probable cause, the law requires that I transfer the case to circuit court so the defendant can be tried as an adult." He looks at Mitchell Taylor and then at me. "Any questions?"

"No sir," I answer. But it's a lie. In truth, I do have one question: how in the world did we get stuck with Overstreet? Judges are assigned to cases randomly in J&DR court. And when Brad briefed me on the six possible candidates, he didn't have anything good to say about Overstreet.

"C'mon," I said. "You can't tell me the man doesn't have one positive trait."

Brad thought for a moment. "You're right," he admitted. "At least the man's predictable. Whatever the commonwealth's attorney wants, Overstreet does."

I chuckled at the time. But I'm not laughing now.

Mitchell Taylor, on the other hand, looks absolutely giddy. He rises to his full height, stands ramrod straight, and calls his first witness.

For the next two hours he hammers our case with bulletproof scientific evidence. The medical examiner, a grizzled old warhorse named Albert Fancher, testifies about the cause of death and basically reiterates what Mitchell told me in Harlan Fowler's office. I do my best to cross-examine the old codger, emphasizing how abusive James Bannister was to his wife and children, but Fancher brushes off my questions with monotone answers that make it clear he regards me as a lightweight. He's a hard witness to control because his answers tend to become lengthy scientific lectures about the commonwealth's evidence, having little to do with the question I asked. The more he lectures, the more I sweat, my voice occasionally changing pitch in the middle of a question. The third time that Overstreet asks me how much longer I will be, I take the hint, and Fancher steps down unscathed.

Mitchell strides back up to the podium, more confident than

before—if that's possible—and calls his next witness, Detective Louis Gonzales. The detective is young and brings a lot of energy to the courtroom, contrasting nicely with the dry delivery of the medical examiner. Gonzales is dark and handsome with bright, expressive blue eyes and thick black hair. I make a mental note to be careful about selecting single young female jurors if, God forbid, I have to try this case before a jury. I also lean over and tell my client to quit fawning over this guy with her eyes.

"He's hot," Tara informs me.

"And he's trying to make sure you grow old in prison," I remind her.

"Nobody's perfect," she mumbles.

CHAPTER EIGHTEEN

I take some solace in the fact that the police department switched the lead detective on this case from Detective Anderson, the seedy cop who tricked a confession out of Tara, to the cool and confident Gonzales. When he disclosed his witnesses, Mitchell gave me some lame excuse about Anderson's caseload and the need to off-load some files. I knew at the time that they just wanted to distance Anderson and his spotty disciplinary record from this high-profile case. I will make it a major issue if we take this case to a full trial. For today, however, Anderson will not even darken the doors of the courtroom.

Mitchell and Gonzales focus entirely on the first-degree murder charge, since Mitchell has not yet amended the indictment to include the gun charges. He probably reasoned that doing so would give me an excuse for a continuance. He and Gonzales have prepared several colorful charts and mounted a lot of grisly crime-scene photos for the benefit of Overstreet, who seems ready to rule even before he hears my cross-examination. They confirm the coroner's testimony about entry wounds, stippling, and tattooing.

"Only the bullet wound to the chest has any hemorrhaging associated with it," says Gonzales, pointing to one of the photographs, "meaning that Mr. Bannister was already dead when the other bullet, the one to the head, was fired into him."

Mitchell then places an enlarged photo of the chest wound on an easel, and Gonzales testifies about the lack of smudging, stippling, or tattooing around the entry wound. "This would be expected if the suspect had been closer than about twelve feet," Gonzales says. Mitchell next places some photos of the recliner chair with closeups of the blood spattered on the chair. Based on the pattern, Gonzales speculates, over my objection, that James Bannister was sitting in the reclining chair when the first shot was fired.

"Where was the defendant when she fired that shot?" asks Mitchell.

"Objection."

"Overruled."

"Thank you, Judge," Mitchell says with his marinelike intensity. I half expect him to salute.

For my part, I just stare at the judge. This is rank speculation. "Sit down, Ms. Connors."

I sit.

"The defendant was most likely on the other side of the room," Gonzales answers. He is standing up now, using a pointer to illustrate on an enlarged picture of the family room. "About twenty-five feet away."

Overstreet removes his reading glasses and studies Tara for a moment with little weasel eyes. Then he turns back to the witness.

"Twenty-five feet?" he asks.

"Just on the first shot, Judge," emphasizes Gonzales. "On the last shot, she was most likely standing over him. But by then, of course, Mr. Bannister was already dead."

Overstreet looks at Tara again, condemning her with his eyes as only judges can do. She stares back, practically snarling. I nudge her under the table, and she gives me one of those "What did I do now?" looks.

But I don't have much time to worry about my uncooperative client's facial expressions, because Gonzales is busy hitting me with some more good stuff.

"Did you check the defendant for gunpowder residue on the night of the attack?" asks Mitchell.

"Yes."

"What did you find?"

"The defendant tested positive for gunpowder residue on her right hand." Gonzales pauses for effect. "Her shooting hand."

Mitchell's strategy is clear. He is trying to establish probable cause, including premeditation, without using Tara's confession. I guess he didn't like the bruises on her face anymore than I did.

"Did you recently obtain a supplemental search warrant," Mitchell asks, quickly shifting gears, "authorizing a search of the defendant's computer files, including her e-mails and instant messages to her friends?"

"Yes."

"Tell the court what you found."

Gonzales dramatically places a stack of documents on the rail in front of the witness box. "From the hard drive of the defendant's computer, we were able to retrieve dozens of e-mails and instant messages where the defendant talked about killing her father."

Overstreet leans forward; I can see something change in his eyes. My mouth goes dry, my throat clenching. We've lost. I can sense it. I haven't had a chance to ask the detective a single question, and we've already lost. The reality of it hits me, and it makes me physically sick.

This is justice?

"Did you find any instant messages from the day of the murder?" asks Taylor.

"No sir."

"How about from the night before?"

"This one." Gonzales waves it around a little, like he's displaying a trophy. "Would you like me to read it?"

I knew the detective had taken the computer from Tara's house the day before she first came into my office. But I've never seen the messages. I'm on my feet, temper flaring.

"Your Honor, I've never seen these documents," I say, shooting an accusatory look at Mitchell Taylor. "I'm entitled to do so under the discovery rules."

Mitchell looks at the judge without blinking. "We picked up the computer on May 2 but had to hire an outside firm to retrieve the IMs from the hard drive. We just received these last night. Counsel is entitled to the documents prior to trial, but not necessarily prior to this hearing."

Overstreet swivels his gaze back to me. "Ms. Connors?"

I don't have any idea if Mitchell's right or not. This is my first criminal case. "Fundamental fairness, Your Honor," I manage to sputter. "How can I be prepared for this hearing if the commonwealth's attorney doesn't notify me until the witness is on the stand?"

"Judge, the commonwealth is not required to—"

Overstreet shuts Mitchell off with a raised hand. "Give Ms. Connors a copy of the documents now," he orders. Then he turns to me, "If you need a recess before cross-examination, I'll grant one."

"Thank you, Judge," Mitchell says.

I sit down without thanking Overstreet for his unfair ruling. He glares at me for a moment. Mitchell waits, probably trying to highlight my sullenness. Let him wait. Stubbornness is one of my strongest traits.

Mitchell passes me a stack of documents and then asks Gonzales, "Would you mind reading the highlighted exchange on the top document for the court?"

Gonzales reads loud and slow. "It starts with a message from Richbrat; that's Tara's screen name." He is working hard not to smile. "James is being an A-1 jerk, as usual..." he stops, looks at Mitchell. "The defendant always referred to her stepfather by his first name..."

"Go on," Mitchell prods.

"This is an IM deal, so her friend, a girl with a screen name of

Wiccarules, writes back, tells her she needs to 'Menendez the old fart.' 'Menendez' appears to have been a code word that she and this particular friend used a lot. It apparently refers to the Menendez brothers who shot their father—"

"Objection," I say. I'm kicking myself for being so slow to make it.

"Sustained," says Overstreet. But he already has the gist of it.

"What did the defendant say in response?" asks Mitchell.

"Gunshots would be too quick," says Gonzales, reading the e-mail. "She says she prefers torture and then a Laci Peterson type of beheading—"

"Objection," I yell. This time I'm on my feet quicker, sounding like a real lawyer.

"On what grounds?" asks Overstreet.

I run through a quick catalog of objections from law school and begin to panic when I realize that nothing fits. It just sounded so bad, I figured it must have been improper—

"On what grounds?" repeats Overstreet.

"Prejudicial," I say.

"That's a new one on me," Overstreet says. "I'm assuming it's prejudicial to your case if Mr. Taylor is bringing it out. That doesn't mean it's inadmissible." I drop back into my seat. "Objection overruled." He turns to Gonzales. "Please finish."

"I basically did," says Gonzales. "She just makes this statement about beheading her stepfather, and then they change the subject."

"Nothing further," Mitchell says dramatically. He turns to take his seat.

CHAPTER
NINETEEN

I stand on weak knees, knowing there is a lot riding on my cross-examination. I'm torn between the nerves grinding my stomach and the anger that burns from Mitchell's surprise evidence. I need to change the momentum quickly. I decide I can't afford to ask for a recess and allow the weasel's preliminary thoughts to harden into concrete.

"Do you want to take a few minutes and review the instant messages?" Judge Overstreet asks.

"No thanks, Judge," I swallow hard. "I'm ready."

"Suit yourself," says the weasel.

"Twenty-five feet," I say to Gonzales as I stand next to my counsel table. "About the distance from me to you?"

He considers this. "Approximately."

"Not very far, is it?"

"Matter of opinion."

I put my hand on my chin and nod. Then I pick up three photographs from my table, have them marked as exhibits, and then show them to the witness.

"Do you recognize the woman in the pictures?"

"Yes."

"It's not easy, is it?"

Gonzales hesitates. "I don't understand the question."

"It's not easy to recognize Trish Bannister with her face so bruised and swollen, is it?"

I see the first hint of caution flash in his eyes. "I recognize her easily enough. But she has been beaten."

"Have you watched the videotape of my client's alleged confession on the night of the murder?"

"Yes."

"And do these look like still photos of Trish Bannister taken from that video?"

Gonzales recovers his look of bravado. "If you say so."

I next show him a picture of Tara, the mark on her cheekbone clearly visible. "And is this a still photograph taken from that same video, showing the bruise on my client's face?"

"Appears to be."

"Now, Detective Gonzales"—I hover next to the witness as my nervousness gives way to anger—"are you saying that my client and her mother somehow staged their brutal beatings on the night of the murder as a pretext so that Tara could kill her stepdad?"

"No," he answers quickly, "I never said that."

"Those are real bruises, aren't they?"

He nods.

"Real choke marks on Trish Bannister's neck?"

"Of course." His tanned face is reddening.

"And that's real swelling around her eye and cheekbone, isn't it?"

"Obviously."

"And real swelling on Tara's face too."

"To a lesser degree, yes. And I would note there are no choke marks on her neck."

"In your experience, do abusers always leave marks when they choke somebody?"

"No."

"Detective Gonzales, would you agree that people act in self-defense when they have a reasonable apprehension that their life is in danger?"

"Objection," calls out Mitchell. "Self-defense requires an imminent threat of personal harm or death."

"Sustained," says Overstreet before I can respond.

"Fair enough," I say, inching even closer to Gonzales. Maybe I'm just trying to think positive, but I swear tiny beads of sweat are forming on his forehead. "Let's stick with that definition, 'imminent threat of bodily harm or death.'" I take the photo of Tara out of his hand and pin him back with my eyes.

"Are you saying that a sixteen-year-old girl who is confronted with a drunken father who weighs... About how much did Mr. Bannister weigh, Detective?"

He ponders this. "Maybe two-twenty."

"About two hundred twenty pounds. And how tall?"

"Six-one, six-two."

"Okay," I say, winding up again. "Would you say a sixteen-year-old girl the size of my client who is confronted with a drunken step-father who weighs about two-twenty and stands about six-two and has already assaulted her at least once"—I wave the photo at him—"would you say that this girl just might be under an imminent threat of bodily harm or death?"

I am proud of the question and pleased that Gonzales lets it hang in the air for a moment before answering.

"Not when her father's on the other side of the room," he says gamely. "Maybe even asleep in his recliner."

I stare him down for a moment as if that is the most ridiculous answer I've ever heard. He squirms but maintains eye contact.

"Detective," I use a sarcastic and scolding tone, "do you have any evidence that suggests Mr. Bannister was sleeping?"

He hesitates. "The angle of the entry wound suggests he was reclined in the chair."

It's time to resort to a neat little trick I learned in law school. When a witness doesn't answer the question, you ask the exact same question again, highlighting his evasiveness and emphasizing your point.

"My question, Detective, was whether you had any evidence that Mr. Bannister was *sleeping*."

"Other than the fact that he was sitting in the recliner...no."

I decide that's as good as I'll get on that point. *Keep moving.* "Now, your belief that Mr. Bannister was sitting in the chair is based in part on the angle of entry of the bullet, is that correct?"

"Yes."

"But the angle of entry could be affected by a struggle for the gun, couldn't it? I mean, if Tara's dad was choking her, and she tried to shoot him, but maybe he grabbed her wrist and the gun got wrenched up higher than his chest"—I demonstrate this possibility as I talk, holding an imaginary gun—"maybe she twisted the gun barrel down toward her father and managed to pull the trigger, or maybe he squatted down at the last minute, trying to avoid a shot. Aren't there lots of possibilities that might explain that angle of entry?"

"No," Gonzales says confidently. "All of those scenarios are based on the defendant and her father being less than an arm's length away. Because there is no stippling or tattooing around the entry wound, the shot could not have been fired at point-blank range. My estimate is that the defendant was about twenty-five feet away."

"And thus," I say, "couldn't possibly have been in fear for her life."

He gives me a look of puzzlement, wondering why I would help finish his thought. "Precisely," he says guardedly.

Perfect. I hand him the photo and head back to my counsel table. I notice that Gonzales has now placed the pictures of Trish Bannister on the rail in front of the witness box. I wonder if I should go through with this next ploy. It was Brad's idea, something that fits his courtroom style but not mine. To me it seems way too dramatic. I'm not even sure I can pull it off.

If it backfires, I'll look like the biggest fool who ever tried a murder case.

But I am desperate. And I did dress for this—just in case—flat-soled shoes, a pantsuit instead of a dress. I take a deep breath and screw my face into a nasty scowl.

Here goes.

"Mr. Gonzales," I say, my voice thick with venom, "pick up that top picture of Trish Bannister and look at it."

Mitchell stands and objects, setting the stage more perfectly than I could have planned. He claims I'm badgering the witness.

I ignore him. "Pick it up," I demand, my voice rising.

"Judge," implores Mitchell, his arms spread.

But Overstreet seems momentarily paralyzed by my intensity. I point at Gonzales and watch him stiffen. "Pick it up," I demand. My voice shakes a little. Leslie the actress.

He picks it up. Mitchell is still standing. "Judge, Ms. Connors needs to treat the witness with a little more respect—"

"Respect," I interrupt, practically screaming. I'm like a lawyer who's come unglued. "He wants respect!" I sneer at Mitchell, my nerves at the breaking point. Gonzales and Overstreet stare wide-eyed at me.

Am I truly crazy? Truly out of control? With conjured anger so real I've convinced myself...I do it. I whirl from Mitchell to the witness and rush at Gonzales, like a possessed woman, anger etched in the crimson of my face. "Give me that photo," I demand of Gonzales. "Give me that!"

I cover the distance between us in a flash. He stiffens and nearly comes out of his seat, holding the photo tentatively, his other hand instinctively bracing against the rail. His head jerks back away from me, every muscle is strung tight, ready to explode. Meanwhile, Overstreet bangs his gavel, calling out my name.

It all happens so fast—my charge, Gonzales's reaction, Overstreet shouting. One second I'm at my counsel table, the next second I'm standing in front of Gonzales, wild-eyed. He's now half out of his seat—ready to dodge or pounce or somehow fend off this maniac standing before him.

And then, without even touching the photograph, I just exhale slowly, relaxing every muscle.

And I smile.

"Ms. Connors," says Judge Overstreet. Now *his* voice is shaking. "I don't know what you're trying to prove. But one more outburst like that and I'll hold you in contempt."

"Yes, Your Honor." I look at the judge, whose face still registers shock, then at Mitchell Taylor, who knows he's been had, then back at the witness. Brad has coached me carefully in what to do next, how to choreograph the next part so that Gonzales has little chance to deny his reaction.

I turn to the stunned court reporter and, with the detached calm of a flight attendant as she gives her preflight spiel, I dictate what just happened. "Let the record reflect," I say, "that I just charged at the witness from my counsel table, a distance that the witness had previously estimated at twenty-five feet." I take a breath; my antics have left me a little short-winded. "Let the record also reflect that when I first turned and verbally accosted the witness, even before I moved toward him, the witness tensed, sat bolt upright in his chair, and stared at me with saucer-shaped eyes. When I moved toward him, still shouting, Detective Gonzales came partway out of his seat and braced himself against the witness rail in front of him."

I lean toward Gonzales and, in the most affable tone possible, ask, "Is that an accurate description of what just happened, Detective?"

He knows it is, Mitchell Taylor knows it is, and most important, Judge Overstreet knows it is. Gonzales ponders his predicament for a beat and apparently decides there's no sense denying the obvious.

"I suppose so."

I nod appreciatively, and now it's me who's smirking. "Twenty-five feet doesn't seem so far away when you've got a crazy red-headed woman coming after you, does it?"

"No," says Gonzales gruffly. "But I didn't shoot you either."

Beautiful. I love it when a witness tries to fight back on points that are oh so obvious.

"Fortunately for me," I remind him, "you didn't have a gun."

"Objection," says Mitchell, but I've already turned and headed toward my seat.

"Sustained," says Overstreet, though I hear the amusement in his voice. And out of the corner of my eye, I can see the weasel smiling.

CHAPTER
TWENTY

T hat was awesome!" whispers Tara when I return to my seat.

"Thanks."

I try to act indifferent—ho-hum, another day at the office—but inside I'm sky high, my heart jackhammering against my chest. It's the adrenaline rush from cross-examination, the feeling that makes trial work so addicting.

It is a feeling and a victory that are short-lived.

Mitchell the marine takes his feet for redirect examination and stands as ramrod straight as ever, like he's ready to order the assault on Iwo Jima. His voice is just as confident and strong as it was before my cross-examination.

"Tell the court," says Mitchell, "whether the evidence indicates that Mr. Bannister was charging at the defendant or sitting in his chair when he was shot."

"Sitting in his chair."

"What evidence supports that?"

I'm up. "Objection. That's been asked and answered."

"Well, apparently Counsel did not understand it the first time," Mitchell replies.

I give him a look which he ignores. "Overruled," says Overstreet. Of course.

Gonzales shifts in his seat, and the muscles on his face relax a little. "There was a blood-spatter pattern on the reclining chair—tiny droplets of blood sprayed from a gunshot wound—but none of those droplets showed up on parts of the chair that would be covered by a person like Mr. Bannister if he were sitting in it. Moreover, there is a small degree of what looks like pooled blood on the crease in the chair between the back of the chair and the seat—about where you'd expect it to be if someone was shot while sitting in the chair."

Mitchell waits a moment as Overstreet writes some notes.

"Now," says Mitchell, "let me redirect your attention to that stack of IMs you've placed on the floor next to your chair—the stack that Ms. Connors ignored."

I start to object and then reconsider. Why bother?

"Do those documents contain a hard copy of IMs from Friday, April 29?" Mitchell asks.

Uh-oh. While Gonzales riffles through his stack, I thumb furiously through my copies. I feel my heart pound its machine-gun rhythm as I think what this might mean.

I nudge Tara and raise my eyebrows at her as I shuffle papers.

"I dunno," she whispers loudly. "I write lots of stuff."

"Here are the pages from April 29," announces Gonzales. I locate the same pages as he waits for Mitchell's next question. "She's talking to her friend Wiccarules."

"Can you read the highlighted portions?" asks Mitchell.

I'm already reading them and my head starts spinning. I've been set up! Mitchell held these entries back, deciding to end Gonzales's testimony this way, blunting the force of anything I did on cross-examination. As I read, I start feeling sick to my stomach. I'm mad at myself for not taking a break and reading this garbage before my cross-examination. And I'm furious at Tara for what she has written.

I focus so hard on the words in front of me that the voices of Gonzales and Mitchell fade to background noise, like they're speaking at the end of a long tunnel.

Wiccarules: Beach on Sat?

Richbrat: Can't. Mom won't let me.

Wiccarules: Why?

Richbrat: Let's bolt for Canada instead—lots of hot guys with cool accents!!!!!

Wiccarules: Canada????

Richbrat: and Speedos. You in?

Wiccarules: Speedos. Gross. What's wrong with Nags Head?

Richbrat: It gets old.

Wiccarules: Serious?

Richbrat: About Canada?

Wiccarules: Yeah.

Richbrat: ABSOLUTELY!!!!!

Wiccarules: Cause you think you're going to jail for shooting your dad?

Richbrat: Nah. My lawyer will get me off on self-defense ☺

Wiccarules: Cool. Your dad was a jerk.

Wiccarules: Was it?

Richbrat: Huh?

Wiccarules: Self-defense.

Richbrat: What do you think?

Wiccarules: Dunno.

Richbrat: More like payback. I shot him once for beating mom and once in the head for mouthing off to me.

Wiccarules: Cool. I'd like to do my dad sometime.

Richbrat: lol. You should have seen him beg.

Wiccarules: Now he knows how your mom feels.

Richbrat: Hope he rots in hell. Should have shot him once for my brother, too, but I forgot. ☹

Wiccarules: Oh well.

Wiccarules: But Canada?

Richbrat: gtg someone at the door.

Wiccarules: later

Richbrat: later

My blood boils as I think about how stupid my client is—how cavalierly she talks about shooting her dad. I glance at the judge as the IM trail is read—Overstreet is stewing. I put down my pen and stop taking notes. I'm so mad at Tara I can hardly see my legal pad anyway. Any chance I had at this hearing has been washed away by this mindless, heartless stream of teen bravado. The deal we so indignantly rejected now seems like a bargain.

I glance sideways toward the prosecutor's table and notice the pained look on Harlan Fowler's face. He doesn't seem to be liking this any more than I am. I then turn toward Tara, who is doodling, trying to act unimpressed, though she cannot hide the slight tremor in her hand. The color has drained from her face, and her shoulders droop forward while the entire courtroom eavesdrops on her IM conversation. All during law school, my non–law school friends would ask me: "How can you represent someone you know is guilty?" Maybe that should bother me more, but right now that's not my problem. I fume at my guilty-as-sin client, not worried about how I can represent someone this *guilty*. My concern, and my only concern right now, is how in the world I can effectively represent someone this incredibly *stupid*.

CHAPTER
TWENTY-ONE

Ten minutes after Overstreet rules against us, lecturing Tara in a stuttering display of righteous indignation, I march down the steps of the courthouse with Trish and Tara in tow, ignoring the cameras and microphones thrust in our faces. As we part ways in the parking lot, I deliver one last stern rebuke.

"Don't talk to anybody about the case ever again," I say to Tara for the third time since court adjourned, my voice still raw with anger. "That includes telephone conversations, e-mail, IMs, snail mail, smoke signals, and everything else. Do you understand that?"

Tara gives me a quick nod without looking up. Though she keeps her eyes fixed on the ground, I can tell the eyes are glistening with tears, her dark eye shadow beginning to run. It's the first hint of remorse I've seen from Tara since I took the case.

Good.

The sharp edges of my anger are blunted ever so slightly by a pang of sympathy. "And stay away from this girl Wiccarules," I chide. "I mean, what kind of kid has a screen name like that anyway?" I'm so frustrated with Tara, it doesn't bother me that I'm sounding like my mom.

Another quick nod of the head and Tara takes a swipe at an errant tear. "Will you stay on the case?"

"What?"

She looks at me, her eyes rimmed with tears. "Are you still going to be my lawyer?"

I notice that the reporters are starting to wander our way from the courthouse steps. I take Tara by the arm, see the scared little girl, and feel my anger melt away.

"As long as you do what I say," I pause, allowing the point to sink in. She looks at me unblinking, and I sense that a lot is being left unsaid. "We've got to talk," I say. "Regroup." I take a half step closer, looking over Tara's shoulder as the reporters head our way. "Are there some things you're not telling me?"

Tara glances quickly at Trish, as if she's seeking permission to share something. But Trish's face is a blank mask—What's going on here?—and Tara just gives me a quick headshake.

"One more question, Ms. Connors," barks one of the reporters as he leads a small pack toward me.

"We need to talk," I tell Tara, then I let go of her arm and we both head toward our cars.

"Ms. Connors, will you still be arguing self-defense in circuit court?"

I turn and glance over my shoulder, shake my head in disdain, and pick up the pace as I head toward the far corner of the parking lot.

The good news is that the reporters don't follow me to my car. The bad news is that when I reach my humble little Accord, there is an imposing man standing next to the driver's-side door, arms crossed, in a custom-fitting Brooks Brothers suit. He looks a little like a tanned and older replica of Mr. Clean—the bald and muscular floor-cleaning genie. He wears a pair of Oakley shades, and the sun ricochets off his shaved head. He is the last man on earth I want to see right now.

The very last.

"Saw you in court today," says Mack Strobel as I approach my car. "Good for you."

Strobel and I have some bad history. During my final year of law school, I helped Brad try a highly emotional case with Strobel on the other side. Strobel was tenacious, underhanded, unethical, and insanely conceited. Unfortunately, he also turned out to be very good.

I come to a stop in front of him. "You're blocking my door."

He turns and looks at the car, as if he hadn't noticed. But he doesn't move. I put my thumb on the Alarm button of my remote.

"I represent a client whose interests coincide with yours," he says in the authoritative tone of his that drives me nuts. "And I have some confidential information that may be of interest."

I grind my teeth, frustrated at the way this guy sets me off. *"I have some confidential information that may be of interest,"* says this self-possessed man, as if he's reading from a low-budget movie script. Who talks that way these days?

"E-mail me," I say. Then I hit the Alarm button and the car wails in response. Strobel shakes his head and steps aside. Heads all over the parking lot turn our way. I push the Alarm button again and the car falls quiet. Strobel watches as I throw my briefcase in the backseat and climb behind the wheel. I roll down my window, put on my own shades, and look up at him.

"What is it?" I ask.

He leans over and lowers his voice. Another movie script move. "Insurance information," he says, the stale lunch on his breath nearly knocking me backward. "And it just might give you some leverage over our friend Harlan Fowler. Personal leverage."

The commonwealth's attorney! I think about this for a moment. My mind flashes to the look on Fowler's face a few hours ago when Mitchell unveiled the damning instant messages. Fowler looked shocked, my own surprise and outrage mirrored on his face. And when Overstreet ruled against us, I noticed Fowler slump a little in his chair, as if some of the life had just been sucked from his body.

At the time, I wrote it off to his emotional attachment to this case. Who could blame him? Losing a friend, then hearing the testimony about the unremorseful IMs from the friend's stepdaughter.

But now Strobel is suggesting something more. My instincts—call it women's intuition if you want—tell me that Strobel is right.

"Get in."

Strobel shoots me a condescending smile and walks slowly around to the passenger side. "I'm glad we're on the same side of this one," he says as he settles into the passenger seat.

CHAPTER
TWENTY-TWO

W hen Strobel gets into the car, I pop a mint in my mouth and offer him one, which he refuses. *Darn.* For several minutes neither of us says a word. I drive down North Landing Road in traffic, still simmering with frustration about the hearing, waiting impatiently for Strobel to tell me his big piece of confidential information. I sense that he's hoping I'll suggest we stop for coffee or lunch someplace. *Fat chance.*

"Well?" I say, when it becomes painfully apparent that he has no plans to speak first.

"Thought you'd never ask." He pulls a thick, legal-sized envelope out of his suit-coat pocket. "What has Trish Bannister told you about the insurance policies?"

"Nothing."

He ponders this for a moment. "That doesn't surprise me." He then dramatically places the envelope in my glove compartment. "A copy of the declarations page for each policy is in that envelope," he says. "Check them out after you drop me off."

"Okay," I say. He is plainly having a lot more fun with this secret agent stuff than I am. I pull into a parking lot, turn around, and head back down North Landing Road in the direction I just came from. "Since we've got about five minutes before I get back to your car and drop you off, why don't you just tell me about it now."

Strobel chuckles. "I've always loved that feistiness about you, Connors. That's why I'm glad we're on the same side this time."

"You haven't convinced me we are yet."

"All right," Strobel says, settling back into the seat. "Then let's resolve that issue right now. James Bannister had two very large life insurance policies in effect when he died—both of them through my client, Benefit Financial. One was a term policy that he purchased with his own money; the second was a keyman policy that was purchased by his company."

"How large?" I interrupt.

"His personal policy was two mil. The keyman policy was five, with a double indemnity clause for accidental or homicidal death."

"Whoa."

"My thoughts exactly," says Strobel. "And here's where it gets interesting. The keyman policy was taken out about six months ago, right after the first round of layoffs at TalkNet, Bannister's company. Of course, all the proceeds go straight to the company. It's not unusual for these types of policies to exist; they help cushion companies from the death of a key leader. But the amount of this policy, the fact that it was purchased when the company was struggling, and the timing so close to Bannister's death…naturally has my client a little suspicious."

Strobel takes a deep breath. He is enjoying unfolding this tale gradually, keeping me in suspense. "The personal policy, on the other hand, has been in existence for a long time—ten years or so. James Bannister is the insured. The proceeds would go one-half to Mrs. Bannister and one-half into a trust fund for the kids with Mrs. Bannister as the trustee. If James Bannister and his wife died together, the proceeds would all go straight to the trust fund, with Harlan Fowler serving as the trustee. Nothing unusual about that setup."

"But there's obviously a catch," I say. Fowler's involvement has piqued my interest.

"Obviously." He takes another long, infuriating pause. "First catch is the way Bannister set up the original trust fund. Under its terms, Jamie would get twice as much as Tara."

Though I'm not surprised, this makes my heart ache for Tara. I wonder if she knew. "Favored son versus stepdaughter," I say. "Not that surprising."

"Second," he says, "Bannister changed the beneficiaries about three months ago. He kept the basic structure in place, half to the primary beneficiary and half to the trust. But he changed the primary beneficiary and the trustee from his wife to… Are you ready for this?"

I've just pulled back into the courthouse parking lot, and I am snaking my way toward Strobel's car. "To Fowler," I say, hoping it's true.

"See," says Strobel. "That's why I want to be on your side of this one. You're always one step ahead."

I park the car right next to Strobel's and put it in park. "He totally disinherited Trish?"

"Yeah. About three months ago. You know any reason he would change beneficiaries about three months ago?" Strobel turns and looks at me as he asks the question.

That's when the phone calls began. That's when the alleged affair began.

I shake my head no and look back at Strobel. My mind is racing as I try to piece this together. Fowler is a beneficiary. Interesting, but it doesn't really make much difference to either my case or Benefit Financial's duty to pay.

"Has Fowler collected on the policy yet?" I ask.

"He hasn't officially filed his notice of claim. The company found out when the local agent who wrote the policy called them. And we have absolutely no intention of paying Fowler or anyone else until we complete our investigation."

"Into what?"

This is apparently the question that Strobel has been waiting for. He reaches for the handle and opens the door. Before he steps out, he turns to me in another melodramatic move. "Find out everything you can about these policies and Fowler's relationship with the family,"

Strobel commands, as if I've just been transformed into his personal paralegal.

"Why should I?" I ask indignantly. "That's your job. I've got a murder case to defend."

Strobel just shrugs and steps out. "Suit yourself." With one hand on the door, he lowers his voice, though there's nobody within thirty feet of my car. "Would it change your perspective if I had a confidential witness who could testify that Trish Bannister and Harlan Fowler were having an affair?"

What?! He closes the door and hops into his car faster than I can roll the window down and call out after him. As I watch him drive away, my head is swimming with the implications of what he's just told me. Marital infidelity, even if it's true, is no basis for Benefit Financial to avoid paying under an insurance policy. The only basis for avoiding such a payout is one with staggering implications for my case. Can Strobel really be suggesting this?

It's one of the first rules you learn in insurance law class. No person can benefit from a life insurance policy if that person causes, directly or indirectly, the murder of the insured.

The commonwealth's attorney? My head is throbbing with the thought of it.

CHAPTER TWENTY-THREE

W hen Brad gets back to the office at five o'clock, I unload about five minutes worth of my "you really should have been there" lecture. I'm on the edge emotionally, and I'm aching for a fight. But Brad's too smart for that. He gives perfect answers, delivered softly and lovingly. "I'm sorry." "I really tried to get out of this hearing." "What did you want me to do?"

After a while I give up, convinced that I will never win an argument married to this guy. I totally capitulate, letting him hug me and then tell me how awesome I must have been. I tell him that my one bright moment was when I charged Gonzales. We laugh about that and then bemoan the stupidity of our client and her IMs. We are in my small cubicle of an office, and Brad is sitting in my one client chair with his legs sprawled out in front of him. He has tossed his suit coat on my desk, and I am pacing back and forth on the small patch of carpet between my desk and the side wall. I never paced before I met Brad.

I tell Brad about Strobel. He listens without interruption. I then hand him the declaration pages of the insurance policies and watch him read. His face twists into a skeptical frown, and he places the policies back on my desk.

"A confidential informant," he says sarcastically.

I nod.

"Let me ask you a question," he says. "Fowler's a reasonably intelligent man, right?"

I give him a "you could have fooled me" look.

"Work with me," he says.

"Okay. *Reasonably* intelligent."

"And his motive for murder is what?"

I've been thinking about this all afternoon but still don't have an answer. "I don't know. Maybe he's sick of James Bannister beating on Trish. Maybe he's worried that Bannister is going to find out about the affair. Maybe he wants some money for himself and Trish."

"That's good enough," says Brad. "Pick any one of those. Now, why would a reasonably intelligent man allow himself to be named as a beneficiary of James Bannister's life insurance policy if he's planning to kill Bannister? It's like painting a neon sign on his chest that flashes 'Suspect.' Why not just allow Trish to stay on as the beneficiary, then he could split the money with her and never be suspected."

"Maybe he didn't know he was the beneficiary."

Brad looks up at me like I've lost my mind. "You're saying that Bannister just names his good friend Harlan Fowler as a beneficiary for 50 percent of a $2 million life insurance policy and never tells him?"

"How should I know?" I turn up my palms in frustration. "I mean, if Bannister is mad at his wife for having an affair, why didn't he just leave the money to his kids? Why name Fowler in the first place?"

Brad stretches his back and brushes his fingers through his hair. "I thought I was asking the questions. And I haven't asked my most obvious one yet."

"I'm waiting."

"If Fowler's our killer, why did your client confess?"

"*Our* client," I remind him.

"Okay, *our* client," he says. "The one with gunpowder residue on her shooting hand."

Three hours later I'm sitting in Trish's living room, trying to find out the answers to some of Brad's questions. On the way over I decided to confront Trish about the affair without Tara being present. Trish has enough challenges in that relationship right now without her daughter thinking she was sleeping around with Fowler.

I am sitting on the sofa next to Trish, talking face to face while Jamie fights the demons on his video games in the back room. Incredibly, Trish has let Tara go out with some friends, a clear violation of bail. Perhaps Trish is hoping Tara will be able to momentarily forget about her miserable day in court. I wonder if Wiccarules is one of the friends. I sense that Trish just didn't have the energy to make Tara stay home.

Trish looks gaunt and frail. Her eyes are vacant pools of defeat. She has a habit of looking down when she talks. Just looking at her makes me hate James Bannister even more. What was she like before he started humiliating her? Was there life there? Was there more confidence? More passion?

I finish telling Trish about my conversation with Strobel. Trish takes it all in while sipping coffee. When I get to the part about the alleged affair, she almost chokes. She places the cup down with a trembling hand.

"Is it true?" I ask softly. "Are you having an affair with Fowler?"

Trish sits there speechless for a moment. She starts to talk, then hesitates. Her face has lost all color. When she finally speaks, it's with a level of conviction I've never heard from her before. Her eyes are still focused downward, but there's the slightest hint of steel in her voice this time.

"Absolutely not," she says. "I was faithful to James every single day of our marriage." Her lip is trembling, and I find myself believing her. "The thought of this..." Her voice trails off and she stops. "Absolutely not," she says again.

I spend the next few minutes asking Trish about the phone call they received on the night of James Bannister's death. Trish claims it was just one of many similar calls. They started about six months ago and occurred mostly when James was home on nights and weekends. Whether Trish answered or James answered, the caller would just hang up. The caller ID always showed a different random number, Trish says. When they called the number back, they would get a message explaining they had returned a call to a prepaid calling-card system and that the person they were calling could not be reached at that number. Even after the Bannisters had their home number changed, the calls continued.

I make a mental note to have Bella subpoena the Bannisters' phone records. I'm pretty sure their local phone company has a computerized log of all incoming calls.

Then I turn my attention to the issue of insurance. "Did James have an insurance policy where he named Fowler as a beneficiary?"

She nods. She picks up her coffee cup to take a sip, then places it back down without drinking from it.

"Why didn't you tell me about it?"

Tears start to pool in her eyes. "Because it was embarrassing, I guess. And I didn't think it had anything to do with the case. Plus Harlan has been trying so hard to help us through this, lobbying for us on the bail issue and everything."

I slide a little closer to Trish and drill into her eyes. She's still not looking at me, which is troubling. "Trish," I say gently yet firmly, "how can you think it's not relevant to the case? It gives Harlan a motive for murder."

Her head jerks back a little, like she had truly never thought of this before. "How could it?" she asks haltingly. "He didn't even know he was a beneficiary until I was going through James's stuff a week after his death and found the policy. I called Harlan myself."

Trish is so naive. "You're saying Harlan knew nothing about this when you called?"

"I don't think so. He sounded surprised and asked a lot of questions."

I snort in disbelief, recalling Brad's question to me about this very issue. I confront Trish with it: "Your husband leaves a million bucks to his best friend and never even tells him about it?"

"Oh," says Trish, letting out her tension in a big breath, as if a major mystery has just been resolved. "James didn't leave Harlan a million bucks. He only got about a hundred thousand."

I reach to fish the dec pages of the policies out of my briefcase and then think better of it. "Let me have a look at those policies," I say to Trish.

CHAPTER
TWENTY-FOUR

It takes me about twenty minutes to review all the paperwork Trish hauls out. Strobel is right about the policy. It has a $2 million face value. Half goes to Fowler in his personal capacity. The other half goes to Harlan Fowler as a trustee for Jamie and Tara. Of that amount, two-thirds goes to Jamie's trust and the other one-third goes to Tara's. Under standard insurance law, if Tara is convicted or pleads guilty of murdering her stepfather, Benefit Financial will not have to pay Tara's share. Fowler, as a trustee, is entitled to an annual fee of 2.5 percent of the trust account, or about twenty-five thousand dollars per year.

But Strobel is apparently unaware of another document in Bannister's life insurance file. It is a letter to Harlan Fowler that Trish says was in a sealed envelope marked, "Deliver in the event of my death." Trish says her curiosity won out—she opened the envelope herself, then read and copied the letter. She delivered the original letter to Harlan in another envelope she sealed and marked in the same way.

I scan the two-page letter. It begins by thanking Harlan for being such a great friend and explains that he is being asked to handle these insurance proceeds because James has lost his trust in Trish, who he suspects is sleeping around. As I read those allegations, I glance up at Trish and notice how wounded she looks about this. It is easy to see why she's trying to keep this quiet. And I have a hard time imagining this lady having an affair with anyone. I make a mental note to press Strobel for the name of his alleged witness and keep reading. In the letter James gives very specific instructions for how Harlan should handle the million dollars left to him.

I want this money to be used for the benefit of my
family, for you my friend, and for some worthy charities. As
for my family, though I suspect my wife has been unfaithful
to me, I never stopped loving her and still feel an obligation
to provide.

I think about the swollen face of Trish Bannister in the police
video, and my anger burns.

Therefore, please take a substantial portion of this amount,
no less than three hundred thousand dollars ($300,000) and
set up a trust fund for Trish, to be administered by you, for
living expenses. I am trusting you not to let her live lavishly,
or to let her spend this money foolishly, but to make sure she
is provided for with these funds. She will probably need to get
a job to supplement these amounts, and that is fine.

James Bannister was such a control freak that he's trying to exercise an incredible amount of what lawyers call "dead-hand control"—
he's still trying to manipulate Trish from the grave.

The letter continues:

I also want you to set up a trust fund for the kids. Keep
this trust fund separate from the other million-dollar trust
fund. The main trust fund should be used for standard
expenses of the kids—school, medical care, housing, etc. This
one should be used by you for the kinds of extra money a
father would have given—help on a car, graduation gifts, paying for weddings, down payment on a house, that type of
thing. Put no less than two hundred thousand dollars

($200,000) into trust for Jamie and one hundred thousand dollars ($100,000) into trust for Tara.

This should leave about four hundred thousand. I want you to have at least one hundred thousand of that for yourself. You've been a great friend, and I'm asking you to do a lot for me even after I've passed. The other three hundred thousand dollars ($300,000) should be used for two purposes: to support worthy charities and to elect worthy Republicans to local office. A list of my favorite charities is attached. You, more than anyone, know which candidates are worthy of donations. I leave that entirely to your trust.

I look at James's signature and then up at Trish's blank face. I wonder how much bad news this woman can continue to take, but before I can deliver it, I notice Jamie standing in the doorway.

He is wearing the same low-hanging shorts he had on the other night, his boxers again showing. He flicks his hair from his eyes and plops down on the other side of his mom. I watch him warily, not wanting to repeat the unpleasantness of the other night. Since Trish is directly between us, I assume that I'm out of his spitting line of fire.

"Going to bed?" Trish asks.

He nods and gives her a hug. She holds him a second longer than I anticipated, and I immediately feel guilty for disliking this kid. Tonight Jamie is nothing more than a pudgy-faced preadolescent. Like all kids, he needs a mother's hug.

Much to my chagrin, he snuggles in next to his mom like he's going to sit here for a while and listen. Trish puts her arm around him.

"Got your homework all done?"

"I did it during *American Idol*."

That oughta be good.

"Great," says Trish. "Tell you what. You go get ready for bed, and

Ms. Connors and I are going to finish talking about a few things. Then I'll come up and tuck you in."

I tense, wondering if this will cause an explosion. "You can do that now—" I start to say, anxious to make peace.

"Okay," Jamie interrupts. He bounces off the couch and heads for the door with another flick of his head.

"Night, Jamie," I say.

"Good night," he responds without looking back. Trish and I both watch him climb the steps.

"I'm really sorry about the other night—," she begins.

I cut her off with a wave of the hand. "Don't worry about it. I know it just comes with the territory." She smiles, as if to say, "You'll never know," then looks back at the documents in front of us.

"Have you made a claim under the policy yet?" I ask.

"No. Harlan said we had sixty days and we ought to wait as long as possible. He said that was all he could tell me at this time, given his position as commonwealth's attorney. I think he meant that the policy could be used as evidence against Tara if it came to light, since she only gets half as much as Jamie."

"Does Tara know about this?"

"I don't think so," Trish says. "I haven't told her."

I try to make sense of all this, but nothing's falling into place. I'm beginning to think that Strobel is grasping at straws, hoping to keep his client from having to pay what is owed. But there *is* one thing I'm sure of.

"This letter isn't worth the paper it's printed on," I say to Trish, holding up James's instructions to Fowler about the trust. She looks at me with wide eyes, confirming my suspicion that Fowler has never told her this. "It's what lawyers call a testamentary document with precatory language. And a court will never enforce it." Now she looks confused. "If you want to tell people what to do with your money or belongings after you die, you have to execute a formal will or leave an entirely handwritten document called a holographic will. Your husband did neither. Language like this in a letter that is merely suggestive—we call it precatory—about how your money should be used after you die has no binding effect. Fowler can follow this if he wants to, or he can ignore it. It's totally up to him."

A look of total exhaustion floods Trish's face. "So, in effect, James didn't leave me one penny of these insurance proceeds?"

"I'm sorry, Trish. It's totally up to Fowler whether to follow these instructions or not. But there's got to be other property in your husband's estate. It would all pass to you as the surviving spouse by matter of law—"

"It's worthless," she mumbles. "This house, every car we own, his company stock—it's all pledged for company debt that is past due, and the banks are coming after the collateral. James was a founder of TalkNet. To get it started, we agreed to secure loans with our personal assets. As the company grew, the loans got bigger too. James and I continued to sign as coguarantors." The tears I saw earlier are now glistening again in her eyes.

"This policy," she says, "is all I have." That hollow look in her eyes, which had disappeared momentarily when Jamie entered the room, is now back. It's as if she's staring into some deep chasm of pain that only worsens if she tries to resist it.

"I thought when he died he would stop hurting me." She sniffs and I can hear the torment in her muffled voice. "I guess I was wrong."

CHAPTER TWENTY-FIVE

Exhausted. I am utterly, completely exhausted, yet still I will my legs onward, one step at a time. My muscles begin to cramp and my lungs scream at me to stop.

But I *will not* stop! I feel as if my life is at stake. To be judged normal, to obtain a clean bill of health, to hang on to all my hopes and dreams, *I must keep going.* One more step. Ten more seconds. One more minute. Then another.

It's Wednesday morning, and I'm at the Norfolk Medical Center, trudging forward on a slightly elevated treadmill, dye shooting through my arteries, electrodes attached to various parts of my upper body. It's what they call a nuclear stress test. I feel like some lab specimen—Dr. Frankenstein, I presume. Dr. Mason Reddick, a thin, balding man with half-moon reading glasses, is standing behind my shoulder, writing on a clipboard. A physician's assistant is reading the machines that monitor my heart as the treadmill drones away and my feet clomp, clomp, clomp out a steady rhythm. The room smells like an odd mixture of antiseptic and sweat.

"How're you feeling?" asks Dr. Reddick.

"Great," I gasp.

"Any chest pains, numbness, or tingling?"

"Nope," I manage. I try to make the word sound normal, but it comes out as a grunt.

"On a scale of one to ten, how tired are you?"

A twelve. "About a seven," I huff.

"Good."

This goes on for another two minutes. My legs are killing me. I'm starting to get dizzy, and Dr. Reddick keeps asking these same inane questions. At nine and a half minutes I would welcome death, and yet the machine just keeps whirring away. My goal, based on my age and moderate amount of daily activity, is thirteen minutes. I finally realize that I can't take another step of this torture.

"A ten!" I concede after a total of nine minutes and forty-five seconds. "I'm at a ten."

"Keep going as long as you can," the doctor says calmly.

Maybe he didn't hear me. "I'm at a ten!" I shout, struggling for breath. A black outline is starting to form at the edge of my vision. That run-down-battery feeling is nailing me again. The PA has a worried look on his face, and the box that now contains my vision is getting smaller and smaller as the blackness around the edge grows.

Without any other warning, I step off the back of the machine. My limbs are trembling, the room is spinning, and the floor is moving under my feet. I stumble forward, grabbing for the handles of the treadmill. I feel Reddick grab me from behind as I collapse, the electrodes still taped to my skin.

Reddick and the PA gently lower me to the floor; I am staring up into their eyes. I try to suck every molecule of oxygen out of the room, but it feels like my lungs just can't get a deep breath, like they won't inflate any larger than a baseball. The good news is that my vision is coming back and the room is not spinning anymore. I manage the slightest trace of an embarrassed smile as I look at Reddick.

"I'd say that's a ten," he says.

Incomprehensible. Twenty minutes later I'm sitting in a chair in Dr. Reddick's crowded office, the walls closing in around me. This is incomprehensible. It can't be happening to *me*. Healthy, thirty-year-old women do not have heart problems. There must be some mistake, some other explanation.

He has already told me the test revealed some bad news. Now he's sharing the particulars. He places his reading glasses on the desk and leans forward. "You have a condition called hypertrophic cardiomy-opathy, a heart condition know as HCM," Dr. Reddick says calmly. He studies me for a reaction. I just stare blankly ahead. My mind can't get past the words *heart condition.*

"HCM inhibits the ability of the heart to pump blood," he continues. "It's why you've been having these bouts of sudden and extreme fatigue. It makes you feel like you can't get a deep breath, because the heart can't keep up with your body's demand for oxygen. If left untreated, it can be fatal."

The bluntness of this assessment disorients me. Suddenly I feel like I'm floating, detached from my emotions, the laws of gravity and bodily habitation no longer applying. My mind flirts with denial. This can't be happening. *Can't be.* There's got to be a mistake. I need a second opinion. These thoughts and a million more dart and swirl through my head, leaving a windswept panic in their wake.

Reddick's words now seem to be coming from the end of a long tunnel two worlds away. The reading glasses are back on, and he's pointing to a diagram in front of me. "HCM basically means that the heart has an enlarged septum, the wall that separates the left and right sides of the heart's chambers." He pauses, circling something on the paper in front of me. "About 80 percent of people with HCM live perfectly normal lives. In the other 20 percent, the septum seriously affects the blood flow, causing blood to back up in the heart. It's what caused you to faint when you pushed yourself too hard at the gym. It also creates a grave risk of heart attack."

Reddick looks at me over the top of his glasses, and I nod. I feel my eyes beginning to tear with the injustice of this. I'm holding it together by a fragile thread. For some inexplicable reason, I feel a responsibility to take this news without flinching, to act the part of a woman with great inner strength.

"The good news is that this condition is correctable through surgery," Reddick says.

That's the good news—surgery?

"We go in and trim the septum back with a small scalpel. If all goes well—and the success rate for this surgery is generally quite high—you'll be back to normal within two months."

I am astonished at how easily Dr. Reddick dismisses the repercussions of open-heart surgery. They will saw through my sternum, crack and pry open my rib cage, connect me to some heart-lung machine, cut away part of my heart, and then staple me back together like a stuffed Thanksgiving turkey. All this for a woman just weeks away from her wedding! Instead of a flawless bride, I can offer Brad what? A heart attack waiting to happen or a woman with a seven-inch zipper scar down the middle of her chest.

"It's going to take some time to process all this," the doctor says. It occurs to me that he's given this same type of speech a hundred times before. "And it's important for you to know there's nothing that you've done to cause this…nothing you could have done to prevent it."

I'm still floating in a state of stunned consciousness, but now tears are pooling in my eyes. The veneer of the strong woman has been stripped away, and the fear of the little girl has taken over. One thought dominates: life is so unfair. I look down and sniff back the tears as best I can.

"We'll need to schedule a time for surgery," Reddick says in that same businesslike tone. "And in the meantime, avoid stress or strenuous activities." He pauses and seems to recognize that the logistics of it no longer interest me. He hands me some tissues that I readily put to good use. "I know this is tough, Leslie. But I've been through this many times. The success rate is very good."

"How good?" I manage, after I finish blowing my nose.

I don't like the brief hesitation. "Around 70 percent of patients have no further complications. Sometimes we get in there and find there's more involved than an enlarged septum. You're young and healthy, and I expect a great result for you."

If this is supposed to comfort me, it doesn't. Seventy percent?! That means 30 percent get opened up twice or keel over from a heart attack sometime after the surgery. This is my life we're talking about!

"I know this is a lot to process," Dr. Reddick says for the second time. He holds out his hands for my used tissues, and I give them to him. He throws them into a trash can behind his desk. It seems that he's ready to move on to the next patient. "And if you have any questions, feel free to ask them. You can call me later with questions if you'd like." He gives me a forced smile, and I have a sudden urge to escape this doctor's office and leave all this behind. I'm so disoriented from the experience that it still seems like I'm floating outside my body. If I get up and leave, I half expect that this other Leslie will remain in the chair, dealing with all the problems I've left behind.

"Do you have any questions, Leslie?"

Just one. And it's nothing you can help me with. It's the one question that nobody can answer, and the only one that matters right now.

Why me?

CHAPTER TWENTY-SIX

I don't know how I ended up on the beach, walking in the wet sand next to the crashing waves, feeling the warmth of the sun on my back and the chill of the water as it laps at my feet. I guess I drove, parked near the boardwalk, and just started walking. It's as if I were drawn here by the waves, the calming effect of the raw power of nature. My thoughts are so disoriented by the news from Dr. Reddick that I feel like I'm still on autopilot. I need a place to think. I need a place to be alone.

I have not told Brad. It was, of course, my first instinct. Pick up my cell phone and pour out my heart. Even now I'm torn between the need for solitude and the strong desire for Brad's comforting arms. But I have willed myself not to tell him for the same reason that I didn't mention the fainting episode, the same reason I didn't mention the appointment I had with Dr. Reddick in the first place.

I don't want Brad to marry damaged merchandise.

I have no doubt that he would stick with me. Actually, that's the problem. I've been through that with Bill. I know what it's like to see your spouse suffer. The helplessness. The despair. The crashing dreams of a fairy-tale marriage. If I truly love Brad, would I put him through this? I think about our honeymoon. At best I'll have a long hideous scar in the middle of my chest.

Why me? I ask the question again and again. *Haven't I suffered enough for one lifetime?*

I carry my sandals and fill my lungs with the salty ocean air. The beach is scattered with early vacationers, the ones who head for the beach the day that school lets out. There are families, kids on Boogie

Boards, teenage girls frying in the sun, lifeguards blowing their whistles and motioning to the swimmers. I absent-mindedly watch the people as I walk, feeling isolated even in the midst of them. I see an overweight dad, his gut hanging over his swimsuit. He waddles as he walks, and I think, *His heart is in better shape than mine.* I see a gray-haired lady in a beach chair, reading a thick novel, an umbrella and wide-rimmed hat giving her shade. *That woman's probably got more days left than I do.*

That's stupid. I've got a heart problem, not a death sentence. A couple my age grabs my attention. The man is rubbing suntan lotion on the woman's back, her already-tanned skin glistening in the sun, except for what's masked by a skimpy white bikini. *A seven-inch scar. A one-piece bathing suit the rest of my life.*

If I'm lucky. If I'm in the 70 percent who have no "further complications."

Right now I don't feel lucky. I feel like everything's changed. Everything I took for granted can no longer be trusted. I can almost visualize my heart, struggling against this oversized septum. *What if I have a heart attack right here? Who would come to my aid? Would I survive?*

HCM. I already hate this medical condition. But the ocean air is starting to clear my head, and I realize I should be grateful that it's treatable. Then again, that's what they first said about Bill's cancer.

A tennis ball plops into the shallow water next to me, and a mangy golden retriever comes splashing after it. I turn to my left and see a young hard body smiling at his dog. "Sorry," he calls out. *I'll bet you are.* I give him a quick and forced smile, then move on.

Today's emotions conjure up the ones I buried long ago on the day of Bill's initial diagnosis. The pain and foreboding all run together, making it impossible to know which is which. The longer I walk, the more determined I am to keep Brad from feeling the same things. Watching a spouse die wounds you in a way that can never be reversed. It's hard to understand if you've never been through it.

But I have. And more than anything else, I want to prevent Brad from feeling that much pain, from losing his unbridled enthusiasm for life. The more I walk, the more I realize I was right not to tell him. If you truly love someone, you'll be willing to let them go. Isn't that what they say?

I think about how painful it would be to leave Brad, and for the first time in my life, I begin to think it might have been better if Brad and I had never met.

CHAPTER TWENTY-SEVEN

After the beach, I head home and research HCM on the Internet. I call Brad to let him know I'm not feeling well and might not be at the office tomorrow. I resist his offers to come and take care of me. I answer what seems like a hundred diagnostic questions. No, I don't think I have a fever. Yes, my stomach is killing me. Which is true—nerves will do that to you. No, I haven't thrown up. Before he prescribes a cure, I decide to blame it on the one thing that always silences men and causes them to change the subject.

"It's a female thing," I say. "Some months it's worse than others." Within a couple of minutes, I'm safely off the phone.

During the phone call I found myself on the verge of telling Brad everything, of begging him to come and hold me so that we could cry together. I hate lying to him. And I know this is not something I can keep from him. If we're going to stay together, we've got to face this as a couple. But right now I don't even know if staying with Brad is the right thing. More than anything else, I just want to spare him my pain. But what would cause more pain: losing a spouse to a heart attack or having someone you love just walk away from you for no reason at all?

The thought of calling my mother crosses my mind. But she would get on the first plane tomorrow and probably never leave my side again for the rest of my life. Plus, to tell my mother is to tell Brad. Even if I made her promise not to say anything, Brad would know within twenty-four hours. Mom would find a way to slip up or drop an oh-so-obvious hint or some other equally transparent ploy to let Brad know.

I might call her to be with me during the surgery, but not just yet.

I call a few law school friends and realize how quickly and how far we've drifted apart. It feels forced to call them for the first time in more than a month and unburden myself to them. Instead I just pretend everything is fine and hurry to get off the phone.

I put on my pajamas and try to go to sleep with the television on. I dread that feeling in the morning when I'll wake up and, just for a second, think that maybe this has all been a bad dream. Then the sleep cobwebs will clear, and I'll realize that I really do have a bad heart. The feeling of despondency will blanket me again. *Will I feel better after some sleep? Worse?*

By 3:00 a.m., I realize that I may never find out. Though I am beyond exhaustion, my eyes are still wide open. Nothing on the television interests me. I give up trying to sleep, pull on some socks, and head down the hall to my makeshift study. I fire up my desktop and start cruising the Internet again, Googling HCM and sifting through more medical advice and treatment options.

My research makes me feel both better and worse. Better because I realize how many people have survived this type of surgery and live perfectly normal lives. Worse because I realize both how quickly HCM can turn fatal and how gruesome the surgery is. I begin to understand that I'm fortunate to be alive. The incident on the elliptical was a warning that may have saved my life. For that I'm grateful, though I'm not really sure who I'm grateful toward.

My views on God changed pretty radically following Bill's death. I grew up a nominal Catholic who attended Mass on important holidays with my family. I have believed in God as long as I can remember, sensing that some greater power put this whole universe into motion. I pretty much bought into the church's notion of a loving God, a gracious Holy Mother, and a suffering Savior who died for us. But after Bill's death I couldn't honestly reconcile those concepts with the unanswered prayers of a cancer widow. Either God was not all-powerful or He didn't really love me.

A sustained argument with God evolved into a more mature and complex spirituality. I started finding more meaning in the simple and beautiful things all around me. The ocean. The quiet of a starry night. The soft cry of an innocent baby. Even the majesty of the law as I studied it in law school. I learned to live more at peace with myself, to be more accepting of others. But now that resolve is being threatened by another blow that seems to come from outside me. Is God trying to get my attention? Is He on some kind of vendetta against me?

The sun is not quite up when I drill down to a Web page that makes my heart race. Not too fast, I hope, what with that deformed septum wall and all. I lean forward in my chair and begin clicking through pages of text, scrolling down as quickly as my eyes will follow. I have found hope on the Internet at 6:00 a.m.

His name is Dr. Dagmar Ostheim, a German cardiologist who apparently specializes in HCM surgery. Unlike his American colleagues, Ostheim does not do traditional open-heart surgery. His unorthodox approach involves a quarter-inch incision on the patient's thigh, through which he accesses the femoral artery and eventually the arteries in proximity to the heart. As I read about Ostheim's procedure, I become more excited and more apprehensive. He sends some kind of guide wire and catheter with a small balloon up through the arteries to the left coronary artery, not that unusual in this day of stints and balloon angioplasties. But when he finally snakes the balloon through the vessels that feed the septal wall, he injects a half teaspoon of ethanol, frying those vessels and all of the tissue that the alcohol touches. This is a controlled heart attack, killing the excess tissue that is blocking the blood flow, causing it to wither and shrink.

It's cutting-edge surgery called alcohol ablation, and it is apparently not yet fully approved in the United States for HCM, though there are a few doctors doing it on an experimental basis. A major complication arises from the fact that the septum is right next to something called the AV node, which is a critical pathway in the heart's electrical system. If the alcohol is injected too close to that node, a pacemaker will be required for the rest of the patient's life. I take little solace in the fact that Ostheim's success rate is higher than most. Fewer than 5 percent of his patients have required a pacemaker, says the article. *That's one out of twenty.* And then there's the other possibility of dissecting the arterial wall with the catheter, a nice way of saying that you puncture the artery and watch the patient bleed to death.

But the complications are not my greatest worry. There is one paragraph in particular that makes me cringe, makes my skin crawl. The operation is done with local anesthesia! The patient needs to be awake so Dr. Ostheim can instruct the patient when to cough, hold her breath, or exhale—all movements that can slightly change the internal circulatory system the doctor is trying to navigate. You've got to be kidding! They want me to lie there awake and take orders from this German doctor while he gives me a controlled but still painful heart attack.

No way. I shudder at the thought of this procedure. No possible way.

Since I've been up all night, I wonder whether I'm hallucinating. Then another thought hits me. There must be some other doctor, someplace, who can do this same kind of surgery without the patient being awake. Another hour of research convinces me there is not.

I print out my research, leave it on my desk, and head back to my bedroom. How could I ever go through with something this bizarre? Then again, the success rates seem to compare favorably with the traditional surgery. If I let them cut me open here in the States, will I regret it every time I look in the mirror, every time I put on my one-piece bathing suit? How bad can it be—this wide-awake heart attack?

I try to sleep by focusing on the positive. Odds are that this surgery would correct my condition. It wouldn't be easy, but I could figure out an excuse to take a few weeks off and fly to Europe for the surgery without Brad even knowing. If the surgery works, my problems are over. But if it doesn't—how could I ask Brad to marry someone with a pacemaker or some kind of incurable heart defect?

A seven-inch scar. A quarter-inch incision. Surgery while I sleep. A wide-awake heart attack. A one-piece bathing suit. A bridal shower with all the usual negligees. I decide to call Dr. Reddick later and ask him about alcohol ablation surgery. But even now I know what I'm going to do. Maybe I've got too much pride or I'm too concerned with physical appearances. Or maybe I just feel like I'm finally entitled to a break. Either way, I'm already starting to plan my excuses for visiting Germany without Brad knowing my reasons.

With that issue settled, I drift off to sleep.

CHAPTER
TWENTY-EIGHT

I wake up about noon with a terrible feeling in the pit of my stomach. Everything has changed. I give myself one day to mourn. Today I will sit around in pajamas all day, play jazz and blues on my CD player, watch some bad daytime television, and feel sorry for myself. Tomorrow, I will go back to work as if nothing has happened.

Right.

After a couple hours of *Judge Judy* and *Fox News,* I call Dr. Reddick. I watch two more judge shows before he calls back. He is not impressed with my plan to let this German doctor cure my heart. He warns me about possible complications, including the risks of a pacemaker and death by a punctured artery. It's nothing the Internet hasn't already told me. When I tell Reddick that a pacemaker is necessary in less than 5 percent of the cases, he sounds particularly skeptical. But I can be a determined woman, even stubborn. And after all, it is *my* body.

"Leslie," Reddick says at last, frustration evident in his voice, "if you're determined to do alcohol ablation, why don't you at least explore doing it here in the States. There's a clinic in Dallas that's doing this on an experimental basis. The surgeon there is an Indian woman, can't remember her name, but she's got a good reputation." *Girl power. Why didn't you tell me about this program before?*

"You're young and a good candidate for successful surgery," Reddick continues. "I could probably get you accepted into that program."

"That'd be great," I say. Reddick warns me that my insurance may not cover this experimental protocol and takes the opportunity to complain for a few minutes about insurance companies in general.

Then he is gone, off to cut and pry open another patient and leave his telltale zipper calling card branded on another chest.

This sends me back to the Internet to research the Dallas surgeon. I find a doctor named Asha Maholtra at the Dallas Heart Clinic. To my chagrin, she doesn't seem quite as experienced as the guy in Germany. Maholtra has performed about a hundred of these alcohol ablations and has had to install pacemakers in fourteen patients. I'm beginning to think that girl power is overrated. But I read further and realize that she is accepting a lot of challenging cases—patients who didn't make good candidates for open-heart surgery in the first place—and my confidence begins to swell.

I'm also comforted by the thought of doing this in the United States and having a female surgeon, one who might understand how important it is for a bride to avoid the long knife. But the thing that clinches it for me has nothing to do with my medical research or science. When I look up her name, trying to figure out how to pronounce it, I discover that her first name means "hope."

Call it women's intuition or an irrational belief in fate. But when I discover this, I feel a flicker of optimism begin to break through. It feels good. I print out that page and get up from the keyboard.

It's time to take a shower.

CHAPTER TWENTY-NINE

I am relieved that Brad is not in the office when I arrive on Friday morning. Bella explains that he is interviewing some witnesses on a case. "You look like death," she says to me.

"Thanks." I keep walking toward my office. I had planned on maybe saying something to Bella, but now I'm having second thoughts. I can feel the tears welling up in my already-puffy red eyes.

"You sure you ought to be in here today?" she asks.

"I'm fine," I say over my shoulder.

Two minutes later, as I try to read my Outlook Task List through the tears, Bella is standing at my door. Bella knows when the phrase *I'm fine* means *I'm dying here*...

"What's going on, honey?" she asks, hand on hip.

I choke on the words for a moment of indecision and then just blurt it out. "I don't want to die," I say, my lip trembling. Bella gives me a look of astonishment, and I'm not sure where the words came from myself. Within minutes I've dumped it all out there, crying the entire time.

"I'm sorry," says Bella as she gently rubs my back. "I'm so sorry." I stand up and give her a hug. When I sit back down, I'm already feeling a little better. I try to smile through the tears.

I tell her about Dr. Maholtra and the insurance not covering this. Bella gets indignant, curses our insurance carrier, apologizes for cursing, then promises she'll get them to pay for it. "What good's insurance," she asks, "if it doesn't pay for getting your heart fixed?"

Her logic is irrefutable, so I don't try to answer.

"I'm gonna pray that God will just heal your heart," Bella

announces boldly. It's a nice thought, but I put no stock in it. Nobody prayed harder than I did when Bill had cancer.

"And I'm gonna call Sarah and get her praying." Sarah is a friend of ours. A former missionary to Saudi Arabia whose husband was killed by the Saudi religious police. She is the most spiritual person I know. Bella calls her the Baptist Mother Teresa.

"I don't know about that," I say. "I would really like to keep this between you and me."

"Sarah won't tell anybody," Bella assures me. "And you really need her praying for you."

It's hard to turn down prayer, so I give in with a mumbled, "Okay...thanks."

"Have you told Brad?"

I shake my head no.

"You really need to tell him," she urges.

"I can't, Bella. Not yet. I just can't."

She seems to accept this and is quiet for a moment. "Well, I really think you should. But you gotta talk to somebody about this. And don't worry. Your secret's safe with me." She pauses for a second, and I try another halfhearted smile. Bella sits down in my client chair. "How we gonna get to Dallas without Brad knowing?" she asks.

"We?"

"You don't think I'm gonna let you go through this alone, do ya?"

That question leads to several minutes of plotting and scheming. Trying to successfully sneak around behind Brad's back takes my mind off my heart, and I dab at my eyes and runny nose. Bella is throwing out some wild ideas, most of which make me laugh. Then out of the blue, she looks at me and asks if I want a cigarette.

"Are you kidding? I thought you were trying to quit."

"Why should I?" she responds. "Here you are, thin as a model..."

I give her a look that says *that's a stretch,* but she doesn't notice. Bella uses a different definition of *thin* and *overweight* than most of us. "You never ate an unhealthy thing in your life, yet your ticker does this septum thing. I figure, what's the use? Might as well do what makes you happy."

Bella's a piece of work. "Having a friend like you makes me happy," I say.

"Don't go getting all cheesy on me now," says Bella. "It would ruin my reputation."

I meet with Trish Bannister later that morning to further investigate the life insurance issue. I have no plans to say anything about my heart to Trish. She's got enough problems of her own.

"You okay?" she asks after a few minutes of banter.

"Yeah. Why?" I'm starting to get paranoid. It's hard for me to hide the fact I've been crying—my eyes get red and puffy, my nose gets red, and my whole face gets blotchy. But I had checked the visor mirror before I came in and didn't think it was that noticeable.

"I guess you just look a little tired," Trish says.

I shrug it off and before long we are in James's study, trying to log on to his computer. His laptop is hooked up to a docking station with an oversized monitor and a broadband connection that probably links directly to the TalkNet intranet system. I had worried that the police might have confiscated his computer as well as Tara's, but Trish says they hardly even looked at it.

Unfortunately, his system is password protected. Of course he never shared this password with Trish.

We try birthdays and addresses, first and last numbers of his social security number, and other likely combinations. After five or ten minutes of this, I decide we'll never guess it.

"Maybe it's the same as his check-cashing card," she suggests. "Occasionally, he would have me get cash using his card."

And it took you ten minutes to think of that? I freeze with my hands on the keyboard and look up at her. "Is there a reason you didn't mention that earlier?"

"Guess I just didn't think of it."

"What's the password?" My fingers are poised over the keys.

"It's like"—she's looking off toward the ceiling—"1B2010. Yeah, that's it. James was always saying he wanted TalkNet to gross a billion dollars by 2010, and then we could retire…"

It works! I'm in! "Good work, Trish," I say. I suddenly feel the need for space. "Can you give me some time to browse around? I'll call you if I find anything."

"Sure," Trish says, retreating for the door. "You want any coffee?"

"No thanks."

I enable the computer's Internet connection, and before long I am on the intranet system at TalkNet. I pull up Bannister's Outlook and start browsing through his e-mails. Fortunately for me, Bannister doesn't believe in deleting many e-mails. Instead, they roll over into an archive file after they've been in his in-box for six months.

I group them by sender and scroll through every e-mail from Harlan Fowler. There are dozens. The men e-mail each other about golf games, trips to Las Vegas, and NCAA tournament pools. They periodically forward e-mail jokes to each other, most of them raunchy. Bannister has apparently made some donations to Fowler's political campaigns, a few thousand dollars, but nothing out of line. He's also taken Fowler on several trips in a private jet that TalkNet leases. Bannister had a private pilot's license and apparently had to log a few hours now and then to stay current. Some of the trips were to Vegas, probably at company expense, but some were apparently fund-raising trips for Fowler, where the two men would take a prospective donor on a one-day golfing trip to some luxurious U.S. golf course. I wonder if Fowler disclosed the value of these trips on his campaign donation forms.

I've gone through nearly six month's worth of e-mails and haven't seen anything about the insurance companies Strobel mentioned. I was hoping that Fowler at least knew about the policies and the fact that he stood to make about a million bucks if Bannister died unexpectedly. But there is no indication from the e-mails that Fowler knew anything about this.

I start scrolling through other e-mails, not sure what I'm looking for. Every twenty minutes or so Trish ducks her head into the study and asks if I've found anything. I guess I would be equally curious if I were in her shoes, but my intuition tells me this is something more than idle curiosity. I still can't see her in an affair with Fowler, but I feel like she's holding something back. And I sense that she's worried I'll discover it on this computer.

"Is there something you want to tell me?" I ask her after she pops into the doorway the fourth time.

Her head jolts back as if her lawyer just turned into a snake. "No," she says quickly...too quickly. "Just checking, that's all."

Two hours of e-mail browsing convinces me that this is a dead end. I decide to change tactics and review Bannister's Word documents, starting with the most current. Bannister was apparently not a prolific writer, so it only takes about forty-five minutes to complete this review. Another dry hole. I notice that Trish has stopped her periodic checks.

It seems strange that there were only a hundred or so Word documents on his computer. I recall seeing tons of documents as attachments in the various e-mails Bannister received. I wonder if somebody has beaten me to the punch and cleaned this computer out. If somebody did, I figure that Trish would be that somebody. But Trish is the one who gave me the password, allowing me to log on to the computer in the first place. And I have a hard time picturing her deleting computer files. I've got a feeling that Trish still thinks a byte is something your dog does.

Even if she did try to delete some files, a good computer expert could always retrieve them.

I open an e-mail attachment just to double-check that it's also in the documents directory. To my surprise, Bannister's computer is set up so that e-mail attachments are not saved as Word files. Instead, they are saved by default to a temporary Internet file, a shared U: drive on the TalkNet intranet, probably to make sure the CEO's computer doesn't get junked up with a bunch of files he'll never need. I navigate my way into this file and discover more than a hundred new documents.

I stand up and stretch, venture out to the family room and talk to Trish for a few moments, then return and hunker back down in front of the monitor to scan these documents. It occurs to me that Bannister may not have realized this drive existed. Bannister himself may have deleted any incriminating e-mails, but if they had attachments that he opened, I should still be able to find them in this directory.

Again I start with the most recent documents. My hope sinks with the passage of every month. This shared drive is set up to save files for two years, and I decide to review them all. I'm looking at last October's attachments now, barely skimming the first few lines of each. Business documents bore me. Profit-and-loss statements, business plans, memos about this personnel problem or that operational issue or some other customer concern. I would rather slit my wrists than become a CEO.

But my diligence is rewarded when a document practically jumps off Bannister's oversized computer monitor. It's like a mirage—a legal document in the midst of business dronings—so completely out of place that I blink to make sure it's real. It stays on the screen, so I begin reviewing it. It's a case, a single case. It's from the Fourth Circuit Court of Appeals, a federal court that has jurisdiction over Virginia and several other states.

Sayers v. Aetna. A widow was trying to collect on a life insurance policy but was having a hard time proving that her husband died. Seems that Mr. Sayers was an avid fisherman who went out into the bay one Saturday and was never heard from again. Three months later his grieving widow concludes that she has seen the last of her husband. She argues that the boat must have capsized and her husband must have drowned. After a two-week trial the district court agrees with the widow, holding it more likely than not that Mr. Sayers would never be seen or heard from again. The appellate court affirmed this ruling, holding that the widow didn't need to produce the body in order to recover under the insurance policy.

My suspicions now raging, I print out the case and stuff it in my briefcase. I review the e-mails that have the same date as the last time this document was accessed, but I don't find anything that would seem to correspond. Who sent this to Bannister? And why?

The timing, of course, cannot be a coincidence. This case hit Bannister's e-mail about a month prior to the issuance of the keyman policy at work. Three months later Bannister changed the beneficiaries on his personal policy. If I could just figure out who sent him this case, I'd have another critical piece of an increasingly mystifying puzzle.

A few minutes later I'm taking a break, talking to Trish at the kitchen table, sipping bottled water. "You guys own any boats?" I ask.

"James had a motorboat that he kept at the yacht club," she says. "I've got to figure out what to do with it now." She takes a casual sip of coffee. "Why?"

"Just wondering," I study her eyes but don't see any flicker of understanding. "James ever do any fishing?"

This brings out a little chuckle. "James?" she asks. "Never. He bought the boat for speed. Same thing with all his toys—the cars, the boat, the Cessna…"

"The Cessna?" I ask.

"Yeah. We owned a small twin-engine plane once. James had to sell it when TalkNet headed south."

That's it! The company jet! I remember the Vegas trips mentioned in the e-mails. James, Harlan, and their other buddies hopping around the country on that leased aircraft. I make a conscious effort to hide the adrenaline coursing through my body.

"Did James have a pilot's license?" I ask. I already know the answer, but I want to watch Trish's reaction to the question. Her pleasant expression never changes.

"Yeah. He had his private license for years," Trish says. "Though the last couple of years he would generally get a commercial pilot to fly him."

"I think I'm going to need to borrow your husband's computer," I say casually. "There's some stuff on there I'd like to access, but I need help to get at it."

"Sure," Trish says, as if she's not the least bit curious about what I'm looking for.

CHAPTER
THIRTY-ONE

On the way back to the office, I call Bella and explain that I need an expert to check Bannister's computer for deleted e-mail. Bella knows just the person. I also tell her we need to issue a subpoena for the Bannisters' phone records.

"No problem," says Bella. "Now, how're you feeling?"

"Okay, I guess. It only hurts when it's beating."

My lame attempt at humor doesn't draw a courtesy chuckle from Bella. "Did you tell Brad yet?"

"We've been through this, Bella. I'm not going to tell him."

"Sure, honey," says Bella. "But if you change your mind, it's okay. By the way, Sarah says she's praying for you."

"Thanks." Though there's no enthusiasm in my voice, I really am grateful for Sarah's prayers. But right now, I don't particularly feel like talking about my heart.

"Do I have any messages?" I ask.

"Just one," Bella says. "Mack Strobel called. He asked for your voice mail."

"Wonder what he wants."

"He wants you to meet him at the WaterSide dock tonight at six, right where you board the Norfolk-Portsmouth ferry."

"I thought you said he wanted my voice mail."

"He did, honey. But I thought I'd better check it out, just to make sure it wasn't urgent."

I love Bella, but she's so nosy it's ridiculous. I'll change the password as soon as I get back to the office.

"And don't even think about changing your password," Bella

lectures, "or I'll just start rolling all *your* calls into *my* voice mail and handle things that way."

I arrive at the dock a few minutes early. In May, the sun is pretty bright at 6:00 p.m., and tonight is no exception. Though there is a strong breeze blowing from the Elizabeth River, it carries hot and sticky air that blankets me like a steam bath. I start sweating almost immediately in my knee-length black skirt and white cotton top. I take off my sandals and unbutton an extra button on my blouse. Then I remember whom I am meeting and immediately rebutton it. I grab a seat on one of the wooden benches and gaze out over the river.

I am sitting outside Norfolk's premier tourist trap—an eclectic mix of downtown shops bordering the massive Elizabeth River. In front of me are slips for yachts and sailboats. Across the river is the huge Norfolk shipyard, where large military and civilian ships are dry-docked and overhauled. Every Friday during the spring and summer, the city gathers for TGIF at the Town Point Park next to me, listening to some pretty good musicians and drinking enough beer to keep Budweiser in Clydesdales for another decade or so.

Something about the water calms me. Tonight the towering ships on the other side of the river seem to dwarf my problems, reminding me that a power greater than me is at work in the world, even if lately it's been pretty hard to see how. I spread my arms out on both sides of the bench and tilt my head back. I close my eyes behind my sunglasses and drink in the sun. The air hosts a mixture of salt water and the cuisines of the WaterSide—fried seafood, Chinese, Mongolian. The smells are making me hungry, though none of those choices are on my new heart-friendly diet.

"This seat taken?" asks a baritone voice behind me.

"No." I pull my arms in and sit up straight. Strobel flings his suit coat over the bench and sits next to me on my right. He is wearing a starched white shirt and a tie that probably set him back a hundred bucks. The tie knot is pulled snugly in place. Does this guy ever relax?

He gazes out over the water. He, too, is wearing shades. The sun ricochets off his bald head. The beads of sweat glisten as they reflect the harsh rays.

"Thirsty?" he asks.

"No."

He waits an uncomfortably long time. "What'd you find out?" he finally asks.

"They weren't having an affair."

He laughs. "You're going to take her word for that?"

"Until you convince me otherwise."

"Okay." Strobel crosses his legs at the ankles and leans back, still not looking at me. "What'd you find out about the policies?"

"I confirmed the policies and the beneficiaries," I say. "But I didn't find anything to suggest that Fowler even knew he was named as a beneficiary. He and Bannister e-mailed each other about a lot of things, but never about any insurance policies."

"Oh, he knew," says Strobel in that self-confident tone of his. "Did you see any e-mails about their frequent jaunts to Vegas?"

I wonder how much I should reveal. I don't trust Strobel, and I don't think he knows about the document I found containing the *Sayers* case. But he always seems to know more than I think he does. He always seems to be one step ahead.

"Yeah," I say. "These guys did their fair share for the Nevada economy."

Strobel grabs his suit coat from the bench and retrieves an envelope from the inside pocket. He hands it to me and leans a little closer. "Next Tuesday night at seven," he says, his voice low, "go to the

Bellagio on the Vegas strip, blackjack table seven. Play precisely ten hands, win or lose. Then go sit at the bar and wait. The dealer will eventually join you."

I look at Strobel like he's lost his mind, but the man never cracks a smile. "Go alone," he warns. "This witness is very nervous. If he thinks you're not alone, he'll clam up."

"About what?" I ask. "In real life, lawyers call witnesses on their cell phones; they don't travel across the country to meet them in smoke-filled rooms."

Strobel stands and flings his suit coat over his shoulder. "In real life," Strobel says, "the Vegas casinos tend to be very protective of their patrons. They don't like people asking questions or issuing subpoenas. If you want confirmation of Fowler's gambling debts, you take it from any employee who will talk. And you tend to take it on their terms."

"Have you met with him?" I ask. Strobel points to the envelope. "Don't leave that lying around," he says.

"How much?" I ask. "At least tell me how much Fowler owed."

"Enough to commit murder," Mack says. Then he turns and leaves.

"You've got to quit watching those old spy movies," I mumble to myself. But despite my effort to make light of Strobel's melodramatic style, something about the man gives me the creeps.

I watch him walk away, then I rip open the envelope. The only thing inside is a sheet of paper with the same instructions that Strobel gave me verbally, as well as a map showing the layout of the main floor at the Bellagio. Blackjack table seven is highlighted in yellow.

CHAPTER THIRTY-TWO

B y Friday night, I can no longer keep Brad away. He's starving for attention and rebuffs all my excuses—I've got a headache, I'm tired, it's been a long week, even the never-before-failed "it's a girl thing" excuse. He knocks on my door at eight thirty, dressed in khaki shorts, sandals, and a T-shirt. I wear my baggy white pajamas, having removed my makeup at least a half hour earlier. Brad looks me up and down, then gives me a quick hug and kiss.

"You're relentless," I say.

"If we can't go out, we'll do popcorn and a movie here," he announces. He's got the DVD in his left hand, and I can guess without looking which one it is. *My Cousin Vinny*, a romantic comedy about an inexperienced New York lawyer and his girlfriend trying a murder case for the lawyer's cousin and a friend in some small town in Alabama. The case is really the result of a giant misunderstanding, as the boys just happened to be in the wrong place at the wrong time and end up getting accused of killing a convenience store clerk. Any other night I would love to curl up next to Brad and watch Joe Pesci and Marisa Tomei aggravate the Southern rednecks. We've watched it together a dozen times and still laugh in all the right places. But tonight I want to be left alone. Laughing is not on my agenda.

Before I can graciously object, Brad has the movie started and the popcorn in the microwave. I slump down on the couch next to him and sit unusually quiet through the first half of the movie. Brad is doing his usual commentary, but for the first time, Vinny's humor leaves me flat. As the murder trial starts, one of the defendants is represented by Vinny, the other by a public defender. The public defender pats his client on the back and walks confidently toward the jury box. But when he starts his opening statement, his nerves and stuttering problem get the better of him. "We intend to prove that the p-p-p-p"—spit is flying—"the p-p-p-prosecution's case is um, um, um, c-c-c-c-circumstantial and coincidental. Thank you," he says, then he waves at the judge as he heads back to his counsel table. That's it, his entire opening! He sits down next to his shocked client and whispers, "I get a little nervous up there."

Brad guffaws as he always does. "A *little* nervous," he mocks. I smile as best I can manage under the circumstances. Brad tilts his head back and looks at me, concern registering on his face. He grabs the remote and flicks off the television.

"You want to talk about it?" he asks.

I'm not ready for this. Yes, I want to talk about it. I want Brad to tell me that it's going to be all right. I want to hear him say that he loves me anyway. I want to tear down this wall I feel myself erecting between us.

But I also know that Brad will not agree with my decision to do experimental surgery. He'll want me to go the safe route, the seven-inch zipper route, the "never show any of your torso again in public" route. Plus I don't think it's fair to put Brad through this. If something does happen to me, he'll feel obligated to stay with me the rest of our lives, caring for someone with a lifelong disability. Brad's too young for that. I won't let that happen. If I have to get a pacemaker, Brad will never see me again.

"It's nothing, Brad," I hesitate, my lip quivering. "I just need some space sometimes."

Brad's face registers his hurt, but I can't help it. "What do you mean by that?"

"I don't know, Brad. Sometimes I've just got to have some time to myself. I just need a little space."

Brad is serious now, the Vinny humor long gone. "Leslie," he says softly, "in a few weeks we're going to be married. There won't be any private space. And there won't be any room for secrets."

I feel the tears begin to burn in my eyes. This is not how I wanted this to go, not what I need at this critical point in my life. "I'm sorry, Brad." I shrink back and curl into my own little shell. "I know you're right. But we're not married now, and I just need some space tonight."

"Okay," he says. He hesitates, perhaps waiting for me to rethink what I've just said. Then he lets out a deep sigh and rises from the couch. He puts his glass in the sink and goes over to retrieve the DVD. He bends to kiss me on the way out. "See you tomorrow," he says flatly. He kisses me quickly on the lips, without emotion.

I want to call him back and pour out my feelings. How can I go through this without him? But I've already frustrated him, and truthfully, he's made me a little mad with the way he just reacted. If Brad and I have one thing in common, it's our intransigence.

And so I let him leave mad. Now I've got my time alone. Now I've got my space. I use it to cry nonstop for the next half hour. But this time, they are not tears of sadness. They are tears of frustration and determination. I will do this alcohol ablation thing. Nobody will stop me.

And for his own good, I will do it without Brad.

All weekend Brad gives me the space I said I wanted. He calls a few times, but our conversations are short and strained. If it weren't a matter of principle, I would tell him that I really just need to see him again and be held by him. But that would mean admitting I'm wrong. Definitely not my strong point.

By Monday morning I'm ready to see Brad. I struggle to get out of bed and take longer than normal getting ready for work. HCM has robbed my passion for life. It was my first thought of the day, and I can't shake visions of the alcohol ablation operation all morning. My first appointment with Dr. Maholtra is in three days, and if all goes well, I could be on the operating table next week.

I choke down some oatmeal and think about how hard it is to lose weight with my new heart-friendly diet. So much for a size 4 wedding dress.

I straggle into work at about nine and exchange the usual pleasantries with Bella.

"Good morning," says Bella.

"Easy for you to say."

"Mmm," she replies. "PMS three weeks running. Must be some kind of record."

It's impossible to outsarcastic Bella, so I don't try. I shuffle into my office and start thinking about Brad. Within half an hour my legal research has turned into more medical research about HCM. By 9:30 I've decided to make nice with Brad, though I still have no intention of telling him about the HCM. I take a folder from the Bannister case file with me as my excuse for needing to talk with him.

I'm more than a little upset that he hasn't already been down to see me. I mean, how many steps does it take to get from his office to mine? Why do I always have to be the first to move?

I walk out of my office, past Bella, and down to Brad's office—thirty-nine steps. Bella watches me with a bemused smirk on her face. Though Brad's door is closed, I do a perfunctory knock and enter without waiting for a response. Brad is sitting at his desk, facing the door, and a broad-shouldered man with long blond hair is sitting in the client seat. He whirls as he hears the door open. I immediately feel like an idiot.

"Yes?" asks Brad, as surprise and amusement register on his face.

I lift the case file in front of me, like I just remembered this critical sentence I must read before I take my next breath. I peer gamely over the top, feeling like Wilson in *Home Improvement*. Brandon is staring back.

"I didn't know you were busy," I say. "It can wait." I spin and head back out the door.

Bella smirks as I walk back by the reception area.

"Why didn't you tell me he was in there?"

"You didn't ask."

I close my door loudly as I shut myself back in my office. On most days the good-natured banter between Bella, Brad, and me is a lot of fun. But on other days you just need a friend. This morning is one of those other days.

Less than two minutes later there is a soft knock on my door. I pull up some e-mails so it will look like I'm busy. "Come in," I say.

Bella sticks her head in the door and enters tentatively. "Are you okay, Leslie? Or do you need to talk?"

After I vent with Bella for a while, I feel better. She tells me about her battles with the insurance company to get this procedure covered. I tell her about Thursday's appointment at the Dallas Heart Clinic. Bella makes me promise to take a girls' day out with her and Sarah on Saturday.

Just before noon I decide to head over to Tara's high school, hoping to catch her during her lunch hour. She's in her last few weeks of school, and this may be the only place I can talk to her away from her mom. As I approach my Accord, I notice a man in a car about fifty feet away, staring at me. Though I'm used to men looking me over from time to time, they aren't usually so obvious about it, ogling me from a parked car in the middle of a parking lot, as if they've been waiting for me. I can't see the guy's face very well because of a glare on the front windshield. But I'm sure he is watching me the entire time as I walk to my car.

My skin starts to crawl. Is this what it feels like to be stalked?

I decide that I am overreacting. There could be a thousand reasons this dude is sitting in his car in our parking lot. I try to think of a good one. Maybe he dropped somebody off and is waiting for them. Maybe he's stalking someone else, an ex-girlfriend or someone, and just wanted to stare at me for practice.

I back out and intentionally drive by him, casting a glance in his direction. He has pulled down a visor. I can't make out the face, but I get a real good look at the car. It's a small silver sports number, some kind of foreign model. Two-door, the kind that was designed to be a convertible, but this is the poor man's hardtop model. It's a late-model car with a dent in the left front panel. The first three letters of the license plate are DMQ. There are some numbers that follow the letters, but I can't catch them with my quick, casual glance.

My panic meter raises a few more notches as I glance in my rearview mirror and watch the guy pull out behind me. As I travel toward the interstate, I notice my stalker hanging several hundred feet back. I think about calling Brad on my cell, but that feels like a sign of weakness. Besides, it's not at all unusual for somebody to drive from our parking lot to the interstate, using the same route I'm using.

Is it?

Once I hit I-264, I decide to outrun him in the left lane. I get the Accord up to about eighty-five, knowing that if I get pulled over by the cops, my stalking problems will be over. I think about who this might be. I'm not a celebrity, and there are no ex-boyfriends running around. Basically, I live a pretty boring life. The only thing that makes sense is someone associated with Tara's case—that's the only truly controversial matter I'm handling right now. Maybe this is part of Strobel's cloak-and-dagger routine.

When I hit my exit, the stalker follows me. I can no longer deny that this guy is after me. My hands are starting to tremble, but I know that the best thing in life is to confront your fears. I decide to pull over at some safe location and get a good look at the guy.

Two blocks later I find the place. There's a 7-Eleven on the right corner with a police cruiser in the parking lot. I pull in at the last second and watch my rearview mirror for my stalker. I'm hoping that he gets stopped at the traffic light just in front of the parking lot. He does not, and he drives by with his hand up next to his face, talking on a cell phone. He's white, fairly thin, wearing a baseball cap, and sitting low in the front seat. That's all I could tell. Looks like I've narrowed it down to about twenty million American males.

I walk into the store and find, not surprisingly, they don't sell mace. I go for the next best thing—an aerosol can of Arid XX deodorant. I notice the police officer, a small thin woman who looks like she probably gets tired wearing that thick police belt with all the heavy equipment. I stuff the Arid into my purse and, properly armed, head back to my car.

I check my mirror about twenty times the rest of the way to school. The stalker's not there. I register at the office, explain that I'm Tara's attorney, and learn that she's in the cafeteria. Visions of my high-school days return, sitting with my clique in the cafeteria—the nerds who tried to be cool—giggling and talking about the guys. I expect Tara to be sitting with a pretty rough-looking bunch. I'll bet her friends are mostly boys, and I'll bet they're pretty punked out.

I enter the chaos of the cafeteria and immediately feel at least a thousand years old. A dinosaur would not feel more out of place. I feel the stares of dozens of high-school girls and more than a few adolescent boys—the same boys who would never have given me a second glance if they had seen me in my high-school days. I stand in the middle of the chaos and scan the tables. I finally spot Tara at a table in the far back corner and head that way. To my surprise, she is eating with mostly girls, and they all look fairly normal. To my even greater surprise, the one boy I see at the table is Jamie, sitting right next to Tara and joining in the conversation with the girls around him.

I would have thought that Tara would try to avoid her little brother at school. But here they are, side by side in the cafeteria. As far as I can tell, Jamie is the only kid his age at this table of high-school girls. He must be loving it.

I come up behind Tara. She turns around to see what her friends are gawking at. "Hey Tara," I say, as if I stop by to eat lunch with her all the time. "I don't know how much time is left in your lunch period, but could I talk to you for a second?"

Since Jamie is also looking at me, I acknowledge him, too. "Hey Jamie."

Tara does not seem the least bit put out by my being there. She introduces me to all her friends as "my lawyer—graduated second in her class from William and Mary." Her friends are all polite and duly impressed that Tara is so important that her lawyer would visit her in school. After making a few seconds of small talk with her friends, I turn back to Tara.

"Is there someplace we can talk?"

"Sure," she replies. "And let's talk slow. I've got a quiz after lunch in American history."

As we leave the table, I notice Tara lean over and give Jamie a quick hug. "Don't mess around on your way back to class," she lectures.

"I'll take him," says one of the girls from across the table.

Tara guides me out of the cafeteria, down the hall, and into the gymnasium. We take a spot high up on the bleachers. We have the entire place to ourselves.

"Does Jamie always eat lunch with you?" I ask.

"Most of this year he has," Tara says. "The kids in his class picked on him during lunch, and he got in a few fights, so my mom worked it out so he could eat with us. His class is in PE."

This motherly side of Tara intrigues me. I didn't know it was there. "What does he do when his class goes to lunch?"

"He comes down to study hall with me. They eat before we do."

"Does he ever act out during lunch… I mean, does the Tourette's ever kick in?"

Tara shrugs this off. "Not very often. When it does, my friends understand it's just the Tourette's. Jamie's really a pretty cool kid."

And maybe you are too. A pang of guilt hits me for the way I've reacted to Jamie. My uneasiness around him is more like Jamie's fifth-grade classmates than Tara's more mature high-school friends. I promise myself to fix that.

"Tara," I hesitate, staring down at my hands. "I've got to talk to you about something that may be pretty tough. I don't like talking about this but…well, as your lawyer…you understand."

"Sure…whatever."

"What we say stays between us and only us—right?"

"Yeah."

"Okay." I swallow hard and begin. "You know that Harlan Fowler is a named beneficiary under your stepdad's life insurance policy. In fact, he gets a million bucks...half the policy." I look at Tara to gauge the look on her face. There is no surprise, no change of expression.

"Yeah. My mom said something about that. But I think he's supposed to give most of it to Jamie and some of it to me."

"Actually, Tara, the letter that instructs him to do that has no legal effect. Fowler's free to do whatever he wants with his half of the policy."

I watch a disgusted look flash over Tara's face, her eyes registering her disapproval.

"I believe that Fowler was in a lot of debt from gambling," I continue. "Probably several hundred thousand." I watch her take this all in; her face shows nothing but contempt. "At the same time, your stepdad was under a lot of pressure at work—TalkNet was getting ready to tank. I think that Fowler sent your stepdad a legal case by e-mail about a month before your stepdad revised his keyman insurance policy for TalkNet. That case sets forth the law about what it takes to prove someone is dead so you can collect insurance. I think maybe Fowler and your stepdad were hatching a plot to have your stepdad disappear, maybe while flying his company's plane, never to be heard from again. Fowler would collect on half the insurance policy, your family would get the other half, and TalkNet would collect $10 million on a policy the company took out on your stepdad. Everybody wins, Fowler sends some of the money to your stepdad in some remote location, and your stepdad starts his life all over again."

Tara's look now turns to confusion. She shifts uncomfortably on the bleachers. "So why does all that matter? It didn't turn out that way. I shot him."

Now I look directly into her eyes, but she does not return my gaze. "I know you shot him, but I also believe that Fowler played some role in this. What role, I don't yet know. But I've been asking myself a question. If Fowler and your stepdad had some scheme so that your stepdad could disappear and Fowler could get rich, why would Fowler want to kill your stepdad before they try to pull that scheme off?"

Tara gives me her signature shrug. "Maybe he didn't. Maybe I shot him in self-defense, just like I've been telling you."

"There is one other possibility," I say. "Maybe Fowler was having an affair with your mom." Tara shoots me a sideways "you're crazy" look. "Maybe they worried that your stepdad was going to find out about the affair before this little disappearance scheme could be pulled off. Maybe they talked you into taking matters into your own hands, and Fowler promised you that he'd make sure you got a light sentence." I stop talking and try to determine if the disgusted look on Tara's face is real or a put-on.

"How am I doing so far?" I ask.

She snorts. "About as good as we did in court the other day. I would never, *ever*, do anything to help that jerk. And there is no freakin' way my mom was having an affair with him."

To my surprise I notice some tears of anger glistening in Tara's eyes as she stares across the gym. "No freakin' way," she repeats.

"Then why is Fowler so anxious to help you?" I ask. "Why is he bending over backward to see this case pled out?"

Tara looks straight at me now. There is a deep-seated hatred etched on her face, and it's reflected in her tears. This is no act. She's suddenly a very different girl than the one I met in the cafeteria just a few minutes ago.

"Do you really want to know?" she asks.

"Tara"—I grab her arm gently—"I really *need* to know."

CHAPTER THIRTY-FOUR

Tara leads me out of the gym and back toward the cafeteria. On the way, the bell rings and we are caught up in the bedlam of students changing classes. Tara finds her friend Rachel in the sea of high-school students, and I follow the girls to Rachel's locker. Rachel goes for a fat American history book buried in the bottom. She hands it to Tara and gives her a look that seems to say, *I hope you know what you're doing.*

We part ways with Rachel and head to the school office. "By the way," says Tara, "that was Wiccarules."

At the office Tara explains that I am her lawyer, and I sign us both out. We make our way to my car. "Where to?" I ask, looking nervously around the school for my stalker.

"Can you just drive for a few minutes?" asks Tara. "I've got something to tell you, and it will be easier if you're not staring at me with those buggy eyes. I swear, sometimes I think they're going to pop out of your head."

"Thanks," I say sarcastically. Nobody has ever told me I have "buggy" eyes before. I always thought my big blue eyes were one of my best features. They've been called expressive or sexy or even alluring (once in a review of a high-school play), but they've never been called buggy. I resist the urge to pull down the visor and make sure they haven't changed. My client's in high school—what does she know?

"I didn't mean anything by it," Tara says. "I mean, they're actually kind of pretty." *Nice try.* "They just make me nervous."

As we're leaving the parking lot, I check the rearview and make sure nobody's following us. Tara opens the history book, and to my surprise, the inside pages are carved out to accommodate a videotape. "Guard this with your life," Tara says. Then she closes the book and leaves it on the floor. "I'm leaving it with you."

"What is it?"

Tara takes a deep breath and begins her story in an expressionless monotone. As she talks, sparing no detail, my mind flashes vivid images of the scenes she's describing, with characters so real they are in living color:

Spring break. Sophomore year. Tara is lovin' Las Vegas. She has pouted for a few days about coming when her parents didn't trust her to spend spring break at North Carolina's Outer Banks with her friends. Things really turned south when Rachel got grounded just before the Vegas trip and couldn't come along. Tara thought it would be torture to spend a week in Vegas with just her family and one of her dad's gambling buddies, but she is actually having a good time. She will never tell her parents that, of course.

They are staying at the MGM Grand, one of Vegas's premier hotels, and her stepdad has pulled out all the stops. The hotel suite is fabulous. It's actually three separate rooms—one bedroom with two double beds that adjoins a massive suite, complete with a huge flat-screen television and small kitchen area, and then another bedroom on the other side. Tara and Jamie share the bedroom with the double beds, her mom and stepdad stay in the other, though she probably hasn't seen her stepdad in the last two days. He's too busy losing money with his friend Harlan Fowler and drinking himself silly to actually spend any time with the family.

Tara has spent the afternoon lounging by the swimming pool in her small black bikini, attracting the unwanted stares of dirty old men and the welcome advances of college-age boys. Jamie and Trish have gone to the theme park at New York–New York, so Tara has been completely left to her own devices. Today has been particularly fruitful, as she met a couple of boys while floating on a raft in the thousand-foot-long lazy river pool.

The guys claimed to be UCLA students, and Tara told them she would be starting the University of Virginia in the fall. She made plans to meet them in a few hours at Club 54.

Tara returns to her bedroom to change, then decides to jump in the Jacuzzi for a few minutes before she showers. She heads across the suite toward her parents' room—James insisted that he and Trish have the bedroom with the master bath—and stops just before entering when she hears men's voices coming from the room. Though she can't make out everything, Tara hears the men making lewd comments. They are obviously drunk, talking loud, and probably watching some soft-porn movie on the television.

Her first thought is to retreat to her own bedroom, as far away from these pigs as she can. But that emotion is quickly overcome with disgust, then with an overwhelming desire to embarrass the men. She decides to strut into the room, look aghast at the television, put her hand on her hip, and tell these perverts how disgusting they are. She will take a mental snapshot of the embarrassment on her stepdad's face and throw this incident back at him anytime she needs leverage. This is an opportunity the fates have dropped in her lap. If she plays this right, she will be spending spring break on the Outer Banks next year, partying away with her friends, and James won't even try to stop her.

She slips the room key her mom had given her into the door and enters the room. She surveys the two men—her stepdad and Harlan Fowler—beers in their hands and eyes locked on the television. Then she turns her gaze to the television, and her jaw drops in disbelief!

This is not the professional soft-core porn Tara expected but, rather, grainy pictures of naked girls the same age as her. She stares at the television, then recognizes the girls and looks at the men with even more contempt than before. Fowler is sitting on a stool, in khaki shorts and no shirt, exposing his thick, hairy chest. He has a remote control in one hand, a beer in the other. Her stepfather is slouched on the sofa, in an untucked button-down shirt and shorts, looking like a slug. He takes another swig of his beer as Fowler clicks off the VCR.

"Don't you ever knock?" James Bannister growls.

"You guys are perverts," Tara spits. She stands there frozen inside the door, suddenly feeling exposed in her bikini top and shorts.

Fowler stands. "It's not what you think." His words are slurred, and he takes a small sideways step to catch himself. "We're reviewing some critical evidence in a case I'm handling."

But Tara knows better. As Fowler takes another off-balance step toward her, a wave of nausea hits. The girls she saw on the tape were classmates, the girls' basketball team, videotaped by a perverted assistant coach. It had been all over the papers and the talk of the school. The coach was facing charges of peddling child pornography. Now the commonwealth's attorney is showing the tape to her stepdad.

"We were studying the anatomical differences between sixteen-year-olds and eighteen-year-olds," Fowler says as he moves toward a dumbfounded Tara, leering at her with bloodshot eyes. "Maybe you can help."

He grins lustfully.

CHAPTER THIRTY-FIVE

Tara takes a deep breath and suddenly stops her narration, as if the next part is too painful to recount. The video in my head grinds to a halt. I glance sideways and note that she is in that trancelike mode again, the same shell she crawled into when she told me the story about shooting her stepdad. She is staring out the front window, motionless.

"Did Fowler abuse you?" I ask softly. I can only imagine how degrading this must have been. Her stepdad was in the room—why didn't he stop this?

"He tried," Tara says after a long pause. "He came at me and I started cursing him. He grabbed my arm and squeezed it hard. He pulled me next to him, told me to settle down, said I might actually enjoy a grown man for a change..." Tara's voice falters a little, and I reach over and pat her leg. "He tried to fondle me, but I fought back. James got up and yelled at him to back off. My stepdad said"—she hesitates, then spits the next words out; she has gone from subdued to fired-up in a matter of seconds—" 'She's not worth it, Harlan; let her go.' "

"Did he let you go?"

"For about a second," she says spitefully. "When James yelled, Fowler let loose, so I just stepped back and stared at him like I wanted to kill him. He stared back for a second, then this perverted little smile crosses his face again, and he said to my stepdad, 'How would you know?' So I tried to slap the jerk. He caught my wrist and pulled me up against his sweaty body again. It was sick! My stepdad yelled again, and this time Fowler backed off for good."

She pauses and shudders for a second, wringing her hands like she's trying to get rid of the residue that Fowler left there. "It was so nasty. I would have killed him if I had a gun. Instead, I just glared at them both for a second, then turned and left the room. I heard somebody snickering as I slammed the door shut."

I am embarrassed for Tara even now, more than a year and a half later. To be molested by a friend of your stepfather's while your stepfather is in the same room...what does that do to a kid? Still, I'm relieved that it didn't go further. And I'm impressed by Tara's willingness to fight back. Most fifteen-year-old girls would have been overwhelmed. Even now, as she retells it, I can see the fire in her eyes. She's not an easy person to victimize.

The magnitude of this, and how it changes everything, starts to sink in. This *is* the commonwealth's attorney we're talking about—the head law-enforcement officer in Virginia Beach. "You're saying the commonwealth's attorney assaulted you?" I regret my tone as soon as the words pass my lips.

"You don't believe me, do you?" asks Tara. Before I can answer, she's reached down and grabbed the history book, placing it on the seat. "Watch the tape."

"You've got a tape of his assault?"

She snorts, signaling her impatience with my stupidity. "Are you sure you finished second in your class?" I don't answer. "Not the assault, Leslie. It's the tape of the girls in the locker room."

"How'd you get that?"

"About fifteen minutes later, James comes over to my room and knocks on the door. I wouldn't let him in for about ten minutes. I threatened to call 911...everything. I finally made sure that Fowler was nowhere around and then let James in. He tried to apologize. Fowler didn't mean anything by it, James told me. He's sorry but sometimes Fowler gets belligerent when he's drunk. James said that Fowler was just telling him what a pervert this coach was and then remembered that he had the locker-room tape in the case files he had brought along to work on. He popped it in to show my stepdad right before I walked into the room. It was all a bunch of bull," Tara says derisively. "Total bull. James tells me that I can't say anything to anybody and reminds me of how powerful Fowler is. I told James that if he let Fowler within a hundred yards of me the rest of the vacation, I would file a police report and call a press conference."

This actually makes me smile, though I'm sure Tara was deadly serious about it. Fowler had no idea what he was getting himself into with this young lady. "That still doesn't explain the tape," I tell Tara.

"Yeah, so the next day I rummaged through Fowler's briefcase when he and James were down on the casino floor. I took the tape and mailed it to Rachel. Later that day I told Fowler that if he ever came near me again, I was going straight to the cops, tape in hand, and I would tell them everything. Needless to say, he left me alone after that."

"You stole the tape?" I ask.

"Borrowed."

"Right," I say. "Borrowed. And you've still got the borrowed tape today."

"It's been coming in handy," Tara says. "It's one reason I'm not too worried about my case." She pauses, then adds, "In addition to the fact that I've got a brilliant lawyer, of course."

I think about the tape for a second. The actions of Fowler suddenly become more understandable. But then another thought hits me. "What about that coach?" I ask. "If you had the tape, how'd they prosecute him?"

"It's called a plea bargain," Tara says proudly. "And it's the same thing Fowler will do for me if he knows what's good for him."

I argue with Tara most of the way back to school, telling her in no uncertain terms that I'm marching straight into Fowler's office later this week to confront him. She wants to hold the tape in abeyance and make vague references to it in order to force Fowler to let her off easy.

"What you're doing is blackmail," I lecture. "And I can't be any part of it. We're going to try this case straight up, not blackmail Fowler into a favorable plea bargain. Besides, he's not handling the case. Mitchell Taylor is."

As I drone on, Tara hunkers down into a pouting mode, mumbling that she should have kept her mouth shut. She can pout all she wants, but I've already made up my mind. We've got so much dirt on Fowler that if this case ever goes to trial, it will be a disaster for him. I will meet with the confidential source in Vegas, find out what Fowler owes in gambling debts, then confront Mitchell with some theory of the case that ties Fowler to the killing. The only difference between my approach and Tara's is that I'm putting it all on the table, threatening Mitchell and Fowler with a very messy trial if they don't plead this one out. Tara's threat was more implicit, but I think my approach will get the job done just as well.

Before I drop Tara off, I turn to ask her one more question. "Did Fowler have any role in the death of your stepfather?"

She has crossed her arms now, as if to remind me that she regrets mentioning the tape. "If he did, would I get off easier?" she asks.

"*Tara,* I want the truth," I say sharply. "Was Fowler involved?"

"How can I plead self-defense and say that Fowler was involved?" Tara asks. "If I conspired with him, wouldn't that make it premeditated murder?"

This girl infuriates me. An hour ago, during lunch, I was actually starting to like her. Now she's talking about the death of her father like it's some kind of chess game and she's trying to figure out her best move.

"Never mind," I say. "If you aren't interested in telling me the truth, then I'll figure it out on my own."

She climbs out of the car and slams the door. She's trying to act mad, but I think she's secretly relieved to have this out in the open. I think she's starting to respect me as her lawyer, and if I need any proof of that, I'm staring at it on the front seat. She has left the tape behind, giving me custody of her precious secret weapon. I will need to handle it carefully. A man's career is at stake and a young girl's freedom is on the line. This case has had enough twists and turns already. But as I watch Tara stalk away, I've got a discomforting feeling that there are other secrets yet to come out.

I begin to pull away and, as usual, check my rearview mirror. My heart leaps when I see him—a man pulled up to the curb about fifty yards back in a faded silver sports car. I immediately jump out of my car, stare back at him, and march straight into the school office to file a report.

By the time the police come, he's gone. I can see the officers struggling to act interested as I tell them my story. The officer in charge jots down some information, promises to run a check on all license plates beginning with DMQ to see if any known felons turn up, and then tells me to be careful. "If you see him again, try to get the entire license plate," the officer says politely. "That might give us a little more to go on."

I never would have thought of that, I want to say sarcastically. Instead, I thank the officers and realize that my report will never command another minute of their time. I feel like they ought to pat me on the head as they leave, tell me not to worry my sweet little self. I hate being patronized. And nobody can do it better than Virginia Beach's finest.

O n Tuesday morning I have Bella issue a subpoena for all records relating to the TalkNet plane that Bannister used. I subpoena records from the Hampton Roads Airport, where the plane is hangared, and from TalkNet's administrative offices. I am hoping to find a flight plan filed by Bannister for a trip to some out-of-the-way location, where he might have planned to disappear off the face of the earth.

I also learn that Bella's computer expert cannot resurrect the e-mail that had the legal case of *Sayers v. Aetna* attached to it. It seems that Bannister's e-mail was actually hosted by TalkNet's server, so any draft or deleted e-mails were never actually on Bannister's hard drive, only on the TalkNet system. Though I'm 90 percent certain that Fowler sent him the case on how to prove death for an insurance claim, I'll never be able to prove it unless I can get at TalkNet's computer system. I think about the hassles of trying to enforce such a subpoena against TalkNet—they'll claim Bannister's e-mails are confidential, proprietary, and irrelevant to our case—and realize immediately that it's never going to happen.

Brad shows up in my office by midmorning, kicks back in my client chair, and fills me in on his theory of the case. He says he has been thinking about it since yesterday afternoon when I called him.

"I like to start with things that we know are true," he says. He then lists them on his fingers. "Number one, Tara stole the locker room videotape. Number two, Tara hated her stepfather and wanted him dead. Number three, insurance policies exist on the life of James Bannister that will make Harlan Fowler a lot of money. Number four, somebody sent Bannister a legal case by e-mail convincing Bannister that if he just disappeared, his beneficiaries could collect on the insurance policies."

Brad rubs his face for a moment and pauses. This is the sign that he thinks he's really clever, really onto something. "The one thing that didn't make sense about Tara's story," he says, "is that she didn't really use that videotape to her advantage until *after* she shot her father in"—here Brad makes quote marks with his fingers—"self-defense." He pauses and looks at me. "She goes to all the trouble of stealing the videotape and then says to Fowler, 'If you come near me again, I'll squeal'?" Brad shakes his head. "From what I know of our client, she's far more resourceful than that."

The phone rings and Brad yells down the hallway, telling Bella to hold all our calls. "She loves it when I do that," he says, smiling. I'm sure that right now steam is coming out of Bella's ears.

What Brad is saying makes sense, but I'm having a hard time concentrating. I'm thinking about how much I want to talk to him about *us,* about how hard it is to pretend things are okay when in reality I feel this terrible wall between us. I want to tell him about my heart. But I *can't* tell him about my heart.

"I think Tara blackmailed Fowler *before* she shot her stepdad," says Brad. "Maybe she found out that Fowler was having an affair with her mom—" I shoot Brad a disapproving look; he knows I don't buy that. "Hold on," he says, palms up, "and hear me out.

"Tara's not just going to go to Fowler out of the blue and tell him she's thinking about shooting her stepdad," he argues. "As far as Tara knows, the men are still friends. So something must have spurred her to conspire with Fowler…"

"Who says Fowler was in on it *beforehand?*" I ask. "I mean, there's no evidence to support that."

"But it makes sense," Brad counters. "Tara goes to Fowler and says, 'I know you're playing around with my mom. And don't forget about this videotape I've got. Now, unless you want me to tell my mom about how you assaulted me, and my stepdad about your affair, then you might want to think about helping me eliminate a mutual problem.'"

Brad shifts in his chair, sitting up and leaning forward as he approaches the culmination of his theory. "So Tara tells Fowler she'll take care of the dirty work as long as he ensures that she gets off easy. Now here's where it gets interesting. Fowler agrees so long as Tara promises to wait a few months before she takes action."

The phone rings again. "Hold the calls!" Brad yells. Bella yells something in return that I can't quite make out. It's probably just as well.

"What Tara didn't realize is that Fowler was using this as an opportunity to get out from under his gambling debts," continues Brad. "After he cut his deal with Tara, Fowler made a few phone calls to Trish, disguising his voice, at times when he knew James would be home so that James would get suspicious. Fowler probably said a few things to James about how Trish was acting funny just to fan the flames. Then Fowler cuts a deal with James. Since your wife's fooling around with some other guy, I've got an idea. You substitute me in place of her as a beneficiary on your insurance policy and then disappear. Your company will get $10 million on the keyman policy, and I'll collect a million bucks on your personal policy and send half to you. Once James agreed to it, Fowler double-crosses James by going back to Tara and giving her the green light to kill her dad. James dies and Fowler gets his gambling debts paid off. The only fly in the ointment is that strait-laced Mitchell Taylor gets involved in the case and refuses to give Tara a lenient plea agreement in juvenile court. So now Tara feels double-crossed, and she brings the videotape to you."

Whew. He's got my brain doing backflips. I try to focus on Brad's theory rather than on Brad. The whole time he's been talking, I've been staring at him, thinking about how badly I want things to be the way they used to be. No secrets. Total trust. But that would mean telling him about my heart and risking his reaction. I'm just not ready for that yet.

"So what do you think?"

His question jerks me back to the issue at hand. Something doesn't sit right with me about his theory. Though it makes sense on a logical level, it doesn't ring true on an emotional level. "I just can't see Tara entering into any kind of a deal with Fowler. She hates the guy."

Brad ponders this. As usual, he's got a response. "As much as she hates her abusive stepdad? Maybe this was Tara's pact with the devil. Or maybe she's going to kill two birds with one stone. Pick your metaphor. The bottom line is that Tara knew she could get back at her dad *and* punish Fowler by forcing him to be complicit in the murder of his good friend."

My woman's intuition is flashing red. I can't see Trish having an affair, and I'm equally sure that Tara would never willingly deal with Fowler on anything. But I don't have a better explanation right now, so I take a different approach.

"How does that help our client?" I ask. "Under your theory she goes from self-defense to premeditated murder."

"True." Brad walks around the desk and starts giving me a back rub. I don't fight it, but I don't relax the way I used to. "We've just got to figure out what happened first," says my fiancé, "then we'll find a way to turn it to our advantage."

The phone rings again, and this time I answer it. "Tell Brad that the attorneys on the *Girl Next Door* case are on line one," says Bella. "And tell him next time he wants me to hold his calls, he can pick up the phone and tell me in a civilized manner."

"I'll tell him," I say. Then I hand the phone to Brad.

A half hour later Brad has handled his crisis. Now I'm in his office, focused again on the Bannister case. It has taken me this long to process his theory. His theory is plausible, but I still don't buy it. And I can't even fathom the implications.

"Brad, are you seriously suggesting that the commonwealth's attorney...*the commonwealth's attorney*...conspired to murder one of his best friends in order to defraud an insurance company of a million dollars?"

"Yep."

"Listen to what you're saying." I'm standing next to the door, leaning against the wall, while Brad is doing his usual three things at once—responding to e-mails, listening to me, and checking his stocks online. "Have you ever seen anything that would suggest Fowler is capable of murder? And why would he trust his entire future—heck, his very life—to a volatile sixteen-year-old girl?"

Brad hits the Send button and turns toward me. "Corruption rumors have been following Fowler since the day he took office. Is he capable of murder?" He jots a note on a yellow sticky, puts it on a file, and flings it into his out-box. "Aren't we all? Besides, we don't have to prove that Fowler is guilty. We've just got to have a good enough theory so that he knows we're serious. We confront him with it, and this case will plead out the next day."

Now my fiancé is making me uneasy. He suddenly sounds a lot like Tara. "Just Fowler? I thought we would take it to Fowler and Mitchell Taylor together, put everything on the table."

"Why would we do that?" Two more stickies find their mark, one on a letter, the other on a folder. He scribbles something that only Bella can read. "Once Fowler's secret is out—once Mitchell Taylor knows—we lose our leverage. For all we know, Mitchell might just haul off and prosecute everybody, make a real name for himself."

Something about this conversation is making me uncomfortable. My ethics professor in law school warned that the best protection against unethical practices is a finely tuned conscience. And he warned it will often be the people we respect most who first suggest we violate our conscience. *Even Brad?*

"Isn't that just a fancy way of saying we blackmail Fowler?" I ask. "How can that be ethical?"

Brad pauses his scribbling on yellow stickies and looks up. He puts down his pen and gives me his undivided attention. "Our number one ethical duty," he lectures, "is to get the best result possible for our client. As long as we don't lie, cheat, or steal to get there, everything else is secondary. All I'm saying is that we maximize our leverage and try to get this case pled out. That's not blackmail, Leslie, that's negotiation. Maybe it's hardball negotiation. But it's no worse than what Mitchell Taylor has been doing to us this entire case."

I hate it when he lectures me. Especially about ethics. I just stare at him for a moment, using my best weapon: silence. He writes a few more notes to Bella, and then the silence breaks him down. It always does. "Look," he says, his palms open in a sign of surrender, "you do whatever you think is best. It's your case. I'm just trying to help you think through some issues with some pretty big repercussions."

"I know," my tone is soft now. He's irresistible when he surrenders. "I'm just a firm believer in putting it all on the table and dealing with it that way. But in this case, you may be right. Maybe we should start with Fowler. We can always bring Mitchell in later if things don't get resolved."

"Whatever you do, I'll support you," Brad replies. "I like putting it all on the table too." He gives me that intense look that makes me feel like his eyes are piercing my soul. I get the distinct impression that he's no longer talking about the Bannister case.

"What's that mean?"

Brad sighs, then apparently decides to plow ahead. "I feel like you're holding back on me." He gets up and walks over to me, taking my hands. "Are you sure you're ready to move forward with this next step?"

I can hardly stand to look at the pain in his eyes.

He adds, "I'm not willing to do this if you've got any doubt about whether it's the right thing to do."

I want to tell him that I'm certain, but for some reason I just can't say the words. Everything in my life is up in the air right now, and I'm no longer sure how I feel about anything, including Brad.

"I guess that's my answer," Brad says after a few seconds of silence. He's looking at me, but now I'm studying the floor. "Maybe we just need to back off a little. Take things a little slower."

I nod my head, unable to answer. I bury my head on his shoulder, and he holds me for a while. "Can we talk about it later?" I whisper.

"Sure," he says. Then he kisses the top of my head, squeezes me tightly before letting go, and leaves his office. I close the door, sit down in his desk chair, and cry.

CHAPTER
THIRTY-SEVEN

Vegas does nothing for me. As far as I'm concerned, it's one big excess—miles of steamy concrete, gaudy neon signs, glittery shows, and loud game floors. Yet I am immediately overwhelmed by the sheer magnitude of it—any one of the major casinos is bigger than the hometown I grew up in. You need a map just to keep your bearings on the gambling floors—endless tables of blackjack, poker, roulette, and keno. Because I have arrived in Vegas several hours early, I take the opportunity to tour some of the larger casinos. It seems like half the civilized world is gathered around the slot machines and gambling tables. I'm struck by the number of tourists from other countries and the glazed looks on the faces of those who sit like zombies at the slot machines. I find myself wondering how long they've been there, how much they've fed the one-armed monsters.

Though it's midafternoon when I first arrive, I lose sight of that fact as I wander through the casinos. Inside the casinos, the bright lights, loud music, and swarm of activity make it feel like a perpetual happy hour. But still, I don't see all that much joy on the sea of faces around me. I'm guessing that most people in the casinos at this time of day take their gambling pretty seriously.

After the first hour all the gaudiness becomes a blur, and I start feeling very much alone. Vegas is not a place that's fun by yourself. I wander among the blackjack tables and start noticing the contrast between the lone gamblers, those who look like a day at the casino is another day at the salt mines, and the occasional happy couple—clinging to each other and laughing the time away as the dealer rakes in their money. I wonder how many of them are on their honeymoons, which in turn makes me miss Brad, which in turn makes me think of my visit to Dr. Maholtra tomorrow.

Duly depressed, I decide to concentrate on watching a few games of blackjack so I can at least have a vague idea of what I'm doing later. Of course, being Leslie Connors also means that I have researched blackjack on the Internet, memorizing the rules and copying a little strategy chart that I've stuck in my purse. Brad has given me a thousand dollars of firm money for my ten hands of blackjack. I intend to return with at least a thousand and one.

Before I know it, it's six thirty and I'm still a few blocks away from the Bellagio. I wander back to my hotel, check the schematic of the main floor that Strobel gave me, and make my way over toward blackjack table seven.

The Bellagio is over the top. The cavernous main floor is cluttered with noisy slot machines, blackjack tables, roulette wheels, and other card games that I don't even know the names of. Everything in sight flashes and buzzes and explodes into dizzying arrays of lights and sounds. I finally locate the table with fifteen minutes to spare. The dealer is a young Hispanic kid with a thin mustache and slicked-back black hair. His nametag says Julio. I nod, but he doesn't acknowledge me. I wander around for a few minutes and time my arrival back at Julio's table. It is now precisely seven o'clock.

The table is a half moon facing Julio. There were four players here a few minutes ago; it's now down to two. I grab a seat in the middle and plunk down five hundred dollars for chips. I had already noticed that this is one of the house's most expensive tables, requiring a minimum bet of a hundred bucks. For a moment, the thought crosses my mind that this might be Strobel's idea of a cruel practical joke, just trying to get me to Las Vegas to lose a bunch of money. But that would require Strobel to have a sense of humor, something he is definitely missing.

On my right sits a chubby, pale, middle-aged guy in a Hawaiian shirt. His equally chubby and pale wife stands at his shoulder, commenting on his luck. On my left is a man who looks like a seasoned gambler. He is probably sixty-five years old with leathery skin and the proverbial poker face. I doubt if he would change expressions if he won the lottery. Surprisingly, Hawaii has more chips than Pops does.

Julio deals us each (including himself) two cards, with his first card being face down. He then looks around our little circle, and we have to decide whether we want another card or not. The object is to have your cards add up to as close to twenty-one as possible, without going over. Face cards count ten; an ace can be either one or eleven. Each player is playing against the house, and Julio gets to see what we do first.

Hawaii is real animated, trying to sound cool by saying things like, "Hit me," or a confident, "I'll stand." Pops just motions with his fingers if he wants another card or taps the table to hold. I decide to follow his lead. The first two hands go the same way. I get dealt two cards. I add up my cards, look at the one card that is face up in front of Julio, and consult my little chart. Both times my chart says to take another card, and both times I go "bust," meaning my cards add up to more than twenty-one. On the third hand, Julio deals himself an ace and a queen, so all three of us lose automatically. In about three minutes I've lost three hundred bucks. My palms are sweaty and my mouth is dry. But the crazy thing is—I'm having fun.

Julio is starting to look a little worried for me. Maybe he thinks I've only got five hundred dollars, and if I don't start winning, I won't be able to play the ten hands that was supposed to be the signal. Whatever the reason, on my fourth hand he actually cuts me a break. I've been dealt a nine and a seven. Julio has an eight showing. Hawaii goes bust and now it's my turn. My chart says take another card, on the odds that Julio might have a ten as his down card and thus a total of eighteen. I motion with my fingers, very cool like my buddy Pops, but Julio raises an eyebrow. I decide to trust him and quickly tap the table. Pops motions with a finger, and Julio deals him another card. I notice that it's a six, meaning that it would have bumped my hand over twenty-one. I give Julio a subtle nod of the head. Pops's hand is now at nineteen. He holds.

And here's where it gets interesting. Julio flips his other card up, and sure enough, it's a face card—ten points. The house now has eighteen. He's already beaten Hawaii, since Hawaii went bust. If Julio holds, he also beats me, though he will have to pay Pops. Still, the house will have won two hundred and paid out one hundred. Everybody on the table expects Julio to hold.

Instead, he draws another card. It's a five, busting Julio. The result—he's turned my losing hand into a winner and the house pays both me and Pops.

"Holy cow," says Hawaii. "What'd you do that for?" But even as he speaks, it apparently dawns on him. Julio gives me a wry little smile, and Hawaii looks sideways at me, as if seeing me for the first time. It's obvious that Hawaii thinks Julio has the hots for me and will now throw hands just so I can win. "Sit down here, Louise," says Hawaii to his wife. He antes up a thousand dollars, while Louise stares at him like he's lost his mind.

"Herbert, you know I don't—"

"Don't ask any questions," Herbert says. "Just sit down." She does, but she looks scared to death. Her skin was pasty before; now she's white as a ghost.

I grin to myself and watch as Pops never changes expressions but quietly doubles his bid. Then Julio deals the cards, and everyone loses but me. In fact, I go on this uncanny winning streak, reading Julio's arched eyebrows instead of my chart to determine whether to take another card. Julio's determination to let me beat the house also benefits the others at the table. At the end of ten hands I have turned my five hundred dollars into fifteen hundred. Hawaii and Pops have done quite well too, with even Louise coming out ahead by following her husband's instructions. It takes all my willpower to cash in my chips after ten hands, especially with Hawaii begging me to stay.

Vegas is now officially in my blood. This is actually fun! I tell myself that I will head back to the blackjack tables after my little rendezvous with Julio. I won't put any more than the original thousand dollars at risk, I promise. Well, maybe a few hundred of my own, but no more than that. I remind myself that I'm here on business, but it's no use. I'm starting to understand how Fowler could accrue some hefty gambling debt.

I head over to the bar and order a Bloody Mary mix on ice. While I wait for Julio, I take out a pen and start calculating how much I would have made if I had bet the maximum of five hundred on each hand instead of the minimum of one hundred. I lust over the number I have calculated on my napkin, and I promise myself that I'll take more chances next time. Maybe we could pay for our wedding this way? Stop it, Leslie! This is such nonsense. Only the foolish gamble away their hard-earned money in Vegas. Right? Then why am I eying the main floor even now, scoping out other blackjack tables with hundred-dollar minimums and dealers who might like redheads?

CHAPTER THIRTY-EIGHT

Ten minutes later Julio climbs up on the bar stool next to me. He orders a gin and tonic. "I'm glad you're not fat and ugly," he says. "What's that supposed to mean?"

Julio grins, showing off rows of perfectly aligned white teeth. "It'd blow my cover story. If anyone sees me talking to you, they'll just think I'm trying to pick you up. If you were fat and ugly, they'd assume I was trying to rip off the house."

Julio's big grin and laid-back style put me somewhat at ease. But I also wonder if this might be his low-key way of seeing if I'm interested. I casually place my left hand on the bar, showing off my impressive engagement diamond.

"Another Bloody Mary for the lady," Julio announces to the bartender. *Is this guy blind?* Then he leans in toward me a little. "To really make this story convincing, maybe we should meet up later," he suggests.

I smile disarmingly because I don't want to alienate a critical witness. "Sorry, Julio," I say. "I've got to fly out tonight. Besides, I'm one of those strait-laced stiffs who never mixes business and pleasure."

"Too bad. I think we'd make a good team."

We banter back and forth for a few minutes, with Julio trying to flirt his way back into the game. I swirl the second drink around a few times, though I never take a swig. I'm starting to get frustrated; I've hinted at the information I need several times, to no avail. Finally, I decide to take the direct approach.

"I was told that you have information about the gambling debts of Harlan Fowler. If so, it's critical information in a murder case I'm trying." I give him the most sincere look I can muster—pleading with my eyes. "I could really use your help on this."

He smiles again, then takes a cool sip of his gin and tonic. "I know," he says. "But information's no good unless you can back it up in court, right? I mean, you really need someone who will not just give you the information but will also testify about it."

My hope inflates. "That would be ideal."

Julio looks around and leans in. "Witnesses sometimes get paid, right?"

I tilt my head skeptically. "Only experts."

"Okay," he says. "Some witnesses get paid. But you've got to understand, if I testify, I lose my job. And my job pays real well, supports my family…"

Your family? Then why are you flirting with me?

"It would have to be worth it," he says. "Do you know what I mean?"

I know exactly what you mean. It's called bribing a witness.

"Julio, I can't pay you." I make my voice firm. "That would be unethical."

This makes Julio laugh. He leans in again. "What we're doing is unethical. It violates Mr. Fowler's privacy rights and every rule of my employment. The only issue is whether I get paid for it."

This is not going well. I'm starting to think that I might get out of here without getting the information I came for. I need to change my approach. If I can just get Julio to confirm the gambling debt, I may be able to get some hard evidence later by applying to a Nevada court for a subpoena.

I turn sideways and face Julio, crossing my legs in the process. "Let's take this in two steps," I suggest. "First, you let me know if Fowler owes money to the Bellagio, and if so, how much. I'll protect your identity so you don't jeopardize your job. Then if the case goes to trial and I need your testimony, I understand that we'll have to make it worth your while."

Julio stares back for a moment. "As in six figures worth of my while?"

I've got to be careful here. Though I never intend to pay Julio a dime, I can't tell him that just yet. I've got to have this information about Fowler's gambling debts.

"If we proceed to trial and use your testimony," I say.

Julio considers this for a moment, then nods his head. "Jimmy," he says, waving to the bartender. "You got a pen?"

I hand him my pen, and Jimmy smiles, then discreetly steps away. Julio writes on his own napkin. He puts his name at the top, then two phone numbers, one for home, the other a cell phone. Now he leans over and puts an arm around me, his lips practically touching my ear.

"The cell phone number is real," he says. "Just in case you forget to make it to the airport in time for your flight. The home phone number is not. The first three numbers are the Vegas area code. The last seven numbers are the amount that Mr. Fowler owes the Bellagio as of last Friday." He gives me a kiss on the cheek and then leans away. "Had to make it look real," he says.

I'm starting to really dislike this guy, but at least I've got what I need. "Thanks," I say, looking down at the home phone number. (750) 029-0350. Fowler was in deep. I fold up the napkin and stick it in my purse.

"Don't mention it." Julio gulps the rest of his gin and tonic, then says, "Got to get back at it."

He leans toward me like he might try for another kiss, and I instinctively lean back. "Can I give you one last piece of advice?" he asks.

"Um…sure."

"Stay away from the blackjack tables," he says, climbing off the bar stool. "You're terrible."

CHAPTER THIRTY-NINE

I stare at the Bloody Mary for several minutes before pushing it away. I know how good it would taste, and I certainly know my nerves could use it. But I also know that I probably wouldn't stop with one drink. And Leslie Connors drunk is not a pretty picture. Besides, how could I go to my appointment with Dr. Maholtra tomorrow nursing a hangover?

I finally talk myself into rising from the bar. I start walking through the maze of Bellagio's main floor. Before my rendezvous with Julio, I was too nervous to eat. Now that it's over, I'm famished. I decide to take Julio's advice and avoid the blackjack tables, though I'm convinced that I'm not nearly as bad as Julio claims. I can't wait to see the look on Brad's face when I plunk down a thousand dollars of the firm's money and another thousand of my own winnings. I don't want to jeopardize that moment, so I make my way back toward the bank of elevators. It's time to get out of this skirt and into my pajamas, find a good in-room movie, and call out for room service.

When I turn to take one last glimpse of Julio, my heart catches. I think I'm being watched. He's a stocky middle-aged man wearing a blue blazer. He has a dark tan and bushy black eyebrows. Though I've never seen this man before, he's staring straight at me. A sliver of fear crawls up my spine. Am I being paranoid—seeing stalkers in every crowd? I decide to stop and glare back at him for a moment.

He looks away and keeps walking, eventually moving past me. My breathing returns to normal. All of this cloak-and-dagger stuff has me seeing ghosts. Just to be sure, I start walking in the other direction, away from the elevators. I make a big swing around the main floor before I work my way back toward the elevators. I glance constantly over my shoulder, stopping occasionally to look around, just to be certain that nobody is tailing me.

I arrive at the elevator just as one closes and heads up with several people. I jam the button and soon another car arrives. I step into the mirrored box of the elevator—man, I look tired!—and push the button for the thirty-second floor. As the doors close I see a man walking rapidly toward my car. I reach over to punch the Door Close button, trying to make it look like I'm reaching for the Door Open button. "Sorry," I say as the doors slide shut.

But the man is quick, thrusting his hand in at the last second. The door edge makes contact and the doors retract. *Darn!* He steps on the elevator facing me, with humorless eyes peering out from under bushy black eyebrows. It's the same guy I saw a few minutes ago on the main floor!

As the doors close behind him, I measure my chances of sprinting by him or calling for help or mashing the Emergency button. But my hesitation seals my fate. The doors close, then the man turns and stands next to me, staring at the numbers on the display above the door.

I steal a glimpse of him in the mirrors, then stare straight ahead, wondering why he didn't push a floor number. I don't really want to consider the possibilities. I try to appear calm and resist the urge to move away from him. I can't let him sense my fear.

"Good evening," he says. "Any luck on the blackjack tables?"

"Do I know you?" I ask.

He smiles and reaches into his inside suit coat pocket. I tense—should I spring for the Emergency button now?

"Relax," he says. He whips out a wallet with some ID and a badge. His name is Robert Mackey. "Hotel security," he grunts. "If you don't mind, I'd like to ask you a few questions. You're not in any kind of trouble; we're just investigating one of our employees. Thought maybe you could help."

Though my lawyer instincts tell me something is wrong with this picture, I agree to answer his questions. I ride back down with him to the main floor and follow Mackey across the casino and through a door that magically appears in a mirrored wall. I follow him past banks and banks of video screens being monitored by men and women in blue blazers. Mackey ushers me into a small office with glass windows all around the top half of the walls. He offers me a modern-looking black leather chair that seems to float on some kind of Plexiglas base. Mackey takes a seat behind his glass desk and offers me something to drink. After I refuse, he picks up the phone and calls someone that I assume is his partner. We are soon joined by a tall, gangly man with facial features so sharp he reminds me of a vulture.

Mackey introduces me. The vulture's name is Victor Bernidini. I wonder if I'm about to get a good cop–bad cop routine.

"You mind if I tape this?" asks Mackey. He places the recorder on his desk and turns it on.

"No. That's fine."

"You understand that this is a voluntary interrogation," says Mackey. "You are free to go at any time, and you are free to refuse to answer any of my questions."

Not quite a Miranda warning. But you don't need to give a Miranda in a noncustodial setting. Hearing his little disclaimer increases my jitters, though I know I haven't done a thing wrong. "I understand."

"And you have agreed to voluntarily answer a few questions for us?"

"Yes." As a lawyer, I know that I have an absolute right to stand up and walk out, and there's not a thing they could do about it. But as a person, there are far more powerful psychological forces at play— forces I haven't experienced since the principal's office in junior high. The psychological forces are strong, so strong that I'm determined to answer every question they throw at me, even if I have to fudge the truth a little. I feel a need to *prove* I have nothing to hide—to answer all Mackey's questions and establish my innocence of any wrongdoing. I suddenly have a new appreciation for the way Tara must have felt the night Detective Anderson extracted her confession.

I state my name and address for the record. Mackey asks if he can see my driver's license, and I show it to him. He makes a few notes.

"Do you come here often, Ms. Connors?"

"No."

"First time?"

"Yes."

"Are you here alone?"

"Yes." This generates a raised eyebrow.

"Pretty girl like you just comes to Vegas alone to gamble for the first time ever?"

I fidget in my seat as the glass walls of the office close in a little. I decide to go for sympathy. "I was just diagnosed with a serious heart problem. I'm on my way to Dallas to see a surgeon about some high-risk experimental surgery…" Even as I say it, it feels like I'm talking about somebody else. *Focus, Leslie, focus.* "I needed some time away. So I stopped here first."

"On your way to Dallas from where?" Mackey asks.

"Norfolk, Virginia."

"I see," he says sarcastically. "And being that Vegas is such a bucolic place and right on the way from Virginia to Texas, you decided to stop over to play some blackjack and have some time alone to think."

Well, sympathy is getting me nowhere. "You always treat your guests with such disdain?" I ask. "Maybe next time I'll stay at a hotel that doesn't mind taking my money."

"That's just it," replies Mackey calmly. "We didn't take your money. You took ours."

How much do these guys know? The air in the room suddenly

seems more stale; a thin line of perspiration is breaking out on my upper lip. But I'm also getting a little frustrated with Mackey's attitude. "You mean to tell me that you guys are worried about a measly thousand bucks?" I feel the Connors temper start to rear its ugly head. Intimidation is giving way to a sense of injustice. "There are guys out there right now raking in ten times that much on one hand. Why are you guys picking on me?"

"Julio Rodriguez," says Mackey. "You know him?"

This is getting tricky. They must have seen us together. "Just met him tonight."

My answer is met with a long silence, as if by waiting long enough they can force out another answer.

"Why did he throw games on the blackjack table?" Mackey asks. He has a steady and unblinking gaze that is unnerving.

Should I deny it? They probably have it on tape. "If you think he threw games, you should ask him."

"Do you have any knowledge as to why he threw those games?"

"No," I say quickly. I realize, of course, that I've just crossed the line. But what choice did I have? Once again, I think of Tara, desperate to prove her innocence to Anderson. How much of her story was fabricated on the spot?

"No idea at all?"

"None." The lie gets easier the second time.

"Did you talk about it at the bar?"

"Talk about what?"

"Why he threw those games?"

"Not really."

"What did you talk about?"

"He asked me out. Gave me his phone number."

"Did you accept?"

I flash my ring. "I'm engaged."

"But you took his phone number?" Mackey pauses and a smile pulls at his lips. "Were you planning on calling him later?"

"No," I say with a sneer.

"Do you mind if we look at what he gave you?"

I consider this for a moment. I have no doubt that these two guys would call both phone numbers. They would immediately figure out that the home number does not belong to Julio. That would only raise more questions. "Yes, I mind."

"I see," says Mackey. He thinks for a moment. "So where does that leave us? You're here alone on your first trip ever to Vegas. You just happen to go to Julio's table. He just happens to tank a few games. Then he comes and gives you a phone number, which you take, though you have no intention of calling him." A pause. "And you've still got no idea why Julio tanked those games?"

I cross my legs and look Mackey dead in the eye to show I'm not being intimidated. "Maybe he's a 'legs' man," I say, swinging my top leg just a little for emphasis.

Mackey nods knowingly. "That's what I would have figured too," he replies. "But one thing bothered me about that theory." He puts his elbows on the desk and clasps his hands together, resting his chin on them. "If you sit down at a blackjack table and suddenly discover that the dealer has the hots for you so badly that he's throwing games—why would you get up after just ten hands?"

I scramble for an answer but come up empty. For the first time, the vulture speaks. "Especially if you need money for some experimental surgery."

That's the problem with lies, I realize. The old yarn floats through my head, *Oh what a tangled web we weave when first we practice to deceive.* Tara flashes through my mind as well, even as I assess my own situation.

"Not everybody is greedy," I say.

This actually makes Mackey laugh. "There are very few things in my job I can count on with absolute certainty," he says. "But one of them is this: everybody *is* greedy."

He leans back in his chair for a second and eyes me. "People are so greedy, Ms. Connors, that we've had some customers actually conspire with some of our dealers in an effort to defraud the house. Funny thing is, they usually test out their system first or just take money in little chunks here and there to lessen the chances of getting caught. The first time they pull it off, it might just be for…oh, say a thousand bucks or so." Mackey pauses, allowing the accusation to sink in. "But they're usually not quite so obvious about it, and they certainly don't huddle up at the bar right after they get done pulling the scam. So, for today, as a one-day special favor for someone about to have heart surgery, I'm going to assume you're right. Old Julio is probably just a legs man, and you're probably not cutting him in on any of the action."

A smirk crawls onto Mackey's face. He's proud of his little double entendre. I ought to be indignant, but I'm just glad to get this over.

Mackey turns to the vulture. "Victor," he says, "would you escort Ms. Connors back to the gaming floor." He turns back to me. "And Ms. Connors, would you do me the favor of staying away from Julio's table?"

"I'll try to beat one of your other dealers instead," I say gamely.

"Right," says Mackey, as I head for the door. "Then let me give you one last piece of advice." I stop. "When the dealer is showing an eight, and you've got sixteen, always take a hit. Not many of our dealers are as dumb as Julio."

"I'll try to remember that," I say. Then I follow Victor Bernidini out of the office. I'm tempted to go back to the blackjack tables, just to show Mackey I can win fair and square. Instead, I decide to head to my room.

It's been a long day.

CHAPTER
FORTY

The next day I discover that I like Dr. Asha Maholtra. I don't like what she does to me, but I do like her style. She is small and strong, with a tan and wrinkled face. She has flawless diction. And she doesn't beat around the bush.

She's been working me over all afternoon. She started by shooting my veins full of thallium and conducting a nuclear stress test. This time I didn't try to be a hero and stepped off the treadmill under my own power after a little over eight minutes. Maholtra seemed less than impressed with my effort, but I assured her that I was saving my strength for surgery. She didn't crack a smile.

She also did something called an electron beam tomography, where she made me lie in a long tube while a machine shot electrons at me and took cross-section snapshots of my body at quarter-inch intervals. Afterward we looked at pictures of my veins and arteries on a computer screen. The doctor took great pains to point out all the deficiencies resulting from my enlarged septum. She then quizzed me endlessly, had me fill out enough forms to make an IRS agent blush, and performed every lab test imaginable.

Now that I've survived her needles and scopes, she is telling me all the possible complications of surgery and giving me another stack of forms to initial and sign. I confirm that I am aware of all the risks of the surgery—a list that reads like a medical malpractice lawyer's dream. There is the stuff I already knew from my Internet research—the risk of a pacemaker if the AV node is affected, the risk of dissecting the arterial wall—but there are also some new things to worry about. Like the risk of a blood clot causing a stroke, or the risk of the alcohol killing more blood vessels than necessary. All of these things and a dozen others have the potential of leaving me permanently disabled or in a persistent vegetative state or dead on the table. Being a lawyer, I know that half of this is just boilerplate for any serious operation. But still it makes me wonder if a seven-inch zipper scar would be so bad after all.

"Lawyers," Dr. Maholtra huffs, as I sign the last form. "They make life unbearable."

It's her first attempt at humor all day, so I manage a lame smile. "That's why I want to do this surgery rather than open heart," I say. "Since I'm a lawyer, I don't trust a doctor with a knife hunkering over me while I'm sleeping."

"Mmm," the doctor says. Either she didn't find it funny or she didn't get it. "Leslie, I think you're an excellent candidate for alcohol ablation surgery in all respects except one." Her voice is more serious than ever.

My stomach falls as I digest this sentence. I beat back a panicked thought: *Did I go through all this only to hear I don't qualify?* Suddenly, I want to do this surgery in the worst way. I look at Maholtra with pleading eyes, unable to voice the amount of hope I have placed on this procedure.

"Apart from the hypertrophic cardiomyopathy, you're in excellent health," the doctor continues, matter-of-factly. "You're young, your arteries are relatively clear, and your heart muscle itself appears strong." She hesitates.

"But…" I prompt her.

"But there is a complication regarding the vessels that feed the septum wall. In an ideal case, there would be just one cluster of vessels feeding the affected part of the septum. Unfortunately, in your case there are several clusters that may be feeding the swollen area of your septum, making it difficult to know which of them to target during the procedure. I think there are two main clusters, but until we get in there, it's impossible to know for sure if they are the ones to target."

Familiar tears begin burning my eyes. I focus on maintaining my composure, trying hard not to dwell on the consequences of what I'm hearing. *Left brain, left brain,* I tell myself. I need logic here, not emotions. I can deal with the fallout later.

"Does that mean I can't have the procedure?"

Maholtra shakes her head quickly. "Not at all, Leslie." I let out a breath I didn't know I was holding. "I've operated on patients with far greater risk factors. I just want you to know that there is a possibility, a higher than normal possibility, that this may not be a one-time procedure. For obvious reasons, we want to destroy the smallest number of vessels possible to achieve relief. This may mean we fail to impact a sufficiently large area on the first round and we have to go in more than once to achieve complete relief."

I can't decide whether to be relieved that I'm still a candidate or devastated at this latest setback my faulty cardiovascular system has dealt me. *Left brain, logic.* "What about the other risk factors? Are any of those affected by this multiple-cluster deal?"

Maholtra looks like she's fighting not to smile at my terminology. Sometimes doctors can make you feel so dumb. "No," she says patiently. "In every other respect, you look like an excellent candidate."

I swallow hard and put on my bravest face. "How soon could we do this, doctor?"

She studies me for a moment, as if sizing up my will to endure this procedure. Then she turns to her computer and punches a few keys. "How does next Wednesday sound? I've got an opening at three o'clock. The sooner we can get this done, the better."

No! my intuitive right side screams. *That's too soon! I need time!* But my right side is no longer connected to my mouth. My unyielding left side is fully in control. "That'd be fine," I say. "I'll put it on my calendar. Heart attack. Wednesday, May 25, 3:00 p.m."

Finally Dr. Asha Maholtra cracks a smile.

On Friday, Brad and I prepare to implement a coordinated strategy that will irrevocably alter the dynamics of the Bannister case. Brad's part is to argue a motion in Virginia Beach circuit court asking for an expedited trial date. Mitchell Taylor will undoubtedly oppose. Though the perfectionist in me would like another six months to get ready for trial, Brad has convinced me that we need to push for the earliest date possible.

In typical Brad Carson fashion, he ticked off the points on his fingers, building an impossible case to rebut. First, he said, delays in juvenile cases always tend to favor the prosecution. Tara turns seventeen in August and, like most girls her age, is looking more mature every day. "I want to call her a sixteen-year-old at trial," says Brad. "There's a big difference in a jury's mind between a sixteen-year-old and a seventeen-year-old."

Second, establishing a quick trial date would put even more pressure on Fowler and hopefully force him to quickly accept the plea bargain we are proposing.

And third, argued my fiancé, *if* we go forward with our wedding plans, we need to get this trial out of the way beforehand. "I don't want us spending our honeymoon getting ready for the Bannister trial," Brad said. The "if" part of his statement was an obvious hint for me to tell him what I was thinking about our wedding plans. But since I didn't know what to say, I just kept my mouth shut.

So today, Friday, May 20, Brad will be arguing for a trial date in late June or early July, though it makes my stomach churn every time I think about it.

My part of the strategy is to surprise Fowler with our allegations of his involvement in Bannister's murder. To do so, I called Fowler yesterday from Dallas, or as Brad thought, from Las Vegas. I told Fowler I needed to meet with him today, Friday. It was extremely critical, I said. We needed to meet alone. Fowler hemmed and hawed but finally agreed to lunch. "It better be good," he said.

"It is," I assured him.

Today mirrors my mood—hot and humid with a steady, wind-swept rain. The umbrella whips around in my hand as I make my way into the city's municipal building from the parking lot. My hair frizzes and blows about. I hope it doesn't rain on my wedding day.

At 12:05 I shake my umbrella and roll it up as I enter the reception area for the commonwealth's attorney. The receptionist calls Fowler's assistant, who relays the message that Fowler requested I meet him in Courtroom Number 6. I stew a little at the arrogance of this man—we were supposed to meet in his office, and I've already played through this a hundred times in my head—but then I head to the court building and find Courtroom 6. Fowler is the only person seated in the spectator section of the courtroom, and I join him on the hard wooden benches.

"Thanks for coming," he whispers, never turning his attention from the lawyers arguing at the front of the courtroom.

"Sure."

Tension fills the air as the defense lawyer flings accusations of prosecutorial misconduct at the young female prosecutor seated at the counsel table. Harlan says her name is Keri Massey. "She shows real promise." But right now, Keri is getting pummeled. The defense lawyer is alleging something about withholding key evidence and coaching witnesses. At the end of his tirade, the judge asks Keri, who appears on the verge of tears, several pointed questions. She answers timidly but holds her ground. The judge then delivers a tongue-lashing, but still overrules the defense lawyer's motion for a new trial.

The bombastic lawyer notes his appeal, and the defendant curses under his breath. When the judge leaves the bench, the defense lawyer rams stuff into his briefcase, then stomps down the aisle until he is directly in front of Fowler.

"She's worse than half the clients I defend," thunders the attorney as he jerks his thumb back toward Keri. "You won't get away with this." The man is overweight and slightly balding. His face is beet red, veins crawling all over his skull. "I've got a long memory, Harlan. You slip up, I'll nail you. I'll treat you the same way you treat me."

To Harlan Fowler's credit, he stands there without flinching. I'm looking over Harlan's shoulder at the defense lawyer, who seems ready to settle this matter with fisticuffs.

"Promises, promises," says Harlan, then he brushes past the man to join Keri in the front of the courtroom. The irate lawyer just stands there and glares at the prosecutors for a minute, shoots a menacing glance my way, then stomps out of the courtroom.

I remain in the spectator section, sensing that Keri needs a few moments of reassurance from her boss. Though I can't hear what they're saying, Fowler is plainly telling her that she has done a good job, and before long she has her head held high as she and Fowler walk back toward me.

"Keri Massey," Harlan says, "this is Leslie Connors, a new attorney working with Bradley Carson."

I shake Keri's clammy hand and read the remnants of tension still on her face.

"What was that all about?" I ask, nodding my head in the direction of the door.

Harlan jumps in. "That's Rodney Craft," Harlan says. "Claims prosecutorial misconduct every time he loses." He looks admiringly at Keri. "It was Keri's first time under his cannon fire, so I thought I'd show up for moral support. Turns out she did just fine without me."

Keri smiles lamely. "I never knew putting the bad guys away would be so much fun."

I had no plans of going to lunch with Fowler. I was just going to drop the bomb on him in his office and then leave. But that plan was shot as soon as I walked into Courtroom Number 6. Now he's insisting on lunch. "We can talk afterward," he says. "A man's got to eat, you know."

Reluctantly, I accompany Fowler across the street to the Beach Diner. He offers to share his big golf umbrella, but I politely decline and use my own. He chats about this and that, and I find myself having less contempt for the man than I did when I drove to the courthouse an hour ago. Seeing Fowler play the reassuring mentor to Keri has softened me a little. I tell myself that he's probably just trying to put some moves on her, too, and this restores my conviction for what I need to do.

As we reach the restaurant, Fowler holds his umbrella over my frizzy head while I fold mine up. He opens the door for me like a polished southern gentleman. He greets everyone in sight, introducing me to them like I'm some long-lost friend. He probably just likes being seen with younger women, I tell myself, trying to maintain the appropriate level of spite for the man. It's hard to do, however, when he greets our waitress by name. "Sally," he says, to the weathered woman in her late forties waiting on our table, "this is my friend Leslie Connors." Sally smiles and nods. "But don't start any rumors" —Fowler winks—"she already has a fiancé."

I blush a little. This is ridiculous. But I'm starting to see why Fowler gets reelected every four years.

"Good thing, Harlan," Sally says to Fowler. "For a minute there I thought you were two-timin' me."

Fowler laughs, then Sally takes our drink orders and leaves us alone.

To maintain the appropriate level of contempt, I remember the scene painted so vividly by Tara. That helps a lot. But Fowler is adamant about eating lunch before we talk business. "No sense ruining a good meal with shoptalk."

I protest but it's no use. I set my file down on the floor and prepare for a long lunch. This is not at all the way I pictured it—a cordial lunch at a small table in the middle of a busy greasy-spoon diner. Nevertheless, I know my time will come. I order a house salad—"low-fat dressing, please"—and listen to Fowler tell quirky war stories about Virginia Beach judges. I hate to admit it, but his personality is a little like Brad's.

Halfway through the meal I get a call on my cell phone from my fiancé. "June 27," Brad says triumphantly. I nearly choke on my salad. Five weeks away. "What did Fowler say?" he asks.

"We haven't had that conversation yet. Can I call you back?"

I hang up the phone and tell Fowler about the expedited trial date. "You guys work fast," he says.

"No point in stalling when you've got a strong case."

At this he just smiles. I sense he doesn't want to pick a fight over lunch. Somehow he veers the conversation back to other matters, and we are soon talking about the hearing we attended that morning.

"Keri's a good lawyer," says Fowler, taking another bite of his juicy burger. He chews for a minute, then washes it down. "Just lacks a little confidence." Now he looks directly at me. "Doesn't seem to be your problem."

I let it pass. "You handled that hearing pretty well," I say, trying to be civil.

He gives me an aw-shucks shrug. " 'A leader is a dealer in hope,' " he says. "Know who said that?"

"No."

"Napoleon Bonaparte, one of the greatest military commanders of all time." As I watch Fowler attack his fries, it occurs to me that he reminds me of a stocky Bonaparte, only with white hair. The Little White-Haired General. "Five years ago, I quit studying law and started studying history," he says. "I realized that the commonwealth's attorney is not so much a lawyer as a leader. To be a good leader, you've got to study great ones from the past…Bonaparte, Lincoln, Lee, Patton. My job is running an efficient office and mobilizing the troops." He pauses, as if I should be taking notes while he dispenses these great pearls of wisdom. "Five years ago I would have chewed Keri out for being intimidated, would have told her to practice civil law if she couldn't take the heat. Now I know that you motivate people by encouragement. It takes ten compliments to offset one criticism, that type of thing."

I take a bite of salad, wondering what his cheeseburger and fries are doing to his heart. "Mitchell Taylor seems to be pretty sure of himself," I say. "Bet you don't have to waste many compliments on him."

Fowler gives me a look that says I don't know the half of it. "Mitchell's hero is Stonewall Jackson. That should tell you everything you need to know. He'd indict his own mother if he caught her jaywalking."

Great. I could be dealing with somebody like Keri, somebody with a heart. Instead, I draw a Stonewall Jackson protégé. "No chance you could reassign him to more important cases than mine, is there?"

" 'Fraid not," says Fowler. "I've got so much personal involvement with the Bannister family, I've got to avoid the appearance of impropriety."

A little late for that.

"How's Trish, anyway?" he asks.

This catches me off guard. "About as well as can be expected," I say, watching his eyes carefully, trying to read between the lines of his question. "Why do you ask?"

He shrugs, his face displaying no emotion. "She's been through a lot. If I were you," he says, "I think I'd be more suspicious if a good friend of the family didn't ask."

We talk around the case for another ten minutes until the bill comes. I've lost my desire to confront him in this diner. It's too busy, there are too many people around, and the whole tone of the lunch has been far too amiable. I ask him if we can meet in his office for a few minutes. He checks his watch and tries to beg off, but I insist. We walk back to his office under overcast skies, but at least it has stopped raining.

Five minutes later I am sitting across the desk from Fowler in his spacious office, with the hardwood bookshelves and Persian rugs reminding me that this is a powerful man's office, a powerful man that I'm about to accuse of some pretty despicable conduct.

Unlike at the restaurant, Fowler does not remove his suit coat when he takes the chair behind his desk. "I've got to be in Judge Richards's chambers at 1:30," he says, checking his watch. "I really don't have much time."

"I'll be quick." I suddenly notice a chill in the air. The cordiality of lunch is gone. This is better; it feels more like combat. I reach into my file and place a folder and a videotape on his desk. I draw a deep breath and start. "You stand to directly inherit a million dollars in life insurance as a result of James Bannister's death. Though Bannister requested that you put some of that money in trust, his request is unenforceable."

Fowler raises his hand, a look of relief on his face. "Is that what this is about?" He stands. Before I can answer he adds, "I'm actually relieved you brought that up. I didn't know if Trish had mentioned it to you, and I didn't want to violate her confidence by saying something if she hadn't.

"Yesterday I sent a certified letter filing our claim with Benefit Financial. And don't worry, even though I'm not obligated to do so, I fully intend to set up the trusts requested by James. The whole insurance policy thing was a surprise to me." He blows out a relieved breath. "I'll sign whatever you want to make sure we legalize the requests about putting that money in trust." He checks his watch again. "Now, if you'll excuse me…"

"You might want to let me finish," I say. "Unfortunately, there's more."

CHAPTER FORTY-TWO

Fowler sits down heavily, then motions for me to continue. His eyes never leave mine. "Did you have an affair with Trish Bannister?" I ask.

He jerks back a little and his eyebrows come together in a look of complete disbelief, like he's sure this is some kind of joke. "You're kidding, right?"

"I'm dead serious, Harlan. Did you have an affair with her?"

He sighs and shakes his head. "Not that it's any of your business...but no. That's utterly ridiculous."

"Did you know that someone was calling and e-mailing Trish in the weeks prior to James's death? Did you know they would hang up if James answered the phone?"

Now Fowler leans a little forward, placing his forearms on the desk. His eyes narrow and his demeanor changes. The amiable politician is gone. "I don't play forty-eight questions, counsel," he says. "If you're accusing me of something, I don't have much time, so you'd better spit it out. But you also better be darn sure you can back it up."

I let his words hang in the air for a few seconds, trying to reorganize my scattering thoughts. He'd rather hear my closing argument than my cross-examination. Fine.

"Oh, I can back it up, all right. First, there's the matter of the insurance policies. Second, there's an e-mail you sent to James Bannister about a month before he procured the policies, sending him a copy of the Sayers versus Aetna case, which basically is a road map on how to collect on life insurance death benefits even if a body is never found." As I talk, I gauge his expression—it is a blank mask. I see unchanging intensity in his dark eyes, but there is no hint that I've struck any chords.

"Third," I continue, "is the fact that I have witnesses. One who will testify that you and Trish Bannister were having an affair, and one who will testify that you owe the Bellagio casino nearly three hundred thousand for gambling debts." The truth is that Strobel has yet to produce a witness about the alleged affair, but I want to see how Fowler responds. Still no reaction from the stone-faced Napoleon. I pause before I hit him with the good stuff.

"And fourth, about a year ago you sexually assaulted my client at the Bellagio." Fowler stiffens; I've hit a nerve. "I'm assuming you remember the night you got wasted and watched video footage with James Bannister of high-school girls in the shower." Fowler's face darkens, a storm brewing in the eyes. "Tara says that she walked in on you that night while you were watching the videotape. You groped her as she tried to leave the room. Later that week she took the videotape and threatened to expose you if you ever came near her again."

I stop and let the impact of this sink in. The only sound is Fowler breathing heavily through his nose. His face is now taut, as if stretched to the breaking point by tense shoulder and neck muscles.

"I've researched the case of the assistant coach charged with producing that video," I add, my voice brittle with tension. "He received an eighteen-month sentence, with all but three months suspended. He also got work release. Pretty good deal for a sex offender." I push the videotape forward a little on his desk. "Maybe his prosecutor was missing some key evidence."

Lunch now feels like a million years ago. I look into Fowler's eyes and think about how he humiliated Tara. This man is a pervert, and I feel nothing but contempt.

Fowler leans back and checks his watch. He punches a button on his phone. "Carmen, please call Judge Richards and let her know I'll be five minutes late." I hear Carmen start to protest, but Fowler hangs up. He stares at me, measuring my resolve, then sadly shakes his head. "That's pretty desperate, Leslie." He's talking in a deep, controlled voice. "I'm used to claims of prosecutorial misconduct—it comes with the territory. But this"—he sweeps his hand across the desk, symbolically encompassing all my points—"is a new low."

"I did not have an affair with Trish Bannister, regardless of how many lying witnesses say otherwise. Have I gambled some in Las Vegas...yes. But I do not owe the Bellagio anywhere close to three hundred thousand dollars. I have no idea what you're talking about with that Sayers versus somebody-or-other case. And finally, the claim that I sexually assaulted a teenage girl is just"—he searches for the right word—"just ludicrous. It does not surprise me that Tara is willing to say anything to help her case, but this..." He falls silent, shaking his head.

I tap the video. "Then how do you explain this?"

He sighs. "Tara stole a copy of that videotape out of my briefcase when I was with her family—most likely. I knew somebody either stole it or I misplaced it, because I couldn't find it after that trip to Vegas. I never dreamed that she had it." Suddenly, his eyes light up just a little. He stands. "Wait here," he says.

Fowler leaves his office and returns a few minutes later with another videotape. "Coach Barker did get an eighteen-month sentence, with all but three suspended." Fowler hands me the tape. "Because he cooperated with us, not because we lost the tape. We nailed a half-dozen co-conspirators in this child porn scam based on Barker's grand jury testimony alone. Here's a copy of the locker-room tape I just pulled from Barker's file." Fowler returns to his side of the desk and throws a few files in his briefcase. "You can watch it in our conference room if you want. I'll have Carmen set it up for you." He stops packing for a moment and looks straight at me. "But this one doesn't leave the premises—it's the original."

I'm working hard not to show my surprise. The tape was my one piece of hard evidence backing up Tara's claim. Does this kid ever tell the truth? On the other hand, just because Fowler has another tape doesn't mean that he never touched Tara. Why would she make that up? And she certainly didn't tell it like it was a figment of her imagination. The look on her face said it was real. Still...

"Leslie," Fowler says, "Judge Richards is a stickler for being on time. Is there a point to all this—other than your joining the ranks of other defense lawyers who want to take cheap shots at the commonwealth's attorney? How does this possibly advance your case?"

That, of course, is the million-dollar question. Watching Fowler focus on it so quickly reminds me again that I'm not playing with a lightweight here. "We have a theory that connects these events together in a way that exonerates our client," I say.

Fowler raises his eyebrows, daring me to share it with him.

"Of course," I add immediately, "I'm not at liberty to say what it is at this point."

Fowler grunts. "Of course."

"But I will say this: Tara's case will get very messy if you force us to raise all these issues in court. It won't just be Tara's reputation at stake... it will be yours." I prepare to deliver my pivotal line with just the right amount of conviction. "I don't want to drag everyone—including you—through this media circus. This case needs to plead out."

Fowler eyes me warily. "On what terms?"

This is the question I hoped he would ask...knew he would ask. I pull in a breath and give my scripted response. "Here's what I would recommend to my client: she pleads to voluntary manslaughter and the gun charges...as a juvenile. She serves until age eighteen in a juvenile detention home."

"Blackmail," says Harlan, without hesitation. "Let's just call it what it is." His bluntness shocks me. I start to respond but he speaks over me. "I've heard you out, Ms. Connors. Now you listen to me." He stands, his briefcase in one hand, pointing at me with the other. His words are clipped, shattering the silence in staccato bursts. "You think you can waltz in here, make some unfounded and spurious accusations, and somehow blackmail me into helping you get an incredibly lenient deal in this case? Let me tell you something, Leslie. I'll help you. I've been helping you. Why? Because I believe in this family. Because I think they've suffered enough. But I won't recommend that Tara get sentenced as a juvenile. We won that probable cause hearing…remember? And just so you don't think you have any leverage on me…"

Fowler reaches down and jabs the button on his speakerphone again. "Yes, Mr. Fowler," says Carmen.

"I need a meeting with Mitchell Taylor and Detective Anderson right after my hearing," demands Fowler. "Tell them it's urgent."

Carmen manages a "yes sir" before Fowler cuts her off.

"I'll tell them all about your half-cocked accusations," promises Fowler. "So it will all be out in the open. Nobody can accuse me of trying to hide anything."

He reaches out to shake my hand as he prepares to leave. Despite his display of bravado, I notice that his palm is moist, the same way it was the first time we met. "Leslie, you seem like a nice enough kid," he says when the handshake is done. "And I know you've got to accept what your client says at face value." He drops his tone and the face relaxes slightly. "But before you go out and try to ruin my career, think about the consequences of making these claims. Sure, I get dirty in the process. But does it help Tara? There's an old saying that you might be too young to appreciate: when you wrestle with a pig, you both get dirty, but only the pig likes it."

Now it's my turn to narrow my gaze at him. "What's *that* supposed to mean?"

"That neither one of us is a pig," Fowler says with a wry smile. "And neither one of us will like it if the mudslinging begins in earnest."

As I fumble for an appropriately caustic response, Harlan Fowler walks out the door, leaving me alone in his office.

CHAPTER FORTY-THREE

Brad is pacing, wearing out the carpet in his office. "Taylor didn't even oppose my motion," he says. "He said he would welcome the earliest possible trial date. I was actually hoping for something in July, but the only open date the court had was in late June."

"That's fine," I say wearily. "Plan a wedding, try a case"—*have a heart operation.* "Who needs sleep?"

"So tell me about Fowler," Brad prompts.

I give him a blow-by-blow of my meeting with Fowler, and he can't stand still.

Normally, his pacing brings me a strange sense of both security and anticipation. Security because there's something rhythmically comforting about it—Brad paces as he wears a problem down with relentless logic, bringing order out of chaos. Anticipation because his pacing often yields a major breakthrough, something I wouldn't think of in a million years.

But tonight his pacing is just annoying. My headache started while driving back to the office. It began as a dull throb around the temples, keeping beat with the windshield wipers as they fought the new wave of rain that moved into the area. Now the pain shoots across my skull, and Brad's pacing is not helping any. *Why can't he be still!*

"He's bluffing," Brad proclaims as I finish my story. "He'll call back early next week and tell us they want the deal."

Harlan Fowler did not act like a man bluffing to me. "I don't know, Brad. I think we weakened our hand by playing it this way. We should have just called a meeting with Mitchell Taylor and put all our cards on the table. If Fowler really does tell Mitchell about our meeting, it will look like we tried to go behind Mitchell's back." I shift in my seat, reading the lines of worry pulling at the corners of Brad's eyes as I criticize his plan. "I think we made it harder on ourselves."

"We'll see." He paces in silence for a few more seconds. I try to ignore the pain ripping at my scalp. I took Tylenol when I hit the office, but it doesn't seem to be helping.

"I still think Harlan's just trying to act tough in front of you," Brad continues. "I'll bet he never told Taylor or Anderson about your conversation. Right now he's sitting in his office, chewing his finger-nails, trying to figure out a way to make Mitchell take our deal."

I watch Brad some more. I rub my temple. "Sounds like wishful thinking to me."

"Tell you what," he says, turning on me with a spark in his eye. "I'm so confident I'll put money on it." He raises an index finger. "No, here's a better prize…an early honeymoon night as soon as Fowler calls us."

Despite the headache, this makes me smile—something I haven't done much around Brad recently. "And what do I get if I win?" I ask.

His eyes go from a spark to fireworks. "That *is* if you win," he says.

"Oh, how foolish of me. And what do you get if you win?"

"*Two* early honeymoon nights," says my fiancé.

I laugh, and then Brad bends over and kisses me. I would love to just focus on him and forget about this case, but I can't. "Seriously, Brad. What happens if Fowler doesn't take the deal?"

He starts rubbing my neck. There's still magic in his hands.

"Then we figure out a way to pin this whole case on him," Brad says.

"Even if our client says she shot James in self-defense?"

Brad stops the magic fingers for a moment. "What's your gut telling you, Leslie? Was it self-defense or is Fowler somehow involved?"

"I honestly don't know."

"Then we keep all our options open," says Brad, "which includes implicating Fowler. We'll figure out at trial which way to go."

Unheeded, Fowler's saying about rolling around in the mud flashes through my mind. My fiancé, the man I love, seems to relish the slosh pit. But for me, the ambivalence of this case is driving me mad. Sometimes I think I'd rather be prosecuting Tara than defending her. And this whole angle with Fowler seems so much like...well, like blackmail. What does his assault on Tara have to do with this case?

"Don't do this to yourself, Leslie," Brad says. The hands are kneading into my neck muscles, but my head is still pounding. "You're overthinking everything. In a case like this, you just pursue every angle. Throw stuff up against the wall. See what sticks."

"How do you live that way?" I scrunch up my neck and he stops rubbing. It was an instinctive response, but I sense he has taken offense.

He comes around and sits on his desk in front of me. "You okay?" he asks. The concern is wrinkled into his brow.

"My head is killing me." *And I don't need a bunch of questions right now either.*

"You want to come over to my place and just crash?" he asks. "I feel like I haven't seen you in a week."

It's Friday night—date night. And I know we've spent a lot of time apart this week. But I also know how I feel right now. Tired. Irritable. And my head feels like I've squeezed a size 7 head inside a size 5 helmet.

"Let's do a rain check," I say softly. "I probably just need to get some sleep."

This precipitates a long sigh from Brad, followed by "Leslie, we've got to spend more time—" He purses his lips and cuts himself off in midsentence. "Never mind," he says. "Sorry."

"What, Brad?"

"No, really. That's fine. Let's just do a rain check."

I stand up and give him a soft hug. I walk down to my office and pack my briefcase. I notice that Bella has left a note on my desk—she's picking me up tomorrow morning at ten for our girls' day out. I would love to just call her and cancel but decide I've already got half my office mad at me; there's no sense alienating the other half.

Brad walks me out to my car and tells me he loves me. I assure him that I love him too. We hug again, and he kisses me on the forehead.

"I'll call you tomorrow night if I can get rid of this headache," I say.

"Don't worry about it," he says, and I drive away, wondering what he meant by that last comment.

On my way home, Mack Strobel calls on my cell phone. This guy has the worst timing I've ever seen.

"Did you talk to Julio?" he asks.

"Yes." I want to tell Mack that I also talked to Harlan Fowler and that Fowler denies he owes the Bellagio that much money. But if there's one man in the world I don't trust, it's Strobel. I'll tell him no more than absolutely necessary.

"And?"

"He says Fowler owes about three hundred grand."

There is silence on the phone. I'm half expecting Mack to demand another movie-script meeting—maybe in an abandoned warehouse this time. I can't wait to tell him what he can do with his meeting.

"You gonna change your defense now?" he asks at last.

"What?"

"You gonna change your defense?"

"To what?" I ask, trying to make it sound like a ridiculous idea.

"The SODDI defense," says Strobel confidently. "Some Other Dude Did It. But in this case, that dude just happens to be the commonwealth's attorney."

"And put gunpowder residue on Tara's hands in the process," I say sarcastically.

Strobel chuckles. It's a condescending laugh that aggravates my headache like fingernails scraping on a blackboard. "Who headed up the investigation?" asks my tormentor.

"Anderson."

"Ask your partner what he thinks about Detective Anderson."

I try to wrap my throbbing head around Strobel's implications. My thoughts are like weak headlights in a dense fog. "Are you saying Anderson planted evidence?"

"I'm saying that Lawrence Anderson makes Mark Fuhrman look like the pope," replies Strobel confidently. "You can take it from there."

I want to get off the phone, but I've got to know whether Strobel is onto something. After all, he's been right about every other aspect of the case.

"Tara swears it was self-defense," I say. "She doesn't impress me as someone who would take a fall for Fowler."

"Unless," muses Strobel, "he promised her that he'd get her sentenced as a juvenile and then maybe split his portion of the insurance proceeds with her."

I think about this for a second. Then I remember how Fowler reacted when I suggested that Tara get sentenced as a juvenile.

"And then," says Strobel, "your opportunistic little client decides to go one better and claim self-defense. She figures she can get Fowler off the hook, earn half a million, and not even spend a day in a juvenile detention home."

In silence I watch my wipers swat away the rain. Strobel probably thinks he's stumped me. He hasn't. I'm quiet because I'm thinking about the fatal flaw in Strobel's theory, a flaw he couldn't possibly know about.

If Tara was working in cahoots with Harlan Fowler, then why would she tell me about the night he abused her in Vegas? As I focus on that question, the tightly wound spring that is my headache coils even tighter. I finally get off the phone with Strobel, more confused and frustrated than ever.

CHAPTER FORTY-FOUR

O ur girls' day out starts with the three of us watching Sarah's son Steven play soccer. The boy is thirteen years old, all arms and legs. He's got a graceful stride and handles the ball pretty well. He has endless reservoirs of endurance, playing midfielder and running down balls that others don't even chase.

Sarah and I stand back from the sidelines, cheering politely and talking. Bella stalks the sidelines like an out-of-shape coach, huffing and snarling at the refs, sometimes under her breath, sometimes loud enough to embarrass the real coaches.

"I don't think she's missed a game all year," Sarah says.

I love Sarah, though to be honest, she makes me a little nervous. I feel like I've always got to be on my best behavior around her, like she's got a level of faith that I'll never have. A former missionary to Saudi Arabia, Sarah's husband was killed by the Saudi religious police. Brad and I represented her in a grueling case against the nation of Saudi Arabia that tested every fiber of Sarah's character. She passed on every count.

I haven't seen her since that case concluded last year, and she seems to be aging pretty quickly. I think she quit coloring her hair or something, because it's now streaked with layers of gray that I don't remember from before. Her skin is showing some signs of age too, deep wrinkles at the corners of her eyes when she smiles, but she's just as comfortable in it as she's ever been. She is wearing shorts, a sleeveless cotton top, and sandals. And she seems to like being a mom as much as ever.

"Steven's fast," I say.

Her face lights up, pride evident in every wrinkle. "Takes after his dad."

"Yeah, but those long legs are yours."

This brings another grin. "In sixth grade the kids used to call me the stork," she responds. "I was the tallest kid in my class. You wouldn't believe how exciting it was in junior high when some of the boys passed me up."

I think of those awkward junior-high years. "Thing One," I say.

"Huh?" Sarah says, but then she is distracted by the action on the field—a breakaway by Steven. "Yes!" she yells. "Cross it, cross it!" Steven takes it into the left corner of the field and turns on the ball, crossing it in front of the goal with a perfect kick. A teammate heads it, but the goalie reacts, deflecting it wide of the goal.

"C'mon," I hear Bella yell in frustration from about ten yards down the field. "That was a perfect cross," she says loud enough to be heard. I'm sure the mom of the kid who missed the header doesn't appreciate Bella's commentary.

"Thing One was my junior-high name," I repeat, "because I hung out with another red-haired girl they called Thing Two."

Sarah chuckles. "But I thought Thing One and Thing Two had blue hair."

"Details don't matter in junior high."

"Kids can be cruel."

And so can fate. I keep the words to myself because I know Sarah doesn't believe them.

Despite Steven's heroics, his team loses by a goal. Nobody is as upset as Bella, who is sure the refs have been bribed. Sarah gives her son a hug and some last-minute instructions before he heads off with a friend. It's been a while since I've seen a thirteen-year-old boy show so much outward affection and patience with his mom.

We decide to travel in Sarah's minivan and then circle back to the park at the end of the day to pick up the other vehicles. Though I woke up this morning with an urge to just stay in my duplex, it doesn't take long before I'm really grateful that I came.

The "girls" take me to look at wedding dresses. Sarah thinks that I look stunning in everything. Bella volunteers opinions before anyone can ask, most of the time commenting on the prices of the dresses. "Good thing Brad's got more money than he knows what to do with," she whispers to me and Sarah after the clerk leaves to fetch another dress.

Next we spend some time at the mall, trying on perfume at Dillard's and loading up on lotions and bath oils at Bath & Body Works. I pick up a pair of jeans and a tank top at Old Navy, both on sale, and we proudly calculate the amount of money I saved. By two o'clock we are all famished, and Bella talks us into going to the Sweet Tomatoes restaurant. "I'm trying to eat more salad," she says.

Turns out she isn't kidding. Bella piles her plate high with lettuce and fixin's, and then smothers it in creamy Italian dressing. To keep the weight off, she decides on a Diet Coke.

It is only after Bella has polished off her salad, a bowl of chicken noodle soup, and started on a small dish of pasta that the conversation turns to my upcoming heart operation.

"I can't believe they just give you a heart attack while you're lying there awake," says Bella, twirling some spaghetti strands.

I'm thankful I've already finished my salad. This subject tends to wreak havoc on my appetite. I take a swig of iced tea. Even the usually diplomatic Sarah seems at a loss for words.

"It's hard to believe how small that thing must be that they slip up through your veins or arteries or whatever," continues Bella. She looks up at me as she takes a bite and must notice the fear in my eyes.

"Oops," she says, chewing. "Sorry." Another few bites. "I thought Steven really played great today."

Sarah turns in the booth to focus on me. "Are you worried?"

"What's to worry?" I say, my throat clenching. "They just run this little Roto-Rooter doohickey up your arteries from your thigh all the way to the heart, navigating its way through twists and turns, any one of which could be fatal. Then they shoot some alcohol into your heart, fry your septum, cause unbelievable pain, and hope they don't nail the wrong spot or they have to set you up with a pacemaker."

Though I try to keep my voice light, the bluntness of my words seems to unnerve Bella a little. She puts her fork down and looks at me, then Sarah, as if to say, *You're a missionary—say something.*

"You don't have to do this, you know," Sarah says softly. "Bella tells me that traditional surgery would be safer and less painful."

I shoot Bella a "thanks for blabbing" look, and she becomes engrossed in her spaghetti, focusing like a laser on the next forkful.

"I know," I say to Sarah. "But I've got to have an operation. And I'd rather go through this than have them pry open my chest and leave a huge battle scar."

There is silence for a moment as we watch Bella eat. The tears catch me off guard. I guess I just haven't given myself time to think about this in the past few days, and here, surrounded by friends, the emotions I've been avoiding bubble to the surface.

Sarah puts a hand on top of mine and says quietly, "I understand." Bella puts down her fork and looks at me with a softness I've seldom seen in her.

"I'm just scared," I admit. The words are escaping before I can stop them. "I'm afraid I'll lose Brad, I'm afraid I'll end up with a pacemaker, I'm afraid she'll puncture an artery..." I'm really fighting hard to keep the tears at bay, but they're pooling in my eyes. My voice breaks off, and Sarah puts an arm around my shoulder. The poor waitress picks the wrong moment to wander over to our table and check our drinks. Bella shoos her away.

"I want you to know that Bella and I will be praying for you," says Sarah.

I mouth the word, *Thanks.*

"And, Leslie, you don't have to be afraid of dying."

I nod my head as the tears fall. "I know."

I check my purse for tissues but come up empty. Bella hands me some napkins, which I use to wipe away the tears and slow the spigot. Then I notice that Bella has been crying too, which has caused her dark blue mascara to run. She looks like a raccoon.

I take a deep breath as I come out of the other side of my emotional woods. "Sorry," I say.

"Hey, what's a girls' day out without a good cry?" asks Bella.

I force a smile and try to think of something else to talk about. But Sarah is not done.

"I don't believe anything bad is going to happen on that operating table," she says as she folds and refolds one of the napkins. "But if it did, Leslie, are you ready?"

I give her a blank look with red eyes.

"I mean," she says, "are you spiritually ready?"

Though I know Sarah means well, this doesn't seem to me to be the time or the place for a sermon. "I guess so. I believe in God and all that. I'd just prefer not to meet Him just yet."

My friends don't smile at my lame attempt at humor. Sarah slides forward on her seat just a little, apparently struggling with what to say next. "Can I share something with you?" Sarah asks. "About what it takes to be ready?"

I want to say no, but I've never found it easy to be rude, especially to someone I respect as much as Sarah. "Sure."

Her next line shocks me. "Scripture says that the demons also believe in God." She delivers this rebuke as softly as possible, but it jolts me as if I've been hit by lightning. "Belief is a matter of the head," she continues. "But commitment is a matter of the heart." She shifts in her seat again so she is looking right at me, right through me, though I'm now tinkering with the utensils in front of me. "I faced death at the hands of the Saudi religious police. I watched them kill my husband. Peace came from knowing that death isn't the end, it's just the beginning. I had peace because I had already surrendered my life to Christ, and I knew that He would raise me up by the same power that brought Him out of the grave."

She pauses and tries to measure my silence. I don't know if I want her to stop or continue. I love Sarah, and I know that this religion thing works for her—I've seen the proof of that. But I'm equally sure it could never work for me.

When I don't respond, Sarah takes one more run at it. "Leslie, I'm only saying these things because I care about you as a friend. And I would never forgive myself if I didn't share the greatest thing that's ever happened to me—a personal relationship with Christ."

"And you know how much He's changed me," says Bella, double-teaming me from across the table. I give her a sideways look, and we all laugh. "Okay, I didn't say He was finished," Bella admits.

"I appreciate your prayers," I say. "And I'm so thankful for your friendship." I eye them both so they'll know how sincere I'm being. "But I'm just not ready to go where you are spiritually. To be honest, I'm still mad at God about Bill's death."

Bella starts to say something, but Sarah cuts her off. "I understand," says Sarah. "We just want you to have the same sense of peace we've found."

"Maybe someday I will," I say in a tone that makes it clear I'm ready to change subjects.

"You guys want any low-fat ice cream?" asks Bella.

Several hours later, we arrive back in the parking lot where my trusty Accord is waiting. Before I get out of the van, Sarah asks if she can pray for me. Who can refuse an offer like that?

Her prayer is like nothing I've heard before. It's not sanctimonious or formal, like most public prayers I've heard. Instead, it's sincere and authentic, as if Sarah is talking to an old friend rather than some faraway force who created the universe. She prays hard about my operation, and Bella peppers the prayer from the backseat with a steady stream of amens. I can't resist opening my eyes a couple of times during the prayer to sneak a glimpse at my friends. Their eyes are closed with intense concentration, but I also sense a peace in Sarah's face that is hard to describe. And when she's done praying, I actually feel more optimistic about the operation. It would be a stretch to say I feel peaceful, but I feel less foreboding, more certain that I'm making the right choice.

As I leave, Sarah holds out one more piece of ammunition that she's apparently been keeping in reserve. It's a thin paperback book titled *Mere Christianity*.

"It's written by C. S. Lewis," Sarah explains, "one of the great philosophers and writers of his day." I reach out and take the book. The name sounds vaguely familiar. "Like you, he had some doubts about the claims of Christ," Sarah continues. "And like you, he was very bright and had a very logical mind. And since he lived in England during the Nazi bombardment, Lewis also wrestled with the same thing you do—how could a just and powerful God allow certain things to happen?"

She shrugs as she gives me the book. "Maybe if you have a hard time sleeping at night, this will help."

I thank Sarah and eye Bella suspiciously. First the dinner conversation, then the prayer, now this. I don't like being the object of other people's attempts to proselytize. Why can't people realize that because something works for them does not mean it works for everyone else? Could it be that this entire day has been nothing more than a setup to get me to read Mr. Lewis's *Mere Christianity?*

I decide to give them the benefit of the doubt. They're just trying to help. And all in all, it *was* a really fun girls' day out.

I toss my Old Navy bag, purse, and C. S. Lewis book in the backseat of my car. My stubborn streak immediately decides that I will never crack the cover of this book. In fact, the only thing that will keep *Mere Christianity* from immediately hitting the trash can is my longstanding rule that I never, ever, throw away books. *Mere Christianity* will find its way into the spare bedroom where I have stockpiled boxes of textbooks and novels and self-help books from the days following Bill's death. None of those books helped me deal with the pain then. And there's equally little chance that a long-dead British philosopher could say anything that would help a twenty-first-century pragmatic lawyer now.

I thank the girls for a wonderful time, hop in my car, and hustle home so I can try on my new jeans and tank top.

O n Sunday afternoon Brad drags me into the office to do some blue-sky work on the Bannister case. "Bella says you'll be out of the office on Tuesday and Wednesday doing depositions," Brad says, "and Monday's swamped. So this may be our only chance to get our theory of the case straightened out."

I'm thinking that Sunday afternoon should be for the beach, but Brad's not just my fiancé, he's also my boss. "Okay, but I want time and a half," I say.

"You and Bella," moans Brad, but I can tell he's looking forward to the time together. In fact, I suspect that's the whole purpose of this "meeting" in the first place.

When I arrive, it's obvious that Brad has already been at it for a while. The conference room table is cluttered with pages torn from a yellow legal pad as well as deposition transcripts, pleadings, interview summaries, and other aspects of the *Girl Next Door* case. The windows overlooking the parking lot are divided into five panes. On the middle three panes Brad has taped several three-by-five index cards of various colors, each with a cryptic note written on it with a black Sharpie. At the top of the center pane is a single sheet of paper with the phrase *fraudulent inducement* written on it. Brad is leaning back in a swivel chair, his bare feet on the table, poring over some documents with a highlighter when I enter. He has on cargo shorts and his favorite baggy T-shirt, a dark blue shirt with yellow letters on the front. "You have the right to remain silent," it says. "Anything you say will be misquoted and used against you in a court of law."

"Hey," I say.

"Okay," he says. "I finally got the court to enforce a subpoena for the show's financial records. Two of the three *Girl Next Door* finalists definitely got paid by the producers to make Brandon hate them." He pauses. "But then there's Annie."

I grab a seat at the other end of the long conference table. "Annie?" I ask, taking the bait.

"Yeah, she's one of the finalists Brandon ditched for the transvestite. She swore in her deposition that the producers didn't pay her anything to make Brandon dislike her; she says she really fell for the guy and tried to win his affections right down to the final week. The problem is…I think she's telling the truth."

"That is a problem," I say sarcastically. "What's the practice of law coming to these days—truthful witnesses and everything."

Without warning, Brad jumps up and comes at me. I'm up in a flash, fists raised, ready to fend off an attack. It's no use. He grabs my wrist, twists me around, then bear hugs me from behind. He growls something like, "When I want your sarcasm I'll ask for it," then kisses me on the neck. For a second I try to wiggle free. Not very hard, of course, because then I might actually succeed. Once I put up my perfunctory little struggle, I become perfectly still. He kisses me on the neck again, and this time I turn to him. Another kiss, warm and tender. *Man, how I've missed this!*

What happened to our feud?

But then he pulls away—darn it! "I will not allow you to seduce me," he insists. *What? Seduce him?!* "We've got work to do," he says somberly.

"Okay, Bradley Carson. I'll remember that."

"I'm sure you will," he replies. But we both know I'm lying.

Brad pushes all the papers, pleadings, pens, and files down onto half the table. I hate it when he does this—just pushes stuff aside so that it sits there in a state of impossible disarray, mocking me as I try to resist the urge to put it in neat little piles. He throws some colored index cards and two black Sharpies on the clean half of the table. "The Brad Carson patented case-building system," he announces.

I stare at him like he's lost his mind. I helped him on a few cases during my third year of law school and never encountered this. I lower my eyebrows in skepticism.

"Actually," he says, "I just started the method on this *Girl Next Door* case when I couldn't get past some mental blocks. I haven't actually filed for the patent yet." He begins taking down the cards that are taped to the windows and throws them on the junky end of the table. *That end of the table makes a nice metaphor for the* Girl Next Door *case. Chaos.*

Brad takes a few minutes to explain his system. We will write one critical fact or piece of evidence on each card. Orange cards are for undisputed facts. Green cards are for highly probable facts. Yellow cards are for possible facts. And pink cards are for facts that are really nothing more than suspicions and don't have much chance of being proven true. I argue about the color-coding for a while—shouldn't pink cards be for undisputed facts?—just to warm up my arguing muscles. Brad is unmoved. When I make up my own unique, patented system, I can choose whatever colors I want, he argues. In the meantime, we will use his.

On a sheet of paper we will write a theory of the case and tape it to the top of the middle pane of windows. We will then tape the cards to the window. If the fact on the card is consistent with the theory, it goes in the same windowpane as the theory. If the theory doesn't explain the fact one way or the other, then the card goes on the pane to the left of the center pane. But if the fact on the card is inconsistent with the theory, then it goes to the right of the center pane.

It takes us about half an hour to write out all the known facts in the case. Brad then gives me the honor of proposing the first theory. "Self-defense," I say, "just like our client says."

"Write it down," instructs Brad.

Five minutes later I am staring at the glaring weaknesses of this theory. I knew all these things before, but somehow Brad's little system brings them into stark relief. Of course, I would never let him know that.

The middle pane has a fair number of cards on it, but they are not the ones that concern me. To the left of the middle pane there are a lot of orange cards. *Fowler's gambling debts,* says one. *Fowler benefits from insurance—one mil,* says another. A yellow card also is taped to that pane, though Brad argued that the card should be pink. *Fowler assaults Tara,* it reads. I am troubled as I realize how much the self-defense theory does not explain.

But even more troubling are the cards to the right of the middle panes, the ones totally inconsistent with the theory of self-defense. The really bothersome aspect is that most of them sound so scientific. And most of them are orange.

Blood pattern on recliner chair. Tara's bloody footprint upstairs. Angle of entry for bullet. No stippling or tattooing for first shot. No hemorrhaging for second shot. No blood spatter on towel.

Brad stands back and surveys his handiwork. He probably suspected that he couldn't just argue me out of the self-defense theory, my mind was already made up, so he wanted to show it to me in graphic form. "Usually," Brad says in his casual tone that is not fooling me, "I will reject a theory if even one orange index card is on the right-hand pane. It's hard to prove a theory that contradicts an undisputed fact."

I can think of no logical argument, so I turn defensive. "Then you suggest a better theory."

He thinks for a moment, a nice dramatic touch, then writes *Fowler did it* on a single sheet of paper and replaces my paper in the middle pane. It takes about ten minutes to rearrange the cards, most of the time spent arguing about what card goes where. We survey our handiwork, and though it looks a lot better than my theory, it's still not perfect. At the top of the right pane, in orange, is the card that says *Gunpowder residue on Tara's hand.* There is also a yellow card on which Brad has scribbled *Tara's confession.* It's in yellow because Brad doubts it's true. "But we've still got to explain why she would take the heat if Fowler killed her dad," I say.

There's also an orange card on the left-hand pane, meaning that it is not explained by this theory, even if it is not totally contradicted by the theory. That card reads *Bruises on Tara's face.* I look at the cards for a moment and remember that something is missing. I pull out another orange card and write, *Bannister receives an e-mail copy of the Sayers case.* I stick it on the left pane. Nothing in Brad's theory explains it.

Now I sit on the conference room table and give Brad my own satisfied smile. "Generally," I say, staring at the orange card in the right pane, "I will reject a theory if even one orange card is in that right pane. It's hard to prove a theory that goes against an undisputed fact."

"Very funny."

We both stare at the windows for a moment. I think about all the scientific evidence that keeps tripping us up, I remember my visit to the Bannister's living room, and I recall the words of Strobel. Looking at all those orange cards, it hits me. *When is scientific evidence not scientific evidence? When does it belong on a green card or maybe even a yellow one?* Anybody familiar with the O. J. Simpson case knows the answer—when the investigating police officer is shown to be a liar.

I scoot forward to the edge of the conference room table. "Detective Anderson was the lead detective on this case. Right, Brad?"

"Uh-huh."

"And you don't trust him, do you?"

"Nobody trusts him, Leslie."

"You think he would plant evidence?"

Brad snorts. "Is the pope Catholic?"

"Then let's look at it this way," I suggest. "Which of these orange index cards could be caused by Anderson's manipulation of evidence?"

"Good question." Brad moves closer to the window. "Not the blood-spatter evidence on the chair or the lack of blood spatter on the towel. Not the stippling or tattooing or hemorrhaging evidence—that's the medical examiner's job. And certainly not the bruises on Tara's face." He reaches out and looks at the sole orange card on the right-hand pane. "But the alleged gunpowder residue on Tara's hand..." Brad thinks for a moment. "The lead investigator could certainly sweep the surface of the gun and contaminate that test."

Though I don't like where this is headed, I'm compelled to follow my own logic. "Which means," I conclude, "that if Fowler did it *and* cut Anderson in on this deal, there wouldn't be any undisputed facts on that right pane."

"Which means that the only things we have left to explain are: number one, why Tara would be willing to take the fall, and number two, why she would bruise up her own face in the process." Brad says this with excitement and a sense of finality. I can tell he's relishing the task of trying to implicate the commonwealth's attorney. He can already see the headlines.

But that theory assumes facts I just can't accept. An affair between Fowler and Trish Bannister. Tara cooperating with Fowler, whom she hates. And why would she tell us about the video? The problem with Brad's "patented case-building method" is that it leaves no room for women's intuition.

"I still think it's self-defense," I say. I can almost hear the air escaping as I burst Brad's bubble of hope that my previous comments had created. "I don't care what your little orange cards say."

"I need a drink," announces Brad.

On Sunday night, like most nights recently, I have a hard time falling asleep. I lie in bed, watching first the news, then a *Friends* rerun, and then I just flip from one channel to another. I've got a long day tomorrow, it's 1:00 a.m., and I'm nowhere close to sleeping. The wind is howling outside my window, spraying rain against the windowpanes in what the locals call a nor'easter. I think about calling Brad, but then he'll want to know what has got me so worried, and then I'll lie to him again, and then his instincts will tell him that I'm holding back. The wall between us will grow...and it's high enough already.

I finally decide that if I can't sleep, I can at least get some work done. I am wearing one of Brad's old T-shirts—high schoolish, I know, but it makes me feel closer to him. I throw on a pair of socks and sweatpants. I wake my sleeping computer and fire up Westlaw for some legal research. Soon, however, I find myself gliding around the Internet, soaking up more information on hypertrophic cardiomyopathy, rehashing things I already know. Only 20 percent of those with HCM ever experience a problem. Even for them, it's treatable through surgery. Alcohol ablation surgery is still considered experimental in the United States. Possible complications include the need for a pacemaker, the risk of stroke, or the risk of a perforated artery. In rare instances, puncturing the arterial wall has resulted in death.

Death. The word glares at me from my computer, nearly pulsating its way off the screen. Death. Uncertainty. Dante's inferno. No more Brad or Bella or Sarah or Mom. One minute I could be lying on Dr. Asha Maholtra's table, watching on a screen as she snakes the catheter through my arteries, and the next minute I could be gone. Nothingness. I stare at the word, frightened like a child.

Death. When you are thirty years old, you don't think much about death. You are invincible. Even if you watch your husband die, you still assume it can't happen to you. And then one day you faint while you're running on an elliptical, and the next thing you know, a doctor is talking about a life-threatening heart condition. Mortality becomes real. Life is fragile. Death is certain and maybe not that far away.

I think of God and tremble. If there is a God, am I ready to meet Him? Is He the God of the Bible? Could the rest of the world—the non-Christians—be that wrong? Will He approve of the way I've conducted my life, the choices I've made? Deep down inside, I doubt it. What have I really done to better the lives of others?

Odds are that I'll survive the surgery. But who likes playing the odds when it's your life you're talking about? I recall how Bill faced death, almost welcomed it, with a stoic intensity. But then, Bill was suffering so much that anything would be an improvement. And Bill was always so much stronger than I am.

I leave the computer. It's making things worse, not better, but the morbid thoughts keep pounding through my head. How do some men and women have such peace in the face of death? I think about Sarah—the way that she and her husband were prepared to die as martyrs for Christ in Saudi Arabia.

I find myself at the kitchen table, unpacking some leftover blank index cards from my briefcase. I get some celery and carrots from the refrigerator to munch on. I pull out a black Sharpie and then walk to my printer in the other room and grab a blank piece of paper. Returning to the kitchen, I write *Christianity* on the paper and tape it to the front of my refrigerator. I improve on Brad Carson's patented case-building system by deciding that pink will be for undisputed evidence, yellow for probable, and light blue for speculative. I will put the index cards on the front of the refrigerator if they support this thesis, on the left side if they are not relevant, and on the right side if they contradict the thesis. Brad's words from earlier in the day echo now—generally, a thesis can be invalidated by even one undisputed piece of evidence on the right side.

I start with some low-hanging fruit. *The empty tomb,* I write on a yellow card. I'm no expert, but it seems to me that the empty tomb is more or less a prerequisite for Christianity getting started in the first place only a stone's throw from where Christ was crucified. If the tomb wasn't empty, then Peter and the other disciples would have been stopped in their tracks. *What are you delirious men talking about? Walk with us to the tomb of Christ—we'll show you the body!*

I'm vaguely familiar with some non-Christian theories used to explain the empty tomb, and they don't seem to hold much water. Was it a fraud by His disciples—stealing the body of Christ? Then how do you explain their willingness to die for a cause they knew to be false? Did Christ merely pass out, fainting on the cross only to be revived in the cold, damp tomb? Remnants of my catechism training seem to disprove this idea. If Christ merely "swooned," then how did He roll away the huge rock and overpower the Roman guards stationed to guard the tomb? Plus, like most of America, I saw *The Passion of the Christ.* Nobody could survive what Christ went through and live.

The *empty tomb* card goes on the front of the fridge. I chew on some carrots and pull out a pink card. I write *Christ's teachings* on it with my black Sharpie. I don't know anybody who disputes the fact that Christ was eons ahead of the other moral teachers of His time. Turn the other cheek. Love your enemies. Forgive. Seems to me that the teachings of Christ were far superior to the more revenge-minded teachers like Mohammed. But then again, that doesn't necessarily mean that Christ was God. There have been a lot of other great teachers—Gandhi and Confucius come to mind. I place the pink card on the left side of the refrigerator.

Next, I write *the universe* on a yellow card. Admittedly, this is painting with some pretty broad strokes here, but then again, we *are* dealing with some pretty big questions. I don't honestly see how anybody can look at the design of the universe, the fine-tuning necessary to support life on this planet, the intricate design of our bodies, and argue that it's all some huge cosmic accident. I've been taught to frown on things explained as "coincidence" in the courtroom when the events are more logically explained by some type of conspiracy or design. No use suspending that rule now. *It's design, not coincidence,* I tell myself, and *the universe* goes on the front of the fridge.

Next I grab a pink card and write *martyrs* on it. There's no speculation here, so I'll use pink—history is replete with Christian martyrs. Men and women with their tongues cut out, burned at the stake, impaled. Men and women who died without flinching—something that I'm not prepared to do. But on my way from the table to the refrigerator, I'm struck with another thought—the Christian faith is not the only faith with martyrs. What about the Muslims who flew planes into the World Trade Center? They were martyrs too—misguided, yes, but still unflinching. I think about this for a moment, and my mind locks on the story of Charles Reed, Sarah's martyred husband. He died trying to reach the people of Saudi Arabia. The religious police killed him because he refused to divulge the names of other Christians. And now Sarah says that when her youngest child goes to college, she wants to head back to Saudi Arabia, to risk her life among the people she loves.

I take out my Sharpie again and write *love* on the card so that it now reads *love martyrs*. It seems to me that this is the aspect that sets Charles and Sarah Reed apart. Men and women die for a cause or trying to gain power or as a matter of principle. But Charles died because he loved the Saudis too much to retreat to safety. This merits a pink card, and it goes right in the middle of the front of the fridge.

I put a few more cards on the front, supporting the thesis, before I write out the three cards I've been dreading. The problem is that they're all pink. And they all belong on the right side of the fridge, directly contradicting the thesis on the front. The first card is labeled *evil men go unpunished.* How can I reconcile a loving God who is all-powerful with the fact that evil men—like Harlan Fowler?—so often get away with their plans and schemes.

It is joined by another card, more devastating than the first. This one simply says *Bill,* but it represents a lifetime of unanswered prayers and deep hurts. God supposedly loves me and has a wonderful plan for my life. Yet my husband loses an excruciating fight with cancer while I sit helplessly by his side. How could a loving God allow this?

The third card is labeled *hypocrites.* I'm tempted to write in the names, but that seems a little meanspirited. I remember vaguely that somebody important once said, "I would have been a Christian but for the Christians I knew." That's the gist of this card. If Christianity is so good, then why has it spawned so many hypocritical people?

As I sit down at the kitchen table to study my work, I am exhausted. I am too wound up to sleep, but I know that sleep is exactly what I need. Wednesday looms before me, just a few days out, like some cosmic deadline demanding answers I don't have. How can I face death so uncertain about my future? I feel like I've been handed a death-penalty case with only a few days to prepare. But in this case, I am both lawyer and client.

That's silly, I tell myself. *You're not going to die. Plenty of people survive surgery a lot more complicated and risky than this.*

Then why can't I sleep?

Thoughts of sleep trigger Sarah's parting words yesterday, said mostly in jest. *If you have a hard time falling asleep, maybe this will help.* In the privacy of my own duplex, I am a desperate woman with nothing to lose. I rise from the table, put on a pot of coffee, and find the book by C. S. Lewis in one of the boxes in my spare room.

As I glance through it, I get the feeling that Lewis must have been reading my refrigerator. Or maybe, as a former atheist, Lewis knew all about objections raised by those who, in the words of Brad, "overthink everything." Though it takes me a while to get used to the somewhat stilted English vernacular, I am soon enthralled by the logical thread of truth that Lewis weaves through his writings. Sarah was right—this man thinks like me.

Which means, of course, that he wrestled with the fact that evil men sometimes go unpunished. While our day has its share of Osama bin Ladens, Lewis saw the indescribable atrocity of the Holocaust. He lived through the Blitzkrieg. The man experienced evil on a personal level.

But Lewis turns this issue on its head, causing me to question the placement of my pink card. The fact that we recognize universal norms of good and evil, Lewis argues, is evidence of a transcendent moral law that is, in turn, evidence of a creator God. *Human beings, all over the earth, have this curious idea that they ought to behave in a certain way, and cannot really get rid of it.* This is the law of nature, Lewis argues, and the fact that it exists is a powerful argument for the existence of a God who established right and wrong.

Lewis's phrase rings a bell. *The law of nature and nature's God,* a phrase contained in our own Declaration of Independence, cited by Thomas Jefferson as the basis for seeking independence from Britain. When I first read that phrase, as a junior-high student, I knew exactly what Jefferson meant.

I read on, as Lewis describes the arguments he made against God as an atheist: *My argument was that the universe seemed so cruel and unjust. But how had I gotten this idea of* just *and* unjust? *A man does not call a line crooked unless he has some idea of a straight line…just as, if there were no light in the universe and therefore no creatures with eyes, we should never know it was dark.* Dark *would be a word without meaning.*

I give my head a vigorous little shake, then take a sip of coffee. Is it just the late hour or is Lewis making sense? I need to get some sleep but decide instead to read one more chapter.

In it I find Lewis taking a shot at another one of my index cards. Christ was a good teacher, I had decided. Nobody would argue with that. Nobody, that is, except for my intriguing new friend from several decades ago. Christ claimed to be God, Lewis argues. What kind of good teacher would feign to do that? And then Lewis says something that literally shocks me: *A man who was merely a man and said the sort of things Jesus said would not be a great moral teacher. He would either be a lunatic—on the level with a man who says he is a poached egg—or He would be the Devil of Hell. You must make your choice. Either this man was, and is, the Son of God; or else a madman or something worse.*

I read those words again and feel the weight of them on my chest, as if they are squeezing my heart. *You must make your choice.* What Lewis says makes sense. The simplicity of it jolts me. Christ as God or Christ as a lunatic: that's my choice. No more Jesus as a good teacher. Like a magician pulling the tablecloth out from under the dishes, Lewis has yanked away one of my foundational beliefs almost quicker than my eye can follow. But unlike the magician, Lewis has unsettled and shattered the fine china of my presuppositions, confounding my thinking with his new dilemma.

I put the book down and contemplate this for a few minutes. I suddenly realize why I resist so much the thought of Christ as God. God allowed Bill to die. If Christ is God, then Christ allowed Bill to die. He heard my desperate prayers, sat idly by, and watched as I lost the best thing that life had ever sent my way.

I remind myself of Brad's cardinal rule: one undisputed fact inconsistent with the thesis will doom the entire thesis. The problem is that I still have two such facts. I rise and pour the remaining coffee down the sink. The pink card with the word *hypocrites* on the front is still taped to the right side of the refrigerator. Right next to it, the pink card labeled *Bill* taunts me, demolishing the logical arguments articulated so eloquently by Lewis. I head back to my bedroom and lie awake for hours with these theological thoughts and counterthoughts swirling through my head, creating a vast whirlpool of unanswered questions.

In the midst of life's complications, the title of the book suddenly seems ironic. *Mere Christianity,* Mr. Lewis called his succinct little book. Unfortunately, things in life are seldom so simple.

By Monday afternoon the lack of sleep is catching up with me. My eyes are bloodshot and swollen, and my whole body feels bloated and gross. This is not helped by the fact that I am sitting with Brad in the office of Mr. D. J. Landers, a sleazy criminal defense attorney who has single-handedly done as much to exacerbate the bad reputation of lawyers as any person I know. I could practically feel the grease slide across my palm as D. J. withdrew his hand after shaking. This guy would give sharks the jitters.

D. J. sits behind his large mahogany desk, his face all angles and points, like somebody squeezed it in a vise and elongated it. He has a thin black mustache and the kind of jet-black hair that comes straight from the coloring bottle. His tan is either spray-on or tanning booth, an uneven and unnatural shade that couldn't possibly be the work of the sun.

Brad and D. J. banter like fraternity brothers. Brad has always been dearly loved by legal reprobates like D. J., probably because Brad is just as antiestablishment as they are. Plaintiff's lawyers (like Brad) and criminal defense lawyers (like D. J.) both tend to have independent rebel streaks. I listen to the two men trade barbs for a while and think of the old saying that a man will be known by his friends. If it's true, my fiancé is in trouble.

After the two men have insulted themselves out, Brad finally gets down to the reason for our visit. "Coach Freddie Barker," Brad says. "Child pornography charges. Was he one of yours?"

D. J. eyes Brad for a moment, as if trying to discern the reason for the question. "Pled him out," D. J. says. "Eighteen months, all but three suspended."

"Must have coughed up some pretty big names," says Brad.

D. J. smiles. "Don't worry, Brad. He held yours back."

"Ho, ho, ho," says Brad. "Who did he rat out?"

D. J. stares again, his eyes narrowing. "I'll tell you the same thing I told Mr. Mitchell Taylor when he asked the same question," says D. J., as if we should be taking notes. "All information regarding Barker's case, other than the fact I represented him, is covered by the attorney-client privilege."

I slide forward on my seat. *Mitchell Taylor?* Brad picks up on D. J.'s hint and crosses his legs, trying to act casual. "How long ago was it that you discussed this case with Mr. Mitchell Taylor?"

D. J. searches the ceiling for a minute. "Three, four months."

"Are you sure?"

More thinking by D. J. "Yeah, pretty sure. Had to be at least three months. May have been four or even five." D. J. throws up his palms. "Time flies."

"Why would Taylor be asking you what names Barker gave up?" Brad wonders. "Mitchell's a deputy commonwealth's attorney. He ought to know who else was prosecuted."

"That's what I told him," says D. J.

"And then?"

"And then he left."

Brad digests this; I can almost see the gears grinding. Then he shifts in his seat and says the next words more as an offhand comment than a question. "Seems to me the other folks prosecuted would be a matter of public record, not attorney-client privilege."

D. J. nods, as if Brad is following the trail of bread crumbs very nicely. "The other persons prosecuted, the fact that my client cut a deal to testify against them, the sentence he received—that's all a matter of public record." D. J. pauses, then speaks even slower, making sure Brad and I get the point. "But the names my client authorized me to divulge to the commonwealth's attorney, to Mr. Harlan Fowler himself, those names are protected by the attorney-client privilege."

"I see," says Brad. "And if, for some reason, one of the names that Barker divulged did not get indicted, then that name wouldn't be a matter of public record."

"Exactly."

"In fact, that information would be known only by you, Coach Barker, and Harlan Fowler."

D. J. nods encouragingly.

"And if I could locate Coach Barker, he could tell me," says Brad.

D. J. makes the noise of a buzzer going off. "Wrong answer. As soon as Barker finished serving his three months, he left the area. Even I have no idea where to reach him. Second, everything he told Fowler is confidential. Barker's deal depended on testifying before the grand jury to the questions Fowler asked and nothing more. If Barker opened his mouth about other things or other persons, he could risk revocation of the deal."

I glance at Brad to see if he's following this any better than I am. He rubs his face for a second—a good sign—then looks out the window behind D. J. "More or less a don't-ask-don't-tell plea bargain," Brad muses. D. J. nods his head. "And as long as your client gets a sweet deal," Brad continues, "you don't really care who else does or doesn't get prosecuted."

"You ought to handle more criminal cases," says D. J. "With a little work, I could have you thinking like one of us."

"Spare me," I mumble, bringing glances from both men.

"Sure wish I could see that file," Brad says.

There is silence for a moment, then D. J.'s beady gray eyes glow bright. He stands up and walks past us to his secretary's cubicle outside his office. We hear him ask for the Barker file. In a few minutes, he brings it back in and ruffles through it as he sits at his desk. Finally, he looks up at Brad. "No can do, bucko. There's just too much privileged stuff in there," he says. He calls his secretary and gives the file to her but leaves several pages of handwritten notes from the file on his desk.

"I understand," says Brad. But I don't notice any resignation in his voice. Instead, it's the way you say "I understand" after seeing the key to unlocking a protracted math problem.

"I'm sure you do," says D. J. Then he turns to me. "Thirsty?" he asks.

A strange question. "Not really." Brad reaches over with his foot and nudges my ankle. *What is that all about?* "I could go for a glass of water," I say.

"Great," says D. J., standing. "Tell you what, I'll show you where—"

"You don't have to—" And then it hits me, a split second before Brad has to nail my ankle again. "Great," I say, finally figuring out Brad and D. J.'s little charade. But a little voice in my head does not think I should go along. The voice, as always, sounds a lot like my grandfatherly law school ethics professor. *The greatest danger to your ethical compass will come from those you respect most.*

Even as I rise to follow D. J., I wrestle with my decision. I know why Brad is doing this—to protect me and to serve the client. He knows I'm a stickler for ethics, so he wants me out of the room while he riffles through the notes. D. J. is an all-too-willing accomplice, a man without an ethical bone in his soulless body.

The ghost of my professor is telling me to speak up even as I silently leave the room. But creating a scene would mean embarrassing Brad, and I don't have the energy to argue with him right now. Besides, as Brad so often reminds me, a lawyer's first ethical obligation is to zealously represent her client. But sometimes Brad acts like that's our *only* ethical obligation.

I'm halfway to the kitchen with D. J. before I make up my mind to just register my objection later. Brad is going to do this, whether I object or not. And so I fall in step as D. J. leads the way.

After an exceedingly long ten minutes of nursing a bottled water and listening to D. J. talk about himself, we head back to D. J.'s office. The notes are still sitting on D. J.'s desk, and Brad is talking to D. J.'s secretary. The men trade one last set of barbs, then Brad and I are on our way.

I have the good grace to wait until we get into Brad's car to get on his case. I slouch down in the passenger seat and look out the front window. "Brad," I begin, "if we resort to that kind of stuff, what makes us any different than D. J. Landers?"

Brad shoots me a sideways glance, sees that I'm not kidding, then probably swallows some smart-aleck answer that was on the tip of his tongue. "By 'stuff,' I assume you're referring to these lists I made after reviewing D. J.'s file notes?" he asks, placing a page of handwritten scrawls on the seat between us.

"I'm talking about the unethical way we got that information." I look at the paper like it's poison, as if by touching it I become a co-conspirator.

"Okay, counsel," Brad says. "Tell me the ethical duty we violated."

"We violated the attorney-client privilege," I say without hesitation.

Brad has now backed out of the parking spot and is headed to the highway. "What privileged information from our client did we reveal?"

I hate it when he does this. "You know darn well it's not our client." There is an edge to my voice. "But we encouraged Landers to breach a duty he owed to his client."

Brad turns on the radio as if this conversation is no big deal. "Do *we* have an affirmative duty to make sure Landers never violates an ethical code? Who appointed us his moral policemen?"

"Brad Carson, you know that's not—"

"I'm serious, Leslie," he interrupts. "Our client's on trial for murder. Do you want me to tell her that we could have obtained a critical piece of information but decided not to because it might result in D. J. Landers breaching a duty of confidentiality to a porn peddler who can't be located?"

Now I am truly confused. This all sounds like a rationalization, but I can't find the hole in his reasoning. "It doesn't feel right, Brad."

"Would you have looked at the file if D. J. had just handed it to us and never said a word about privileged information?"

I think about this for a moment. "I don't know. I guess."

"Of course you would have, so what's the difference?"

I shrug off the question. This whole argument is wearisome.

"Leslie, you're a good lawyer," Brad's voice is softer now, the pointed questions gone. "But even you can't win cases if you are constantly second-guessing yourself. Sometimes I feel like we're in a basketball game, and you're always calling fouls on yourself while the other team is just bowling over us."

Okay, I decide, he may have a point. But I don't need his lecture right now. I fight back with silence, the sound of the radio amplified by the absence of words. Brad reaches over and puts a hand on my leg. I know he wants me to reciprocate—put my hand on top of his, hold his hand, lean over and kiss him on the cheek, whatever. Instead, I just sit there, and before long the hand is withdrawn.

Sulking, I reach down and pick up the paper. There are two lists of names.

"The list on the left contains the names of people implicated by Coach Barker," Brad says. There is no emotion in his voice, none of the sideways smiles at me that he normally intersperses with his driving. "I got the names from some notes to the file that Landers made when he first interviewed Barker about the child porn ring."

I survey the list of seven names. I don't recognize any of them.

"The list on the right," continues Brad, "is the names of those indicted by the grand jury after Barker's testimony. According to Landers's notes, all six of them pled guilty and cut a deal with Fowler. Most of them served a minimum of six months."

I do a quick comparison of the list of names. There is one name that is on the left side but not the right. "What about this guy Melvin Phillips? What happened to him?"

"Don't really know," says Brad. "But here's what I pieced together. Barker told D. J. Landers, his own attorney, the names of people that Barker would be willing to testify against. That list included Phillips as well as the other six. Landers then went to Fowler and cut a deal— Barker pleads guilty and cooperates in the prosecution of these other seven members of the porn ring. In exchange, Barker gets off with eighteen months, all but three suspended. But the grand jury only returns six indictments—everybody but Phillips. Grand jury proceedings, as you know, are secret and not even defense lawyers get to attend. But there are some notes I reviewed where Landers asked Barker about his grand jury testimony. Seems that Fowler didn't ask a single question about Mr. Melvin Phillips."

"Why not?" I ask.

"That's not really clear. Landers probably didn't care one way or the other since his client got the deal with or without an indictment of Phillips. Maybe Fowler couldn't get any corroborating evidence against Phillips. Maybe Barker changed his mind before he went into the grand jury room and wouldn't name Phillips after all. Could be a dozen innocent reasons why Phillips didn't get indicted."

"And one or two not-so-innocent ones," I add.

We are now stopped at a traffic light and Brad turns to look squarely at me. "Do you know who Melvin Phillips is?" he asks.

I quickly search my tired memory banks. "I told you I'd never heard of any of these guys."

Brad is still looking at me, anxious to watch my reaction. "An eccentric but brilliant tax lawyer," says Brad. "Who also happens to be a partner of Mack Strobel."

I feel like we just had a head-on collision and my airbag exploded in my face. "Wow!" I manage. My head is spinning with this new information. I can't begin to process it right now, but I instinctively know that it will play a major role in our case.

The light changes and Brad turns his attention back to the road. "Good thing you've got an unethical partner," he says.

On the way back to the office, Brad mentions that he is late for a meeting with Brandon Matthews. Trying to avoid Brandon, I slip into the women's rest room on our floor while Brad goes straight to the office. I give Brad enough time to usher Brandon into his office or a conference room, then I leave the bathroom, walk down the hallway, and enter the reception area for the office suites of Carson & Associates.

To my surprise, Brandon is already leaving Brad's office and heading straight toward the reception area. He is no more than thirty feet away with his head down or he would have already seen me. Unless I just turn tail and leave, I'm about to be discovered. After he puts two and two together, he'll marvel at what a big coincidence this is and then he'll tell Brad. The secret of my fainting in the gym will be blown wide open, resulting in endless questions from Brad that I don't want to answer.

Before I can turn around, Bella takes over. She stands, looks right at Brandon, and shouts, "Get out!"

He stops in his tracks, wide-eyed, and focuses on her. She now has her hand over her mouth. "Oh. My. *Goodness!*"

I slip unnoticed out of the reception area and down the opposite hallway toward my office.

"What?" I hear Brandon say.

"Has anybody ever told you," Bella asks dramatically, "that you look just like Fabio? I swear, you two could have been separated at birth."

"You're not the first one who's said that," Brandon replies, sounding relieved.

I'm now walking down the hallway with my back to Brandon. A few more steps and I'll be turning into my office.

"I just love Fabio," Bella says. "And if you're not the spittin' image."

A friend is someone willing to look stupid so you don't have to. I make a mental note to order some flowers for Bella.

As I drive home from work, I decide that I am too tired to wrestle with God or the Bannister case or even the demons that keep me from sleeping. I stop at a Revco and pick up something called Sonata, which boasts that I will get a good night's sleep with minimal side effects. I will only take it for the next two nights—but I've got to get some rest before my surgery.

As I leave the drugstore and climb into my car, I notice a middle-aged man in a dark blue sedan watching me. I exit the parking lot, and he follows two cars back. He takes the same turns as I do for about two miles. Then, just as I am ready to dial the nearest police station and let them know I am coming, he drops out of sight.

When I reach my duplex, I check my mirrors and make sure he's not around. I deadbolt and chain-lock the door, then fix myself dinner, periodically checking the two-car driveway out front by peering through the blinds. I ignore a couple of calls from Brad, deciding that I'm too tired to spar with him tonight. I finish dinner and then throw in a load of wash. I know if I get on the computer, I'll find new things to ratchet up my already-frayed nerves. Instead, I pick up my copy of *Mere Christianity*, almost against my will. There's something strangely mesmerizing about this little book, even if it does mess with my head when I read it.

Tonight's message from Lewis is clearly not designed to make me feel better. He is arguing that *none of us is really keeping the Law of Nature.* Is this guy an English philosopher or a Puritan preacher? The thought no sooner hits my mind than Lewis tries to answer it in the next few sentences. *I am not preaching, and Heaven knows I do not pretend to be better than anyone else. I am only trying to call attention to a fact; the fact that this year, or this month, or, more likely, this very day, we have failed to practice ourselves the kind of behaviour we expect from other people.*

This very day, says Lewis. I think about the shady transaction with D. J. Landers. Is that what Lewis is talking about? Or is it the way I'm misleading Brad so that I can—what?—make sure I don't end up with a surgical scar. Would I expect Brad to tell me if he were having heart surgery? Of course I would.

But this is for Brad's own good, I reason. I am trying to keep from hurting him deeply, the way I was hurt when Bill died. If this surgery isn't successful, I can't handcuff Brad to a disabled wife, someone who will, at best, drag him down or, at worst, leave him a widower. *There may be all sorts of excuses for us,* continues Lewis. *A string of excuses as long as your arm. But if we do not believe in the Law of Nature, then why should we make excuses for violating it?*

I don't need this. My conscience already works overtime without Mr. Lewis piling on. I put down the book and head for a long, hot shower. A few hours later I check the driveway and the street out in front of the duplex one more time, triple-check the locks on the doors and windows, take my Sonata, and climb into bed. Like the medication promised, in less than an hour I have left all of my troubles safely behind.

CHAPTER FORTY-NINE

Mitchell Taylor calls me on my cell phone Tuesday morning while I'm driving to the airport.

"Harlan Fowler told me about your proposal," says Mitchell. This is not good news. I never should have let Brad talk me into doing it this way.

"It's blackmail," Mitchell continues, his righteous indignation pouring over the phone. "And we will not be blackmailed." He pauses for dramatic effect.

"It's not blackmail," I respond. I wonder if Mitchell can sense the lack of conviction in my voice. "These are serious allegations against Mr. Fowler, and we thought he was entitled to know about them before we filed them."

"Why? So you can get Fowler to pressure me into letting Tara off easy?"

I let the silence be my answer. After a moment, Mitchell fills it. "If you were serious about these allegations, Leslie, you should have come to *me* with them, not Harlan. I would have let Tara tell her story to a grand jury. I still will if you want to move forward. We'll see if they believe her or Harlan."

Mitchell must think I'm stupid. He wants to question Tara in front of the grand jury, where defense lawyers like me aren't allowed, just so he can get her testimony on the record and then figure out a way to impeach her at trial. Why should I give him a preview of Tara's testimony, especially when there's no chance he'll actually indict Fowler for this assault?

"If you haul her before the grand jury, I'll have her take the Fifth,"

I say. "Unless, of course, we've worked out a deal on this murder case first."

"Now we're back to blackmail again," says Mitchell. "And our original offer stands. Voluntary manslaughter…as an adult. Two to five."

More silence. "Hello?" says Mitchell.

"I heard you," I say. "But you're making a big mistake."

Within minutes I am off the phone. Though it's small solace, I know that my luck can only get better.

Or so it seems.

I arrive at the Norfolk airport on Tuesday morning nearly two hours before my scheduled departure time. I have packed light and dressed comfortably—jeans, sandals, and a pullover with a V neck. I've piled my hair on top of my head and gone light on the makeup. It's hard to garner much enthusiasm for how you look when you are getting ready to lie mostly naked on an operating table while medical personnel snake a catheter through your body and talk about you like a lab specimen. I try not to dwell on the indignities of surgery.

I slide through the security lines without too much hassle and repack my computer into my carry-on luggage. I start walking down the concourse to my gate—always at the end—wheeling my garment bag behind me. My briefcase—jammed full of work I'll probably never touch and the little book by C. S. Lewis just in case—is piggybacking on my garment bag.

I'm thinking about food.

The last few days I've been so nervous that I haven't eaten much. Now I'm under doctor's orders not to eat in these final twenty-four hours before surgery, so I'm suddenly famished. Plus my head is throbbing from lack of my usual morning coffee and caffeine, another one of the doctor's unreasonable orders. I wonder if Maholtra would really care if I just had one cup of coffee. But I've never been a rule breaker, so I wander over to a concourse newsstand and bookstore and pick up a bottle of Dasani water. As I am preparing to pay, I reach down to grab a copy of *USA Today*.

That's when I see it. On the row of papers, sitting right next to *The Virginian-Pilot*, is a tabloid called the *National Inquisitor*. And there, above the fold, is a headline and boxed-in photograph that nearly buckles my knees. Lightheaded, I pick up the paper as if looking at a mirage. I flip the other *National Inquisitors* over so the headline cannot be seen.

"Are you okay?" asks the clerk.

"Yes…sure. Um…" I thrust the paper and water at her. She rings them up, and I pay without saying another word. This can't be happening! The clerk glances at the paper, then at me, then…I'm almost sure…back at the paper.

Reeling, I head for the nearest seat on the other side of the concourse, away from the prying eyes of the clerk. It's a gate with no outgoing flights right now, so I'm pretty much alone. Only then do I allow myself to focus on the lead article. My chest tightens, and I bite my lip to keep from crying.

"*Girl Next Door* Bachelor Still Hot!" screams the headline. Beside it is a box with four grainy photos showing our very own Brandon Matthews kissing or coddling four different women. This will undoubtedly wreak further havoc on Brad's already hopeless case, disproving Brandon's spurious allegations that he can no longer find any girls interested in dating him. But that's the least of my concerns. The tightness developing in my chest has absolutely nothing to do with Brandon's litigation chances. Instead, my attention is riveted to the top right photo, a closeup shot of Brandon looking down into the eyes of a woman who appears to be lying beneath him, though it's hard to tell since the photo only shows their head and shoulders.

The woman has her eyes closed, and she appears to be wearing a skintight white Lycra top. Her hair is falling back on the carpet around her, and Brandon is inches away, looking at her with tender concern in his eyes.

I remember the look well, the worry on Brandon's face as I first regained consciousness that day at the gym.

It takes ten minutes for my embarrassment to become anger. I read the article, such as it is, which details Brandon's various liaisons even as he claims in a lawsuit that his love life is on the rocks. I am only mentioned in the article once. *On at least one occasion, Brandon has also been observed spending some one-on-one time with his attractive female lawyer—in a decidedly nonlegal environment.*

Those jerks.

I will sue them for every penny they have. Defamation of character. Invasion of privacy. Punitive damages. I walk quickly down the concourse toward my gate, conjuring up images of me cross-examining some fat, cigar-smoking weasel from the *National Inquisitor,* exposing his lies. My anger is fueled by every magazine stand I pass, every stranger who looks at me a moment too long, every thought of what this will do to my reputation in the legal community.

I will put the *National Inquisitor* out of business if it's the last thing I do.

I arrive at the gate and check in with the boarding agent. I'm still more than an hour early, so I grab a seat in front of the large windows overlooking the runways, my back to the concourse. *Why does all this stuff happen to me? Don't I have enough to worry about already?*

I think about calling Brad on my cell phone. The story probably just came out this morning. He's bound to hear about it today, bound to see my picture splattered all over every supermarket and magazine rack in North America. But if I call him now, I will have to explain everything. He'll want me to wait on this surgery or maybe cancel altogether. I've come too far to jeopardize that now.

I stare out the window, numb with the implications of this story. How can these people live with themselves—spreading rumors for profit, ruining innocent lives? Why did Brad ever agree to take this stupid case in the first place? I think about all my efforts to avoid Brandon in the last few weeks. And now *this*.

I feel myself slipping from anger to self-pity. This is, without doubt, the lowest point of my life. I am heading for serious surgery, scared and alone. I have just been made the laughingstock of the Tidewater legal community. A shaky relationship with the man I love has just been further jeopardized. Brad will realize I've been lying to him for weeks.

I feel the tears begin to sting the back of my eyes. *Don't cry. What good will that do?* But sometimes you can't help it. Whether they are tears of anger or fear or frustration or sadness, I don't know. I only know that it's hopeless to try to hold them back. I begin dabbing at my cheeks with the palm of my hand, sniffling as I fight a losing battle. I am surprised to feel a hand rest softly on my shoulder. When I turn, I find that the hand belongs to Bella. When we first talked about the operation, she had told me she would go to Dallas with me. But in recent days we had decided she needed to stay at her desk and provide cover with Brad.

"You didn't really think I'd let you go through this alone, did ya?" she asks. She sits down next to me and, like my mom used to do, wraps her arms around me.

"I'm scared," I say, and the tears begin in earnest.

CHAPTER FIFTY

Wednesday morning. I am lying on my back on a narrow operating table in the heart-catheter lab at the Dallas Heart Clinic. I am awake, wearing nothing but a hospital gown and my underwear. I am cold. Dr. Asha Maholtra is sitting on a stool beside the table, just below my waist, looking at two large monitors that I can also see. One displays my vital signs, the other is an echo-cardiogram of my heart. The bulky echocardiogram equipment hovers just over my chest. My arms are stretched high above my head, grasping a metal bar. I am squeezing the bar so tight that I'm sure I will cut off all circulation to my arms.

"Relax," says Dr. Maholtra.

Yeah, right.

Dr. Maholtra is not very talkative today, and the room is quiet except for the rhythmic beep that keeps time with my heart and the magnified *whoosh* of blood flowing through my veins. I wonder if it's too late to opt out.

"This may pinch a little bit," says my doctor as she swabs at one thigh and then the other. "I'm just administering a local anesthesia."

I flinch and jerk a little.

"I haven't done anything yet," says Maholtra. Then I feel the prick of the needle. I now know why they don't let you eat in the twenty-four hours before surgery. My stomach is flopping back and forth, back and forth.

In a few minutes Maholtra has apparently made her quarter-inch incision. "I'm going into the femoral artery now," she says as if she's doing a play-by-play of the operation. I feel some blood trickling down my thigh and wonder if that's supposed to happen. "I'm using a flexible guide wire, and we're slowly working our way up to your heart," says Maholtra. Her voice is calm and steady, but it doesn't help my nerves. "We're going past the intestines…behind the stomach… past the liver…"

I am watching Maholtra out of my peripheral vision, and she has me worried. Instead of one smooth motion, she is pushing the cable in a little, then reeling it back, then twisting, then sliding it forward another inch. I swear that I can feel each movement, like a small snake squirming its way through my body. *Be careful,* I want to say.

I hold my breath as I watch the guide wire worm its way up to my heart. A gentle tug, another pull, *whoosh, whoosh…* "It's going fine," says Dr. Maholtra, "but I need you to relax a little."

This, of course, causes me to tense up even more. I am starting to feel lightheaded and decide to look away from the monitor. I fight back the panic, concentrating on the ceiling, thinking of nothing, knowing full well that I am not prepared to die.

"Okay," says the doctor. "Now we're going to slip a tiny catheter over the wire…this part won't take long at all."

What Maholtra isn't saying, but what I know from my Internet research, is that she's using the catheter to park two electrodes at the bottom of my right ventricle. The electrodes are hooked up to an external pacemaker. If she has to use them, I will be on a pacemaker for the rest of my life.

Now Maholtra moves to the most dangerous part of the surgery. She punctures an artery in my other thigh and begins snaking another catheter with a small balloon attached to the tip up toward my heart. When she gets it in place, she will inflate the balloon. More pushing and tugging. I watch the monitor as she approaches the spot just above the heart where the blood vessels take a sharp turn. *Dead man's turn,* a former patient called it in a journal he posted online. It's the spot where a few doctors have punctured the arterial wall.

Please, God. Help me through this.

Even as the words speed across my thoughts, I feel the guilt. For the first time in years, I'm pleading with God—not the benign god of nature that I tried to make my peace with after Bill's death but the God of C. S. Lewis, the one I've been fighting with since Bill died.

Please, God. I don't dare say more. If He's as real as Lewis says He is, and as all-knowing, I don't need to say more.

I tense, Maholtra pushes…and the catheter snakes around the corner. I breathe.

Thank you.

"We're going into the left coronary artery now," says Maholtra. "And then into some of these smaller vessels that feed the septal wall."

I'm watching the monitor again, but I'm focused more on the prayer I just completed. I called. He answered. This same God I've been disrespecting was there for me. Can it be that simple?

"I'm glad we got at this when we did," says Maholtra. "Not much blood is getting through."

Maholtra has now sealed off the flow of blood out of the offending vessels by inflating the balloon at the end of the catheter. She then shoots a small amount of contrast medium into the tube that runs through the catheter from my thigh all the way up to the tip of the catheter next to the vessels feeding the septum. I watch on the screen as the medium floods the vessels, turning them black. No contrast medium leaks back out past the balloon, meaning that the seal is holding.

It also means one other thing. Maholtra is now ready to give me a heart attack.

I squeeze the bar up over my head. "Slow and steady breaths," says Maholtra. "You'll experience some burning for a few minutes, but then you'll have a fresh start." The words echo in my ears, along with Maholtra's earlier statement, "Not much blood is getting through."

Despite the chilly temperature of the room, I break into a full body sweat. I think about the sorry state of my heart. I prepare for pain unlike anything I've ever felt. C. S. Lewis springs to mind. His diagnosis: *This very day we have failed to keep God's law.* The consequences: *separation from God.* His solution: *Christ's death can put us right with God and give us a fresh start.*

I'm struggling to hold it together. So many things can go wrong. A stroke…a pacemaker… "I'm going to inject a little morphine," says Maholtra, fiddling with my IV. I squeeze the bar above my head.

Save me, Jesus, I pray. *Forgive me, God.* The morphine hits my bloodstream, relaxing every muscle, and a peace sweeps into the deepest part of my being. Like ocean waves smoothing the sand, it washes away every footprint of my paranoid thoughts.

I breathe, slow and steady, and look down just in time to see Dr. Maholtra pick up the syringe of pure ethanol.

CHAPTER
FIFTY-ONE

I t starts slow, a light burning in my chest, like somebody is pushing down hard right in the middle of my sternum. But then it builds and intensifies, a white-hot pain that is excruciating. Still, I almost float above it. The pain is there, so fierce that I want to scream out, but it's almost as if it belongs to someone else.

It seems like hours rather than the minute or so that Maholtra predicted. I squeeze the bar above my head so hard that I'm sure I'll leave imprints, swallow hard, and try to focus my fuzzy thoughts. Just when I think it's unbearable, like a constant gunshot striking my body, just when I've got to yell for Maholtra to stop, the pain subsides. Five seconds, ten, fifteen…the fire is leaving my body.

All is quiet now, perfectly still, except the gentle noises of the machine. *Beep, swoosh, beep, swoosh.* My mind floats, unanchored by the cares of this world. But when I glance down at Maholtra, even through the fog, I can sense that something is wrong. She looks troubled and she's not saying anything. *Beep, swoosh.* At least my heart is still pumping.

Breathe, I tell myself. I vaguely remember that I am supposed to experience some sort of immediate relief, like someone who had been standing on my chest has just stepped off. I take a deep breath…at least I try. But my lungs do not fill, the pressure is still there. *Beep, swoosh, beep, swoosh.*

Maybe I should panic or maybe right now I don't really care about much of anything. I remember Maholtra saying she was injecting a "little" morphine, the same way doctors say this might hurt a "little." At least the operation is over, the intense pain is gone, and I'm still alive. For some reason, I find myself smiling.

Beep, swoosh, beep, swoosh. Through the fog, I try to focus on the positive. My heart is still beating its steady beat. *Too steady?* I form the question in my mind but my lips won't cooperate.

I am sooo relaxed. I am vaguely aware that Maholtra is removing the catheter from my left thigh. My breathing is still shallow, still a little forced, but it occurs to me that it's nothing to worry about right now. I'm riding the clouds and the pain is over.

Beep, swoosh. Beep, swoosh. Oh yeah, I remember. This time my lips form the question that floats in and out of my consciousness.

"Pacemaker?" I ask.

The next hour or so is pretty much a blur. I'm not sure if I got an answer to my question or not, but for some reason it seems immaterial. I eventually become aware that they've wheeled me into a recovery room. The *Mona Lisa* smile slowly leaves my lips.

I am in and out, like I'm swimming through a soupy fog. Before my mind is completely clear, I open my eyes and see Brad Carson standing over me. He takes my hand and I let him.

"It didn't work, did it?" I ask.

Brad slowly shakes his head. "No, it didn't."

I nod. It occurs to me that he shouldn't even be here. The paper. I remember the nightmare of the paper. "Did you read the paper?"

"What?"

"The paper. Is that why you're here?"

"No," says Brad, leaning down to kiss me on the forehead. "Bella told me."

"I like that," I say, referring to the kiss.

Brad smiles, but there's sadness in his eyes. I try to smile back, but I'm still swimming in the soup.

"Pacemaker?" I ask.

Brad looks puzzled.

I nod toward the machines hooked to my body. "Am I on a pacemaker?"

"No," he says softly. He leans down close to me. "There's no pacemaker. It's just that Dr. Maholtra will probably have to do this again. There's another bunch of vessels feeding the septum that she didn't zap. She said this really didn't do what she hoped it would."

I nod like I understand. In truth, the only thing I understand right now is that Brad is with me. I hold his hand, close my eyes, and relax some more.

Time goes by, how much I don't know. I open my eyes and look for Brad—was it just a dream? No, he's still here...sitting in the chair by my bed.

"Sue those idiots," I say.

"Huh?" He stands up and comes near my bed.

"The paper. What's their name? Sue 'em."

"We'll worry about that later," Brad says.

But I'm feeling belligerent. "Why don't you want to sue 'em? Me and Brandon are not..." I make my hand wiggle a little bit.

"I know," Brad says reassuringly. "But technically, what they printed was true."

"Half truth is a lie," I spit out. It's something my mother used to say all the time.

Brad looks at me like he's bothered by what I just said. "That much I know," he says. "Let's talk about it later."

Because I don't have the energy to argue with him, I close my eyes and head back for the clouds.

CHAPTER FIFTY-TWO

Eventually the fog lifts. I still feel woozy, but the floating sensation is gone. My body feels like the Russian boxing team just used me as a punching bag. I look around the room—Bella is sitting in the chair where Brad was before.

"Is Brad here?" I ask.

Bella nods. "In the hallway on his cell phone, of course." She stands up and moves to my bedside. "How you doin', kiddo?"

"Okay." I nod bravely. "I'm a little thirsty."

Bella grabs a plastic cup, and I eagerly suck down the cold water through a straw.

"It didn't work, did it, Bella?"

"Not exactly, hon. But now the doc knows which bunch of nerve vessels to fry next time. Look at it as a good dry run."

I manage a frail smile. "Don't ever go into medicine, Bella. Your bedside manner's a little gruff."

She smiles back. Then she comes over and squeezes my hand. "I started worrying as soon as they took you back for surgery. I called Brad. He has a buddy with a private plane..."

Bella's eyes are red and watery, a rare occurrence. I reach out my arms, and she bends over and gives me an awkward hug.

"Thanks," I say.

When she stands back up, she asks again if I'm okay.

"I really am," I reply. And it's true. The peace that hit mere seconds before the morphine is still there. "Something happened in there spiritually," I tell Bella. "I'm not sure what it was, but I called out to Christ and somehow I felt like He answered."

Bella's glistening eyes light up. She pulls the chair over as close to my bed as she can manage and sits on the edge of it. "Tell me all about it," she says.

For the next several minutes Bella pries every detail out of me and then pronounces my eternal salvation. When Brad reenters the room I give him a small but sincere smile—the first time in weeks I've smiled at him without feeling hypocritical.

"You look great," he says, coming toward the bed.

"Liar."

"Maybe I should leave you two lovebirds alone," says Bella, slipping out of her chair. She leans over and kisses me on the forehead, then whispers in my ear, "No making out in hospital rooms."

I snort. But I'm suddenly self-conscious about how bad I must look. I know my hair is snarled and knotted on the pillow, and my mouth feels like I'm breathing fire.

Bella leaves and Brad sits right on the edge of my bed. "How's Sleeping Beauty?"

I take a deep breath and feel the emotions welling up inside me, bubbling over. "Brad, I'm so sorry—"

He puts a finger to my lips. "Shh…we don't need to talk about it now."

But I shake my head. "We do, Brad. I mean, at least I do. I can't let unspoken things keep building up between us."

He is holding my hand, rubbing his fingers over the back of it, gently massaging.

I take a second or two, trying to figure out how to start. But the emotions are building, and my rational dam is powerless against them, my words coming out in a flood. "I just didn't know how this would all work out. I was scared of being scarred for life, scared of having a pacemaker, scared of making you marry someone who would be disabled and slow you down or die in your bed on your honeymoon or never be able to do things with you…" My tears choke out the words as Brad bends down to hug me. I squeeze his neck with my left arm, my non-IV arm, and the tears roll down the side of my face, soaking my pillow.

"I love you, Leslie Connors," he whispers. "I love you."

It is two minutes, maybe three, before Brad senses that my tears have abated enough for him to end our embrace. He leans back up in the bed and tenderly wipes the tears from my face with his fingers.

"I don't love you because you're perfect," he says softly—so softly that I can barely hear him. "I don't want to marry some flawless, untouchable diva... I want to marry *you*. I love you, Leslie Connors, just like you are. I want us to be in this together, for the good times *and* the bad times... I *especially* want to be there for the bad times." As Brad's talking, I'm nodding, my heart nearly exploding inside me. He has no idea how beautiful these words are to me or how much I needed to hear them.

"I don't care if you've got a pacemaker and a colostomy bag and an oxygen tank." The thought of all this makes me smile, putting my problems in perspective. "I'll love you anyway. It's you I'm in love with, all of you, not just your body. I want to spend my life with you; I want to grow old together."

"In that department, you've got a pretty good head start." Brad smiles at my lame joke and I sigh deeply. What did I ever do to deserve this man? Here I am, lying in a hospital gown with no makeup, gnarly hair, dragon breath, and he's pledging his love to me. And then it hits me. It's the same love I feel for him—not Brad Carson the trial lawyer or Brad Carson the nice-looking and rich Virginia Beach bachelor. It's deeper than that. I will love him on his worst day as much as he loves me right now.

He has now bent closer to me, so that his forehead is almost touching mine. "I love you, Leslie Connors, and nothing will ever change that."

The fullness inside me tingles its way to my lips, curling them into a small but content smile. "Bad breath and all?" I ask.

As if to answer, Brad kisses me like he's been waiting his entire life for this moment. When he pulls back, he looks at me with unconditional love.

"Bad breath and all."

CHAPTER
FIFTY-THREE

There is still one final surprise before I leave the Dallas Heart Clinic. She shows up later that afternoon, smothers me with love and concern, and throws out not-so-subtle hints that I should have let her know about my heart.

"Thanks, Mom," I say as she fluffs a pillow or gets me some fresh water or refolds my clothes in my gym bag in the corner of the room.

"I think your dad had some cholesterol problems," my mom says, as she flits around the room, making me tired. "I'm pretty sure he's on Lipitor or Zocor or something like that."

This almost makes me smile. My mom has been here for a half hour, and this whole thing is suddenly my dad's fault. This same woman who insists that I invite my dad to my wedding is now blaming my heart condition on him. Everyone in the room has the good sense to let it pass. Everyone except Bella.

"With all due respect, Mrs. Humphreys"—Bella insists on calling my mom by her maiden name and addressing her as Mrs., though Bella is actually a few years older—"I don't think high cholesterol problems have anything to do with this heart condition that Leslie has. As I understand it, HCM is more of a hereditary defect that can sometimes be dormant for several generations."

Mom folds a newspaper—"Anybody reading this?"—and throws it in the trash. "I think some of Joe's people had some other heart problems, too," she says. I glance over at Brad who rolls his eyes.

Mom bends over and kisses my forehead. "How're you feeling?" she asks.

Like something the cat dragged in. "Okay."

I must be frowning or furrowing my brow or something because my mom suddenly looks concerned. "Penny for your thoughts," she says.

That I can't wait to get out of here so I can get some rest. "They're not worth that much," I tell my mom.

I don't get any more time alone with Brad until we're on the flight home. I finish off the last ounce of my Diet Coke and close the novel I've been pretending to read. I run my fingers across the cover. Brad takes the hint and puts the case he's been highlighting down on the little tray in front of him. He looks at me over the top of his reading glasses. I take off my own reading glasses and place them on the tray in front of me.

"Everything all right?" he asks.

"Yeah, actually it's real good."

Brad reaches over and puts his hand on top of mine. I lean a little closer.

"Brad, something happened on that operating table. Something significant. Something spiritual."

"Okay," he says tentatively. "Want to tell me about it?"

I squeeze his hand a little. How do I describe this? Will he think I've turned into some kind of religious nut? A snake handler?

"Well, it's not like I saw a bright flash of light or the earth opened up beneath me or anything, but I prayed..." I pause to collect my thoughts, "I prayed to Jesus; I asked God to help me...to, um, I don't know...to save me." As I say the words, I suddenly feel more at peace again, a warmth spreading through me. It's right to share this with Brad, though I'm fumbling around for the best way to express these new emotions. "It was like, before I prayed I felt scared...alone, just freaking out basically. But afterward, even while I was praying, I suddenly felt like it was going to be okay, almost like everything had changed."

Brad squeezes my hand a little, a sign of acceptance though no words are spoken. *Man, I love this guy!*

"I guess the shot of morphine didn't hurt either," I say.

He chuckles. "Pastors ought to give that a try," he says. "Replace the wine and bread with morphine. Might help their attendance."

"But it was more than that," I say, looking directly at him. "I've still got this sense of calm even after the operation, even though I'm facing another one. It's like…none of this caught God by surprise… and that's enough for me."

I sense this is making him uncomfortable, and I can't really blame him. Twenty-four hours ago we were two skeptics stumbling through life, relying on our own grit and savvy. Now one of us is sounding like a revival preacher. How many surprises can Brad handle in one week?

"Are you okay with all this?" I ask.

He smiles warmly. There is not an ounce of condemnation in his steel blue eyes. He sets his glasses on the tray, wraps an arm around me, and gives me a kiss on the forehead.

"You're not going to become a nun or anything are you?"

"No, silly."

"Then I'm okay with it, Leslie. It's part of who you are and therefore part of the person I love."

I want to talk more about this; I want Brad to experience it too. To have his blessing is awesome, but to have him understand this on a heart level—the level where we find real forgiveness and peace— that's what I want more than anything in the world.

But there are times to push and times to back off. And I sense that if I push Brad right now, I will only be pushing him away. We will have plenty of chances to talk about this in the next few days.

"Thanks," I say softly. "I love you." Then I lay my head down on his shoulder and close my eyes as if I'm going to sleep. Instead, I begin to pray…

CHAPTER FIFTY-FOUR

Brad forces me to take Friday off. I call Bella to check my messages and to let her know that I'll be dropping by on Saturday morning to get my mail and check on e-mails. She runs through a list of several callers, including my mom, a few clients, and Brandon Matthews. "Says he just wants to apologize for dragging you onto the front page of the tabloids," says Bella. "He didn't know he was being followed. He said he really wanted to tell you in person, but I told him you wouldn't be in today." Bella pauses.

"What aren't you telling me?" I ask.

"He's actually a pretty nice guy," Bella says tentatively. "And I think he wanted to ask you to help out on his case."

"Fat chance."

"You might want to just hear him out," suggests Bella.

"Okay. I'll hear him out sometime and then tell him no. Is Brad in?"

"Yeah," says Bella. "And don't you dare try to stop by for 'a few minutes.' He's guarding the door with a shotgun. If you get by him, you'll have to deal with me. You need your rest."

"Front door or back?"

Like a good girl, I stay away from the office all day, and Brad rewards me by coming to my duplex on Friday night for date night. He brings a movie and a couple bags of microwave popcorn. In a nod to my increasingly annoying diet, he has brought only low-fat popcorn. While it cooks, Brad melts half a stick of butter. When the popcorn finishes popping, he dumps part of it into a green bowl and the other part into a matching yellow one. He pours melted butter over the popcorn in the yellow bowl.

"Yellow is for butter," he says. "That way we can remember which one is mine."

"When's the last time you had your heart checked?" I ask.

"Mm, let me think," says Brad, popping a handful in his mouth. "Never."

"You need to."

"Let's take it one heart surgery at a time," he replies.

Before we get the movie started, we get caught up in a reality show. Brad soon finishes his bowl of popcorn and starts in on mine. "Needs more salt," he says, shaking it on like there's no tomorrow.

One of the contestants has a tattoo on her back—some large sun-looking object.

"You like tattoos?" I ask Brad.

"On you?" he looks at me like I've lost it.

Though I have no intention of getting one, I'm offended that he should think it's so out of the question. "No, on my mom," I say. "Of course on me."

Brad looks me over and shrugs. "Tattoos are cool," he decides. "Just don't put it on your bicep."

I give him a flex, and he squeezes the tiny lump on my arm. "A little Clearasil will make that go away," he says.

Just like that I'm on him. Punching, tickling, just basically mauling him. "Watch your heart, watch your heart," he says as he tries to fend me off.

He eventually surrenders, and we turn our attention back to the show. "Tattoos are okay," says Brad. "But scars are really sexy."

"What's that supposed to mean?"

He hits the Mute button. "I've done a little research on this operation you had," Brad says tentatively. His face is scrunched up a little, like he's expecting an explosion. "Open-heart surgery would be safer."

"I don't want to do open-heart surgery." My voice is firm. I can't leave any room here for hope. "It takes you out for four to six weeks, it leaves a huge scar, and it's *not* any safer."

Brad takes a deep breath, as if he's trying to figure out whether to jump into this debate or not. "I just want you to consider it, Leslie. Don't put your life at risk just because you're worried about a scar that nobody will see. I mean, it's not—"

"I knew you would do this," I snap. "It's why I didn't tell you in the first place. I knew you would try to make this decision for me, tell me what to do."

My accusation is met by silence. Brad furrows his brow, hurt and confused.

"I'm sorry, Brad. I just need to make this call myself. I need your support."

"Sure," he says. "I just wanted to talk about it."

I lean over and give him a little kiss. "I know," I say. "And I'm sensitive about it, I guess. This is a big deal to me. I just need your support."

"Okay," says Brad, "you've got it."

He's telling me what I want to hear, but I also sense that this isn't over. We've entered a cease-fire, but Brad will come at it again from another angle. That's the challenge of being engaged to an attorney.

A half hour later I am sitting with my legs straight out and resting on Brad's lap. When the reality show finishes, I decide to pick another fight. I'm starting to feel better, even a little feisty, and since I can't go to work and argue with other attorneys, Brad will have to do.

"Are you going to drop Brandon's case?" I ask, knowing full well that Brad is not.

"What do you think?"

I grin to myself. Brad is trying to avoid this topic. He's reluctant to upset me when I'm not fully recovered. Sensing an advantage, I zero in.

"He's lied to us at every turn," I say. "Cut your losses."

"Our losses, Leslie."

"Even more reason. Cut *our* losses."

Brad thinks for a minute, rubbing his hand back and forth on my cheek. "What about our duty of loyalty to our client?"

Oh, brother. Is that the best he can do? "Seems to me that he forfeits that loyalty when he lies to us," I reply. "C'mon, Brad, it's a waste of time."

"So I guess we'd better drop the Bannister case too."

"What?"

"It's pretty clear she lied to us."

"That's different."

"In what way?"

I give him a dirty look, and he just smiles, palms held up and out.

"Do you ever stop being a lawyer?" I ask in exasperation.

"Hey! You're the one who brought it up."

"You want anything to drink?" I ask, getting up from the couch. I've learned the hard way—if you can't outargue him, just change the subject.

"No thanks."

In the kitchen, I notice the pile of index cards on the counter next to the refrigerator. The cards remind me of the night I wrestled with God and the way those philosophical questions became irrelevant on the operating table. The cards also remind me of how badly I want Brad to experience this same new sense of peace and fulfillment that I now have.

Brad has started the movie and I go back to the couch, snuggling pretty close, and looking for an opportunity to work the conversation around to God. By the time the movie finishes, I'm still searching.

Brad flicks off the television and I say a quick prayer—the only kind I've mastered so far. "Brad, before you leave, can we talk about something?"

"Must be serious."

"It is, kind of." I pause. This is so much harder than I thought. My leg starts bouncing up and down, a nervous little habit. "I don't really know how to explain this, or what even happened for that matter, but Brad, on that operating table—when I prayed—it was the beginning of something special. I mean, I know we talked about this on the plane, but…well, I, um…I wish you could at least give Christ a chance."

I give him "the look," convinced I can do better with my eyes than I am doing with my lips. Bella said that God would give me another chance as well as the words to talk with Brad about this. But it's hard to believe that God orchestrated this bumbling attempt.

"Leslie, I think it's awesome where you are spiritually," he says slowly, tentatively. "But I'm at a different place, you know that." Almost against my will I nod.

"I've always envied folks who have an authentic faith in God," Brad continues. "Especially those who find refuge in Christ. But I've just got too many unanswered questions."

"So did I. But those questions melted away the first time I really prayed with my heart, prayed to Christ."

He starts to say something, then swallows his words.

"Say it, Brad," I urge. "Don't hold back. I want to know—need to know—what you're thinking."

"It's just…how can you justify your belief that God is a God of justice?" asks Brad. "Christ dying for our sins and all that—how can a just God require an innocent man to die for guilty men? What would you think of a judge who says to you, 'Ms. Connors, I know you've proved the innocence of your client, but I'm going to sentence him to death anyway because I know the next guy who comes in my courtroom will be guilty, and I'm going to let your client take his place'?"

Though I'm used to sparring with Brad, I sense that more is at stake in this conversation than the usual banter about our court cases. I also feel totally unprepared to answer his objections. But I must try.

"He's not just a God of justice. He's also a God of love. That's what makes Him different from other judges; that's where your analogy breaks down. God loves us so much He wasn't willing to sentence us the way we deserved. He sent His own Son as a proxy to take our punishment."

"So He didn't love Christ?" asks Brad.

I sigh, sensing that I am losing ground. It seems so weird to be arguing for the traditional Christian view, the view that I have rejected for so long. "All I know is that I was scared to die before my surgery, but now things have changed."

"And I'm telling you how much I respect that," says Brad. "I even envy that." A pause. "But I just can't embrace *that* for myself."

My heart sinks at the finality of the statement. But just as I want Brad to respect my budding faith, I've got to respect his views.

"Okay," I say, nodding my head. "I accept that. But it doesn't mean I'll stop working on you."

We both sense the tension leaving the air, and as usual, Brad wants the last word.

"Tell you what," he says. "If we win the *Girl Next Door* case then I'll start believing in a God of miracles. Who knows, I might even become a priest."

On Saturday morning I sneak back into the office, anxious to do some legal work and take my mind off my bad heart. Since it's Memorial Day weekend, Brad has suggested a relaxing day at the beach, but this time I'm the one who wants to spend it working. We've compromised with plans to head for Sandbridge late in the afternoon, a small family beach just south of the tourist-crazed Virginia Beach strip. Summer is officially starting, and my skin is still white and freckled. At this rate I'll have to use that spray-on tan that D. J. Landers uses, or they'll confuse me for a ghost at my wedding.

It takes most of the morning to catch up on e-mails and paperwork from the week. The phone company provided the records that Bella subpoenaed. She has done a lot of work with these numbers, highlighting the calls she identifies as coming from calling cards, which began precisely when Trish said they did—about six months earlier. They are all a few seconds in duration and occurred on nights and weekends when James Bannister would likely be home. According to Bella's memo, attached to the phone records, further investigation revealed that the caller used a number of different AT&T calling cards from various pay phones in the Tidewater area. Untraceable. Not much help to our case, but the information is consistent with my belief that Trish was not having an affair.

The documents that we subpoenaed for the company airplane that Bannister used also came back. There is no indication that he had planned a trip over the Bermuda Triangle or any other destination where it would be easy to disappear. Bella has also had a forensic expert examine the towel that Tara claims she wrapped around the gun when she went downstairs. Though a bullet was fired through the towel, and James Bannister's blood was smeared on the towel from when Tara covered his face with it, the expert could find no blood-spatter evidence that would indicate the towel had been close to Bannister when the gun was fired.

I can't seem to get a break in this case, and now the trial is just one month away. I realize that I've got to spend more time with Tara. Somehow I feel like the key to understanding this case will be getting to know Tara better. She's got to trust me enough to tell me the truth, not what she thinks I want to hear. I've got to get inside that girl's head.

I have skipped breakfast, meaning that I'm starving by the time lunch rolls around. I also need a break, so I drive a few blocks to a Schlotzsky's. I grab a salad, a bottled water, and a bowl of vegetable soup and find a table outside. The weather is unseasonably cool— only about 75 degrees. Strong gusts of wind and dark, threatening clouds make me think that our late afternoon at the beach will probably get rained out. *Good. I could use a little more time at the office.*

I pull out one of the newsletters that I brought to review while I eat—*Virginia Lawyers Weekly*—an update on important cases decided in the state last week. I am minding my own business when one of my napkins blows to the ground. I reach down to grab it, and when I sit back up, I find myself looking into the flat gray eyes of a man standing next to my table. He is tall and thin, with a pockmarked face from a bad case of childhood acne, and short dark hair gelled back. He is wearing long pants and a black T-shirt, and I know I should recognize this guy from somewhere, but I can't recall where.

"Mind if I join you?" he asks.

"Actually, I'm busy." I nod toward my newsletter.

He sits anyway. "This will just take a minute."

He places a folder on the table in front of him. "Detective Lawrence Anderson," he says, reaching out his hand to shake mine. "I was the lead investigator on the Bannister case."

Recognition and fear crawl up my spine. I stiffen a little. "What are you doing here?"

"Just saw you having lunch all by yourself," he replies, his voice flat. "Thought I'd join you for a minute."

This guy gives me the creeps. I glance around the mostly deserted restaurant. "Is this even proper?" I ask. "Meeting without Mitchell Taylor or Harlan Fowler?"

Anderson laughs. "Proper," he repeats sarcastically. "You're worried about proper."

He slides forward and puts his elbows on the table, drilling into me with those dark eyes. I don't want to appear afraid, but I can't help leaning back in my chair a little, resting my elbows on the armrests.

"You're new at this, Ms. Connors," he says. It's a statement, not a question. "But there are certain unwritten rules in the practice of criminal law that nobody transgresses. It's the only way the system works." He twists his face like he's thinking about how to phrase this. "You see, Ms. Connors, there are good guys and there are bad guys. Harlan Fowler, he's one of the good guys—he's given his entire life to putting away the creeps who make life miserable for the rest of us. And he's one of the most ethical men I know."

I'm so stunned by Anderson's lecture that I don't know what to do. His condescending tone is making me angry, but at the same time, his brazen arrogance worries me. He's playing by a different set of rules. I purse my lips and stare back, trying to act strong. My leg is bouncing quickly up and down under the table, nervous energy being expelled from my body.

"There are boundaries," Anderson continues. "Guys on your side of the bar allege prosecutorial misconduct and police incompetence all the time…comes with the territory." Anderson shrugs, then slides an inch or two closer. "But what you're doing here is over the line, Ms. Connors. Accusing an innocent man of molesting a teenage girl."

I start to talk, but Anderson waves a single bony finger at me. "Let me finish," he demands. "Because two can play this game. You see, I'm not officially here today to talk to you about the Bannister case, to ask you to back off on Fowler, to show you where all this might lead. I'm here on another matter."

"Then make it quick," I say, my voice betraying me with a quiver. "My soup's getting cold."

Anderson gives me a sardonic smile, bringing crow's-feet to the edge of his eyes. Then the eyes go flat again. "There's an OxyContin ring operating at your client's school," says Anderson. "You know what OxyContin is, don't you?"

I nod. "I've heard of it."

"Of course you have—drug of choice for rich young kids these days. Doctors prescribe it as a powerful painkiller. Thing is—we've busted a few kids at the school who are now cooperating with us. One of them, this young lady"—Anderson withdraws from his folder a picture of a teenage girl talking to Tara. He places it on the table where I can see it. I don't recognize the girl—"is willing to testify that she gets her supply from Tara, one of the biggest peddlers at the school. And get this"—he shifts his gaze from the picture to my eyes—"according to this girl, Tara gets her stash from her lawyer."

Anger flashes through my brain, the bouncing of my leg intensifies. "That's total bull," I say, contempt now filling my voice.

"Maybe," says Anderson. "But then there's this man"—he withdraws two pictures of me and Julio; one where we are talking, the other of Julio kissing me on the cheek; *where did he get these?*—"who is prepared to testify that you offered him a hundred thousand dollars to falsely testify that Harlan Fowler owes the Bellagio a ton of money and is also prepared to testify that you asked him where in Vegas you might be able to get your hands on some OxyContin." Anderson tilts his head and gives me a sideways look of curiosity.

"Leave," I sneer. "Get your sorry butt out of here. This is a sham, and you know it."

Instead of leaving, Anderson just gives me an arrogant half smile and pulls a minicassette recorder out of his pants pocket. He places it on the table between us. "Just in case you have some half-cocked idea of reporting our meeting," he says, "I want to make it clear why I'm here talking to you."

Before I can think to respond, he's turned on the recorder. "This is Detective Lawrence Anderson. The time is twelve thirty-five on Saturday, May 28. I am interviewing Ms. Leslie Connors about any possible knowledge she has regarding a drug ring at—"

I reach over and shut off the recorder. "The interview's over, Anderson." Now I lean forward, my anger and contempt fueling my courage. "Leave."

"Okay," he says, with disgusting nonchalance. He returns the pictures to their folders and the recorder to his pocket. Then he tries to stare me down one last time, the gray eyes narrowing. "But be careful what you do in this case," he warns. "Things can be taken out of context."

He deftly slides two more photos out of his folder. I gasp, then stare back at him with intensified hatred. "You jerk."

I swat my soup and it spills all over the photos and into Anderson's disgusting lap. I rise indignantly and savor the look of shock as he jumps to his feet.

"I'll let you clean it up," I say. "You're good at cleaning other people's messes."

I grab my purse and newsletter, then turn on my heels and leave a smirking Anderson standing at the table, wiping his pants with my napkin.

The two photographs are searing anger into my brain, branding my determination to follow this case wherever it leads. The photos by themselves are not shocking—I've seen them before. But the fact that Anderson or his goons took them—that blows me away.

Though my thoughts are distorted by anger, I try to force myself to think logically. I just surfaced the allegations against Fowler about a week ago. Before that, nobody even knew that he might become an issue in this case. Nobody, that is, except for me, Brad, Harlan Fowler, Trish Bannister…and Mack Strobel.

So why was one of Anderson's men following me around that day in the gym—more than a week before my meeting with Harlan Fowler? And what is Anderson doing with the original photo of me lying on the floor while Brandon Matthews hovers over me, inches away from my face—the same photo that just appeared on the cover of the *National Inquisitor?* Could he have copied it from the *Inquisitor?* But I remember how grainy the picture appeared on the front of the magazine. The one Anderson just showed me was crystal clear.

How likely is it that Anderson now has my greedy little friend from Vegas in his hip pocket? I reach into my purse and pull out the napkin containing Julio's cell phone number. I call it and my heart sinks when I hear the female voice of a prerecorded message.

"The T-Mobile customer you are trying to reach is no longer taking phone calls at this number. Thank you for using the T-Mobile system."

CHAPTER FIFTY-SIX

I head straight to Brad's house. I find him in the backyard, cleaning the pool. The dark clouds have thickened and it's starting to sprinkle. Thunder booms in the distance. We head inside to the kitchen, and I tell him what happened with Anderson while Brad fixes some iced tea. By the time I finish my story, Brad is furious.

He grabs his cell phone, starts pacing the kitchen, and dials directory assistance. He eventually gets through to the Virginia Beach Police Department. He demands the number for Anderson, but Brad's anger is no match for the police department's bureaucracy. He gets passed from clerk to clerk, each one making him angrier than the last, his voice rising in frustration. He gets cut off twice but finally finagles his way into Anderson's voice mail. He leaves a two-minute message so vitriolic that it makes me blush. But it also makes me feel great. Every woman needs a knight who thinks it's his full-time job to defend her.

"C'mon," says Brad. "We're gonna file a complaint with the Internal Affairs Department."

This does not surprise me. Brad's instincts are to run toward the battle, not away. But I'm not sure this is a good idea. I can get pretty fired up too, but I don't believe in seeking out trouble. It usually does a good enough job of finding me.

"Are you sure that's smart?" I ask. "The whole thing is just my word against his. What if Anderson follows through on his threat to frame me for drugs? Why keep raising the stakes in this thing?"

"He's bluffing," says Brad confidently. He grabs his car keys from a drawer. "They couldn't get past a preliminary hearing. The student's testimony would be hearsay, and Julio would get his head taken off on cross-examination."

Visualizing a preliminary hearing with me as the defendant is not much comfort. "He's bluffing." I repeat the words with a sarcastic edge, following Brad toward the front door. "Just like Harlan was bluffing. Just like Harlan was going to cave in and take our deal."

We're heading down the front steps now, and it's obvious that Brad's mind is made up. "Don't you ever get tired of being wrong?" I ask.

He jumps into the driver's side of his Jeep, but I just stand next to the passenger door in the light rain, refusing to open it. Brad jumps back out and leans on top of the Jeep, looking at me with pleading blue eyes. They stand out like diamonds against the backdrop of dreary rain and dark clouds.

"You can't just let them push you around like this, Leslie. They're testing you. It's the schoolyard bully. You've got to fight back."

I'll bet Brad got beat up by more than a few bullies as a kid. He never backs down. And while he may be right, it feels as if things are escalating out of control, like two heavyweight boxers standing toe to toe, punching and counterpunching, neither backing down, both suffering major brain damage.

"Where does it stop?" I ask.

Just then the wind gusts, the rain starts coming a little harder, and a bolt of lightning flashes across the sky. A second later the thunder follows, bringing a smile to Brad's face.

"It's a sign," he says. "The gods are with us."

"Or maybe He's telling us to back off," I say. But I climb into the Jeep, buckle my seat belt, and prepare to throw another punch.

The rest of the weekend passes quickly. I spend Sunday morning in church with Bella, Sarah, and her kids. At first, the small church is disconcerting to me. The informal nature of the worship, the homey style of the pastor, the casual dress of the church members—it's all so different from the churches I attended as a child. But somewhere between the third and fourth "praise song," something happens. I look over at Bella, who has her eyes closed as she sings loud and off-key. Then I just focus on the words and the God we are worshiping.

It's not like He suddenly makes the challenges of the week manageable; it's more like I suddenly don't care all that much, at least not at that moment. This is the God who heard me on the operating table, the same one who sent His Son to die for me. He was there when I desperately needed Him, and this is my opportunity to give back. I want the chorus to go on forever; I feel like a lifetime of repressed praise and spiritual emotion is bubbling to the surface. My intellectual objections, my index cards, even the prose of C. S. Lewis seem a lifetime ago, as if I harbored them in another universe. But in this lifetime, in this universe, right now, God is real, I am experiencing Him, and He deserves my praise.

When the service ends, I am still processing a lot of emotions. Now, more than ever, I want Brad to feel the same forgiveness through Christ, the same sense of renewed communion with God. When Sarah asks me to join her and Bella for lunch, I can't agree fast enough. I use the opportunity to pick Sarah's brain about the best way to approach Brad.

"Don't push," counsels Sarah. "He knows where you stand and how important this is to you. If you try to push him toward Christ, it'll just drive him away."

"Yeah," echoes Bella, the pushiest woman I know. "Strong-arming people on religious matters doesn't work." She smiles, then takes another big bite of eggplant. "I've tried."

"Your responsibility is to live in such a way that Brad can see the difference Christ is making in your life," says Sarah. "He'll be drawn to Christ when he sees Christ at work in you."

This suddenly seems like such a heavy responsibility. Brad knows me too well. I'm no saint. I'm not even a former missionary like Sarah or a confident and growing Christian like Bella. I'm just a new convert working hard to figure out how this whole thing works. What if I mess up? Or more likely, what happens *when* I mess up? Does Brad's chance to experience the grace of Christ really depend on how well I live my life?

"What's Plan B?" I ask.

Bella smiles. "You are Plan B," she says. "I was Plan A."

CHAPTER
FIFTY-SEVEN

On Monday morning, Memorial Day, I wake up at 8:00 a.m. and panic. The Bannister trial is four weeks away, and I don't even know what our theory of the case will be. Worse, the wedding is just a little over two months away, and I'm not close to being ready. I've been so focused on my heart operation these last couple weeks, and things have been so tenuous with Brad, that I couldn't even think about the wedding. Calls and e-mails from my mom, blunt hints from Bella, follow-up calls from bridal stores we visited—all of them went unheeded or unanswered.

I let the phone ring itself out, assuming it's another call from my mom. I roll over, fluff my pillow, and close my eyes. It's no use. I start making a mental list of all the things that I still need to do before August 6. My wedding, the day that I thought might never come, is just around the corner. And Leslie Connors, one of the world's most organized planners, is going to throw her own wedding together at the last minute? How did I get this far behind on something this important?

To make matters worse, Detective Anderson has Brad all riled up and chomping at the bit to get revenge. I know because Brad calls me at 8:30.

"Did I wake you?" he asks.

"Not unless you called me about half an hour ago."

A pause tells me he did. "Sorry. Were you thinking about coming in today?"

He puts it in the form of a question out of respect for my heart. But I know what Brad really means. Yesterday we talked about possibly filing a motion first thing Tuesday to disqualify the commonwealth's attorney's office from handling the case and thus rid ourselves of Mitchell Taylor. The motion would be accompanied by a brief we would file under seal, alleging that Fowler is the killer and therefore his entire office has a conflict of interest. We would need Tara's permission to file this motion, because she would have to retract her confession and be willing to testify that Fowler is, in fact, the killer. It's my job to confront Tara today and see if this is what really happened.

"Do I get double time?"

"Hard work is its own reward," says Brad.

I scoff at this. "Where do you get these sayings, anyway?"

"That's from the Old Testament," says Brad. "Book of Ezekiel."

I'm not sure if he's kidding, so I let it pass. "I'll be in about ten," I say, rolling out of bed.

"Ten?" Brad says, sounding alarmed. "If you weren't so cute, I'd fire you."

"Right. You probably say the same thing to Bella."

"Don't have to," Brad replies. "She's already here."

"You guys need to get a life. It's 8:30 on a holiday, and you're already at the office?" I hang up the phone and wonder what kind of firm I've gotten myself into.

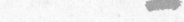

When I arrive, Bella is puffing on a cigarette at the reception desk.

"Where's Brad?" I ask, trying not to gag on the smoke.

"In his office, working on the motion."

"I thought this was a nonsmoking area."

"It's a holiday," snorts Bella, as if that explains everything.

I get through the reception area without taking another breath. In fact, I hold my breath all the way down the hallway until I get to my office, just to be safe. I start glancing through some legal memos

Bella has put in my in-box. Beneath them are two bridal magazines. Bella has tagged several pages with little pink flags. I know she's just trying to be helpful, but seeing the magazines renews my anxiety attack.

Two months. Just two lousy months.

I've suddenly lost my appetite for legal work, so I boot up my computer and start searching the Internet for all things wedding. I start by looking for a place to hold the reception. A few minutes later I think I hear Bella lumbering down the hallway toward my door. I shrink the Web site for the Williamsburg Lodge and click on my Outlook icon. When I turn to face the door, Bella is standing there.

"Find anything?" she asks.

My cheeks are burning a little. *Why should I be embarrassed about planning a wedding on a holiday?* It's not like I don't work hard for the firm. "Not really," I say, returning the Williamsburg Lodge site to its full-screen size.

Bella comes over and takes my mouse. She clicks on a few things and then shakes her head disapprovingly. "You could be at Kingsmill for the same price," she says.

"Huh?"

"Wait here," says Bella, as if I might otherwise sneak out the window. A few minutes later, she's back, hauling a big black three-ring binder. On the front it is labeled, "Trial Notebook: Parish Case." She plops it down on the desk in front of me.

My stomach knots. I can't handle one more responsibility right now—if Brad is trying to pawn this case off on me, a case I've never even heard of before today...

"Open it," Bella says. When I do, the first page says *Trial Date, August 6.* The writing is in beautiful flowing white letters with a picture of Bruton Parish, the quaint little church for our wedding, in the background. August 6—our wedding date.

"It's going to be beautiful," says Bella as I stare at the picture. She is looking over my shoulder, with that cat-who-swallowed-the-canary look. The smell of stale cigarette smoke hovers around her, like the dust cloud that goes with Pigpen in the Peanuts comic strips. She reaches down and turns the page. "I figured that if you two kids were really gonna do this wedding, which for a while I seriously doubted, then we had a few decisions to make."

The first few pages contain photos of four gorgeous places in Colonial Williamsburg for the reception, including sample menus and prices. There are brochures for each one slid neatly into a little plastic pocket that Bella glued to the pages. I flip to the next page— a list, including phone numbers and quotes, from three different photographers. Next to the middle one, Bella has scribbled, *I like him best.*

"I've got samples of their work at my desk," she says proudly.

"I can't believe you, Bella," I say. I could hug her, but I've probably already used up Bella's quota of hugs for the month. I flip the page. *His and her blood tests,* it says. *Dr. Satterwhite, 9:30 a.m., June 23.*

I twist my neck and look up at Bella. "Does Brad know about this?" I ask.

She shakes her head, her chubby face resplendent with pride. "But for his benefit, I do have a rough budget at the end." She smiles. "He may have to sell a few of his toys."

The next page contains pictures of cakes, together with prices and sampling dates. Then there's the page simply labeled *Invitations.* Under the heading it says, *See supplemental books.*

"There's more?" I ask.

"Of course. I've got scrapbooks full of sample invitations."

"Wow."

I flip a few more pages. Bella has covered it all, even looking up places for a rehearsal dinner and posting reminders to register for gifts.

"This is unbelievable," I say for the second time. "You've thought of everything."

"Well, not quite everything," confesses Bella. "This just gets you through the wedding. For the honeymoon, you kids are on your own."

I place my hands over my mouth and stare at the book, just trying to absorb this incredible act of friendship. Perhaps sensing an emotional moment, Bella quickly turns the book back to the first page and starts describing each of the reception locations.

My phone rings and Bella picks it up. "She's busy," she tells Brad. "She's right in the middle of some important research and can't possibly be disturbed." Bella hangs up the phone and smiles at me.

"That'll get him down here," she says. "That way you can decide on the reception together."

"You're incorrigible," I sigh.

Bella looks down at her watch. She waits a few seconds and then says, "Five…four…three…two…one…," then looks toward the door.

It takes a few more seconds before Brad pokes his head around the corner.

"What took you so long?" asks Bella.

CHAPTER FIFTY-EIGHT

I head to the Bannister house a few minutes before 6:00 p.m. I had called earlier that afternoon, explaining that I needed to talk to Trish and Tara. "We're having a little family cookout tonight," said Trish. "Why don't you join us for dinner?"

On the way I think about Jamie. How could I not? The first time I set foot in the Bannister place he spat on me. But I know I can't blame him. The kid has Tourette's syndrome. And in the last few days, saliva has taken on a whole new meaning for me.

My epiphany took place late Friday morning as I stayed home for the second day in a row. When I told Bella about coming to Christ on the operating table, she told me I needed to start reading the Bible. "Three chapters a day," said Bella. "Whether you feel like it or not." It was, said Bella, the same advice that Sarah gave her when Bella became a Christian. She dropped a brand-new Bible by the duplex first thing Thursday morning.

"Start reading the gospel of John," said Bella. "If you start with Genesis, you'll never get past the genealogies."

On Thursday I started. By Friday morning, I was on chapter nine. Halfway into the chapter, I had to put the Bible down and just think. *Now as Jesus passed by, He saw a man who was blind from birth. And His disciples asked Him, saying, "Rabbi, who sinned, this man or his parents, that he was born blind?"*

The question immediately caught my attention. I thought about my pink card on the refrigerator. Why do evil men go unpunished? And a related question. Why do innocent people suffer? I thought about Jamie and Tourette's syndrome. Who sinned—Jamie or his parents?

Christ's answer: *Neither this man nor his parents sinned, but that the works of God should be revealed in him.* Then Christ did an absolutely amazing thing for the man born blind. Christ spat on the ground, made some mud with His saliva, and put it on the man's eyes, healing him. *Wow!* I thought. *This is a Messiah who gets His hands dirty—a Healer who's not afraid to touch those whom other people ignore or avoid.*

I thought about my own reaction to Jamie, how I had avoided him—blamed him, really—for making my life uncomfortable. How was God glorified in Jamie's life? I thought about the way Jamie loved on his mother and hung out at school with his sister—the way Jamie brought some sanity to this family by just being Jamie. I thought about the way he coped with the Tourette's every day, and I felt ashamed when I thought about my treatment of Jamie as compared to Christ's treatment of the blind man. Spit drove me away. Christ used it as a balm of healing. I heard C. S. Lewis chiding me one more time—*This year, or this month, or more likely, this very day we have failed to practice the kind of behaviour we expect from other people.* I closed my eyes and prayed that the next time I met Jamie, I would behave more honorably.

Later that day I shared my epiphany over the phone with Bella. She had a far more pragmatic view of the passage. "That one always befuddled me, too," she said. "I mean, why didn't Christ just say the word and heal this guy instead of using a mud pie to do it?"

"Yeah," I said. "I wondered the same thing."

"Know what I think?"

I knew she was going to tell me anyway, so I just waited.

"It just proves that Christ can take the grossest stuff in life and make it a blessing," she continued. "I call it 'holy spit.'"

Jamie answers the door when I ring the doorbell. He is wearing some baggy cargo shorts that are one good tug from falling down to his ankles and a ratty black T-shirt with a few small holes in it.

"Hey bud," I say.

"They're out back," says Jamie, turning and walking toward the back of the house. I shut the door behind me. *Compassion, Leslie.* "You havin' a good weekend?" I ask cheerily.

He doesn't acknowledge the question. "Mom!" he calls out. "That lawyer's here."

Trish greets me and starts chatting as Jamie heads out back. At least he's not playing video games.

"Tara's out by the pool," Trish says. "She's not very happy. She wanted to hang out with some friends, but I told her you needed to talk with us."

Great. Make me the bad guy. "Can I help with anything?" I ask.

I expect Trish to say something polite like, "No thanks, we've got it all taken care of" or "Just make yourself at home while I finish the fruit salad." Instead, she gives me a package of hamburger patties and another patty all by itself on a plate. I don't have the heart to tell her that I don't eat red meat anymore.

"If you don't mind," she says. "The grill's out back by the pool. If you could throw these burgers on"—she hands me a spatula—"I could finish up a few things in here." She notices the look on my face but misreads it. "The one on the plate is a soyburger," she says. "Tara doesn't eat red meat."

"Oh."

I head out to the pool and find Tara. She's wearing a small black bathing suit top and a pair of cotton shorts over her bikini bottoms. And she's bouncing on the trampoline with Jamie. His shorts are now closer to his knees than his waist and would have fallen totally down if he wasn't holding them up with one hand while bouncing.

They are both laughing as Tara tries to double bounce her little brother by hitting the tramp just before he does to send him flying. She has a hard time since he outweighs her, but after a few bounces she succeeds. Jamie goes bouncing higher than usual, loses control the next time he hits the tramp, and ends up tucked into a little ball while his sister bounces him all over.

The lawyer in me wants to lecture them about how dangerous this is. Somebody could get hurt, you know. Spinal cord injuries, paralysis, then who'll be laughing? Instead, I smile and wave at Tara, then head to the grill.

"Wanna try it?" she asks.

"Next time."

A few minutes later, Trish sticks her head out the back door. "Why don't you help Ms. Connors with the burgers?" she yells to Tara.

"It's no problem," I say politely, though I sense that Trish is just trying to give my client and me some bonding time.

Tara keeps right on jumping.

"Tara," Trish says more sternly.

"Man," Tara grunts. She trips Jamie up one more time, setting off a round of whining. Then she climbs down from the tramp and trudges over to stand in front of the grill with me. Trish says, "Thanks, Tara," then goes back inside.

Now Tara is just standing there with her arms crossed. I soon discover how hard it is to carry on a conversation with a sulking teenager.

"School over?"

"Yes."

I start to ask her if she's got big plans this summer, then I catch myself. We all know what her plans will be if the case goes south. "You're pretty good on the tramp," I say.

She shrugs it off. "Not really."

Hmm. What else is there to talk about?

"Your mom doing okay?"

This garners a "that's a dumb question" look. "Sure."

This is painful. I've decided that everybody better like their burgers rare.

"You being careful on your instant messages?"

"Of course."

There are a few more long, uncomfortable seconds of silence.

"I think I can handle the grilling, Tara." I look over at the tramp, where Jamie is working on a seat drop. "Feel free to go bounce your brother into oblivion."

"Okay." But instead of heading back to the tramp, Tara goes over to a lounge chair by the pool. She takes off her shorts, applies liberal amounts of body oil, then dons her shades and lies back to catch a few more early evening rays.

"C'mon," says Jamie from the tramp. "I've got a new trick to show you."

Since Tara doesn't answer, Jamie begs for a few more minutes. Just as I am taking the burgers from the grill, Jamie climbs down from the tramp, whips off his shirt, and, still wearing his cargo shorts, does a flying cannonball into the pool, splashing water all over Tara.

"I'm gonna kill you!" she screams.

Poor choice of words.

We eat dinner at the table in the cutout area of the kitchen that overlooks the cut-stone patio, the enormous pool, and the manicured backyard. I sit at one end of the rectangular table, Jamie sits at the other—*out of spitting distance*. Tara and her mom sit on opposite sides. I try to engage the kids in conversation, but my knowledge of Xbox games, extreme sports, and teenage boys is rather limited, so we don't have much in common.

Jamie, who has changed into a dry pair of shorts to go with his ratty T-shirt, is constantly flipping his hair, blinking his eyes, and sniffing. He eats mostly with his head down, but he occasionally steals a glance up at me, as if he's forbidden from doing so. I try not to stare when he grimaces, making these contorted facial expressions like he's just seen someone disemboweled. It seems that he grimaces the most when I'm talking or when I've just finished talking. Maybe he can sense how uncomfortable I am around him and it somehow makes the Tourette's worse. I tell myself to loosen up, but that just makes me more tense as well.

This is turning out to be a long meal.

After a few bouts of prolonged silence, Trish starts talking to me and the kids start bantering between themselves. They are talking about what kind of animal parts they would eat on *Fear Factor* for fifty thousand dollars. Though Trish is trying to keep my attention removed from that conversation, I eavesdrop enough to figure out that Jamie will eat just about anything.

"You're sick!" Tara exclaims at one point.

This makes Jamie grin.

"I saw you on the cover of the *National Inquisitor,*" Trish says to me in a sympathetic tone soft enough so the kids won't catch on. But Tara's head jerks toward us, and she looks puzzled.

"You were on the cover of the *National Inquisitor?*" she asks.

"You've heard of it?" I ask, trying to change the subject.

"Of course," she says. "Who hasn't?"

"I haven't," says Jamie.

"What for?" asks Tara.

"It's not important," says her mom.

Then why'd you ask? I want to say. But I don't have to, because apparently the same thought is going through Tara's mind.

"You can't just bring up something and then say, 'Oh, never mind,'" Tara chides her mom, then turns to me. "What were you doing on the *National Inquisitor?*"

I find myself explaining the whole situation with Brandon, carefully leaving out any references to a bad heart. Like Brandon said, people pass out all the time at the gym for a variety of reasons.

"You rock!" Tara proclaims when I finish. "My friends already think you're cool. Wait till I show them this!"

Great. My only hope is that the magazine featuring me has already been replaced at the stands by this week's latest scandal.

"Ms. Connors doesn't need this spread all over Virginia Beach Academy," Trish says. But I can tell from the look in Tara's eyes that the horse has already left the barn. "I think we need to let it drop."

Jamie grimaces.

"Sure," says Tara. But when she looks at me, I still see a spark in those hard brown eyes. I think about how seldom I've seen much life there. "What gym do you work out at?" she asks. "I want to join!"

After dinner, Trish is doing dishes, Jamie has retreated to his computer, and I finally have an opportunity to talk with Tara alone. We are sitting at the formal dining room table, with Tara slouched low in her seat, arms folded in studied defiance. I am explaining the recent developments in the case, including Mitchell Taylor's rejection of the plea offer I made to Harlan Fowler.

"That's why I didn't want you telling everybody about what that jerk did to me," says Tara. "Now everybody thinks I'm lyin', and Fowler will no longer be trying to help us with the case."

Since I don't really have a great response, I just sit quietly for a moment. She may want an apology, but I'm not going to apologize for doing the right thing.

"At least when nobody else knew about Fowler trying to hit on me, we could use it against him," Tara says sullenly. She's staring at the table. "I could threaten to rat him out. Now it's out there, the damage is done, and he's got no reason to help us out."

"Well, it's not really out there," I say. "Mitchell Taylor knows about it, and Detective Anderson knows about it, but the public doesn't know yet. Fowler's still got every reason in the world to keep us from going public."

Just then the doorbell rings. Tara and I both listen as Trish goes to the front door and answers. It turns out to be a handful of Tara's friends. Tara yells for them to come on back to the dining room. She introduces me to them, apparently decides not to brag about my appearance on the cover of the *National Inquisitor* just yet, then excuses herself and her friends for a few minutes. "I'll be right back," she says.

After Tara gets her friends settled into the theater room in the basement, she comes back up to the dining room table to finish our conversation. "They said they're going to wait for me before they start the movie," she says in a clear signal for me to make it quick.

I take a deep breath and hope for the best, realizing that there is a lot riding on these next few moments. "Brad thinks that Harlan Fowler shot your dad," I say. "He thinks that Fowler might have been in a physical relationship with your mom, or at least the beginning stages of an emotional connection…"

Tara quickly gives a derisive little laugh and a sarcastic smile. Then the stone face returns.

"He thinks that you came home that night and found your dad dead. He thinks that Fowler convinced you to take the blame on the basis that you could be sentenced as a juvenile and with the promise that Fowler would get you a light sentence. Brad thinks that Fowler also promised you something like half the insurance proceeds and told you that, because he was the trustee for the life insurance policies, nobody would be able to collect a dime if he was convicted of the murder. Brad thinks that Fowler might have talked Detective Anderson into doctoring the test for gunpowder residue on your hands."

I study Tara's face, but my words are having no discernible impact. It feels like throwing pebbles against the side of Mount Rushmore—the words are hitting, but the expression never changes.

"Brad and I both thought it was a little unusual that Fowler was the first one on the scene. Your mom told police that she called him right after she went downstairs with you to look at the body. By then you had already called 911 several minutes earlier. So it seems strange that Fowler got there first. Plus you never mentioned your mom calling Fowler when you gave your statement to police."

"Maybe I forgot."

"Maybe." I pause. *Man, I wish this kid would look at me.* "Or maybe you didn't kill your dad at all. Maybe Fowler did and then said he'd frame you if you didn't cooperate, but he'd make you rich if you did cooperate."

Finally, Tara looks up at me with those lifeless brown eyes.

"What if he did?" she asks.

"Then we would file a motion to disqualify anybody from the commonwealth's attorney's office from trying this case, including Mitchell Taylor. We would try to prove at trial that Fowler killed your dad. You would have to recant your police statement and testify under oath about what really happened. They would put you through hell on cross-examination."

I stop and let her mull that over. There are other repercussions, but this is enough to think about for now.

"But Tara," I say, leaning forward and emphasizing each word. "I'm not willing to build my case on a lie. I've told you what Brad thinks. And most of it makes sense. But you're the only one who knows. Is that how it happened? Did Fowler kill your dad and pressure you into saying that you did it?"

Tara searches my eyes for a moment, as if looking for the answer. Then she nods her head ever so slightly and sets her jaw.

"That's exactly how it happened," she says.

CHAPTER
SIXTY

On Tuesday morning Brad and I file a motion asking the court to disqualify the commonwealth's attorney's office from prosecuting this case based on a conflict of interest. This motion is purposefully vague. We allege that factual support for the motion can be found "in the accompanying brief, which is filed under seal."

In order to file the brief under seal, we called one of the judges in advance and obtained an order "sealing" our brief, meaning that it cannot be viewed by the public. This, says Brad, is the surest way to guarantee that the newspaper and television reporters will be all over this case, trying to unseal the obviously juicy brief so they can find out what's inside. "It's like slashing your wrist and swimming with sharks," says Brad. "The feeding frenzy will be incredible."

Brad is determined to make it worth the sharks' time. He seems absolutely giddy about raising the stakes in this case, boldly predicting that Fowler will force Mitchell Taylor to accept our plea bargain as soon as they lay eyes on our brief. "They'll fold like a cheap suit," predicts my ever-optimistic fiancé.

In the brief, Brad has outlined our evidence against Fowler, throwing in spicy details about Fowler's assault on Tara in Las Vegas, Fowler's gambling debts, and Fowler's alleged insurance fraud scheme. The only thing missing from our brief is the alleged affair between Fowler and Trish Bannister. Brad put it in the first draft, but I refused to sign it until he eliminated any reference to the affair. I still don't believe Trish had an affair, and even if she did, we don't need to put it in this brief.

"If we get a hearing on this motion," warns Brad, "we'll have to bring up the affair—it's strong evidence of motive."

"I know. But let's not put it out there until we absolutely have to."

I hand-deliver the motions and briefs to the court, then hand-deliver a copy to the commonwealth's attorney's office and Mack Strobel's office. I constantly check over my shoulder while I'm walking and my rearview mirror while I'm driving, but I don't catch a glimpse of anybody following me. After I drop off the papers, I try calling Strobel several times, but his secretary makes excuses. Strobel's reluctance to take my phone calls makes me nervous. First Julio, now Mack.

As I run around town and drop off these legal bombs, I find my thoughts constantly wandering to my next surgery with Dr. Maholtra. The pain of my alcohol-induced heart attack still lingers in my memory, like a phantom stalking me, the headless horseman to my Ichabod Crane. I can't shake the memory of that cold, sterile operating room or the fear that wracks my body as I wait for the alcohol to snake its way through my arteries and up to my heart. I no longer fear death as I once did. But my newfound religion has done nothing to alleviate my fear of the pain, and that fear still holds me tightly within its grasp. That may explain the slight tightness in my chest today, or it might be caused by the HCM or the stress of this case or the memory of Detective Anderson shuffling pictures onto the table in front of me, smiling like a blackjack dealer who has an ace in the hole while I bet the farm.

I'm starting to understand why lawyers have one of the highest heart-attack rates of any profession out there.

On Wednesday morning Mitchell Taylor fires back with his own brief under seal, calling our motion "frivolous" and "a desperate attempt by a desperate defendant to divert the court's attention from the real issues in the case." Mitchell's brief is accompanied by a notice for a closed hearing on Friday. The brief argues that our motion implicating Fowler has no merit and thus the commonwealth's attorney should not be disqualified.

So much for Brad's prediction that they would want to plead the case out as soon as they read our brief. After I finish Mitchell's brief, I head down to Brad's office, walking brusquely past Bella at the reception area.

"I wouldn't go in there if I were you," warns Bella.

I brush it off. The hearing is only two days away, and we've got a lot to do.

I open the door and barge through. "They'll fold like a cheap suit," I say, my voice thick with sarcasm. "I think those were your exact words."

I wave the brief in the air. "Doesn't look like a cheap suit to me."

Brad is staring at me from behind his desk, but he's not the only one. Sitting in front of Brad's desk, turned halfway around in his chair and gawking at me as well, is none other than Brandon Matthews.

I freeze.

"I believe you two have met," says Brad.

I feel my face burn and mumble an awkward apology.

"I was so embarrassed that day in the gym," I say. "And then afterward, it just got so uncomfortable that I didn't know what to say."

"Don't worry about it," Brandon says. "Seriously. I probably would have done the same thing."

We both take a few minutes to vent about the idiots at the *National Inquisitor* and the sorry state of American journalism. Somewhere during the conversation, I plunk myself down onto the small leather couch in Brad's office. The phone rings and Brad punches the speaker.

"Line one," barks Bella. "WVEC."

Brad pops on his headset, motions at us with a finger, and stands to pace. "I can't comment on that," he says. "It's filed under seal."

While Brad talks, Brandon leans toward me on the couch, looking me over with his droopy eyes. He is wearing a skintight T-shirt and a pair of tightfitting jeans. His hair is pulled back in a small ponytail.

"Haven't seen you at the gym in a while," he says. "You doing okay?"

I scrunch up my nose. "Planning a wedding. Not much time to work out."

"Oh." He glances over his shoulder at Brad, then back at me. "You could never tell that you're not working out. Brad's a lucky guy."

I feel another blush coming on. "Thanks." I shoot a look at Brad who ignores me as he gabs with the reporter on the phone.

"I think you can assume it's pretty shocking stuff," Brad is saying. "Judges don't seal court records without good reason. You know how fond they are of the First Amendment and free press." Brad chuckles, still ignoring my "get off the phone" look.

"Brad and I were actually just talking about you," admits Brandon. "I told him it would be great if you could sit at counsel table with us on my case, maybe even handle a few witnesses." Brandon's voice is even, but his big, blue sympathetic eyes are pleading. He crosses his legs and lowers his voice a little more. "Frankly, it wouldn't hurt to have a woman on my side in the courtroom."

Just then Brad catches my eye, and I shoot flaming arrows in his direction. He'd better not ignore me this time.

"That's all I can say for now," he says into his headset. He holds up one finger to me, then tells his caller that he really has to go.

"I'd love to," I say to Brandon. Even while my lips move, I'm praying for forgiveness for shading the truth. All right, for lying. "But your trial starts next week, and I've got my first murder case starting just two weeks later. I really can't."

Brad puts down the headset and settles back into his seat.

"Brandon was just telling me how you were discussing my

involvement in his case," I say to Brad. I keep my voice cheery, in that tone that makes others think everything is fine but also promises Brad that he'll pay later. "And I was just telling Brandon how his case will probably run right up to the start of the Bannister case."

"Well, we are a little heavy on the testosterone at the plaintiff's table," says Brad. "We thought a pretty, sophisticated, smart woman like you might balance the team out a bit."

Brandon is nodding with his whole body, but I'm not buying it for a second. "That's the most transparent thing you've ever said, Brad Carson. If you think that flattery will—"

"No, it's not," Brad interrupts.

"Not what?"

"It's not the most transparent thing I've ever said."

I immediately realize that this is like one of those knock-knock jokes. At this point, I'm supposed to ask him what the most transparent thing is that he's ever said to me. Instead, I just scowl at him, refusing to give him even this minor pleasure.

"The most transparent thing"—he is unfazed by my lack of cooperation—"was that time I told you that I loved you for your brains."

Out of the corner of my eye, I see Brandon's lips curl into a small smile before he forces them back into a straight line. He is apparently unsure if I'm going to shrug it off or explode.

At that moment, so am I.

CHAPTER SIXTY-ONE

After Brandon leaves, Brad gets an earful. I start with my cross-examination. What are you trying to do to me? Don't you know how much I detest Brandon's case? Why didn't you tell him right from the start I couldn't do it, instead of making me tell him? What were you thinking?

Brad knows he's not really supposed to answer any of these questions, so he just patiently allows me to punch myself out. After a few more questions, I flame out and plunk myself down on his sofa. "I felt like a jerk telling him no," I say.

"You can always change your mind."

"Bradley Carson, if you even suggest—"

He raises his hands in surrender. "Okay, okay, I get it. You're not going to help on Brandon's case. That's fine."

"But I don't understand why you didn't nip it in the bud," I respond. I'm not going to let Brad surrender this easily. Surrender ought to be a little painful. "You made me tell him no. Why didn't you tell him no when he first raised it?"

Brad looks at me for a moment, letting the silence build. "You really want me to explain? Or would you rather have me just grovel around and apologize some more?"

"Actually, I haven't even heard the first apology," I say. "But what I really want is an explanation." This had better be good.

Brad stares into space for a moment and then speaks deliberately. "Brandon is going to be able to help us some on the Bannister case, Leslie. When I learned that, I didn't have the heart to just blow off his request without asking you."

"What do you mean, 'help us some on the Bannister case'?" I cross my arms and put on my stern look.

Brad rubs his face for a second. "I can't say. You've got to trust me."

"What do you mean you can't say?" It suddenly feels like everyone, including my fiancé, is playing games with me.

"You've got to trust me on this, Leslie." Brad walks around to the front of his desk, pushes some papers aside, and sits on it. He's now just a few feet from me. "Brandon has some information that may help us in the Bannister case. But here's the problem"—Brad's steel blue eyes bore in on me—"some of the judges in Virginia Beach are strongly biased toward the prosecution. They don't like the fact that the rules basically require the prosecutors to show us their file but that we don't really have to disclose our witnesses or evidence. They think that the rules unfairly favor criminal defendants."

This is not exactly news to me. "So."

"So some of those judges will do things to level the playing field. For example, you might be arguing some type of motion, and the judge will say, 'Now, Ms. Connors, do you have any other evidence to suggest that somebody else killed Mr. Bannister?' Or, 'Ms. Connors, do you have any other evidence to suggest that the police tried to frame your client?' The point is that the judge will ask these questions at some hearing well in advance of trial, basically forcing you to show your hand. If you don't reveal something to the judge, but try to use it later at trial, he'll accuse you of sandbagging the court and the prosecutor. Sometimes the judge will then exclude the evidence altogether."

I take a deep breath and uncross my arms. "I still don't see what this has to do with Brandon."

"Everything," says Brad. "You see, Brandon can testify to a few things that will really help us in the Bannister case. But if you know what his testimony's going to be, then some judge might weasel it out of you at this hearing on Friday or at some other pretrial hearing. Brandon's testimony will only help us if it is kept under wraps. If the prosecution knows what Brandon will say, they can work around it at trial. Since you'll be arguing all the motions, the judges will be asking you about potential evidence, not me. If I'm the only lawyer on our team who knows what Brandon might say, then we can ambush Detective Anderson with it at trial."

My head is starting to throb at the temples. Is Brad serious about this? He expects me to prepare this case while staying in the dark on a potentially powerful piece of evidence?

"Did you say Detective Anderson?" I ask. I see the relief in Brad's eyes as he realizes that I have picked up the hint.

"Did I say that?" asks Brad. He shakes his head in mock frustration with himself. "Well, at least I didn't tell you that Brandon's testimony could seriously jeopardize the detective's credibility if he dares to take the stand and testify at trial."

As I shuffle past the reception area on the way to my office, Bella is chewing out a couple of young men. One is wearing jeans and a polo shirt and holding a notepad; the other is wearing jeans and a T-shirt and holding a huge camera in his right hand, letting it swing freely as he listens to Bella with strained patience. I'm guessing it's a crew from the paper.

"I assume you two are both educated men," Bella is saying. "Probably been to college and grad school both. And I'm further assuming that you therefore know the meaning of the words *under seal*—"

The men spot me, spin on their heels, and head in my direction. "Ms. Connors," the guy with the notepad calls, "you got a second?"

Bella is now standing at the reception desk as I stop midstride. "Not on your life," she announces.

"I really don't," I say earnestly. "I'm pretty swamped today." I start walking away.

"It'll just take a second," says the persistent little newshound with the pad. Meanwhile, the second guy has aimed his camera at me and snapped a picture.

"Apparently, they don't teach you the meaning of no in graduate school either," Bella says, as she steps in front of them. This allows me to head down the hallway unmolested. "So here's a free lesson in newspaper etiquette…"

I hustle into my office and close the door.

There's an e-mail waiting for me from Brad. *Subpoena Strobel for Friday's hearing,* it says. *We'll teach him to ignore our phone calls.*

I forward the e-mail to Bella. Nobody would take more joy in hand-delivering a subpoena to the arrogant Mack Strobel than Bella. I add my own note as I forward it along.

Please don't hurt him, my e-mail says. *We really need him alive and able to speak at this hearing. Which means,* I add as an afterthought, *that you might want to leave the gun at home.*

I am only half-kidding. It is well known around town that Bella packs a Beretta nine-millimeter repeat-action handgun in her over-sized purse. It is also well known that she is not afraid to use it.

CHAPTER
SIXTY-TWO

Virginia Beach judges, as a whole, break every Hollywood stereotype about men and women who wear the robe. For the most part they are a hardworking bunch, issuing quick, fair, and even courageous decisions. Most of them are young and athletic, hanging out at the popular Wareing's Gym and drawing more than their share of admiring stares from star-struck jurors.

There are a few exceptions among the nine judges who inhabit the circuit court bench. Most notable among them are an aging but highly respected little man named Franklin Silverman Jr. and a former prosecutor named Gerald Farley, a man of excess and ease who has been on the bench so long that he has forgotten what it's like to put in an honest day's work. In appearance, Farley reminds me of one of the great Caesars without his laurel crown—his skin is chalky white and hangs almost in folds around his oval face. His eyes look so small peering out through his meaty face that you get the feeling somebody put him together wrong, like a Mr. Potato Head, the beady eyes of Danny DeVito inside the skull of Jabba the Hutt.

And rumor has it that his eyes dwarf the size of his brain.

The way my luck has been lately, it does not surprise me when we draw Farley for our Friday morning hearing. After shuffling through the other motions on his docket at a less-than-inspired clip, he surveys a still-crowded courtroom—full of lawyers and the press—and sighs audibly. "All of this for just one motion?" he asks wearily. "Let's get it started."

Without fanfare, Brad, Tara, and I take our seats at the defense counsel table while Mitchell Taylor and Harlan Fowler stand behind the opposing counsel table. The members of press row scoot forward, pencils and laptops poised. I begin unpacking my papers but notice that Mitchell has made no move to do so. He just stands there with his hands behind his back, like a marine waiting for a command, his gray suit coat hanging perfectly on his solid frame. Finally, Judge Farley glances up, and Mitchell takes that as a cue to launch his argument.

"This is a hearing concerning a matter that has been filed under seal, Your Honor," Mitchell begins. "It concerns scurrilous and frivolous accusations by the defendant with absolutely no evidence to support those accusations. Giving defense counsel a chance to air these attacks in a public setting, before Your Honor has a chance to determine if they are relevant to this case, would be a great travesty."

There is no movement in press row except for small amounts of saliva that is undoubtedly drooling down the chin of every reporter. Scurrilous accusations—what could be better? Mitchell turns and solemnly looks at Harlan Fowler, standing next to him. "These are personal attacks against Mr. Fowler, Your Honor. Untrue, vicious, and wholly unsubstantiated." Though I don't turn around and look at the reporters, I'm sure this description has generated more saliva. "Mr. Fowler should at least have a chance to disprove this nonsense in private, before these sham accusations are allowed to create a public stain on Mr. Fowler's distinguished career of public service."

"Your Honor," says a confident female voice behind me, I turn my head along with the others, "my name is Carmen Francone, and I represent several media clients present in this courtroom. The First Amendment requires that this hearing be open to the public, in full view of the citizens of this commonwealth, and not in some smoke-filled back room, hidden away from public scrutiny. We're not talking about accusations against a private citizen. These allegations are against the commonwealth's attorney, the chief law enforcement officer in this city."

The fight is on, back and forth, a legal slugfest that generates about twenty minutes' worth of fierce debate, until Jabba finally bangs his gavel and silences the lawyers.

"Ms. Francone," he says wearily, "there is no greater proponent of the First Amendment than me. But that does not mean that *every* hearing has to be conducted under the intense spotlight of the media. This trial will be a public trial. And any critical motion that might affect the outcome of this trial will be held in public. But the motion before me today is not even a motion about the merits of this case. Instead, it's a motion alleging a conflict of interest on the part of the commonwealth's attorney. Courts have a long history of resolving such matters outside the public domain. That is why, for example, all disciplinary proceedings against lawyers are held in confidential proceedings without public access. Accordingly, I will conduct a preliminary hearing on this matter in my chambers. If there is any evidence that the accusations contained in the defendant's sealed brief are true, or that they might impact the merits of this case, we will reconvene in open court immediately and deal with them here."

"I object," says Francone.

"So noted," says Judge Farley. Then he surveys me, Brad, Tara, Mitchell, and Harlan Fowler. "In my chambers," he orders.

We tramp in single file out the back door of the courtroom and into Farley's cramped office. He settles in behind his big oak desk while Brad ushers Tara into one of the comfortable leather chairs directly in front of the judge's desk.

Farley eyes the rest of us who are still standing. "You may need to run to the conference room next door and grab some more chairs."

In the corner of the office is a table with a couple of wooden chairs. Brad grabs one of those and places it right next to Tara. He motions for me to sit in it. Mitchell walks next door to fetch another chair while Farley and Fowler exchange pleasantries. I whisper into Tara's ear, "You ready for this?"

Tara nods in reply, but I can tell she's nervous. Her lips are set in a taut, straight line, and she keeps smacking her lips, betraying the cotton mouth that has beset her. She looks as comfortable as a cat who stumbled onto the set of *101 Dalmatians*.

Eventually, we all crowd around Farley's desk, side by side in uncomfortable chairs, with nowhere to put our legal pads or case files. Everyone except Brad, that is. Brad is leaning casually against the side wall, his arms crossed as he stands behind the rest of us in our little ring of chairs.

"You don't want to sit, Mr. Carson?" asks Fowler.

"I'm fine."

I pull out my legal pad and place it on top of my crossed legs, hunching my shoulders together like you do when you're in the middle seat of a commuter flight. Tara is on my right; Mitchell Taylor sits to my immediate left. This is hardly the way you envision it in law school, a crucial hearing being held in a space and setting that makes you claustrophobic.

"Ms. Connors," says Judge Farley, shifting back in his seat and folding his hands over his stomach, "this is your motion."

"The defense calls Mack Strobel," I say. "He's under subpoena, and I believe I saw him sitting in the hallway outside the courtroom."

Farley blows out a breath as if I'd just requested that he fly in the President of the United States for interrogation. He looks around his small office, which seems to be growing tinier by the minute. "Okay," he says at last. "We'll need another chair. I guess we can put the witness up here next to me, at the side of my desk."

Farley looks up to the sheriff's deputy who is standing in the doorway to his office. "Frank, could you please get Mr. Strobel?"

While the deputy finds Strobel, Mitchell Taylor earns a few more brownie points by running next door and grabbing another chair. He puts it in place just in time for Strobel's grand entrance, a disruptive affair that includes Strobel shaking hands with everyone in the office except Brad. Judge Farley swears Mack in as a witness, and he settles into the small wooden witness chair.

I flip to my notes for Strobel's examination and begin laying the foundation for his involvement in this case. In a booming voice that seems two sizes too large for this setting, Mack affirms that he was retained by Benefit Financial Insurance Company to investigate this case. I get Mack to authenticate copies of the life insurance policies made payable to Fowler as a beneficiary and trustee, all to the great boredom of His Honor, who hasn't bothered to take a single note.

Now for the good stuff.

"Did there come a time," I ask, "immediately following the transfer hearing in this case, where you and I discussed the common interests of our clients?"

"Objection," says Mitchell. "Hearsay."

"I'm not going to ask him what was said," I respond. "I just want to establish that we had the conversation."

Mack answers even before the judge can rule. "Sure," Mack says, "we had a conversation."

Mitchell spreads his palms, as if to ask what happened to his hearsay objection. Judge Farley ignores him.

"And did you tell me—"

"Hearsay," says Mitchell, louder than before.

"Sustained."

I uncross my legs and then recross them, so the other one is now on top. "Regardless of what you told me, did there come a time when you learned, in the course of your investigation, that Mr. Fowler had incurred rather substantial gambling debts at a certain Las Vegas casino."

Strobel lets the question hang out there for a second, probably giving Mitchell a chance to object. When no objection is forthcoming, Strobel answers in that deep, strong voice of his. "Any such information, Ms. Connors, if I even had such information, would be protected by the attorney-client privilege and attorney work product."

"I agree," says Farley.

"Not if he told me the information," I say. "He waives the privilege when he tells me." I realize now that Strobel intends to fight me all the way and has probably found a willing ally in Farley.

I turn back to Strobel and give him my best "don't mess with me" look. "You tipped me off to a confidential source who worked at the Bellagio and could confirm Fowler's gambling debts. Isn't that true?"

"I put you in touch with a confidential informant. I have subsequently learned that he will say just about anything for the right price."

I purposefully drop my notepad on the floor and lean forward in my seat, steeling my gaze at Strobel. "You told me, did you not, that Harlan Fowler and Trish Bannister were having an affair?"

"Objection," says the jarhead sitting next to me. "Hearsay."

I want to slap Mitchell Taylor.

Without waiting for the judge to rule, I ask my next question. "Did your investigation turn up evidence of an affair?"

"That's protected by the attorney-client privilege and work product doctrine," says Strobel.

"Sustained," says Judge Farley, as if anyone asked him.

"This is ridiculous," I mumble.

Farley's head jerks back as if I just let out a stream of profanity. "What did you say, Ms. Connors?"

My eyes go big with fear as I stare back at an angry judge. This man, I remind myself, has the ability to throw me in jail.

"I hope she said that this is ridiculous," says Brad from behind me. "Because it is."

All heads swivel around and stare at my fiancé. My heart is *rat-a-tat-tat*-ing against my chest. *Is this normal?*

"This man"—Brad points at Mack—"is representing a client who refuses to pay out on a million-dollar life insurance policy because they believe that this man"—Brad points toward Fowler—"committed murder." This just about brings Fowler out of his seat, his square jaw and fierce eyes turn first on Brad and then to Judge Farley. "So why don't you quit hiding behind all these legal loopholes and evidentiary objections and just tell the judge what's really going on?" Brad challenges.

This prompts a loud chorus of angry responses from Harlan Fowler, Mitchell Taylor, and Mack Strobel. Judge Farley shouts them down, causing an eerie silence to settle in on the chambers. I glance quickly at Tara who looks scared out of her mind. I turn my attention back to the judge.

"Mr. Carson," Farley says. He is seething now, the beady eyes smaller than ever, his double chin jiggling in anger. "In these chambers, we follow certain rules of protocol, certain rules of evidence. Your showboating and hotdogging, for which you are so famous, will not get you anywhere back here. In case you've forgotten, I excluded the press from this little hearing, so there's nobody to be impressed by your antics."

I'm thinking to myself that Farley is wrong. I was impressed by Brad's little speech. If nothing else, it ratcheted up my courage. Maybe that was the whole point.

"Now," says Farley, in a slightly calmer tone of voice, "I believe Ms. Connors is lead counsel for this hearing. If you have anything else to say, Mr. Carson, you can whisper in her ear and let her tell me. Otherwise, you can wait out in the hallway for this hearing to conclude."

Farley is now glaring at Brad, who I assume is glaring right back. Farley waits for a moment, probably to give Brad a chance to apologize. It's a waste of time.

"Given the Court's obvious bias," Brad says, hurling his words like knives across the chambers, "I would suggest that Your Honor recuse himself from this case. I originally thought that Your Honor could put aside the fact that you and Mr. Fowler used to work side by side in the commonwealth's attorney's office earlier in your career. Given the way you've conducted this hearing so far, that obviously is not the case."

CHAPTER
SIXTY-FOUR

Ten minutes later the in-chambers hearing resumes without Brad, who has been banished to the courtroom after the judge ranted against his ill-advised motion for recusal. Now it's me and Tara against the collective might of the good old boys' club of Virginia Beach and their newest apprentice, Mr. Mitchell Taylor.

"Isn't it true, Mr. Strobel, that your client, Benefit Financial Insurance Company, has refused to pay the death benefits to Mr. Fowler on the basis that he may be implicated in the killing of Mr. James Bannister."

"No," says Strobel confidently. "That's not true."

"Excuse me?"

"That's not true," repeats Strobel. "We have decided to pay. We've settled our dispute with Mr. Fowler, subject only to court approval since there are minors involved."

This news rocks me back in my seat. Now it's obvious why Strobel has been avoiding my calls. What to do next? Where is Brad when you need him?

Remain calm. "Isn't it true that you initially refused to pay the benefits because you had suspicions about Mr. Fowler's involvement in the death of James Bannister?"

"That is true," Strobel replies. He looks pleased with himself, as if I just swallowed the bait—hook, line, and sinker. "But now that we've completed our investigation, we've decided it would be prudent to settle the matter and pay out the benefits."

"Then why do you need court approval, if you're just going to pay out the benefits?"

"Because we want to make sure that neither Mr. Fowler nor the minor beneficiaries bring a bad-faith action against us for failing to pay immediately. Part of the court approval process is a waiver of all future claims by the beneficiaries."

I glance at Tara. "Beneficiaries like my client," I say.

"Yes. Like your client."

"But you didn't even bother to tell her or me that you had settled this matter and now intend to pay?"

Strobel blinks, but his voice is still confident. "We just proposed the settlement to Mr. Fowler earlier this week. A letter to your client is in the mail."

"In the mail," I repeat sarcastically. "The phones still work at Kilgore & Strobel?"

"Objection," says Mitchell Taylor.

"Sustained."

But Strobel answers anyway. "Your client will be getting every dime she has coming to her under the policies. We didn't think she would object."

Now I'm seeing red. Strobel and Fowler worked out a settlement, then purposefully kept me in the dark so they could make a fool of me at this hearing. What makes me really mad is how well it's working.

I glance at Fowler who is sitting there with a smug and pompous look on his face. The contrast between him and my frightened client is so stark that I honestly believe, perhaps for the first time, that Fowler might just be the killer after all.

"Ms. Connors?" prompts Judge Farley. "Any more questions for Mr. Strobel?"

Though Brad is gone, his advice rings so clearly in my ear that he might as well be leaning over my shoulder, whispering to me. *Trust your instincts, Leslie. Trials are won and lost by split-second decisions. Go for it.*

"Isn't it true, Mr. Strobel, that the reason you settled the insurance case is because Mr. Fowler agreed not to prosecute one of your law partners for child pornography in return?"

"Whoa," says Tara under her breath.

The men in the room are so shocked by the allegation that it takes a second for them to catch their breath. When they do, it's like the Fourth of July.

"Objection!" yells Mitchell.

"This is unbelievable," growls Fowler.

"You've got quite an imagination," says Strobel.

"Order," Farley demands. He slides forward in his seat so he is now leaning on his desk. "Order!"

I am glowering at them all, one at a time, just the way Brad would be doing if he were here. "Can I get an answer?" I ask the judge.

"I object," repeats Mitchell. "There's no possible relevance for this question. This is nothing but a fishing expedition; throw stuff up against the wall and see what sticks."

"Next thing you know," chimes in Fowler, "she'll be claiming that a Martian landed at the Bannister home and committed the murder."

I snort and lean forward so I can look down the row at Fowler. He ignores me.

Farley studies me for a second, indecision wrinkling his face.

"Your Honor," says Mack Strobel, his calm voice filling the room with reason. "I would love to answer that question and clear up the innuendos being so casually thrown about by Ms. Connors. But even a first-year lawyer"—Mack shoots a condescending look my way— "knows that my reasons for settling the insurance case are protected by the attorney-client privilege."

"I agree," says Farley. "I don't see what possible relevance this line of questioning has. Now, Ms. Connors, if you have any direct evidence linking Mr. Fowler to these murders, I think you'd better let me hear it."

I think about this for a long minute but can't see any way to get around this attorney-client nonsense that Mack keeps throwing out. I finally concede that I have no further questions, and Mack Strobel asks if he can be excused.

"Of course," says Farley.

While he leaves, I touch Tara gently on the elbow. "The defense calls Tara Bannister," I say as soon as the door closes behind Strobel.

I have again sucked the air out of the room.

Heads turn toward Tara, and she is suddenly frozen by their stares. Instead of standing and shuffling to the witness chair, she just sits there, her eyes suddenly moist.

"Tara," I say, gently squeezing her arm.

"I can't," she whispers.

"What?"

"I can't." She leans toward me. "He didn't do it," she says it so softly that I can barely hear, though her mouth is just inches from my ear. "I did."

I nod my head and then study the faces of the good old boys. "I think I need a moment with my client," I announce.

CHAPTER SIXTY-FIVE

I have never felt more empathy for Tara than I do at this moment. We are huddled in the hallway with Brad, and Tara is wrestling with her emotions and her unbending obligation to tell the truth. She looks very much like a vulnerable teenager, confused and frightened as she fidgets from one foot to the other.

"I can't stand Fowler," she says through clenched teeth and wet eyes, "but I can't hang him out on this." She looks at me. "I'm sorry, Leslie. I know how much you wanted to nail him."

"Tara, this isn't about nailing anyone," I say. "I just want you to tell the truth."

I can tell from his body language that Brad does not share my warm and fuzzy feelings toward our client right now. "How many times are you going to change your story?" he asks Tara. I watch Tara's eyes turn instantly hard. "You make it nearly impossible to defend you when you keep switching back and forth like this," Brad lectures.

"Yeah," Tara quips. "Especially when you've got to do it from the hallway."

I suppress a grin and decide that I like this kid better all the time.

A few minutes later Tara and I walk back into Farley's chambers, interrupting a perfectly good hunting story being told by His Honor. Fowler is busy laughing generously in all the right places.

We take our seats and the room goes silent.

"No further witnesses," I say.

Jaws drop all over the room as Farley eyes me suspiciously. "That's it?" he asks incredulously. "You make this big hurrah about evidence implicating the commonwealth's attorney, file a seventeen-page brief under seal, bring a big-shot lawyer in here to testify under oath, get every media outlet in town licking their chops, and *that's it!* That's your evidence?"

I don't really know what to say, and my senior partner is still banished to the hallway. *Tara changed her mind? Strobel sandbagged me? Oops?* I finally settle on "Sorry, Your Honor." I stare down at my shoes and try to look sympathetic. "Things obviously didn't work out the way we planned."

Farley scoffs and leans back in his chair. I have made his decision easy. "Before I rule," he says, "I want to make sure you've presented all your evidence. I don't want this court second-guessed later based on evidence that wasn't presented at this hearing." He pauses for emphasis, then adds, "Are you aware of any other evidence that might implicate the commonwealth's attorney's office or anyone associated with them in the death of Mr. James Bannister?"

I immediately recognize what Farley is doing. Just as Brad predicted, the judge is trying to make sure that the commonwealth gets a sneak peek at any evidence that might incriminate law-enforcement officials.

"No, Your Honor."

"Are you aware of any other evidence suggesting that the commonwealth's attorney's office or anyone associated with him has acted improperly in this case?"

"Other than indicting an innocent girl?" I ask.

"You know what I mean."

"No, Your Honor. I have no other evidence at this time."

"All right then," says Farley. "Here's my ruling." He looks at the wall above my head for a minute, deep in thought. Then he turns his attention to the court reporter.

"I cannot, of course, keep the defendant from arguing any theory of the case she wants to argue to the jury. But, Ms. Connors, you must have some evidence to support your theories. And the next time you come waltzing into my courtroom with evidence this thin, you will find yourself in contempt of court and will be paying the attorney's fees of every other lawyer who has to waste their time disproving this nonsense. Do you understand?"

"Yes, Your Honor."

"As for your motion to disqualify the commonwealth's attorney from prosecuting the case, I find no merit to the motion and deny it with prejudice."

"Thank you, Your Honor," chimes in Mitchell.

"One final thing," says Farley. "Defendant's brief was filed under seal and this hearing was closed to the press and public." He looks directly at me. "There's a good reason for that. If any of this leaks out, Mr. Fowler will be crucified in the press, though it's clear to me that he's done nothing wrong. Consequently, everybody in here is subject to a gag order. You are not to discuss this hearing with anyone, anywhere, at anytime. Is that clear?"

We all assure him that it is.

Farley looks directly at me. "And this gag order applies to Mr. Carson as well," he says.

"I'll tell him, Your Honor."

"Good. Mr. Taylor, I would ask you to draft an order that I will sign reflecting the court's ruling."

"Be glad to," says Mitchell Taylor.

I can't get out of the cramped chambers fast enough.

I huddle with Tara and her mom in the hallway, explain the ruling to Trish, and then warn Tara to keep her thoughts to herself. "You can't tell anybody about what went down in there," I warn. "Especially on IM."

"I know," says Tara. "I wasn't born yesterday."

Brad and I then "no comment" our way through the gauntlet of reporters and head toward our cars in the parking lot. I am thinking about us as a legal team and how our roles are the opposite of what you might expect. Leslie Connors, red-headed female associate, the logical one who likes researching, arguing the law, and keeping it low-key. Brad Carson, her experienced male counterpart, who responds with emotion, trying his cases on a visceral level that makes me uncomfortable. And at least in today's hearing, left me alone.

Once we are safely out of earshot of the reporters, I let him have it.

"We need to get you some anger management," I say, only half kidding.

"Farley's a jerk," Brad replies. "He'd made up his mind before he even heard the first witness. Somebody had to show him we wouldn't be pushed around."

"You really showed him." I reach out and grab Brad's arm with my free hand. He switches his briefcase to the other hand so we can hold hands as we walk on in silence.

"It was mostly just theater," Brad admits. "I wanted to make a point. I'll make it up to you, I promise."

"I know what you have in mind. I'm not that easy."

He laughs. "I can't believe you think I'm so one-dimensional. I was just thinking about a nice back rub and a romantic dinner."

"There aren't enough back rubs and romantic dinners in the world," I say, trying to sound at least a little upset. The truth is that I know exactly why Brad did what he did. He's like a basketball coach who gets himself thrown out of the game in order to fire up his players and get some sympathy calls from the referee. Even if it didn't work today, Brad knows that this escapade will be repeated to the other judges. When it's time for trial, they'll know that we're prepared to fight for every issue in this case.

"Name your price," Brad says.

Suddenly, an idea pops into my head. *Is this even fair?*

"Go to church with me on Sunday," I say.

"Name another price."

"No, seriously, Brad. I think you'd like it. There's no pressure and it really helps your perspective on all this stuff." I stop walking for a second, turn to him, and trot out "the look." "Please!"

"I don't know, Leslie. I'd feel so awkward." He looks down, unable to stare down "the look" and tell me no. "There are so many people I know who attend your church. I mean, I represented Pastor Bailey in the abortion protest case, I represented Sarah Reed, and Bella's there. I'd be so conspicuous, the visiting infidel, like a warlock hanging out at a conclave for priests."

His voice is soft and I can tell he's weakening. "Then let's go to another church," I say. "A big church where we can blend in and nobody will know you. Just one time." He glances back up at me and I know I've got him. "I won't ask again."

"Oh...all right."

"Serious?"

"Just once. As penance for getting thrown out of Judge Farley's chambers."

"Just once," I promise. Then I stand on my tiptoes and kiss him.

"They must've won!" shouts one of the reporters from halfway across the parking lot.

CHAPTER SIXTY-SIX

F irst Baptist Norfolk is big enough for Brad to get lost in a crowd, Sarah Reed assures me. The music is contemporary, the pastor is engaging, the dress is casual, and they do an altar call every Sunday. It sounds perfect, so I decide to drag Brad there on Sunday morning in order to worship with a congregation that, on its Web site, calls itself *First Family.*

Brad shows up at my duplex at about nine o'clock in his jet-black Dodge Viper—fifteen minutes late, but he knows I won't complain since I'm so happy he's going to church at all. Consequently, he doesn't waste one of his vintage "sorry I'm late" apologies this morning. He is wearing a golf shirt, khaki pants, and ultracool Ray-Ban sunglasses. If we weren't already engaged, it'd be love at first sight.

"You look great," he says, the minute he lays eyes on me. I shrug it off but in truth I'm excited he noticed. I'm wearing sandals and a light cotton sundress with lots of bright colors that contrast nicely with my all-too-white skin and nonexistent tan. I took about half an hour this morning to straighten my naturally curly hair, then I brushed it back and held it in place with a matching headband. I'm wearing a gold necklace with a cross on it and some understated earrings.

"You look so good I almost attacked you," I say.

"I'm glad you didn't," says Brad as he gives me a quick peck on the cheek.

Huh?

"It'd just be one more thing to confess in church."

First Norfolk is strategically located off Interstate 264, its steeple visible to thousands of motorists each day. We are waved into the parking lot by smiling attendants, then follow the flow of traffic around the building.

"There's a sign for visitor parking," I point out.

Brad scoffs. "If we park there, they'll jump us before we can get out of the car. We'll have do-gooders and fund-raisers knocking on our doors every night for a month." The Viper is now being waved into a grassy field since all the regular lots are full. "Remember, Leslie, whatever you do, don't put your address on anything."

"You're so cynical, Brad Carson. This is a church."

"And a big church that undoubtedly has lots of debt"—Brad is weaving his way through the grass, trying not to bottom out—"and evidently needs a new parking lot. No addresses, Leslie."

"Whatever."

We walk hand in hand toward the back door of the church, falling in step with the others. We are greeted as we enter by another smiling face who welcomes us to the church while handing us a bulletin and a list of Sunday-school classes and teachers. "Wonder if that painted-on smile is latex or oil-based," Brad whispers.

"Cynical, cynical, cynical," I reply.

It's now 9:50, and the service started at 9:45. I wonder if the rest of my life will be spent arriving late at things, married to the ever-tardy Brad Carson. The doors to the main auditorium are closed, since the service is now in progress, and a couple more greeters are standing in front of the doors with their own pasted-on smiles.

We stand in a group with several others, also waiting to get in. "They're praying," explains one of the ushers.

"Probably for me," whispers Brad. I elbow him and give him a "behave" look.

The prayer apparently ends and our little throng is ushered into the large church auditorium. There are pews arranged in a giant horseshoe pattern around the stage, with a huge choir behind the podium area on the raised platform and stained-glass windows to one side. Everyone is now standing and singing some kind of praise song, and before I know it, we are being ushered down toward the front of the section just to the right of the stage. I know what Brad's thinking—*Where are they taking us?*—and I notice he's dropped half a step behind me and the usher, probably digging in his heels.

The usher deposits us in the second pew from the front—I will have to remind Brad later about who made us late in the first place—and a family of five shoves down so we can join them. We begin staring at the words on the big screen up front and singing along as best we can.

"Don't sing too loudly," I whisper to Brad, "or they won't invite us back."

"Don't worry," he says. I see him warily eye the huge television cameras that are scanning the crowd. I hadn't realized that First Baptist was on television, and the cameras are disconcerting as they hover around the front of the church on their extended mechanical arms and relay our intimate worship scene to all of Tidewater, Virginia. I am fairly certain that if one of those cameras takes aim at Brad, he will hit the deck of the church and hide under the pew until I assure him it's safe to come out again.

Before long, I've forgotten about how uncomfortable my fiancé must be, and I've lost myself in the singing. Though I love Sarah's little church, there's just something special about this huge choir, the orchestra that sits in front of the stage like they're in the pit at a Broadway play, the enthusiastic music minister, and the people singing at the top of their voices all around us. I'm not sure that I've ever experienced worship quite like this before, almost like you're floating toward God's throne on the wings of these songs, or like God is leaning a little closer as we praise Him, or maybe a little bit of both. Whatever it is, the songs end too quickly, and I check our bulletin in hopes that we didn't get there so late that we missed most of the singing for the day.

Sure enough, we did. Still more punishment for running on Brad Carson time.

We are now seated, and the young, energetic pastor is explaining the "great First Baptist ripoff." All visitors are supposed to fill in the flap of our bulletin with our name, address, e-mail, and so on, and then rip the bulletin along the perforation. He has the entire audience rip their bulletins at the same time, presumably so visitors like us won't feel so conspicuous. "We promise you," says the pastor, "that this won't be used to harass you or drop in unexpectedly or to compile an address list for anybody else. This is just so we will have a record of your visit."

Brad leans toward me. "Give me five minutes of cross-examination," he whispers.

Despite his skepticism, I notice that Brad dutifully fills in every blank. He folds it in half and drops it in the offering plate when the ushers bring the plates around.

"I can't believe you actually filled it out," I whisper.

"Strobel will have a hard time believing it too," whispers Brad.

"You didn't."

He nods. "And I checked the box that says he wants a personal visit from the pastor."

While the ushers are collecting the rest of the cards and the offering, I skim through the bulletin and Sunday-school list. "Hey, look at this," I nudge Brad and point to one of the Sunday-school teachers for young couples. *Mitchell Taylor*, it says.

Brad makes a face. "Probably a different guy, same name."

"Either that or their standards are pretty low," I whisper.

A little while later, the pastor is into his sermon, and I try to set an example for Brad by taking notes. I am secretly praying for Brad even as I listen, my heart filled with an almost desperate sense that this might be his best chance to understand the love and grace of Christ. Though the pastor is young, he is absolutely brimming with caffeine-laced energy, and he doesn't talk in the kind of tired church clichés that I know would alienate Brad. I find it easy to listen to this guy named Eric—or Rick or something like that—as he bounces around the stage and has me laughing one minute, then seriously contemplating my spiritual condition the next. Though he uses a lot of Scripture, he is not afraid to apply it to common occurrences. I feel a little like C. S. Lewis has slid off the page, ingested a double shot of espresso, and is now prowling around the stage.

My only disappointment is that Brad is not taking notes.

As only God could orchestrate, the sermon is a perfect topic, not just for Brad but for me as well. The pastor is preaching about hypocrisy in the church, and about halfway through I quit taking notes for the purpose of serving as an example for Brad and start taking them just for me. I recall the pink cards on my refrigerator, especially the one that targeted this very issue. It occurs to me now that I never really resolved those issues logically, that I just took a leap of faith even though pink cards—indisputable facts—still existed that were irreconcilable with the faith I now embrace.

"There are bad doctors and bad lawyers and bad financial consultants," the pastor is saying, "but that doesn't mean you fault their entire professions or quit seeking the help of those professionals. Okay, maybe with lawyers."

Ouch. The audience chuckles a little and Brad bristles.

"And you've got to remember that the real issue is not whether those who claim to be Christians are perfect, but whether Christ is doing a work in their lives, changing them from the inside out, making them more like Himself. In other words, you may be thinking to yourself that a certain person is pretty rotten, or pretty hypocritical, but you don't know what they were like before they met Christ. You think they're bad now, you should have seen them before."

The preacher closes his Bible and says he wants to close with a brief illustration, because sometimes we are quick to point out hypocrisy in others but slow to see it in ourselves. As he talks, he moves to the front edge of the stage. In fact, he claims, sometimes the very same conduct we would condemn in someone else as hypocritical, we excuse in ourselves as just putting on a good front.

"But the truth is, many of us are barely able to hold it together on the outside and are dying inside." He pauses for a second and seems to look right at me. I divert my gaze to my notes, then look back up to see him now scanning a different part of the audience. "This suit," he says, as he brushes his hands down each sleeve, "was custom made just for me and, if you don't mind my saying so, goes rather nicely with this monogrammed white shirt and patterned silk tie. And probably most of you are thinking, Pastor Eric looks pretty dapper today." There are a few snickers as the audience, myself included, wonder where this is headed.

I make a note of the name—Eric something. "But hidden by this impressive suit," says Pastor Eric, "is a shirt that is not what you think it is." As he talks, Eric is taking off his suit coat and revealing, to the literal gasps of a few church members, a white shirt that is torn, muddied, and even bloody in spots.

"Many of you came to church today looking good on the outside," Eric says, "but you are dying on the inside. Torn relationships"—he picks at the shirt—"hurt feelings"—he points to the blood, and I'm wondering where it came from—"and a muddied mess of a family life or financial life or work life or"—he pauses and drives the point home—"even health issues. But many of you are so busy worrying about what you look like on the outside that you won't allow God to heal you where it counts, on the inside, in your heart."

Unbelievable! Now he's reading both my thoughts and my medical records? Then the pastor speaks these words, and it feels like somebody is shaking me by the shoulders and telling me to pay attention, that this is for me: "For the LORD does not see as man sees; for man looks at the outward appearance, but the LORD looks at the heart."

The words slice through me, illuminating my heart as surely as the catheter and scope used by Dr. Maholtra. I am suddenly ashamed of focusing on nothing but the outward appearance, worrying about a surgical scar, and putting everyone I love through untold heartache and pain. I have risked my life, and Brad's and my future together, to avoid marring my outward appearance. I misled Brad for weeks before I had the surgery. Maybe God didn't honor my first attempt at surgery because I was doing it for all the wrong reasons. Do I have to be perfect for Brad to love me? for God to love me? for me to love and accept myself?

The pastor's words take me deep inside myself, and I don't like what I find. There is conceit there. And selfishness. Insecurity. And fear. There is the heart of a woman who is ungrateful toward her God and who is so hung up on outward appearances—judging people by how they look or how smart they are or how much money they make—that she is sure the whole world judges her the same way. And perhaps, most important, there are the remnants of unresolved anger toward God because of Bill's untimely death. The shirt on that pastor is nothing compared to what I'm hiding inside.

Before I know what's happening, the pastor is done preaching and we are singing again. This time, they're inviting anybody who is wrestling with these issues to come down to the front of the church and pray. I am suspended between my desire to go, to get rid of all this junk inside me, and my fear of the embarrassment of going. *What will Brad think? What will I say once I get down front?* It's a tug of war, my heart propelling me forward and my feet superglued to the floor.

I watch others go—five, ten, going alone or with someone—down aisles on both sides of me. And then, "Excuse me," I say to Brad, as I slip past him and into the aisle, then walk a few steps toward a lady with a warm look on her face and an outstretched hand.

"I'm Gail," she whispers, "how can I pray for you?"

I tell Gail why I have come. She asks me to follow her, then puts an arm around my shoulder and leads me out a nearby door and into a room where we have some privacy. It is here that I explain everything I'm feeling—the repulsive look at my own heart, my unresolved anger at God, my vain focus on outer appearances, my fear of upcoming surgery. I tell her how even this morning I was hoping that my fiancé might get something from the pastor's sermon, but it never dawned on me how much spiritual help I needed.

Gail turns out to be a fabulous listener and a wise counselor. In a few minutes we're praying—first Gail and then me. Confessing my shortcomings and self-centeredness to Gail had been nerve-racking, but confessing them to God seems natural. When I conclude, there are tears in my eyes, and Gail hands me some tissues. I dab my eyes from the side, to keep my mascara from running worse than it already is.

"How do you feel now?" asks Gail.

"Like I needed to do that," I say. "I'm tired of being angry at God—" I break off my sentence and Gail places a hand on my knee. I dab a few more times before the tears can start.

"And this whole issue of accepting people for who they are on the inside…" I then tell Gail about Jamie Bannister and she nods knowingly. "From now on, I won't be so quick to judge just on outer appearances."

"And what about yourself?" Gail asks. "Are you ready to give

Leslie the same acceptance that you give others—based on what's inside rather than requiring perfection on the outside?"

I think about this for a moment. "Guess I'll have to," I say, "since the outside is getting ready to sport a seven-inch surgical scar."

Gail and I eventually return to the auditorium and find Brad patiently waiting. Poor Brad. He's probably wondering if he's getting ready to marry some kind of religious zealot. Maybe he is.

"Sorry, Brad," I say. "I just needed to get some things straight." I give him a look that says, "We'll talk on the way home," and he picks up on it.

"No problem," he says. "You spend half your life waiting for me; I don't mind waiting for you for a change."

I then introduce Brad to Gail, and we talk about nothing for a few minutes, then excuse ourselves.

"If you get a chance to come again," Gail says as we are walking down the aisle to leave, "you might want to try a Sunday-school class. There's a great class at 9:45 led by another lawyer. Do you guys know Mitchell Taylor?"

My jaw almost hits the floor, but Brad never even blinks. "I know a guy by that name," he says, without breaking stride. "But I'm pretty sure he's no Sunday-school teacher."

CHAPTER SIXTY-SEVEN

Tuesday morning is my day to make everybody upset with me without even trying. After two days of procrastination, I finally call Dr. Maholtra to cancel my surgery. Fortunately, Dr. Maholtra is in surgery herself and I get an assistant. "Tell Dr. Maholtra how much I appreciate what she did," I say. "But let her know I've decided to go the traditional surgery route."

"Can I ask why?" the assistant says.

You just did, I want to say. *And no, it's actually none of your business.* Instead, I politely inform her that I've decided to go with traditional surgery even though I have the utmost respect for Dr. Maholtra.

I can't get off the phone fast enough.

Next I go in for my appointment with Dr. Reddick, who squints at me over his little half-moon glasses and resists the urge to say, "I told you so." Everything goes smoothly with the balding wisp of a doctor until it comes time to schedule my surgery.

"I think I can fit you in a week from Thursday at 8:00 a.m.," he proudly suggests, after checking his very busy calendar on the computer in the examining room. Before I can even answer, he starts typing it in.

"Actually, I can't do it then," I say.

His fingers freeze on the keyboard as if he doesn't know what to do.

A patient has the audacity to suggest she can't work around the doctor's schedule?

"May I ask why?" he says.

Do they teach them that question in med school?

"I was wondering if you might have something in early July," I respond, dodging the doctor's question.

He straightens at the computer keyboard, turns to me, and stiffens. "With all due respect, Ms. Connors, you have a high-risk heart condition here, and I think we ought to operate as soon as possible. I can't imagine what you have scheduled next Thursday that would take precedence."

Up until now I had avoided telling the good doctor that I'm a lawyer, but now I'm out of options. "I'm defending an innocent sixteen-year-old on murder charges," I say. "And unless you're telling me that there's a much higher risk of heart attack if I wait four weeks instead of ten days to have this operation, then I'd really like to be there to defend her."

Dr. Reddick clears his throat. "It would be preferable to do it earlier," he says. "Every day with this condition untreated is a day of risk. But no, I don't expect that waiting a few more weeks will make a tremendous difference."

Following this concession we both relax a little and work out the logistics of surgery for July 6, the Wednesday after the Fourth of July weekend. He writes another prescription for blood thinners and beta blockers, and then gives me a bottle of nitroglycerin pills to take if I feel a heart attack coming on. I write it off as his subtle way of saying that I ought to be taking this all a lot more seriously.

As I leave, the humorless Reddick gets in one final dig. "Don't suppose it would make much difference if I told you to avoid stress and strenuous exercise," he says.

"I promise you I won't break a sweat exercising," I reply.

"That's what I thought," Reddick grumbles. "Have a nice day."

Brad Carson is the third person I frustrate on Tuesday morning.

"Tell me you're kidding," he says when I tell him about my surgery date.

"Serious as a heart attack," I quip.

"Can we not use that phrase?" he asks, concern wrinkling his brow. "You need to get this scheduled ASAP. We'll get the Bannister case continued until after you recover, Leslie. One thing is certain, your health comes first."

"Continue it until when?"

"After the wedding," says Brad. "September."

"If I remember correctly, there are at least three good reasons not to do that." I start counting them off on my fingers. "One, juvenile cases only get worse with time. Two, we need to keep the pressure on Fowler—"

"That's different, Leslie," Brad interrupts. "I was saying that if we had the choice, we should get an early trial date. I didn't say we should risk our lives to get this case tried early."

"Brad, I'm not risking my life to try this case before my operation. I'm high risk for a heart attack, yes. But I've been high risk for months, probably years. And now I'm on blood thinners and beta blockers. This septal thing is growing very slowly. It won't be any different a month from now than it is right now."

Brad sighs deeply, but I look him straight in the eye and plow ahead. "You were right about Tara Bannister needing a female lawyer, Brad. And besides, I *want* to do this. I can't let my heart condition win. I can't let it keep me from trying this case."

Brad can see that he's not going to win this one, but I love the guy for trying. "You've got to at least let me help, Leslie. Let me take some of the witnesses, reduce the stress a little."

"You've got the *Girl Next Door* case starting next week," I say.

"I'll drop it," he retorts. "I'll continue that one. I'll call the court today."

Though it's tempting, this is no longer what I want. "Brad, I don't need you to drop that case now. I'll work the Bannister case up for trial, then you can step out of your other case as soon as it's over and help me. Let's just keep things on the same schedule as before." I put my palms on the outside of his face and draw closer. "It's really important to me that my heart condition not have the final word. I've got to feel like we're beating this thing, not being controlled by it. Can't you understand that?"

He twists his face in disapproval but is smart enough not to push it. "What about the wedding?" he asks softly. "Should we move that back a little?"

I've thought about little else since leaving Reddick's office. "I'll have four weeks to recover, Brad. Dr. Reddick says that should be enough. Whatever we do…we've got to keep our wedding date. I can't let HCM postpone that. I've got to have something to motivate me during rehab, something to make it all worthwhile." I give him a hug, and he throws his arms around me.

"And the only thing that could make something that bad worthwhile"—I squeeze him close and fold into the security of his arms—"is you."

CHAPTER SIXTY-EIGHT

This is definitely the one," I exclaim as I bring my hands to my mouth. I twirl slightly and stare at the bank of mirrors in front of me, admiring the dress from every possible angle.

"Elegant yet simple," says the fitting clerk in David's Bridal. "Sophisticated."

I don't know about all that, but I do know one thing: I love it! My search is over.

I had seen a dress on the Internet last night that I liked. So this evening I stopped by David's Bridal to check it out, only to experience that familiar lukewarm feeling that comes from looking at a dress that would suffice but not dazzle.

"Can I show you a few more like it?" asked the clerk.

I was tempted to tell her no, since I was already feeling guilty that I wasn't working on pretrial prep in the Bannister case. My ingrained politeness made me stay. Two dresses later, she trotted out *the dress,* and I started smiling as soon as I saw it.

"It looks great on you," the clerk is saying. *It ought to for $950.* And though she's getting paid to say it, I tend to believe her.

It's an Oleg Cassini dress, ivory colored and sleeveless, with a funneled neckline and a simple A-line style. The slit in the neckline ends just high enough to perfectly cover the top of my surgical scar, according to the description by Dr. Reddick of where that scar will run. It has a beautiful band of embroidery and beads that the clerk calls a beaded empire bodice, with a high waistline directly below the bust. I love what it does to my figure as it gradually flares in stunningly simple lines from the bodice to the floor.

I hold my chin high and twirl around slowly one more time. I could stand here all day admiring myself, but I don't want to act as egocentric as I feel. The dress clings snugly on top, then falls in elegant folds of beautiful fabric.

I picture my hair pulled back tightly into a bun at the nape of my neck, and soon I am trying on tiaras. Within minutes I've found the perfect small and understated rhinestone tiara, complete with a bottom row of pearls. This, of course, requires another few minutes of admiring the dress and tiara together, a match so perfect that they should never be sold as separates again.

"Your hair is so beautiful," says the clerk. "It just brings out every hue in that tiara."

I wonder how much it would cost to keep this lady around. I could pay her to throw out these constant compliments, maybe she could even offset the snide comments of Bella...

Bella!

I'm immediately on my cell phone, speed-dialing her number. "Want to see what the lovely bride's going to look like on her wedding day?" I ask.

"Are you serious?" Bella gasps. "I'll be right there."

There is a moment of silence as I smile broadly.

"Where *is* right there?" Bella asks sheepishly.

he next week flies by at warp speed as I work around the clock
on the Bannister case and the Leslie Connors wedding plans.
Through some miracle of time management and the industri-
ousness of Bella, Brad and I manage to get our wedding invitations in
the mail, and yes, one is addressed to my dad. We also issue witness
subpoenas and prepare our exhibits for both the *Girl Next Door* case
and the Bannister case. I spend a full day with Trish and Tara, preparing them to testify. It will take at least one more day with Tara, and
longer if she doesn't start taking this more seriously.

My only break in the last seven days has been to attend First Baptist Norfolk on Sunday morning. This time I went alone.

On Wednesday, Brad starts the *Girl Next Door* case in federal
court while I stay in the office and work on motions and other matters pertaining to the Bannister case. Brad comes back to the office
Wednesday night looking exhausted after picking a jury and com-
pleting his opening statement.

"How's it going?" I ask.

"If our case is half as good as I promised in the opening, we'll do
great."

"Is it?"

"No."

He throws his suit coat over a chair in the conference room where
I'm working and flops his briefcase down on the table. "How's the
jury?" I ask.

Brad slouches into a chair. "Two single females," he says triumphantly. "It might be the only thing that saves us."

I let Brad unload about the case for a few more minutes, avoiding even a hint of my "I told you so" attitude. Right now, he needs my encouragement. Hopefully, after the case is over, I'll get a chance to talk to him about why he stayed with it in the first place.

"Who's your first witness?" I ask.

"Gotta go with the plaintiff," Brad says. His tone makes it sound more like a duty than an opportunity.

"Mind if I come watch?"

He grunts. "Heck, I'll let you question him if you want. Just remember, we're not dealing with the sharpest tool in the shed."

"I'd better let him stick with you. He might not understand some of those big words I have a tendency to use."

"Thanks," says Brad. "You hungry?"

"I'm starving." Then I remember my new wedding dress. "For a nice light salad."

Brandon Matthews looks out of place on the witness stand and is trying hard not to appear nervous. He is wearing a button-down dress shirt and a pair of khakis. The top two buttons of the shirt are unbuttoned, displaying a large gold cross around his neck and blond chest hair that contrasts nicely with his dark summer tan. His blond mane is pulled back in a tight ponytail, displaying another piece of cross jewelry, this one a small gold earring. Even with the long-sleeved dress shirt, you can tell he's ripped, and I'm glad I don't have Tara Bannister with me or the drool would be flowing like a faucet.

Brad has already walked Brandon through the critical elements of his testimony—the way the show misled and humiliated him, the damage to his income as a weight trainer, the snide comments that people make when they see him now. Brandon is answering the questions with great enthusiasm, though it seems to me and probably everyone else in the courtroom that he's trying a little too hard, like an amateur actor who believes that every line needs to be packed with drama.

"Did you subsequently find out that two of the three finalists you chose before Jewel was brought onto the show had been paid off to alienate you during their last date in order to make it more likely that you would choose Jewel the transvestite as the winner?"

Brandon takes a sip of water and puts on a forlorn look that seems manufactured. "I knew something had changed," he says solemnly. "On our other dates there was, well"—he sits up a little straighter, proud of the memories—"those dates were hot. The girls were attracted to me. We, uh, we hit it off pretty good, if you know what I mean. The cameras couldn't even show most of it." At this, it seems that Brandon actually puffs his chest out a little, pecs flexing through the shirt.

"Then, after Jewel showed up...well, the claws came out. And suddenly, my sweet girl-next-door finalists turned into the three"—he pulls himself up short—"the three stepsisters from Cinderella." Now Brandon smiles a little at his own cleverness. "I thought they were just jealous of Jewel."

"But you later learned that two of them got paid for turning against you?" Brad asks.

"That's correct."

"Then what about Annie? Do you know of any evidence that indicates Annie received payment to turn against you so that Jewel would win?"

Brandon looks down and shakes his head slowly. "No," he says. "The way I treated Annie was a mistake." He shrugs his shoulders. "If I had it to do over again, I would work harder on keeping that connection with Annie. She was pretty and fun-loving, and we actually had some pretty awesome chemistry..."

"But?" prompts Brad.

"But I guess I got blinded by Jewel and, well, what she brought to the table that Annie didn't."

Brad knows better than to touch that one, so he quickly changes subjects. "Did you ever speak to Annie after the show?"

I know the answer that Brad and Brandon scripted. Brandon is to say that he spoke to her once and apologized. This, according to Brad, shows just the right amount of contrition without overdoing it.

"Yes," answers Brandon. "Matter of fact, I just spoke to her in the hallway a few minutes ago."

I turn my gaze to Brad, who never misses a stride, though I know the answer was a surprise and he's dying on the inside. He's now forced to ask the question that everyone is thinking. "What did you say?"

I hold my breath, unnerved by the gleam in Brandon's eye. "I told her how sorry I was about not choosing her on the show. I asked her if I could make it up to her with dinner once this case was over."

"And she said?"

"She'd think about it."

I exhale. That wasn't so bad. Maybe Brandon's smarter than we think.

The testimony rambles on, and I start making a to-do list for the Bannister case and my wedding. Then, just before the midmorning break, Brad gets to the questions that drew me here in the first place.

He starts by showing Brandon the cover of the *National Inquisitor*. Part of Brad's case is to show that Brandon's "social life" has been damaged, so he goes through the women pictured with Brandon one by one, proving that things are not as they appear from the pictures in the *Inquisitor*.

When he gets to the picture of me, my hands start to sweat and I can hardly look at the witness. Though the assembled media are intently focused on Brandon for this salacious part of his testimony, it still feels to me like they're secretly stealing sideways glances in my direction.

"Now, the next picture shows you and a woman with red hair who has her eyes closed. It appears that you are leaning down to kiss her. Can you explain the origins of that picture?"

"Sure," says Brandon, as he shifts in his seat. "The woman in that picture is your law partner, Leslie Connors…"

I note out of my peripheral vision that some of the reporters are scribbling notes.

"And I'm actually just checking to see if she might need mouth-to-mouth resuscitation."

At this point I notice one of the jurors break into a broad smile and another puts her hand over her mouth to hide her own smile. A few of the others are looking down, probably trying to hide amused grins.

"You see," continues Brandon, oblivious to the smirks, "Leslie had passed out in the gym where I work"—*Brad should have told him to call me Ms. Connors*—"and I'm just bending over her to make sure that she's breathing okay and to determine if she needs CPR."

The defense lawyer coughs, and it causes one of the jurors to giggle.

"What is she wearing?" asks Brad.

"I think it was probably a Lycra top, and she probably had on running shorts," says Brandon. "That's the type of thing most women in the gym wear."

I look to my left and scan the bemused faces of the reporters. They're not buying this. One is actually staring at me but quickly looks away when I catch her gaze.

"Did you eventually give her a ride home that day?" asks Brad.

"Sure, after we called the paramedics and had her checked out," says Brandon.

"Does that explain this other picture—the one of Leslie and you in her car?"

"Yeah, it does."

"Did you on that day or at any other time have any kind of romantic relationship with Leslie Connors?"

"No, I did not." Then Brandon smiles broadly, the rows of perfect white teeth standing sentinel just below his broad Roman nose. "She was already taken."

At the break, I pull Brad aside in the hallway.

"Put me on the stand," I say. "The jury thinks that Brandon is just making all this stuff up about me passing out and the CPR."

Brad frowns. "You know I can't do that. You're my partner. If you have to testify, then I have to withdraw."

"Well, you're a smart guy. You've got to figure out something to bolster his credibility—some way to make the jury understand that these pictures are just an attempt by a corrupt cop and a shameless newspaper to set me up."

Brad looks around to make sure there are no eavesdroppers. "Oh, we've got a way to do that," he says softly. "But Brandon won't let me do it. By exposing Anderson in this case, it would destroy our element of surprise in the Bannister case. And that's something that Brandon is simply not willing to do."

"The evidence you won't tell me about?" I ask.

Brad nods.

"Why would Brandon care so much about the Bannister case and so little about his own?"

"Maybe he thinks that we can get the testimony we need out of the paramedics that came to the gym," Brad says. "Or maybe he thinks his case is headed south anyway. Or maybe he really wants to nail Anderson for providing those pictures, and he thinks the best way to do it is through springing this evidence on him in the Bannister case."

"Or maybe," I say, "he has an attorney who's on a personal vendetta against Detective Anderson and threatened to withdraw if Brandon didn't agree to defer this damning evidence against Anderson until the Bannister case."

Brad gives me his poker-face look, a confirmation that I've hit a bull's-eye. "I think the judge is getting ready to resume court," he says. He kisses me on the cheek and heads back to the courtroom.

CHAPTER
SEVENTY

On Friday morning, while Brad plows through day three in the *Girl Next Door* case, I head to Virginia Beach circuit court for two motion hearings. One is a routine hearing to get a plea bargain approved for one of Brad's clients. The other is a motion that has been filed by Strobel, asking the court to approve his proposed settlement of the life insurance claims. Since the settlement involves Tara and Jamie, and since the kids are under the age of eighteen, the settlement requires court approval.

Because Strobel is suggesting the settlement, I naturally decide to oppose it.

The paperwork for Strobel's settlement proposes that Benefit Financial pay the entire $2 million due under the policy. One million goes to Fowler in trust for the children, just as the policy says. Jamie gets two-thirds of that amount, Tara gets one-third.

The other million is more complicated. The terms of the policy indicate that the second million is to be paid directly to Fowler. But Bannister had also signed and sealed a letter to Fowler asking him to put most of that money in trust for Bannister's family and certain charities. Because this language was never included in a will or in the language of the insurance policy itself, it is unenforceable. Unless he was the murderer, Fowler could walk away with this million dollars and nobody could stop him.

But Strobel has proposed a compromise. Under Strobel's plan, the million will be paid to Fowler, in accordance with the terms of the policy, but Fowler will then sign a court order agreeing to abide by James Bannister's wishes in the unenforceable letter insofar as Trish and the kids are concerned. Trish will get three hundred thousand, just as James requested, two hundred thousand will go into trust for Jamie, and one hundred thousand will go into trust for Tara. That leaves four hundred thousand. In the unenforceable letter, James instructed Fowler to keep a hundred thousand for his trouble and to put three hundred thousand toward charities and the Republican Party. But there is no mention of that request in the proposed settlement, so I am assuming that Fowler intends to ignore that part of James's letter and pocket the remaining four hundred thousand.

I've got to hand it to Strobel; he's thought of everything. The insurance company pays what it owes but then gets Fowler, Trish, and the kids to sign an order saying they will not sue the company for bad faith. Trish and the kids get every dime they're entitled to under the policy, including money that James specified for them under the unenforceable letter. Fowler looks like a good guy, since he's giving Trish and the kids even more than they are legally entitled to have, but in reality he's walking away with four hundred thousand dollars, including three hundred thousand that James wanted to go to charities and some Republicans. The only parties that might complain, the charities and Republicans, don't have a leg to stand on.

"I'm opposing the motion," I tell Strobel when I see him.

"On what grounds?" he asks incredulously. "Your clients are getting everything they're entitled to and more."

"On the grounds that Fowler should not get a dime, since he may well be Bannister's killer."

Strobel grunts. "That's ridiculous, Ms. Connors. How many judges have to tell you that before you'll believe them?"

"At least one more," I say.

For the hearing, we draw a judge who is known to be evenhanded and patient. According to Brad, Judge Patricia East is a friendly young judge who is known for her fairness and decorum—unless you get her mad at you. "Then what happens?" I asked.

"Just don't do it," he said. "Trust me."

If anybody ought to know how a judge acts when you upset them, it's Brad. I don't plan on finding out firsthand.

Strobel asks for a closed hearing in Judge East's chambers. This time there are no newspaper reporters hanging around to object. Once everybody gets settled in, and after Strobel explains what a great proposal this is, I tell the judge I'm not yet ready to concede. With both Strobel and Fowler glaring at me, I ask the judge for more time to investigate whether Harlan Fowler was somehow involved in the death of James Bannister.

Though Judge East expresses a healthy amount of skepticism, putting on the record that she can't possibly imagine Mr. Fowler being involved in any way, she still reluctantly agrees to at least let me finish the Bannister murder case first to see if anything unexpected comes up. "But if I were you," she warns, looking at me over black-rimmed reading glasses, "I think I'd take the money now. If your client gets convicted, she might get zilch."

"We're willing to take that risk, Your Honor."

"Then I want the first hearing date after the Bannister case concludes to get this settlement affirmed," barks Strobel.

As everyone takes out calendars, I start in with my litany of excuses. First, there is the open-heart surgery scheduled for July 6. Then, as soon as I am healed, there is our wedding on August 6. Then, of course, there's the honeymoon. I let everyone know how sorry I am, but I couldn't possibly attend another hearing on this matter until at least a week after our wedding.

This seems to touch a soft spot in Judge East. We chat for a few minutes about the prospects of my wedding following so quickly on the heels of open-heart surgery. I tell her it's the only thing that might get me through the surgery in the first place. She wishes me luck on both, then sets a hearing for August 12, six days after our wedding.

"I know it's not a full week," says Judge East, "but I'm putting Mr. Strobel and his insurance company at considerable inconvenience by postponing the approval of this settlement. If you still want to oppose it on August 12, then you might have to suffer a little inconvenience of your own by coming back early from your honeymoon."

The judge looks at the furious face of Mack Strobel, then back to me. "Perhaps by August 12 you'll change your mind about opposing the settlement," the judge adds. "If so, I'm sure a letter to that effect will suffice, and you can enjoy a few extra days in Key Largo or wherever."

"Thank you, Your Honor," I say cheerily. I notice that Mack Strobel and Harlan Fowler do not do the same.

"And give Mr. Carson my congratulations," says Her Honor.

Fowler leaves Judge East's chambers quickly, without talking to me. I grab my briefcase and head down the hallway for my second hearing of the morning. Though I try to ignore him, a persistent Mack Strobel is at my elbow.

"We're giving your client every penny she could possibly claim," he says. "Why are you postponing this?"

This man's got some nerve. I stop and face him. "Maybe it's because your compromise is a sellout," I snarl. "Maybe it's because you first convince me that Fowler is involved in Bannister's death and then propose to pay him four hundred thousand dollars. And maybe, before the settlement hearing takes place, I'll have a chance to find something that will disqualify Fowler from ever getting a dime of the family's insurance money."

"You're making a mistake," Strobel says somberly. "Justice is a patient suitor, but she can't wait forever."

"What's that supposed to mean?"

"You'll figure it out."

A few minutes later, with my head still swirling from Strobel's latest melodramatic pronouncement, I enter Courtroom Number 4. Because Friday is motions day, there are a still a number of people milling around. I locate a young African American woman sitting in the last row with two small boys. She is wearing a wrinkled red skirt, a tight black top, and a pair of scuffed flat leather shoes. She is gaunt in the face with dark circles under hard red eyes. Her oldest, who looks to be about five, is playing with some toys on the bench next to her. She's balancing his younger brother on her knee.

Some lawyers in the front of the court are arguing a motion, so I keep my voice down. "Are you Keisha McFadden?" I ask.

She nods. She can't be a day over twenty. "Shh," she says harshly to her son who is making guttural noises with his toys on the bench seats.

Keisha previously hired Brad to bring a personal injury case against a doctor who botched the delivery of Keisha's second child. It was one of the few malpractice cases Brad lost. Out of sympathy or guilt or some other irrational emotion, he later agreed to represent her when she was arrested for buying 1.2 grams of cocaine. She cooperated with the cops, providing names and testimony in exchange for a promise from the prosecutors that they would take her cooperation into account at sentencing time.

"Mr. Carson had to be in federal court today, so he asked me to handle this," I say.

Keisha looks at me suspiciously. "All right," she says warily.

"He's already worked out the plea," I say. "You get eighteen months, all but seven days suspended, which you already served before you made bail. You get twelve months probation, 150 hours of community service, and a five-hundred-dollar fine. You understand, Keisha, that if you get caught with drugs or get in any other kind of trouble in the next twelve months, the court will give you the eighteen-month sentence on top of whatever else you get."

"I know," she says defensively. "It was just 1.2 grams. I'm off it now anyway."

I look into her vacant eyes and doubt it. But I refuse to allow myself to get sucked into this case, too. Leslie the crusader has enough of her own problems right now.

To my relief, I notice that Keri Massey is the prosecutor in the front of the courtroom handling cases for the commonwealth. I remember how sorry I felt for Keri the day that Fowler introduced me to her. I remember wishing that I had Keri instead of Mitchell prosecuting the Bannister case.

I take a seat in the front row and listen as Keri finishes the matter before her. During a lull in the arguments, a young man in a suit slides up to her counsel table and hands Keri a note and then disappears. I assume he's an intern with the commonwealth's attorney's office. Keri reads the note, then gives me a solemn little nod. I nod back.

A few minutes later, the court takes a brief recess. I approach Keri.

"I'm here representing Keisha McFadden on her plea bargain," I explain. "Think we can slide her case through next on the docket?"

Keri looks down at the counsel table and shuffles a few papers. "Actually," she says, "the commonwealth is not prepared to go forward on that case today." She lifts her eyes to look at mine.

"What?"

"Something came up. We're not willing to go forward at this time." She is speaking softly, her eyes pleading with me to understand.

"Does that mean the deal's off?" I ask.

"Not necessarily," she says. "It's just not on today. We need more time."

"Why?"

"Can't say."

I shift from one leg to the other. *What's going on here?*

"When will you be ready to get this deal approved? My client's got two young boys; it's not easy for her to make these trips." I'm trying to sound aggravated, but it's not easy with someone as nice as Keri.

"*If* we go forward," Keri says, "and it's no longer a sure thing, Leslie, but *if* we go forward, it will be after August 12." She studies me carefully as she says this. I feel my face flush in anger.

"Are you telling me—" I'm raising my voice, but Keri stops me with a hand on my arm.

"I've told you more than I should already, Leslie. That's really all that I can say."

CHAPTER SEVENTY-ONE

E ight days before trial I'm in full-blown panic mode. My first murder case, a client I have a hard time trusting, a mound of scientific evidence against us, and Brad Carson will be tied up in federal court for several more days before he can turn his attention to this case. I am chugging enormous amounts of caffeine that is off-set, I hope, by my blood thinners and beta blockers.

This can't be good for my heart.

It's Sunday, and after another morning of solo attendance at First Baptist, I go home to change into shorts and a tank top and then join Brad at the office. I left him there at eleven o'clock last night, and it looks like he's been here awhile today. I wonder if it will be like this our entire married life.

"You eat yet?" I ask.

He shakes his head, as if the thought of food never crossed his mind. He is elbow deep in documents from his case, chewing on a yellow highlighter, his bloodshot eyes peering out through reading glasses. He highlights a few more lines, then takes off his glasses, rubs his eyes, and looks up at me.

"How was church?"

"Great. You okay?"

He hesitates. "Yeah. Well, actually no. I'm getting slaughtered over there."

"I'm sorry," I say. And I mean it. "But Brandon's got the best lawyer possible. If you can't win it, then it's not winnable."

Brad sighs. "Good pep talk. The Packers could use a coach like you."

I go over and sit in his lap, neither of us talking. I kiss the man, the best way I know to cheer him up. I see a little fire return to his red eyes, though I suspect it's got nothing to do with the case.

Thirty minutes later our takeout order arrives. As we spread our lunch on the conference room table, I decide to drop the bad news about Tara's confession.

"I've researched her confession from every possible angle," I tell Brad. "I just don't see any way we can keep it out."

"Good."

I stop playing with my food and give Brad the "are you crazy" look he deserves. The man's been working too hard.

"Why are you working so hard to keep it out?" asks Brad, shoveling a forkful of lasagna into his mouth. "I mean, she explains during Anderson's questioning that she shot her dad in self-defense. Her face is bruised and her mom's face is beat to a pulp. What's not to like about the confession?"

He's losing it. "Well, first, she admits to killing her father. And second, she doesn't exactly act remorseful. Third, you'll remember that Anderson tripped her up on that question about how the blood from the cut on her heel made it into her bedroom. And fourth, she is smart-mouthing her mom the entire interview. Overall, a pretty pitiful performance by a spoiled teenager who acts a lot more like a cold-blooded killer than a scared kid."

"And you think she'll do better if you keep the confession out and put her on the stand live?"

"She can't do any worse."

Brad looks past my shoulder and considers this for a moment. "You understand that you couldn't introduce that videotape into evidence even if you wanted to?" Brad asks, insulting my intelligence.

"Of course I can't," I respond. "For us to try to introduce it would be hearsay. Only Mitchell Taylor can introduce it under the exception to the hearsay rule for the admission or confession of a party opponent."

"Exactly," says Brad. "Which means that you should put up a token opposition to the videotaped confession, just enough to make Mitchell Taylor think you really want it kept out. Then he'll introduce it into evidence, and you can build your self-defense case around the statements in the videotape and keep Tara from ever taking the stand."

I feel like I've been talking to a wall. "You're not listening to me, Brad. That videotape is terrible for us. I can't build my case around that."

"Leslie, you haven't seen terrible. Tara on the stand…that would be terrible."

There is a long silence. I trust Brad's trial skills when he's focused. But right now, he's obviously not focusing on *my* case. Tara will be far better on the stand than she was in that videotape. I should know. I've worked with her, coached her, helped her to learn how to show remorse and act the part of the victim. Sure, she still needs some work, but, she'll be much better than that awful confession.

"Brad, on this one we just disagree. I'll have her ready, I promise."

Brad stands and stretches, rubbing his face with his hands and then running his fingers through his hair. He starts pacing. "You really think so?"

"Yes. I do."

"How far away from here does she live?" he asks.

"Twenty-five, thirty minutes."

"Then bring her in," Brad says, "and we'll see."

Two hours later, Trish drags Tara into my office. My client is not happy that we've interrupted her afternoon tanning time. Nonetheless, she agrees to a dress rehearsal of her trial testimony.

After she sulks through her direct testimony with me, Brad homes in for cross-examination.

"You're glad your stepfather is dead, aren't you, Tara?"

She hesitates a little too long, and I make a note to talk to her about that. "Not really."

"Oh?" says Brad. "You're not?"

"No."

"Who is Wiccarules?" Brad asks.

"Screen name for a friend."

"Do you instant message this friend?"

"Of course."

Brad slides a document across the table to Tara. "Did you tell her that shooting your dad was 'payback'?"

Tara answers without looking at the paper. "Probably."

"Did you say that you hoped your dad rots in hell?"

"I guess."

"Did you say that you should have shot him one more time—three times instead of two times—including a bullet for your brother?"

Tara shrugs.

"Answer yes or no," says Brad.

"Yes."

"And did you tell Wiccarules that it was more payback than self-defense?"

Thunder clouds form on Tara's face as she looks straight ahead. Brad reaches across the table and points out the lines. "Right here," he says.

"I know," Tara replies sharply. "Yes, I said it." She narrows her eyes and looks at me, as if this is somehow my fault.

Brad slides a picture of James Bannister's reclining chair across the table. "Do you recognize this?"

"Yeah."

"What is it?"

"My dad's recliner."

"Now look closely at the bloodstains on that chair. Can you tell the ladies and gentlemen of the jury why those blood patterns make it look like James Bannister was sitting in the chair when he was shot as opposed to standing up and strangling you?"

"I don't know about the blood patterns. I do know he was strangling me."

"Even when you shot him the second time?"

"He was coming after me."

"Then do you know why the scientific evidence suggests that Mr. Bannister had been dead a long time before that second shot was fired?"

Tara shrugs. Her face is dark with rage.

Brad stands. "Isn't it true," he says, his voice stern, "that you shot your stepdad in cold blood while he was sleeping, then you waited a half hour or so and drilled him again, then you bragged to your friends about it?"

"You're a jerk, you know that?" Tara shoots back. "You don't have any idea what that man did to me and to my mom! I'm glad he's dead! And I hope he rots in hell!" She turns on me. "You happy now? Did you both get what you wanted? I do hate him. I did kill him. And I'd do it again."

Brad sits back down and looks at me. The room is silent except for the heavy breathing of Tara and the hammering of my heart.

Eventually, Brad leans back, looks up at the ceiling, and sighs. "I think we've got a little work to do," he says.

CHAPTER SEVENTY-TWO

E ach night of the next week, our final week before trial, Brad and I have essentially the same conversation when he returns from federal court.

"How'd it go today?" I ask.

"Not good."

"You want to tell me about it?"

Brad then recounts that day's woes—terrible witnesses, dirty lawyers on the other side, bad body language from the jurors, testimony dragging on ten times longer than he anticipated—each day it's something different. After he gets done griping about how bad the day went, I remind him what a great lawyer he is. "If anybody can pull this off, Brad—you can." Secretly I'm thinking, *Why didn't you dump this case when I first suggested?*

On Thursday night Brad is particularly forlorn. He describes the weepy testimony of Annie, the only *Girl Next Door* contestant who he didn't have any dirt on. She testified about how committed she was to Brandon and how badly it hurt when he chose the buxom Jewel over her wholesome promises of true love. Brad says his opponent at least three times showed the video of poor Annie leaving in the limo, makeup streaking down her face.

"I just want Brandon to be happy," she sobbed into the camera. "But I never knew his happiness would cause me this much pain."

"Even I felt sorry for her," grumbles Brad.

According to Brad, Annie went on to testify that, though her heart was broken on the show, she never dreamed of suing the show's producers. "We all knew they were making no promises," she said.

"They told us all along that anything could happen, that there would be some shocking twists at the end."

"And the worst part," says Brad, "is that I couldn't lay a glove on her. I didn't have any evidence that she had been paid anything extra by the show's producers to force Brandon away from her and toward Jewel. The jury felt so sorry for her that I couldn't do my usual cross-examination, or they would have hated me for it. Basically, I gave her a walk.

"To rub it in, the show held a press conference after court today. They announced that Annie would have her own show next year where she would get to pick from twelve of America's most eligible bachelors. They're calling it *Revenge of the Girl Next Door.*"

"Looks to me like she already got her revenge," I tell Brad.

Each day of the week also brings disturbing news about how slowly the case is proceeding. This is due, in Brad's cynical opinion, to the fact that the other lawyers are getting paid by the hour and are milking their client. "The trial would have been over by now if they weren't getting three hundred bucks an hour," he complains. And as Monday gradually turns into Friday, one thing becomes crystal clear to me—I will be starting the Bannister case without him.

The old Leslie Connors would have freaked. And even the new Leslie Connors, the one with the new faith and the new self-confidence, is toying with freaking by Friday afternoon when I learn that Brad will begin his closing argument in the *Girl Next Door* case on Monday, the same day that the Bannister trial starts.

"Start off by arguing our motion to exclude the confession," Brad tells me. "That should buy us a couple of hours. Then take your time picking the jury. With any luck, I'll be there by noon, just in time for the opening statements."

I feel my chest clutch a little at the thought of picking the jury without him. "Can we talk about the types of jurors we're looking for one more time?" I ask.

Brad sighs. "Okay," he says. "But it hasn't changed since yesterday."

I spend all of Sunday afternoon, the day before the trial, shopping with Tara. I am determined to have her looking like a sweet, respectable young girl at trial if it kills me. And by 5:00 p.m. on Sunday it feels like it just might.

Tara and I have been arguing all day about what she is going to wear. I prefer knee-length skirts and conservative blouses that button up to her neck and are long enough to overlap the waistline on her skirts. Tara, mindful she will be on television, thinks this is the most ridiculous idea she has ever heard. "The stores where I shop don't even carry that old maid stuff," she says.

We eventually compromise on a few outfits that include thigh-length skirts, a neckline that plunges a little, and an exposed midriff. It's more skin than I want her to show, but Tara says the clothes are so old-fashioned that she's going to burn them as soon as the case is over.

If we lose you'd better get used to orange jumpsuits.

I go to bed early Sunday night—the best lawyer is a well-rested lawyer and all that. But as I watch sitcom reruns until late night turns into early morning, I realize that my nerves are so frayed I may never sleep. This, of course, makes me worry about being tired for my first day of trial, which in turn makes it harder to fall asleep. My mind drifts toward the negative—everything that can go wrong my first day of trial, all that is riding on this case, thoughts of Tara receiving a life sentence for murder.

By two thirty, even the new Leslie has no choice. I rummage

around the medicine cabinet and find my Sonata. I read the fine print about taking the tablets at least four hours before I need to be active again. Four hours will be six thirty—that will work. I pop a tablet in my mouth, promising myself that I will only do this before the first day of trial, then crawl back in bed. The last thing I remember is checking the alarm.

CHAPTER SEVENTY-THREE

t's light out when I finally crack an eyelid. I hover in that half-asleep-half-awake zone for a minute, feeling like I've done this a few times already. My brain slowly registers that the sunlight is sneaking through my closed miniblinds but my radio is not yet playing. *Relax,* I tell myself, *you've still got a few minutes to sleep. Take advantage of it. But that sunlight...*

I bolt up in bed and check my digital clock radio: 7:55! How did that happen? I snarl at the clock, checking the Alarm button. It's off, but I distinctly remember setting it.

I groan, then slam my palm on the bed in frustration and jump out. I'm dizzy, my head's throbbing and my stomach is churning like mad. I grab my watch from the counter: 7:57. I've got to be dreaming...a nightmare. I'm never late. Never.

I rub my eyes and curse. *Of all the mornings! Okay, got to get it together. Think!*

I'm supposed to meet Tara and Trish at the courthouse at eight. Trial starts at nine. It's forty-five minutes on a light traffic day, and today is Monday morning. That thought sparks more cursing. Then I remind myself that the new Leslie doesn't curse.

I throw on clean underwear and a bra, brush my teeth and then my hair with a few quick, furious strokes, twist it into a bun, and then step into my skirt. I put on a white blouse, partially buttoned, and take a quick glance in the mirror. What a disaster! Why does stuff like this always happen to *me?*

I pack my makeup kit—eye shadow, blush, lipstick, mascara, eyeliner—and grab a belt and a pair of heels. Five after eight!

I run out to the car barefoot and throw everything into the passenger seat. Then I run back in and grab my briefcase, eye the coffee pot with envy, and snatch my purse. I sprint back out to the car and realize I'm sweating before I climb into the driver's seat. Deodorant!

I run back upstairs and grab the powder-fresh Mitchum out of my drawer. I apply it by the time I hit the kitchen and leave it on the counter.

I climb into my car for the second time and back out of the driveway, slam my Accord in drive and take off down the street. I've got forty minutes to get my rolling makeup parlor into the court parking lot.

Before I flip down my mirror and start applying any makeup, I speed-dial Bella. Breathless, I explain I'm running late and ask her to call the clients and the court.

"They won't start without you," Bella promises.

Bella was wrong.

I arrive at the courthouse a few minutes after nine, amazed at the stupidity of Tidewater rush-hour drivers. I half walk, half run from the parking lot to the courthouse. I arrive at the courthouse seriously short of breath. My oxygen-starved heart is pounding like a jackhammer, and I make myself slow down—no case is worth a heart attack. I check the bulletin board and find our courtroom assignment. Judge East, Courtroom Number 3. Maybe my luck is beginning to change.

Thank you, Lord. And oh, um, sorry about the cursing.

As I ride the escalators up to the courtroom, I am rehearsing my "sorry I'm late" speech. If Brad's taught me anything, he's taught me how to apologize for not being on time. But when I finally walk through the doors of the courtroom, it's like I've been spun back into the world's most cruel nightmare. Is this some kind of sadistic practical joke?

The courtroom is empty.

Except, seated in the back row, playing a handheld GameBoy, is Jamie.

He looks up through the forest of bangs covering his eyes. "They told me to wait here for you," he says. "They wanted me to tell you that the case got transferred to Courtroom Number 8."

Eight. Judge Farley. "Why?" I ask.

"I dunno. A little while ago everybody was in here. Then the judge came out and asked to talk to the lawyers. That other guy—"

"Mitchell Taylor?"

"I guess so. I dunno. That other lawyer went up to where the judge was sitting, and then she told everybody to go to Courtroom 8."

How can this be happening? Mitchell Taylor is a snake.

"Well, let's go find 'em," I tell Jamie.

He flips his hair, turns off his GameBoy, and rises to follow me.

"Thanks," I say. But as usual, Jamie doesn't respond.

CHAPTER SEVENTY-FOUR

Nice of you to join us, Ms. Connors," snaps Farley. He has taken the bench after his clerk informed him that I had finally arrived.

"Sorry, Your Honor. I slept through my alarm."

"Well, you've kept a lot of people waiting," he says, glaring at me with his dark pea-sized eyes.

"Sorry, Your Honor."

Farley punishes me by remaining silent for a moment as he writes some notes on his legal pad. I stand respectfully at my counsel table, with Tara seated next to me. Behind me, in the spectator section, are members of the press, the entire jury panel, and a few other lawyers and clerks who couldn't resist dropping in on this high-profile case.

I'm not sure if I should remain standing or sit down. I tentatively slink into my seat. As soon as my rear touches the chair, Farley raises his double chin and barks at me. "Ms. Connors!"

I'm immediately back on my feet. I'll bet he's enjoying this.

"Is defense counsel ready?"

"Yes, Your Honor."

"Do you have any motions?"

Motions. In this morning's chaos I almost forgot. "Yes, Your Honor. I do have one motion that we would like to argue before we impanel the jury."

"Which one is that?" Farley asks.

It's a subtle blow by this prosecution-oriented judge. He's trying to make me state the nature of my motion in earshot of the jury, or at least say that I want to approach the bench. Either way, I'll look like I'm hiding something.

"Perhaps we should approach the bench," says Mitchell Taylor, as he rises to his feet and buttons his suit coat.

Both Farley and I look at him the way you would someone who objected at a wedding. Didn't he understand what Farley was trying to do?

"Approach," says the judge.

Mitchell and I shuffle to the bench. I am clutching the twelve-page brief I drafted on this matter. As Brad instructed, it's got enough cases to make it look like I'm trying, but it's weak enough that I'm sure to lose the motion it supports.

"I have a motion to exclude the confession of my client," I whisper. I place the brief on the bench in front of Judge Farley. "You might want to take a brief recess and read our authorities."

"That won't be necessary," says Mitchell. He's looking straight at Farley, with an aura of confidence so thick that you'd think the jury was composed of his Sunday-school class. "We don't intend to introduce the confession."

I look at Mitchell—*are you kidding?*—and Farley looks at me. Then Farley picks up the brief and hands it back to me, gloating. "Guess we won't be needing this," he says. "Now, have you got any other motions?"

"Not at this time." I try to maintain my decorum of professionalism. My mind is already racing with implications. Mitchell will rely solely on the physical evidence. To combat it, I'll *have* to put Tara on the stand.

"Then let's see if we can get a jury in the box," says Farley.

At two thirty in the afternoon, Brad slips into Courtroom Number 8. Tara slides down one seat so Brad can sit next to me at counsel table.

The judge is busy instructing the jury about its role in the case and other aspects of courtroom logistics.

"How'd it go?" I ask. Brad had called at the lunch break to tell me that they had completed their closing arguments just before lunch.

"I've got good news and bad," whispers Brad.

I take a deep breath. "Let's start with the bad."

"We lost," he whispers. "According to what one jury member told the press, it took them fifteen minutes to elect a foreman and then they took a straw vote. Everyone voted against us, but then the jury decided, on a split decision, to order one more free lunch before finalizing their verdict. After lunch, they took another fifteen minutes to review the evidence, then ordered dessert. They announced their defense verdict at one thirty."

I'm not sure what to say. I search for some silver lining in that cloud, but if there is one, I'm sure not seeing it. "And the good news?"

"After the verdict, the producers of the show announced that Brandon will have a chance to win back Annie's heart. He's going to be one of the bachelors on *Revenge of the Girl Next Door.* You should have seen him when they made the announcement. He looked like he'd just won a million bucks."

"How sweet," I say sarcastically as Judge Farley concludes his charge.

"Does the prosecution have an opening statement?" the judge asks.

Brad is tugging on my elbow again. He cups his mouth to my ear as he eyeballs the jury. "How'd you get stuck with them?" he asks.

It's indeed a far cry from the type of jury we wanted. Our first priority was to get a few jurors who had been subject to abuse at the hands of a family member, and there were several on the panel. But Mitchell objected to each of them, and Farley dutifully dismissed them for cause. Next, I wanted some single moms, preferably ones who had been the victim of a nasty divorce. I did manage to get two single moms, but both claimed that they got along pretty well with their exes. In total, the men outnumber the women—definitely a bad sign—there are three singles on the twelve-member jury, and only four jurors have a college education.

"Well," I whisper to Brad, "all the smart jurors were busy in federal court this morning."

He reaches down and gently places a hand on my ribs. Then, ever so slyly, he tickles me!

I jerk hard to the left and almost giggle, drawing a nasty stare from Judge Farley.

It's great that my partner has finally joined me in court. I think.

CHAPTER SEVENTY-FIVE

Mitchell Taylor rises and looks every inch the lawyer in his blue pinstriped suit, red tie, and starched white shirt. He buttons his suit coat and walks to the front of the jury box with no notes, his feet shoulder-width apart, his impressive granite jaw set firm in determination.

"I am Mitchell Taylor," he says. "And I represent the people of the Commonwealth of Virginia."

"Makes me want to salute," mumbles Brad.

"In a few minutes," says Mitchell, "I will talk to you about the people's evidence…my evidence. But first, I want to talk to you about my duty…and about your duty."

Mitchell takes a few steps, looks down in contemplation, then looks squarely into the eyes of the jurors. He seems so in charge, so sure of himself—every hair in place, his suit hanging perfectly on his athletic body. I am amazed that he is doing this without notes. How did Tara get stuck with me?

"When I first became a prosecutor," said Mitchell, "I was sure that the lines would always be crystal clear. I would prosecute bad guys, and my witnesses would be good guys. My victims would always be saints, relying on me to avenge their deaths or their injuries—"

"Objection!" To my surprise, Brad has jumped to his feet and objected to Mitchell's opening. "Could the court ask Mr. Taylor to stick to the facts?" Brad says.

Farley looks as surprised as me. "Are you handling defendant's opening?" he asks Brad.

"No, Your Honor."

"Then why don't we let your co-counsel make the objections?"

Brad grunts something and sits down.

I lean back toward him, keeping my eye on Mitchell. "What was that all about?" I say out of the side of my mouth.

"Rhythm. Knock him off stride."

But he has underestimated Mitchell Taylor.

"My point is this," says Mitchell, "I will not only stick to the facts, but I will follow the facts wherever they lead. That is my solemn duty"—he pauses—"and my pledge. Your duty is to return a verdict based on those facts, however unpleasant that might be. And if either one of us shirks our duty, if I back away because the facts and the evidence don't lead where I wish they would, or if you back away because emotion or sympathy overwhelm your duty to base a verdict on the evidence, then we will have compounded a tragedy and failed in our most important civic duty."

Mitchell lowers his voice as he confides some of the difficulties of his case. "The commonwealth does not get to pick its victims. They are not all Boy Scouts. In this case, the victim was a man with many positive traits, but he was also a deeply flawed man. At times he was cruel to his children. At times he abused his wife. But we have laws against that. And if his wife or children had come to me and asked me to prosecute, then I would have come before you on their behalf, pleading that we deliver the justice they requested."

Mitchell stops and draws a deep breath. "But unfortunately, they did not. Instead, the defendant, sixteen-year-old Tara Bannister"—Mitchell turns and points at her and Tara has that deer-in-the-headlights look—"shot her stepfather in cold blood, while he sat in a chair defenseless, then watched him die, waited some substantial period of time, and then shot him again, in the forehead. She then called the police and lied to them about the way it happened.

"We will show you that the defendant was proud of what she did and bragged to her friends about it. We will show you that she committed this crime not in self-defense but, in her words, for 'pay-back.' We will show you an instant message where she describes how she made her stepdad beg before she shot him—once for herself and then, later, for her mom. We will show you that the defendant's only regret is that she didn't shoot her stepfather one more time on her brother's behalf. We will show you that she talked about doing it ahead of time and illegally acquired the gun she used in the crime. And we will show you, using her own words typed on her own computer, how she thinks she can just waltz into court and fool you into thinking it was self-defense."

I study the body language of the jury and it is not good. They look at Mitchell with intense and stony gazes, and occasionally shoot a fiery glance at me or Tara. He has done a masterful job of creating hostility toward my client while distancing himself from James Bannister. He is Mitchell Taylor, pursuer of justice wherever it leads, and I am Leslie Connors, the slippery defense lawyer who helps guilty clients skate.

For the next twenty minutes Mitchell walks the jury through the scientific evidence. He talks about stippling and tattooing, gunpowder residue and blood-spatter patterns. He trots out lots of pictures, some of which make the jurors wince, and he speaks with the precise authority of a man who has nothing to hide.

About halfway through, Brad is in my ear again. "Stop taking notes," he says.

I wrinkle my brow and look at him. *Why? Mitchell is laying out the blueprint for his entire case, and my partner is telling me to stop taking notes?*

"The jury is watching you," Brad whispers. "Show them that Taylor is saying nothing worth writing down. Show them you're bored."

I put down my pen, stare ahead at the judge's bench for a few minutes and then lean back in my chair with my hands folded in front of me. I pretend that Mitchell is reading from the phone book, and I glance around the courtroom like I'm looking for something worthy of my interest.

"Much better," whispers Brad.

But then Mitchell comes to the end of his opening, and as his voice crescendos, I find it impossible not to lean forward and give him my undivided attention. I stare bullets at him, knowing that the jury is watching, hoping they will pick up on the contempt I have for a man so passionate about prosecuting an abused sixteen-year-old girl.

"Justice is often depicted as a blindfolded lady, with a pair of scales in one hand and a sword in the other," Mitchell says. "The sword represents judgment. But it is used only after a careful and fair weighing of the evidence, and that process is represented by the scales. It's exactly what I've tried to do for you in the last fifteen or twenty minutes. Lady Justice is blindfolded for a reason. In this country, she is not to be swayed by the color of your skin, your economic status, your age, or the fact that you happen to have an abusive father. She is not to be swayed by emotional arguments and passionate appeals to ignore the law and the evidence just because you feel sorry for the defendant. For Justice to be true to her charge, she must also be blind."

Mitchell gazes across the jury panel one more time. "I would urge you to remember that as you listen to the arguments of defense counsel."

CHAPTER SEVENTY-SIX

T he court orders a brief recess after Mitchell's opening, which gives me a chance to fret even more about the one I'm about to give. I don't like the approach Brad has talked me into taking. I would be much more comfortable talking to the jury about the law and the evidence, analyzing the case piece by piece. But Brad has convinced me that we have too many holes in our theory for that approach. He has convinced me to attack and to jack up the emotional level in the courtroom.

But that is not my style and therefore violates the primary rule of advocacy that Brad taught me: be yourself. I tell Brad this as I stand next to him in the hallway, hugging myself defensively, speaking low enough so I cannot be heard by the press or even our client, who is standing a few feet away with her mom.

"Do you want me to give it?" asks Brad.

I shake my head no. We both know that the jury needs to bond with one primary lawyer during a case. That lawyer needs to give both the opening and closing. And we both know that in this case that lawyer needs to be me.

"I'm just nervous," I say. My palms are sweaty, my mouth is parched, I'm shifting from one foot to the other, and I feel like I'm going to puke.

"Heart okay?" Brad asks, his voice a thin whisper.

I nod, though thinking about it seems to make the little monster skip even faster.

"What do you want me to do?" Brad asks. "I mean, you've got to give this thing in a couple of minutes. How can I help?"

I let out a deep sigh. "Quit thinking like a man for about two minutes," I say. "Always trying to figure out a way to fix things. I know I've got to give this opening. I know I'm going to be super nervous until I get started. I know that Fowler and Anderson and Taylor are all going to hate me and be gunning for me after I attack them. Right now, I don't need solutions; I need someone to commiserate with me."

Brad looks like he wonders if the flow of oxygen to my brain has been completely shut off. "I get it," he says. Then tentatively, "I think." He glances around, as if he could be committed to a mental health facility if anybody actually heard this conversation. "You don't want me to suggest solutions; you just want me to listen to how nerve-racking this is for you?"

"Precisely."

"And empathize."

"Right."

"Okay." He nods slowly, staring at me like I'm some new species he just discovered at the zoo. "Then you're right. You should be worried. We're about to take on the entire Virginia Beach law-enforcement community with an opening that is incredibly high risk. If I were you, Leslie, I'd be barfing right now myself, and I've been doing this for years."

"Thanks," I say sarcastically, my lips pursed in a thin, nervous line. "That's better."

***

"Ladies and gentlemen of the jury, my name is Leslie Connors. Together with my partner, Brad Carson, it is our privilege to represent the sixteen-year-old defendant in this case, Tara Bannister."

I am standing behind the podium that Brad moved in front of the jury box for this presentation. I swear my knees are knocking together so loudly they can be heard in the next courtroom, and I hardly recognize my own trembling voice. But I have started, and soon the nerves will recede.

"You have heard Mr. Taylor talk a lot about your duty, but he failed to mention perhaps your greatest duty of all." I pause for a moment to allow them to focus. I am speaking ad lib here, but it needs to be said. "You have a duty to keep an open mind until all the evidence is in. You have a duty to reserve judgment until you hear both sides of the case. And most important"—I turn and wave toward Tara—"you have a duty to assume my client is innocent unless the commonwealth can prove otherwise beyond a reasonable doubt. It's the same benefit of the doubt you would want if you were a defendant."

"Objection!" Mitchell's on his feet. "That's improper." He's referring to the so-called Golden Rule prohibition—lawyers can't ask jurors to put themselves in the shoes of the defendant or the victim.

"Sustained," growls Farley, and it appears Mitchell has won the first legal skirmish. In fact, he has only highlighted my point, just as I hoped he would.

I draw resolve from this objection, like a warrior who's suffered a flesh wound in battle. There's no turning back now. I step out from behind the podium, leaving my notes on the lectern. Who needs them? I've been over this speech so many times that it's chiseled into my memory forever.

"Mr. Taylor says he wants us to follow the evidence wherever it leads. 'That's our duty,' he says. Okay. Fair enough." I pause, turning to Mitchell Taylor. "But is he really willing to do that?"

Now I take a step or two closer to the jury. "The evidence, you see, is only as reliable as those who collect it in the field, those who supervise its chain of custody and compilation, those who safeguard the evidence until it's presented to you. At every link in that chain of custody—crime-scene investigation by the police, preservation and testing of the evidence by investigators, and compilation and presentation of the evidence by prosecutors—there are opportunities to tamper with the evidence or lose certain evidence or alter the nature of it. Stippling and tattooing, gunpowder residue and blood patterns are only as reliable as those who collect, analyze, and present them. In this case, that reliability is zero."

I pause for a moment, recognizing that my words are falling like bombs into a deathly quiet courtroom. Though I've not raised my voice, pounded my fist on the podium, or even used many hand gestures, I have captivated them. These are serious charges, made even more so by my somber delivery and the high stakes in the case.

And the funny thing is, I am no longer the least bit nervous.

"Is Mr. Taylor willing to follow the evidence there?" I ask. "Is he willing to ask the hard questions?

"We will show that his lead investigator, Detective Lawrence Anderson, a man who had the opportunity to affect every piece of evidence collected at the crime scene, cannot be trusted." I take a deep breath before this next line. Brad has insisted that I include it, though he still refuses to tell me the evidence he thinks will support it. "We will prove to you that Anderson is the type of police officer who will do whatever it takes to ensure a conviction, including manufacturing evidence."

"Objection!" Mitchell is on his feet like a rocket. "Judge, she's got no basis for that! Until today, nobody's even mentioned evidence tampering in this case. This is ridiculous."

"Approach," says Farley.

When I get to the judge's bench, I feel Brad at my shoulder.

Farley puts his hand over his mike. His face is beet red and his jaw is clenched. "Ms. Connors, I run a clean courtroom, which means that I require defense attorneys to stick to the facts. You don't just waltz in here and accuse the Virginia Beach Police Department of being corrupt without evidence. Now if you've got something on Detective Anderson, I want to hear about it, and I want to hear about it right now. And if not"—he points a trembling finger in my face— "young lady, you're on thin ice with this court."

If Farley is trying to intimidate me, it's not working.

"I've got evidence, Judge."

Farley turns to Mitchell Taylor. "Has she shared it with you?"

"Nothing, Your Honor."

Farley then glares back at me. "Then let's hear it."

"Not now."

Farley leans forward a little more. "Ms. Connors, you raised it in your opening. I've got to decide whether to instruct the jury to disregard those comments. If you've got evidence, I want to hear it."

I return his stare in silence, my anger in full bloom now. I've got to try this case against both the prosecutor and the judge?

"Judge," says Brad, his voice surprisingly devoid of any anger. "Detective Anderson tried to intimidate my co-counsel into dropping a certain theory of the case. He threatened to manufacture a drug charge against her if she didn't cooperate. We reported this to the Internal Affairs Department of the Virginia Beach Police Department. I'd be shocked if Mr. Taylor is unaware of a disciplinary investigation against the lead detective in this case."

"Is that true?" Farley asks Mitchell.

"Yes, Your Honor, but there's no evidence that he tried to manufacture—"

Farley's hand is up. "Save it for the jury," he says. Then he gives me one last glare. "Be careful, Ms. Connors."

I just glare back, too stubborn to tell him what he wants to hear. "Oh, she will be," says Brad.

As I step back in front of the jury, they seem to be more open to me. You can see it in some of their faces. Maybe they expected the defendant to just hide behind the burden of proof, but we're suggesting a whole lot more. Corrupt police officers, shady prosecutors. At least they know it's going to be interesting.

"Now, Mr. Taylor suggests that my client should not have taken matters into her own hands. In the comfort and safety of this courtroom, he likes to second-guess young Tara Bannister. But Mr. Taylor didn't have to live with an abusive stepfather. He didn't have to come home to a mom whose face he hardly recognized because an out-of-control stepfather had used it as a punching bag. He didn't have to wonder if the next word or the next innocent action might set the man off and drive him into a torrent of profanity and abuse. He didn't have to live with fear every second of his life."

I stop in midstream and look at the ground. This is the part I have dreaded most, the part that could ruin an innocent man's career if I'm wrong. I lower my voice, as if maybe a softer tone can keep these facts just between me and the jury. "And there's a reason Tara couldn't just report these allegations of abuse to the police and let them handle it: because she knew that the police ultimately would bring any evidence they gathered to the prosecutors, and she knew that the prosecutors ultimately reported, each and every one of them, to the commonwealth's attorney, and she knew that the commonwealth's attorney—"

"Objection!" Mitchell sees what's coming and he tries to head it off. "Objection, Judge."

"—is the same man who assaulted her, while Tara's stepfather watched."

"Approach!" shouts Farley.

The courtroom is buzzing as we approach the bench, and my heart feels like it's going to pound right through my chest. I know I'm about to get chewed out again—the price you pay for defending your client. But I also feel I've done the right thing. Maybe other lawyers would not have gone this far, but that's what separates Carson & Associates from everyone else.

"I promised the judge you'd be careful," whispers Brad as he joins me in front of Farley's bench. "Tsk, tsk."

I give him a sharp elbow to his bony ribs and brace myself for the snarling judge.

After my tongue-lashing, I plant myself in front of the jury box for the third time. This time the jury is looking at me wide-eyed, wondering who I might accuse next. I suddenly feel like one of those supermarket tabloids that I so despise—too outrageous to be taken seriously but too juicy to be ignored.

I swallow hard as I get ready to promise them something I was really hoping to avoid. But as a good trial lawyer, I try to act enthusiastic about it. "When we get a chance to present our case, you will hear from Tara," I promise. *And I hope she doesn't lose her cool or say something stupid or dig herself a bigger hole than she's already in.* "She will tell you how her stepfather, James Bannister, assaulted her on the night in question when she first arrived home and then attacked her later that night when she tried to get some ice to keep the swelling down on her bruised face. She will tell you how frightened she was of her stepfather's hair-trigger temper and how she felt the need to have a gun to protect herself. She will tell you why she had to use that gun on March 25 of this year to save her own life."

I pause for a moment and walk over to our counsel table, where Brad hands me three large pieces of foam board with enlarged photographs mounted on each one. They are each the size of a picture that might hang in somebody's living room. I walk back to the jury and lay the foam boards down on the podium. *"Show them, don't tell them,"* Brad had said as I prepared this opening. *"Remember, we're a visual society now."*

"At the end of this case, ladies and gentlemen, you will have to decide whether my client, Tara Bannister, acted in self-defense. The judge will tell you that self-defense requires that someone be under an imminent threat of serious physical harm. But that's a lot of lawyer talk. In reality, you will have to decide if self-defense requires this…" I show them the first photograph. It is a picture of Tara's face from the night of the crime, taken from the police video of her confession. The bruising and swelling on her face are clearly visible.

"This is a picture of what James Bannister did to Tara on the night in question," I explain.

I put the photograph down and pick up the second one. "Or does it require this?"

I show them the photo of Trish taken from the night in question. Her face is badly bruised, her eye nearly swollen shut. "This is what James Bannister did to Trish Bannister on the same night," I explain.

Mitchell Taylor is on his feet. "Judge, I object. Ms. Connors isn't claiming that the defendant acted in order to prevent harm to her mother. That picture is highly inflammatory and not at all relevant."

"I agree," says Farley before I can explain.

"And if the other poster board is a picture of someone besides the defendant the night of the murder, then I would object to that one as well," says Mitchell.

"Is the other foam board a picture of the defendant from the night in question?" asks Farley.

"No, Your Honor."

"Then I'm instructing you not to show it to the jury," says Farley.

I act disappointed, but I can already see the jurors' collective imaginations filling in the blanks. They probably think that there is some third woman who has been abused by Bannister in this other picture

and that her face looks worse than the prior two. The actual picture—
a shot of a casket—was far less powerful than what they are now conjuring up in their minds.

"My point," I say, "is that you must decide how much abuse Tara
Bannister had to endure before she was entitled to act in self-defense.
We believe that when your stepfather punches you and later tries to
choke you to death when you walk by to get some ice for your
wounds…well…we believe you're entitled to use deadly force to protect yourself.

"And when you hear all the evidence, we think you might agree."

CHAPTER SEVENTY-SEVEN

The court calls for a recess, and everybody on our side of the courtroom congratulates me on a great opening. I feel relief that it's over but no great pride in what I did. I suppose it's the same way a prizefighter might feel if he were to walk up to the other fighter during a press conference and punch him in the gut. We've proven we mean business and we're not going down without a fight, but we've still got to back it up in the ring.

To nobody's surprise, Harlan Fowler heads straight into the hallway to face the television cameras and start clearing his name. I have no desire to join him in front of the cameras, so I linger at our counsel table for a few minutes, talking in hushed tones to Brad, Tara, and Trish. This allows me to momentarily avoid the press, due to the standing rule in Virginia Beach circuit court for cases like this. The television stations and newspaper are all allowed one "pool" camera in the courtroom. The feed from the pool camera is made available to all the local affiliates. That way the proceedings can be televised in a non-invasive manner that avoids the chaos of a dozen television cameramen and reporters jockeying for position.

The net result is that the media horde sets up camp in the hallway, mobbing the litigants as soon as they leave the courtroom.

Suddenly, I've got a dilemma. "I don't want to go out there right now and face them," I tell Brad.

"So don't."

"But I've got to go out there," I say, making a face that telegraphs my real meaning, "because it's on my way to someplace else."

Brad furrows his puzzled brow. Sometimes men can be so thick.

"She's got to pee," Tara interjects.

"I knew that," Brad says, and immediately he's got a plan. "We'll go out there together. I'll draw the media fire; you make a run for it."

"Sounds like a plan."

We walk toward the back doors. "Don't say anything inflammatory," I caution Brad, as if I'm now the senior partner since I gave such a stellar opening. "I think I inflamed enough emotions during my opening."

"Don't worry," says Brad. "I'll just issue a few soothing statements to calm things down a little." But I think I detect a slight grin forming on his lips.

I walk through the doors and notice the cameras still circled around Fowler, capturing every word. He is saying something about clearing his name and cheap defense-lawyer tactics.

"Ms. Connors," someone calls out, and the cameras swing toward me. "Can you give us any details about the alleged assault by the commonwealth's attorney that you mentioned during your opening statement?"

"No comment," I say and keep walking. Behind me, I hear my fiancé.

"You want details?" he says. The cameras now swing toward him. "Stick around until our client testifies."

"Mr. Carson, the commonwealth's attorney says these charges are just desperate lies. What do you say to that?"

I'm now past the crowd of reporters, but I slow down a little so I can hear Brad's response.

"Tell the commonwealth's attorney to appoint a special prosecutor for this case so that Mr. Fowler can take the stand and testify," I hear Brad say. "Then I'll cross-examine him and we'll find out who's lying."

That's supposed to calm things down?

I'm now halfway to the rest rooms, but I hear another shouted question.

"Any comments on the verdict from federal court?" I hear some-one shout.

I smile to myself. I'll bet he didn't expect that one.

"I don't want to tell you how to do your jobs," Brad says. "But I think the much better story is this state court trial. If I were you, I wouldn't waste valuable news time talking about the *Girl Next Door* case."

I hear laughter as I enter the ladies' room.

As I emerge from the ladies' room, I notice none other than Harlan Fowler coming down the hallway toward me. I duck my head and angle wide enough to give him plenty of room to pass. Instead, he steps in front of me.

"We've got to talk."

I look him squarely in the eye. "Talk," I say with a shrug.

"Not here." He glances down the hallway. "There's a conference room back there," he says gruffly. "Let's use that."

I don't know why I follow him into the conference room. I should tell him no, tell him that if he wants to talk with me he can talk right here. But instead I go with him. I guess I feel a little guilty for ambushing him in court, or maybe it's just that his voice is so authoritative—telling him no is like telling your dad no when you're still in grade school. For whatever reason, I slide into the conference room with him.

He slams the door.

Anger is etched on his face. It dawns on me that he is blocking my way to the door.

"What you did in that courtroom is wrong." Fowler is seething, speaking through clenched teeth. "I didn't touch that girl, Leslie. It's taken me two decades to build a reputation of integrity, and you destroy it in one sentence…one filthy lie. Two decades, Leslie."

I don't respond. The man is scaring me. There's something in his eyes that is beyond anger.

"What you did is criminal," he says.

There's nowhere to run so I just hold my ground. "What *you* did was criminal," I shoot back. "I'm just doing my job."

"Don't pull that garbage on me," Fowler says sharply. "Defense lawyers do their jobs every day without pulling stunts like that. There are rules, Leslie, unwritten and unspoken…rules that make the system work. You defend your client, but you don't attack the prosecutors personally. We prosecute your client, but we don't go after you personally. You broke the rules, Leslie." Fowler pauses and gives me a sideways glare. "And when you come after us, we come after you."

Every muscle in my body is on fight-or-flight alert. My heart feels like it's ready to explode, and the synapses in my mind are all firing at once. I'm so tense I can hardly think clearly.

"Is that a threat?" I ask. My limbs are now visibly shaking.

Fowler smirks and shakes his head. "I don't use threats, Leslie. I'm just telling you the way it is. I didn't pick this fight. Remember?"

"I think our conversation is over," I say. I try to walk around him, but he steps in front of me again.

"One more thing," he says. "And this has nothing to do with the Bannister case." He is nearly nose to nose with me. "Remember the Keisha McFadden case?"

I nod, still returning his stare. We are like a couple of prizefighters getting instructions from the referee a few seconds before the opening bell.

"Turns out that her drug purchase was within one mile of a school zone," Fowler says. "That's a mandatory statutory enhancement of five years added to any penalty she might get. Looks like we won't be pleading that one out after all. I've assigned it to Mitchell Taylor."

I didn't see this coming, and it knocks the wind out of me. This man is so powerful in so many ways. "She's got a family, Harlan. Two little boys. She can't do five years."

"We've all got families, Leslie," Fowler says in a menacing tone. "And I didn't pick this fight."

Then he turns and leaves the conference room, leaving the door open behind him. I hear him call out in a friendly tone to one of his reporter friends. I am angry, scared, and stunned. I finally manage to reach over and close the door. I sink into one of the padded chairs and stare straight ahead, my heart pounding against my chest. I think about Fowler's last comment, that look in his eyes, everything that lies ahead. Pressure builds in my chest and I find myself sucking for air, hyperventilating. Is this what a heart attack feels like?

I start getting dizzy. I put my elbows on my thighs, clasping my hands, and lowering my head toward my knees. *Deep breaths. Relax. Pray.*

There is no sharp pain in my chest, just a lot of pressure and a racing heart. Still, this can't be good. I stare hard at the floor, forcing myself to think of nothing, willing myself to calm down. *Breathe in, breathe out. I can do all things through Christ who strengthens me.*

Where did that come from? I flash back to the words of the pastor on Sunday. *All things,* I remind myself.

My breathing is slowing down, and I feel myself starting to relax. Should I call 911? If I do, then I'll end up going straight to the hospital and probably under the knife. If I tell Brad, he'll insist that I get checked out immediately. He'll handle the rest of the trial on his own. I know he's ten times the lawyer I'll ever be, but Tara really needs a woman on her side.

Tara needs *me.*

I stand up and take a few more deep breaths. My hands are steady, my breathing is returning to normal. And my resolve is stronger than ever.

A few hours earlier, even a few minutes earlier, I was unsure if Fowler had ever really assaulted Tara. Sure, I said he did it in my opening statement, but that was something I *had* to say. Deep down, I really didn't know who to believe.

But now Fowler has shown his true colors. I'm convinced he assaulted Tara. And he probably would have made a run at me if he thought he could get away with it.

But if he thinks he can bully Leslie Connors, then he has underestimated the pluck of the Irish. As someone who claims to be a student of history, Fowler, of all people, should know better.

CHAPTER SEVENTY-EIGHT

M itchell Taylor plays it smart the rest of the afternoon, grilling Detective Louis Gonzales on direct examination and compiling a mountain of scientific evidence to support his case. I try to act bored while Tara unfortunately seems to hang on Gonzales's every word.

Gonzales teaches the jury about the science of gunshot wounds. He trots out some horrid photographs of bullet wounds from other cases to show how gunshots fired at close range leave pinpoint hemorrhages around the entry wound due to the discharge of burned powder and fragments. He is standing in front of the jury box as Mitchell questions him, so that he can use a pointer and refer to blown-up photos on an easel. "This is called stippling or tattooing," explains Gonzales. He then shows the jury a photograph of the entry wound for the bullet that entered Bannister's chest, puncturing his lung and tearing up some major arteries.

"The absence of any stippling or tattooing around this wound shows that the bullet was fired at a distance of more than twelve feet," Gonzales explains. "Also, if the bullet were fired at a closer range, you would expect to see smoke or soot around the wound. We have neither here."

"Could Mr. Bannister have been strangling the defendant when this shot was fired?" asks Mitchell.

"Not unless he has twelve-foot arms," says Gonzales.

Most of the jurors smile.

Next, Mitchell places another blown-up photograph on the easel for the jury to see. This one, says Gonzales, is a picture of the wound from the second bullet fired, the one that entered just above Bannister's left eye.

"In this photo, you can see some stippling around the entrance wound where the burned powder and bullet fragments hit the flesh." Gonzales points to several dark pinpoints on Bannister's forehead. "But it's not what we would call a contact wound, meaning that the gun was not actually touching the skin."

Now Gonzales turns to face the jury. "But the most unusual thing about this entry wound is the complete lack of any hemorrhaging around the wound."

"And what does that mean?" asks Mitchell.

"That the victim was already dead when this shot was fired," says Gonzales. "And his blood was no longer flowing."

"Impressive," whispers Brad. "Should we just plead guilty now?"

Gonzales returns to the witness chair and gives the jury a lecture on blood patterns and the geometry of bullet wounds. Then, using photos of the scene, including photos where a metal rod protrudes from the bullet wound on Bannister's chest to indicate the trajectory of the bullet, Gonzales leads the jury through his conclusions about the shootings. According to Gonzales, Bannister was sitting in his easy chair and Tara was about twenty-five feet away when the first shot was fired. He deduced this from the angle of entry for the bullet as well as the blood pattern on the chair. The second shot, says Gonzales, was fired as Tara stood over an already-dead James Bannister and shot him again in the forehead.

"How much longer?" asks Farley, checking his watch.

"Just a few more questions," says Mitchell.

"Very well."

"Was there a towel found over Mr. Bannister's face at the crime scene?"

"Yes."

"If someone had been hiding a gun under that towel and shot somebody at close range, would you expect to see a pattern of blood droplets on the towel from the wound to Mr. Bannister?"

"Certainly."

"Did you find that?"

"No. The only thing we found was blood smudged onto the towel where it had come in contact with Mr. Bannister's chest. But there was no blood-spatter pattern."

Mitchell now hands Gonzales the gun used by Tara and has it entered as an exhibit. "Did the police dust Commonwealth's Exhibit 14 for fingerprints?" asks Mitchell.

"Yes."

"And what did they find?"

"Fingerprints belonging to the defendant."

"Any others?"

"No."

"One more thing. Was the defendant checked for gunpowder residue on her hand?"

"Yes. The defendant had gunpowder residue on her right hand, indicating that she was definitely the one who pulled the trigger."

Farley calls it a day after Mitchell's direct examination of Gonzales, meaning my cross-examination will have to wait until tomorrow morning. After court, we run the media gauntlet and huddle with Tara, Trish, and Jamie before Brad and I head to our cars. Brad had asked Trish to bring Jamie into court for the opening statements. After that, he found a vacant courtroom and played with his Game-Boy until court concluded.

"Remember," I say to Tara, "no instant messages about the case—"

"I know, I know," she says.

Jamie is tugging on his mom's arm, but she is trying to brush him off. "How many days will this trial last?" she asks.

"C'mon," whines Jamie. He flicks his hair. "Let's go. I'm hot."

"Probably three," says Brad. "We'll most likely be done by the weekend."

Tara turns to me. "You were great today," she says.

"Thanks."

"Let's go!" says Jamie, tugging harder. He's flicking the hair and grunts a few indecipherable words.

"Just a minute," answers Trish.

Then it starts. Something in Jamie snaps and he starts cursing, pulling his mom's arm and then flailing at her. He spits, but it falls harmlessly on the pavement. Trish lets go of his arm and he throws his GameBoy down, mumbling the whole time. I glance around, embarrassed at the scene, and see one of the news camera guys, about ten feet away, filming this mess!

"Brad!" I exclaim, but he's already seen it. He walks toward the cameraman, placing himself between the camera and Jamie, and starts waving the guy off. "This is a private matter!" Brad yells. "What're you doing?"

Before I can even move I see Tara charging toward the cameraman. "You stupid jerk! You can't film this! Get that camera outta here!"

She is intercepted by Brad, who stands in her way, but can't keep her from cursing at the cameraman. The guy now has his camera trained on Tara, recording the entire scene.

"C'mon," Brad says. He's got an arm wrapped around her, walking her away. I hustle over and grab the other arm. "Let's go, Tara. Settle down."

She finally quits struggling, shakes Brad's hand off her arm, and stops yelling at the cameraman. She turns her back to him and walks a few steps toward her mom and her brother, escorted by Brad on one side and me on the other. She is breathing hard, and I can still see the anger bubbling just below the surface.

By now Jamie has calmed a little bit, and our whole gang starts moving toward the car, leaving the cameras behind us. I'm just about to breathe a sigh of relief when Tara suddenly turns, salutes the camera with her middle finger, then turns back around and huffs off toward her car.

"Smooth," says Brad, as we just stand there and watch Tara go. "Should be a good lead-in for the six o'clock news."

"If we're lucky, maybe they'll lead off with the *Girl Next Door* case," I respond. I force a smile, then Brad and I head to our separate cars.

CHAPTER SEVENTY-NINE

The second day of trial starts off with far less drama. I arrive at court a half hour early, and even Brad Carson gets there on time. Trish arrives with Tara in tow, wearing one of the "old maid" outfits we picked out on our shopping trip. "Sorry about last night," Tara says.

I shrug and give her a look that says she's not getting off that easy. "What's done is done."

After Farley comes rolling in, Gonzales climbs back up into the witness box, and I begin my cross-examination. It will be short and sweet. We've decided that the jury likes Gonzales—it's hard not to. Our script calls for making him the good cop. And I will use his cross-examination to make sure that they have to bring their bad cop into the courtroom to take his licks.

"Good morning, Detective Gonzales."

"Good morning."

"You are the lead detective on the case today. Is that right, Detective Gonzales?"

"Yes."

"But you have not always been the lead detective, correct?"

"That's right."

"In fact, the first lead detective assigned to this case was Detective Lawrence Anderson, is that right?"

"Yes."

"And he was the detective in charge the night the crime scene was investigated, right?"

"Yes."

"I mean, you never saw the crime scene with your own eyes,

right? You have reviewed the pictures, but Detective Anderson was actually there. Isn't that right?"

"Yes."

"And he talked to the witnesses and to my client?"

"Yes."

"He was in charge of collecting the evidence and establishing a chain of custody for it, correct?"

"Correct."

"And he would be the one who would oversee things like dusting the gun for fingerprints or checking my client's hands for gunpowder residue, right?"

"Yes."

"Would you agree, Detective Gonzales, that the integrity of any investigation is only as good as the integrity of the police officers who conduct it, particularly the detective in charge of it?"

Gonzales hesitates for a moment. *Good.* "Yes, I would agree. And Detective Anderson has an excellent reputation for integrity."

"Yet he was transferred off this case and replaced by you?"

"It was part of a routine reassignment of caseloads. Anderson had a lot of active cases and needed help."

I eye Gonzales with my best suspicious look, telegraphing to the jury that we're not getting the whole truth here. "But Anderson is still with the department, right?"

"Yes. Of course."

"Is there any reason that you're aware of, Detective Gonzales, why Detective Anderson could not come here and testify about what he found on the night of the shooting?"

This generates another momentary hesitation. This time Gonzales steals a quick glance at Mitchell Taylor. I decide to capitalize on it, just to make sure the jury caught it. "Mr. Taylor can't answer that question for you, Detective. You have to answer it for yourself."

"Objection!"

"Sustained."

Gonzales now looks confused and turns to the judge. "Do I need to answer the question?"

"You need to answer the original question," says His Honor. "I sustained the objection to defense counsel's last extraneous comment."

"No," says Gonzales. "I'm not aware of any reason he couldn't testify."

"Good. Then we'll save our questions for the detective who was actually there on the night of the shooting." I turn to the judge. "Nothing further."

Sooner or later every case finds its rhythm, and our case does so on Tuesday. Mitchell Taylor patiently builds his case, piece by piece, while Brad and I sit back and ask very few questions on cross-examination. "Sometimes," says Brad, "the best cross-examination is to just sit there and look bored during direct examination." Most of Mitchell's evidence is indisputable scientific evidence and seems to have little effect on the jury. They want to hear from Detective Anderson and from Tara Bannister. Everything else is window dressing.

Tuesday morning is consumed by the testimony of Dr. Albert Fancher, the Virginia Beach medical examiner, who nails down the cause of death and mostly repeats Gonzales's testimony about the bullet wounds and the damage done by each bullet. I notice a few of the jurors stifling yawns, and I keep my cross-examination short and sweet, mostly picking at some of his characterizations of the bullet wounds.

The rest of the day is given to equally dry and monotonous testimony from a ballistics expert, a fingerprint expert, and a representative from the ATF, who testifies that a trace of the gun marked as Exhibit 14 confirms that it was stolen two years ago. I don't deem any of these experts worthy of cross-examination except the fingerprint expert. From him, I elicit the obvious admission that fingerprints could be wiped off a gun if somebody had, in fact, used the gun before Tara did.

At 4:30 Mitchell is asked to call his next witness and finally says the name we've all been waiting for: "Detective Lawrence Anderson."

"How long will Detective Anderson be on the stand?" asks Farley.

"Several hours."

"Then let's start his testimony tomorrow," says the judge. Farley has been fighting sleep most of the afternoon.

After court recesses, I give my standard warning to Tara—no IMs. But tonight I add a caveat. "And no obscene gestures to cameramen, either."

She gives me a sheepish little smile. "I said I'm sorry."

"It's okay."

Then she does something totally out of character. She thanks me again for being her lawyer and then gives me a quick little hug. Nothing cheesy or overly sentimental, just a quick and awkward squeeze.

It so surprises me that I really don't know what to say or do. There is a moment of uncomfortable silence, then I say, "I'm proud to be your lawyer, Tara."

And tonight, I really mean it.

O n Wednesday morning Detective Lawrence Anderson takes the witness stand and hunches his thin frame forward like the vulture he is. Contempt for this man crawls all over my skin. He is wearing a white shirt and red tie, a blue blazer and black pants. His pockmarked face shows no emotion as Mitchell Taylor asks some preliminary questions. He has gelled his hair back like a cop from a 1990 television show. He glances over at me and scowls.

Mitchell carefully walks Anderson through the events on the night in question, and it seems to me, for the first time in this case, that Mitchell Taylor is clearly uncomfortable. It takes him about two hours with the witness to retrace the evidence already introduced through the testimony of Detective Gonzales. Though he spends a little more time with Anderson on chain-of-custody issues, it's obvious to me that Mitchell would never have called Anderson to testify if we hadn't made such a big deal about his credibility to the jury.

"Did you manufacture, alter, or otherwise corrupt any evidence in this case?" Mitchell asks in conclusion.

"No," says Anderson. "Never."

"No further questions."

Brad immediately stands to cross-examine Anderson. I had argued that Anderson should be my witness, but as the senior member of our firm, Brad overruled me. "Besides," said Brad, "I've got some evidence against this guy that I wasn't at liberty to tell you."

Brad takes a couple steps toward Anderson, then stops. He waits for what seems an interminable length of time. "Never?" asks Brad.

"Never."

"How about in other cases? Have you ever manufactured evidence in other cases?"

"Never."

"Have you ever threatened to manufacture evidence in other cases? Have you ever threatened to prosecute somebody based on trumped-up charges if they didn't do what you wanted?"

"No."

"Never?"

Anderson stares at Brad and waits, as if he expects Mitchell Taylor to object. Then Anderson reaches out and takes a slow and deliberate drink of water from the glass sitting in front of him, never taking his eyes off Brad. "Never, Counselor. Not once."

"But if you did," pushes Brad, "and if I could prove you did, would you agree that your word wouldn't be worth much in this case?"

"I didn't," says Anderson sharply. "So it doesn't matter."

Brad paces a little, back and forth, moving closer to Anderson. What a showman. "Isn't it true that on Saturday, May 28, this year, you followed my associate, Leslie Connors, to a Schlotzsky's Deli and threatened to prosecute her for a bogus crime if she didn't stop pursuing one of her leads in this case?"

The accusation, made so matter-of-factly, seems to rock the courtroom back on its heels, sucking the air out of the room. Anderson snickers and shakes his head. "That's the most ridiculous thing I've ever heard, Mr. Carson. But coming from you, it's hardly surprising."

Brad walks over to our counsel table and pulls a copy of the *National Inquisitor* with my picture on the front out of a folder.

"Are you sure you know what you're doing?" I whisper.

"Not really," he whispers and then walks back to the well of the courtroom.

"Now, Detective Anderson, have you ever seen this photograph before?" Brad points to the photo on the front of the *Inquisitor,* holding it so the jury can see.

"I've seen that magazine," says Anderson.

"No, I mean the photograph itself. Have you ever seen the photograph that ended up being sold to the publishers of this magazine and then reprinted on their cover?"

"No, of course not." Though Anderson is still acting confident, I notice a distinctive bobbing in the large Adam's apple that protrudes from his skinny little neck.

"Isn't it true that you or someone working for you took this photograph and sold it to the *Inquisitor?*"

Mitchell is now on his feet, and I'm wondering what took him so long. "Objection, Judge, what possible relevance—"

"If the court will give me a few minutes," says Brad. "I promise that I'll link it up."

Farley lets out a big puff of air and dons an aggravated look, like he doesn't get paid enough to make these earth-shattering decisions. "All right," he sighs. "Make it quick."

Brad forgoes the traditional, "Thank you, Your Honor," and I don't blame him. He turns back to the witness.

"Do you deny ever seeing a photograph like the picture on this cover?"

"Yes." Anderson takes another drink.

"Isn't it true, sir, that at Schlotzsky's that Saturday you showed my co-counsel this photograph and a number of other photographs, including a picture of my co-counsel meeting with a witness in this case in Las Vegas and a photograph of a classmate of Tara Bannister."

"Same objection," says Mitchell.

"Overruled."

"No," says Anderson. "As usual, that's a lie."

"And didn't you use these photographs," says Brad, "to threaten my client with a trumped-up charge of selling drugs? Didn't you tell Ms. Connors that the people in these photographs were prepared to testify against her?"

"There are no photographs," says Anderson.

"Objection!" Mitchell is louder now—and a little late.

"The witness has already answered," says Farley. "But Mr. Carson, you'd better tie this up in about two minutes or you're done."

"Yes, Your Honor."

He rubs his chin and takes a step closer to the witness. "Look at the date on this *National Inquisitor*," Brad says.

"May 24. So what?"

"About four days before this meeting that I'm talking about," says Brad.

Anderson sits straight up and the anger flares in his eyes. "There was no such meeting, can't you understand that?"

"And no photos?"

"No!"

Now Brad takes his time and walks back toward our counsel table. He opens a folder, checks its contents, then picks it up. "I'm getting ready to ask you a hypothetical question," Brad tells the witness. "So pay attention, because this one gets a little complicated."

"Don't patronize me," says Anderson.

"All right," says Brad. He turns and points to Brandon Matthews, who to my surprise is sitting in the fourth row. "Let's suppose, hypothetically, that Mr. Matthews is going to testify during our case to the following facts. First, that the picture on the front of the *National Inquisitor* is actually a picture that somebody took at the gym where Mr. Matthews works as a trainer, while he was tending to my co-counsel after she had passed out. Second, that—"

"Objection," calls out Mitchell. "Mr. Carson can't just stand there and recite all this supposed testimony."

"During Mr. Taylor's questioning the witness gave opinions as an expert witness," Brad shoots back. "And I'm entitled to ask an expert a hypothetical question so long as I can back up my hypothetical facts with testimony—which I can."

"All right," grunts Farley. "But, ladies and gentlemen of the jury, remember that what Mr. Carson says is not evidence and will never be evidence unless a witness comes in and testifies about it."

Brad clears his throat and starts again. "Anyway, assume that Mr. Matthews will say that he felt really bad after this picture hit the front of the *National Inquisitor* and called our office to apologize to my co-counsel. Our receptionist told him that Ms. Connors was not working that day, which happened to be a Friday, but that she would be stopping by the office on Saturday morning. Hypothetically speaking, that is." Brad smiles at the jury. He's such a ham.

"Now let's assume that by the time Mr. Matthews gets by the office on Saturday, Ms. Connors is just leaving the office to grab some lunch. And when Mr. Matthews follows her, he discovers that somebody else is also following her, namely you." Brad takes a deep breath and smiles at Anderson. "Are you following me so far?"

"Yes."

"Let's assume that Mr. Matthews hangs back and watches you approach Ms. Connors at lunch and sit down at her table. Let's assume that he then sees you pull out some photographs that you show to Ms. Connors, which results in a heated conversation. What if he then sees Ms. Connors stand up and swat at her soup, spilling it all over you and the photos? And then he watches Ms. Connors stomp away and watches you wipe off your clothes and then watches as you place the photos back in a folder and throw them away right there at Schlotzsky's. Now, hang in there because this is where it really gets interesting."

Mitchell jumps to his feet.

"Sorry," says Brad, and Mitchell sits back down.

"Assume for a moment that after you leave Mr. Matthews goes over to the trash, pulls out the folder with the photos, which are just copies anyway, and calls me and brings them to my office. And what if I had this gentleman in the second row"—Brad turns and points again, an elderly gentleman nods—"an expert witness named Dr. Johnson, dust them for fingerprints? If Mr. Matthews and Dr. Johnson are willing to testify about all that, then here's my question—"

"Finally," mumbles Farley.

"If you're going to contend that what I've said is not true, if you're going to say that Mr. Matthews and my fingerprint expert are lying when they take the stand and confirm this"—Brad dramatically pulls several large pictures out of the folder, each of them protected by a see-through plastic covering—"and if you've never seen these photos before…then how did your fingerprints end up on every one of them?"

Anderson eyes the photos as if they're poisonous snakes. He looks at Mitchell, but Mitchell returns nothing more than an emotionless stare. Finally, his eyes lock on Brad's. "My fingerprints are not on those photos," he says, though his voice lacks its earlier conviction. "I already told you that."

"Well, let's mark them as exhibits anyway," says Brad. "Just in case."

Mitchell Taylor tells the court he has no objection, and the photos are entered into evidence. Brad waits patiently for the clerk to mark the exhibits, then he turns back to Anderson. "Would you agree, during the next recess, to allow Dr. Johnson to obtain a set of prints from you?" Brad asks with a smile.

"No, I won't. I'm not going to dignify your unfounded accusations by giving you a set a prints as if I'm a criminal."

"Hmm," says Brad, stroking his chin. Then his eyes light up and he reaches into his suit coat pocket, withdrawing a folded paper towel. With it, he carefully reaches out and picks up Detective Anderson's drinking glass, by the lip of the glass, avoiding the areas where Anderson held the glass. Holding the glass gingerly, Brad turns to the court.

"We would ask permission to mark this glass as the defendant's next exhibit," says Brad triumphantly. "And we would further ask that we be allowed to take custody of the exhibit overnight so that Dr. Johnson can test it for fingerprints."

Farley shoots Detective Anderson a menacing look, as do most of the jurors. "Any objections?" Farley then asks Mitchell Taylor.

Mitchell stands, as straight and composed as ever. "No objection," he says, "we'd like to get to the bottom of this as well."

"Then I'll grant Mr. Carson's request," says Farley.

I can barely contain myself as the court orders a recess and the bailiff orders that we all rise. Everyone remains silent as Farley leaves the courtroom, and then, as if the room itself exhaled, everyone relaxes and starts talking at once.

I notice that the prosecutor's table is not a happy place. Harlan Fowler is confronting Mitchell in an animated whisper, hand gestures flying. Mitchell is shaking his head, arguing back. You know things are going well when the lawyers on the other side are arguing with each other.

By contrast, the backslapping at our counsel table is soon joined by both Brandon Matthews and Trish Bannister. "You are unbelievable," I say to Brad. Then I place my hands on his shoulders, stand on my tiptoes, and plant a kiss on his lips.

I turn to Brandon and smile. "And I'm liking you better all the time." I move in for a hug and am instantly confronted with that split-second nightmare that every woman dreads. He's going for a kiss! I turn my head at the last possible moment and give him my cheek.

As we pull away, I notice out of my peripheral vision the mischief in Tara's eyes. "I'm liking you better all the time too," she says to Brandon. "And I don't turn my cheek."

CHAPTER EIGHTY-ONE

Our celebration is short-lived. The rest of the morning is spent listening to Mitchell's computer expert, as he talks about how he recovered the instant messages from Tara's hard drive. At the end of the most tedious hour of testimony I have ever heard, Mitchell finally gets around to having the expert read the messages.

The jury sits transfixed as they listen to Tara, a.k.a. "Richbrat," talk about "Menendezing" her dad. "Gunshots would be too quick," says the worst message. "I prefer torture and then a Laci Peterson type of beheading." The jurors slide even further forward on their seats when Mitchell and his witness get to the IMs written weeks after the shooting. Tara calls the killing "more like payback" than self-defense. "You should have seen him beg," Tara says. "I hope he rots in hell."

At this point some of the jurors have their arms crossed as they glare at Tara, judgment burning in their eyes. I announce that I have no questions for the witness, and then Mitchell announces that the prosecution has rested its case. Farley follows with his own announcement: lunchtime! I can hardly eat during the trial, as my nerves twist my stomach into knots. But Farley looks like a man who hasn't missed a lot of lunches in his day, and he's not about to start now.

Brad and I need time alone at lunch. We hustle out to his Jeep and head down North Landing Road. Five minutes later we find a Subway and stand in line for another five minutes before we order. Brad goes for the Italian sub with everything but onions, then snags a bag of chips and a cookie. I look askance at all the sub rolls and meats and fixin's and my stomach churns. "I don't think I want anything," I say.

Brad gives me a crossways look and I sigh. "Half a veggie sub," I say, knowing I won't eat more than a few bites. We wait until we slide into our booth to start talking strategy.

"We've got to lead off with Tara," Brad says. "Got to change the momentum. We nailed Anderson, but now those IMs are killing us."

Though I like arguing with Brad, I can't find a thing wrong with that assessment. "Agreed." I go for a bite of the sub, but Brad's not watching so I make it more of a nibble. There is *so* much pressure on Tara's testimony. "This whole case will be won or lost with Tara, won't it?"

Brad nods. "Is she ready?" he asks. He has wolfed down half of his sub in about three bites. Didn't his mom ever tell him how many times to chew?

"As ready as she'll ever be. I just don't know if I'm ready."

Brad looks at me and concern darkens his brow. "You okay, Leslie?"

"I'm fine." Truthfully, I'm feeling a little clammy.

"No, I mean it," says Brad. "I want to know how you're really doing. You look a little pale."

I put down my sub and decide it's time to quit pretending. "I feel awful, Brad. Scared. A little sick."

He sits straight up. "Then I'm taking Tara. We aren't playing games with your heart, Leslie."

"It's not my heart," I say. "It's just my nerves."

"Let me take her anyway," Brad says.

I lean forward and take his hand across the table. "You're the best lawyer in the state, Brad. Maybe the country. But this client, in this case, needs a woman. Tara needs me, Brad. And we both know it."

Even Brad has no answer for this one, because he knows it's true. "You sure your heart's okay?"

"If I feel any chest pains, shortness of breath, or anything like that, you'll be the first to know."

The steel blue eyes penetrate the window of my soul, and I fall in love with the man all over again. For the hundredth time. Today.

"Promise me," he says.

"I promise."

CHAPTER EIGHTY-TWO

Tara takes the stand in the afternoon. She is wearing another of the old-maid outfits I forced her to buy, and she looks adorable. Knee-length khaki skirt and a green-and-white oxford blouse. As a concession, I gave her two earrings in one ear and three in the other.

She is nervous and wipes her sweaty palms on her skirt as she takes the stand. I ask her several preliminary questions, and pretty soon I notice that the waver in her voice is gone. Surprisingly, I've been so focused on her that I've forgotten I was also supposed to be nervous. I'm amazed at how calm I feel, my ticker clicking along at a smooth seventy or eighty beats a minute.

We spend the first hour laying bare the details of Tara's dysfunctional family. I think about Pastor Eric's sermon again—how things can look so good on the outside when they are really a mess. Tara talks softly about her stepfather's mental and psychological cruelty toward her. She recounts the shameful details of how her stepdad would abuse her mom and sometimes humiliate her mom in front of the kids. She nearly whispers as she talks about what she heard behind closed doors and how many times she asked her mom why she was tolerating it. It was a home that no teenager should be asked to endure.

Sixty minutes of bashing James has a visible effect on the jury. Arms are no longer crossed, and some are leaning forward a little in empathy. I suspect that a few of the jurors might already be wondering why Tara waited so long to end the life of her miserable stepfather. And everyone is wondering why Trish didn't just leave and take the kids with her.

But I know that Tara still has to survive cross-examination, and that won't be easy. There's the scientific evidence, and her instant messages, and the blood on her heel that mysteriously made it into her bedroom, and her hair-trigger temper. I've been working this case nonstop for the last two months, and I still don't feel like I've really figured out what happened. "It doesn't matter what happened," Brad says. "If they think James deserved it, they'll acquit." That's his theory. I still think a jury will have a hard time ignoring the powerful scientific evidence that Mitchell has amassed in this case.

"Let's turn to the night of your stepdad's death," I say. "Friday, March 25. Do you remember that date?"

"Oh, yes ma'am," says Tara. I'm so proud of her for remembering the "yes ma'am" stuff that I could hug her. "It was Good Friday."

The answer triggers something unexpected. A synapse fires and then another. Good Friday. Of course I knew it was Good Friday, but something—maybe my intuition, maybe a hunch, whatever—tells me that this is important in a way I've never understood. I'm now operating on two levels. I'm running through my script of questions with part of my brain, but the other part is frantically working on this new puzzle. *Good Friday.* What's so significant about that?

"Were you home that night when your stepdad first got home?" I ask.

Tara says she was out with some friends. We have both agreed that the details of their activities are better left unsaid.

Good Friday, my subconscious is repeating.

"When did you get home?"

"I'm not sure. About 11:30 or so."

"And who else was home when you entered the house?"

"My mom, James, and Jamie."

More synapses fire. "Were your mom and Jamie in bed?"

"Objection," says Mitchell. "How could she know?"

"Sustained."

"Were your mom and Jamie in their bedrooms with the doors closed?"

"Yes."

"Where was your stepdad?"

"He was up. He was drunk, and he gets mean when he's drunk. So he came out to the foyer and started yelling at me." Tara and I had also decided not to mention the fact that she was grounded.

"Did he hit you that night?"

She pauses. We've practiced this pause. "Yes, it was the first time."

I take a deep breath. Brad and I agreed it would be best to let Tara tell most of her story uninterrupted. I will now ask her to tell us what happened that night, and she'll tell the entire story, looking at the jury. Then I'll ask some follow-up questions to make sure we hit all the important details. Before I pop the question, I glance at Brad and he encourages me with his eyes, the same eyes that looked so concerned at lunch. I gain confidence from my split-second connection with those eyes, and as I turn, I'm warmed by how much he loves me.

"Tara, I want you to tell the jury, in your own words and in as much detail as you can, exactly what happened that night from the time you got home until the time you shot your stepfather."

Tara swivels toward the jury but looks down, unable to make eye contact. She launches into the answer we have practiced so many times—not so many times that it sounds rehearsed, but just enough so she hits all the high notes. She talks about the way her drunken stepdad assaulted her, how she went to her room, how she grabbed a gun for protection and hid it under a towel, how she came back downstairs to get some ice and show her stepdad she wasn't going to cower from him...

The jury is taking it all in, and I'm listening carefully so that I can fill in any gaps, but still... Something's just not right. All that scientific evidence can't be wrong. Anderson might be corrupt, but he didn't fabricate blood spatter on the chair, couldn't have changed whether the gunshot wounds were stippled or tattooed or whatever, couldn't have affected whether there was blood spattered on the towel... Too many things don't match what Tara is telling the jury right now.

Good Friday. Brad. I think about how Brad volunteered to take this examination for me. How he worries about my heart...my disability. My disability triggers thoughts of *Jamie.* His disability. I remember the cafeteria, Jamie eating with Tara. The way Tara mothers him. Protects him. I remember just two days ago, when Tara went after that cameraman.

And it dawns on me, as breathtaking as my heart attack! How could I have been so blind? It's the story of Good Friday—an innocent person taking the punishment for the guilty. It's what Brad offered to do at lunch—trade places. Tara didn't kill James Bannister!

Jamie did.

CHAPTER
EIGHTY-THREE

I *can't let her do this!*

But what are my choices? I'm in the middle of examining the defendant in a murder trial, while she confesses to a crime she didn't commit. There's no textbook response for this one. *God, why did You show this to me now?*

"Your Honor, may we take a brief recess?"

Farley looks at me like I've just called his mother a dirty name. "Excuse me?"

"I need a brief recess to consult with my client."

Mitchell is up, his arms spread. "In the middle of her testimony? That's unprecedented."

I have never hated that man more than I do right now.

"You can't consult with her in the middle of her testimony," says Judge Farley, as if he's Mitchell's puppet.

"It'll just take a moment, Judge."

In a show of authority, he bangs his gavel. "Objection sustained. Proceed with your questioning."

She's innocent! "Now, Tara, you've heard the evidence during the prosecution's case, right?"

This is not in our script and she gives me a quizzical look. "Yes ma'am."

"And you remember how their expert tried to make it sound like the gunshot to James Bannister's chest killed him, and then a second shot was fired into his forehead after he was already dead."

"That's not the way it happened."

I take a deep breath and walk a few steps toward Tara, leaving my notes at the podium. "Your little brother, Jamie, he's got Tourette's syndrome, doesn't he?"

"Yes."

"Sometimes he gets picked on at school because of that, right?"

Tara shrugs. "Sometimes."

"You even have him eat lunch with you and your friends so he won't get picked on, right?"

Her face hardens a little, but she knows I saw them that day. "I guess so."

"A kid like that wouldn't make out very well in a juvenile detention home, would he?"

Tara stiffens and gives me a sideways look. "What's that got to do with anything?"

"Jamie was home when your mom got beat up by your stepdad that night, wasn't he?"

"Yeah. I already said he was."

"And Jamie can have quite a temper, can't he?"

"He gets mad just like we all do."

"Did he know where the gun was in your room?"

Tara looks at the judge. "Do I have to answer that?"

"Yes."

Tara thinks for a moment, probably trying to assess what I know. "Yes."

My heart is pounding, and I'm so nervous I can hardly think straight. But one thing I know—I'm Tara's lawyer, not Jamie's. And I cannot let her do this. I take a deep breath, swallow hard, then, "Isn't it true, Tara, that your brother shot your stepdad, not you?"

"Objection. Leading."

Tara fires me an angry look. "Are you crazy?"

There's a buzz in the courtroom, and the judge bangs his gavel. "Sustained. Rephrase the question, Ms. Connors."

Think! I've got to figure out a way to phrase this question—to get at this information! I can't ask my own client a leading question; that's why Mitchell's objection was sustained. But what was it my evidence professor used to say? Just start the same question again with the phrase "whether or not."

"Tell me, Tara, whether or not your brother shot your stepdad while he was sleeping in his reclining chair, before you got home."

"That's insane," Tara snaps. "How could you even say that?"

I sense a fleeting opportunity to lay my case before the jury. "Maybe your brother shoots your stepdad and then calls you on your cell phone," I reply. I speak quickly so that Mitchell Taylor cannot interrupt. "You come home immediately. Then you think up a good self-defense story, which requires that you wipe down the gun and handle it yourself, shooting your dad again so you'll have residue on your hand and a bullet hole in a towel. So you fire the second shot into his forehead while he's lying on the floor, already dead… That's how it happened, isn't it, Tara?"

"Objection," Mitchell shouts. "That's not even a question. It's just pure speculation."

Farley scrunches up his face for a moment and then surprises me. "Overruled." Though Mitchell is right, Farley obviously wants to know the answer as much as I do.

"That's not the way it happened," Tara sneers. "How do you think I got the bruise on my cheek? You think my dead stepfather did that to me?"

"No," I answer calmly, "I think your brother did. At your request."

"You're crazy," Tara says. Then she looks at the judge, and I watch the ice return to her gaze. "I want to fire my lawyer."

CHAPTER EIGHTY-FOUR

Farley takes us all back into his chambers, and this time I've really done it. Mitchell's complaining because I've switched theories in the middle of the case. Farley suspects that I'm just trying to get a mistrial. Tara says she can't believe her mom has paid me thousands of dollars in fees so I can just turn against her at trial. Even Brad, always my defender, seems to be at a loss for words on this one.

With each new accusation, my heart pounds harder against my chest, like it's trying to break out.

"Tell you what I'm going to do," says Farley, after a long lecture on legal ethics. "I'm going to leave you and Mr. Carson alone with your client for a few minutes. If she wants to keep you on the case...fine. If she wants to fire you...fine. I'll appoint a public defender. But you're not going to parlay this into a mistrial."

The judge and Mitchell leave, and nobody says a word for a while. I guess Brad and Tara are waiting on me.

"What you're doing is noble," I tell Tara. "Even heroic. But it's also wrong. You can't lie under oath and take your brother's punishment."

"I don't care what you think," snaps Tara. "I'm firing you."

"Brilliant," pipes in Brad, standing so he can pace. "Those public defenders will really do a great job with this case. Probably get you life."

"Tara, the problem is—" I start. But I shut up when Brad gives me "the look"—his, not mine.

"Don't you understand, Tara? Leslie's giving the jury one more thing to hang their hat on if they want to. She's not going to argue this crazy theory in her closing; she's just throwing it out there so they can bite on it if they want to."

What?! Oh, yes I am going to argue this in my closing. But we'll cross that bridge when we come to it. *If* we come to it.

Tara's eyes begin to tear up and some of the edge leaves her expression. "Jamie wouldn't last a day in jail," she says. "And I won't let you put him there."

"We aren't going to put him there," Brad says reassuringly as he paces. "The jury won't hear another word about Jamie shooting your stepdad. They won't have to."

Tara seems unconvinced. And she's not the only one.

"Can I have a word with you?" I ask Brad. "Alone?"

Tara reluctantly agrees to wait in the hallway for a moment. As soon as the door closes behind her, I start.

"In case you've forgotten, Tara's our client, not Jamie," I tell Brad. "How can you promise her that we won't argue that Jamie did it? How can we just let her perjure herself the rest of the case?"

"Whoa," says Brad. "Number one, who's to say she's perjuring herself? And second—"

"Brad, you know I'm right. It all adds up. The way she protects Jamie. The time between the first and second shot. The angle of the shots. Everything."

His face never changes expression while he paces. I wonder how we've missed it this long. Synapses fire and another epiphany hits me. "You've known all along, haven't you?"

Brad stops pacing for a moment and looks me in the eye. "We've got a client who says it's self-defense. That's good enough for me."

Now it's stubborn versus stubborn. "But it can't be self-defense. Not on this evidence. And I'm not willing to go back out there and argue for a theory we know is wrong and let my client lie under oath to support it."

I brace myself for Brad's lecture in legal ethics. We've had similar conversations before. It's the jury's job, not mine, to determine whether a defendant is lying. It's our job, as advocates, to assume our clients are telling the truth. It's our job to build a case consistent with their innocence.

Instead, he takes a totally different approach. "Unless I'm mistaken, Leslie, I thought your entire faith was based on letting Christ take your punishment, even though He didn't do anything wrong. How can you deny Tara the chance to do the same thing for her own flesh and blood?"

As usual, there's no answer for this Brad Carson question. Maybe this is the ends justifying the means. Maybe this is a breach of our legal duty to Tara. But how *can* you deny this girl the ability to protect her little brother?

Confusion now clouds my thoughts to the point that I completely lose confidence in my own judgment. I trust Brad enough to marry him. Maybe I should trust him enough to follow his advice on this case.

"Bring her in," I say.

CHAPTER EIGHTY-FIVE

Tara climbs back into the witness stand as if nothing unusual has happened. We walk through the events on the night of the shooting one more time, emphasizing that Jamie was still in his room when Tara shot her stepdad. Next, I train my sights on Harlan Fowler.

"Mr. Taylor has argued that you should have just called the police and reported your stepdad to them. Why didn't you do that?"

"Because I didn't trust them."

"Why not?"

"Objection," Mitchell calls out. "May we approach?"

Judge Farley waves us up to the bench, and Brad comes with me.

"Here we go again, Judge," complains Mitchell. "She's trying to take this witness back to Las Vegas and the alleged incident with Mr. Fowler that has nothing to do with this case."

"Nothing to do with this case?" Brad says from over my shoulder. He's whispering, but it's so loud the judge is shushing him. I'm not happy that Brad isn't letting me make this argument. She's my witness. "It has everything to do with this case!" Brad's voice has not quieted. If anything, it's a little louder.

"Shh," says Farley.

"Mr. Taylor claims she should have called the police about her stepdad instead of shooting him," Brad continues. His voice can no longer be called a whisper. It's that low voice thing that men do when they're mad but trying not to let their voice carry. The jurors are either leaning forward or craning their necks a little sideways. "How can she go to the police when she knows that the decision to prosecute rests with the commonwealth's attorney," Brad argues, his voice rising, "the same guy who sexually assaulted her during a trip to Las Vegas."

"Mr. Carson," Judge Farley snaps, his own voice a strained whisper. "Keep your voice down."

"Sorry, Your Honor, but this is all so ridiculous."

"Your Honor," says Mitchell, the only person now whispering low enough so the jury can't hear. "Even if everything Tara claims about Mr. Fowler is true, which we don't concede for a second, how could it have any bearing on her claims of self-defense in this case? She says that her stepdad attacked her and was strangling her when she shot him. Is she now contending that she would have just said, 'Let me go, please, so I can call the cops,' if she hadn't had this prior brush with Mr. Fowler?"

Brad turns on Mitchell. "You're the one who said she should have just called the cops. Not us."

Crack. Farley brings his gavel down. "Counsel," he says sharply. Then he glares at Brad. "Mr. Taylor's right. These allegations are irrelevant to your defense. They're not coming into this case. Not on my watch."

"Thank you, Your Honor," says Mitchell Taylor.

Brad reserves his comment until he's walking back to counsel table with me. "They already did," he says with a chuckle.

When Mitchell the marine stands to cross-examine Tara, my stomach clutches. There are so many trapdoors—the unexplainable scientific evidence, her bloody footprint in her bedroom, her illegal possession of the gun (a topic we intentionally avoided on direct examination), and her explosive temper. I keep telling myself that she'll get through it, that I've prepared her for every possible question.

And I know that Mitchell Taylor's got to be careful or it will look like he's beating up on a sixteen-year-old kid.

"Let's begin by making sure that nobody is confused about the suggestions by your lawyer that maybe it was actually your brother who shot your stepdad and not you. Did your brother shoot your stepdad?"

"No."

"Was he even downstairs when you shot your stepdad?"

"No."

"Your lawyer suggested that maybe you were just covering for your brother, taking the fall so he could go free. Is that what's happening here?"

Tara shoots me a mean glance, as if to remind me that these first few questions are my fault. I scribble some meaningless notes on a pad. *Sorry.*

"No," says Tara.

Mitchell pauses for a moment, searching the carpet for his next thought. "Your lawyers are pretty sharp; I'm sure they've discussed with you the principles of double jeopardy. Are you aware of how that works?"

What kind of question is that? Brad is nudging me. *Oh yeah.* "Objection. Attorney-client privilege."

"Sustained."

Mitchell takes a few steps closer to Tara. "Well, did anybody besides your lawyer explain how the principles of double jeopardy might apply in this case, especially as it concerns your brother?"

Tara gives Mitchell a confused look, wrinkling her brow.

"Let me explain," offers Mitchell. "You ever watch television shows or movies about lawyers?"

Tara shrugs. "Sure."

"Have you ever heard that a person can't be tried twice for the same crime? Something called double jeopardy."

I stand to object.

"Yeah," says Tara.

I'm still standing. "Judge, I don't see any possible relevance to this—"

"I'll link it up," says Mitchell, "if you'll give me the same latitude that you've given defense counsel when they asked for latitude."

"Proceed," says Farley.

"But you also understand," continues Mitchell, "that if you're acquitted of this crime, found innocent, nothing prevents me or the other prosecutors from putting your brother on trial for the same crime."

Tara's face turns into hard lines, her narrow brown eyes drilling Mitchell. "He didn't do it."

"I know. That's why I'm asking this question. Because if you were really trying to cover for your brother, you wouldn't be trying to get off based on self-defense, would you? I mean, you understand that a not-guilty verdict for you just puts your brother in further jeopardy, right?"

The question, so deviously astute, hits me like a sledgehammer. And the stunned look on Tara's face confirms my worst fears. There are times when an entire case turns on a single devastating question. My stomach flops in realization that I've just witnessed such a time, and I'm powerless to stop it.

"Objection," I say standing. But Farley waves me off. "Overruled."

"No, it's okay," offers Mitchell. "I'll rephrase. All I'm trying to say is this: if your brother had actually shot your stepdad and if you wanted to take the blame for him, you wouldn't be claiming self-defense, isn't that right?"

Tara sets her jaw and nods her head. "That's right," she says, and I know that Mitchell's got her. He has cleverly insinuated that a not-guilty verdict here will mean a trial for Jamie. He has given Tara every reason to incriminate herself irrevocably during her testimony in order to make sure the jury will never buy her argument of self-defense. And it has all happened because I opened the door on direct examination when I implied that Jamie was responsible.

How can Tara ever forgive me? How can I ever forgive myself?

Every second of this cross-examination is now torture. And Mitchell Taylor still has a whole legal pad full of questions.

CHAPTER EIGHTY-SIX

For nearly an hour Mitchell walks Tara through every piece of scientific evidence that contradicts her testimony. Tara shrugs off his questions with little attempt to fight back, admitting that she has no explanation for the contradictions.

"Did you hear the evidence about the blood pattern on the recliner chair?" Mitchell asks.

"Yes."

"Can you tell the ladies and gentlemen of the jury why that pattern exists on the chair if you shot your stepfather while he was standing up?"

"No."

"Do you see this photograph with the metal rod showing the angle of the bullet that entered your father's chest?"

"Yes."

"Does it look to you like whoever shot your stepfather was holding the gun substantially higher than Mr. Bannister's chest?"

"I don't know. I guess so."

"Do you have any explanation how that could be true if he was choking you at the time you fired the gun?"

"Not really."

On and on Mitchell goes, all afternoon, exhibit by exhibit, handing Tara the shovels she needs to dig herself a deeper and deeper hole. Every question cuts like a serrated knife. Tara's voice seems to grow lower and thinner throughout the afternoon as she shrinks back into the witness stand. Watching, I experience death by a thousand cuts.

Mitchell waits until a quarter of five to ask the question he's been setting up all afternoon. He punctuates it with a long pause and a couple of steps toward Tara.

"Tara, we've been through a lot of exhibits this afternoon, a lot of photographs, and a lot of scientific evidence, and it all seems to point toward somebody shooting Mr. Bannister from more than twenty-five feet away while he was sitting in the recliner, and then firing a second shot into his skull after he had died—"

"Objection," I call out. "That's a speech, not a question."

"Because counsel interrupted me," says Mitchell, "before I could finish it."

"Proceed," says Farley.

"Your lawyer seems to suggest that person might have been your brother. In fact, Tara, that person was you, wasn't it? You're the one who fired that shot into your dad while he was sleeping in the recliner, isn't that the way it happened?"

Tears well up in Tara's eyes as she stares at the rail in front of her seat. I watch in horror as she presses her balled fists to her mouth and the tears start rolling down her cheeks. She now realizes it's time to abandon her self-defense claim completely or risk her brother going to jail. After a few of the longest seconds of my life, she brushes at her cheeks with her palms and looks up at Mitchell, slowly shaking her head. "I shot him," she says, her voice hoarse with emotion, "while he slept in his chair." She pauses, and the look of an assassin creeps into her eyes, transforming this sixteen-year-old in an instant.

"He beat my mother that night while she begged him to stop. He treated her like an animal," Tara says. "One too many times." She glances at me, then back at Mitchell. "So I shot him while he slept.

"And I'm glad he's dead."

When court adjourns there is more than the usual amount of bedlam. Reporters rush out to meet deadlines, phoning their studios to reserve a lead spot on the news. Tara walks like a zombie toward our counsel table, her eyes now red but dry, her face expressionless.

"I'm so sorry that I put you in that position," I say in a tone so quiet that only Brad and Tara can hear. "But it's not over yet. We can put you back on the stand tomorrow. We can—"

"I don't want to talk about it," says Tara with an accusatory glare. "Especially not with you." She is packing up her stuff with quick, angry movements. "You've already said enough for one day." Meanwhile, Trish has made her way to our counsel table and looks completely overwhelmed by the day's events.

"Tara," Brad says sharply, "Leslie didn't cause that. She's been killing herself for you on this case, the least you can do is listen to her."

"Save your lectures," says Tara. She turns her back on Brad and stalks past me. "It's over now."

"Tara!" I call out, but she doesn't turn around. Trish is following her down the aisle of the courtroom, trying to calm her.

"Let her go," says Brad. He comes over and places a hand on my elbow as I watch Tara leave the courtroom. The despair is overwhelming, fueled by the knowledge that I will soon watch another set of doors close on Tara, doors that will not open for many years, maybe a lifetime.

And I have no one to blame but myself.

CHAPTER
EIGHTY-SEVEN

I do not leave the office that night until nearly eleven. Somehow working allows me to postpone the despondency that will certainly overtake me when I get home and dwell on the day's events. Brad has been great, reassuring me that we are exactly where he always knew we would be.

"The scientific evidence against us was so strong," says Brad. "I knew at the end of the day we'd be counting on jury nullification. You can't blame yourself for this. Tara has been lying to us from day one."

But on my way home, I can no longer keep the truth at bay. I have lost this case for Tara. I followed my instincts, tenaciously pursued the truth, and cost my client her freedom. I am too depleted to cry, too beaten down for anger. I feel nothing but emptiness and the same foreboding I experienced when I found out about my heart. I'm like a robot going through life's motions, trying to survive from one minute to the next. First my health, then my career. I must find the will to fight back. But how? And what's the use anyway?

I need a good night's sleep.

I pull into the driveway of my duplex and park in my usual spot, right in front of my half of the house. The other side of the duplex is dark, but their car is in the driveway so I assume that my neighbors are sleeping.

I had kicked off my shoes while driving, so I grab them and my purse, then climb the front stoop of my duplex. The single bulb of my porch light provides all the illumination I need as I insert my key in the door with my right hand. I open the door and find the light switch immediately inside. The light flicks on and I take a step.

Everything happens at once.

A man's hand wraps around my face, covering my mouth, stifling my scream. I feel a gun jammed into the small of my back as panic shoots through my body. I smell cheap cologne and feel hot breath on my neck. I fight for air.

"Scream and you die!" he whispers in my ear.

In a flash, he thrusts me inside and kicks the door shut with his heel. I feel the gun leave my back for an instant, the lights go off, and the gun is back. My panic is now in full bloom. I'm beginning to cry, still gasping for breath as the hand pulls tighter against my mouth. *Think, Leslie!*

God, get me through this!

Thoughts ricochet around my mind like a pinball machine. Who is it? A rapist? A thief? No, thieves strike when nobody's home. Anderson? Fowler? He twists me closer, and pain shoots through my jaw. He tells me to settle down and nobody will get hurt. I realize that I've dropped everything I was carrying into the duplex. I realize that if he really wanted me dead he would have already shot me.

"Put your hands behind your back," he orders.

He's going to tie me up! Kidnap me?

My heart feels like it might explode; there is a sharp pain in my chest. *Air! I need air!*

Instincts take over…survival instincts. I've got to avoid the gun! Desperate, I try to drop toward the floor, and the sudden movement frees me from his grip momentarily. I drive an elbow into his groin on the way down and hear his primal groan just before my world explodes.

I've never felt pain this intense, a debilitating, paralyzing pain that sears every nerve ending and makes me shriek like a wounded animal. I flop powerless to the floor. My skin feels like it's on fire, burning itself free from my flesh and bones. He's on me again before I can even react. He wraps duct tape tightly around my mouth, choking me and suffocating my screams. He duct tapes my hands behind my back as I squirm in fear of another deadly jolt.

A Taser, I realize. I've been zapped with a stun gun. And I'll do anything to avoid another jolt.

My attacker turns me face down on the floor, my face pressed against the cool tile of my small foyer. He places the prongs of the stun gun in my back again, and I flinch. "No! Please no!" I try to beg for mercy, but my words are stifled by the tape and turned into a guttural, "Mmmmmm."

"Shut up," he says, "or you'll fry some more."

I choke back my sobs as best I can. Anything to avoid another round of excruciating pain.

I force myself to think, to process what's happening. It's not Fowler; I would recognize his distinctive baritone. But this guy has a stun gun. Law enforcement?

Anderson?

We stay motionless in the dark for a few moments, the stun gun still wedged into my back, my captor's heavy breathing ringing in my ears. I try to relax, breathe through my nose. But it's impossible to get a deep breath, my chest feels like an elephant is standing on me, and every muscle is tensed by the thought of another jolt from the Taser.

I think about my scream when he first hit me with the Taser. The neighbors—somebody must have heard! But as soon as the thought hits, as if to mock me, I hear the static of a police radio, a dispatcher sending a squad car to some type of numbered code. I realize the sound is coming from my captor's belt. He's monitoring the police frequencies! I listen, hoping for a call referencing my address. Nothing.

After a minute, maybe two, my captor pulls the gun away from my back and tapes my ankles together. I strain my neck and glance back at him. Even in the shadows, I can tell it's Anderson. The same tall, wiry build. He's dressed in black pants and a dark T-shirt.

Though his face is hidden by a stocking cap, I know it's him. Who else could it be? The police radio, the stun gun…the motive. I feel his plastic gloves as he binds my ankles—so tightly I know it will only be a matter of minutes before I lose all circulation.

He catches me looking at him. "Keep your head down," he growls, then grabs me by the hair and slams my face into the floor. I am dizzied by pain that shoots through my nose and across my cheekbones. I feel the blood pouring from my nose, pooling on the floor.

Anderson grabs me under the armpits, and while I hang my head toward the floor, he drags me onto the carpet of my living room. I lie there, face down in my own blood, and listen as Anderson moves from one room to the next, closing miniblinds all over the duplex. I work on my breathing, finding it harder now to suck in enough oxygen through my nose. I am maintaining consciousness by a thread, though I feel the pressure in my chest lessen slightly.

A few minutes later, after what seems like another eternity of fighting for breath, I hear Anderson punch numbers on his cell phone. He gives the address for my duplex, says, "No weapons," then hangs up. As I hear Anderson's footsteps heading back toward my living room, I listen for the sound of sirens, and I pray.

His radio crackles again. More police dispatching and responding. None having to do with me. "You're probably wondering what's going on," he says casually. It's the calm precision of his words, the fact that he doesn't bother whispering, that chills me most of all. He walks up next to me and I flinch, then I feel his shoe wedging against my side. He flips me over with his foot, causing me to lie uncomfortably on my arms, which are wrenched behind my back and ducttaped together. The blood now trickles from my nose down my cheeks, matting my hair. I keep sniffing, trying to stop the bleeding, and it feels like the blood is pooling in the back of my throat.

Then Anderson does something I never would have expected. He walks over to the wall, finds the light switch, and flips on the living room light. I squint as my eyes struggle to adjust.

"I want to see the look in your eyes when I tell you what's going to happen," he says.

CHAPTER
EIGHTY-EIGHT

Detective Lawrence Anderson pulls off his ski mask, tucks it in a plastic bag he apparently brought with him, then spreads another piece of plastic on my couch. He sits on the plastic, stares at me, and crosses his legs.

"Since you've seen me, you probably realize you're going to die," he says, sending chills up my spine. I begin to hyperventilate a little, then force myself to take deeper, slower breaths. He must kill me now, I realize. But he will not take me without a fight.

"If you could talk, you would probably say something stupid like, 'You'll never get away with this.'"

"Mmmmmm," is all I can manage. I cough into the duct tape, then swallow some of the blood trapped in my throat. But I also stare at Anderson with eyes no longer wide with fear. I am finding my courage, spurred on by a faith that gives me hope even in death.

"You would be wrong," says Anderson with a smirk. "Just like you were wrong to continue to pursue this case even after I warned you off."

I shake my head and try to stare him down, blood still running from my nose. He has power over my body, but he cannot control my will. Cannot.

He laughs at my show of defiance, which causes me to find even more resolve, mixed with a healthy portion of anger.

"I've found," says Anderson, "that the best way to pull off a crime is to hire a criminal. And you'd be surprised what convicted felons will do when they're facing a possible third offense under Virginia's 'three strikes and you're out' law." Anderson smiles. "But who am I to lecture a lawyer as brilliant as you on the law."

The radio squawks again, and Anderson pauses to listen. Once again the call has nothing to do with us.

"Take Umberto Rodriguez, for example. Two priors, one for rape, the other for distribution of a controlled substance. Then it's just my luck to be the lead investigator on a third bust—more drugs."

While Anderson talks, I weigh my options. There's no chance of wiggling my hands free from this duct tape, the way they do in the movies. It's so tight it's cutting off my circulation. And he has wrapped it around my wrists who-knows-how-many times. I can't negotiate with him, because I can't say a word. And my ankles are taped so I can't even make a run for it.

"Umberto is looking at a minimum of twenty years under Virginia's wonderful sentencing guidelines for third-time offenders. That's a lot of motivation...twenty years' worth." Anderson looks at me and smirks. "Am I boring you?"

I don't give him the satisfaction of even a head nod in response.

"Anyway, the man does what others have done before him. He cuts a deal with me. You see, Ms. Connors, there are so many different ways that this man never gets prosecuted, never even gets indicted. I lose track of a witness or I have a chain-of-custody problem with some evidence or a prosecutor fails to get a grand-jury indictment. In exchange, the criminal owes me a favor, a crime of my choosing—and guess what? This time, you're the lucky victim."

Anderson stands and walks over next to me, towering over me as I now stare at the ceiling, refusing to look at him. "It's the perfect setup really. And it keeps the police from ever suspecting me. You see, Umberto the rapist will be here in a few minutes. Tonight's crime will be rape and murder, using one of your own kitchen knives to give it that spontaneous feel. Then he'll help himself to a few snacks from your refrigerator. A true psychopath, though a little sloppy with DNA and fingerprint evidence. After you're dead, I'll leave first, and an hour or so later Umberto will leave, making enough noise to alert the neighbors. By then, I'll be with some other cops and will have a wonderful alibi. Since I'm working the graveyard shift tonight, I'll get called in to help investigate, thus explaining any of my own hairs or footprints or DNA at the scene."

He takes a deep breath of self-satisfaction, and I find myself praying for one last chance to send this man to hell. "Meanwhile," he says, "Umberto's on his way to Europe with the passport I'll give him tonight. We find all this evidence against Umberto, but the man is now a fugitive, and the case sits in the inactive file drawer unless Umberto is caught. If he is, I'll make sure he never makes it back to this jurisdiction alive."

I think I hear tires on the pavement outside, but I see no lights coming in my window. Another choking spell hits me, and I swallow some more blood. "Then a year or so from now, I catch another convicted felon with his hand in the cookie jar for the third time, and we do another breaking and entering, this time with Brad Carson. Unfortunately, your man dies in self-defense."

Enraged, I swing my legs around and kick him. I have no leverage and it does nothing except make him mock me with laughter. Then his face turns serious and he takes out the stun gun.

"Feisty," he says, coming toward me.

CHAPTER EIGHTY-NINE

I am granted a reprieve by a soft knock on the door. Anderson looks at me for a long second, then turns and heads toward the door. *Thank you, Jesus.*

He looks out through the peephole, then opens the door quickly and ushers in a muscled man with a goatee and a short buzz cut. The man is also dressed in black, but he is not wearing gloves. He has tattoos on both arms and a studded earring that reflects the dim light.

Anderson frisks him in the hallway while he fidgets. "Is that really necessary?" the goateed man asks. I assume this is Umberto.

Anderson brings Umberto into the living room and explains the plan. The entire time Umberto is jumpy, like he's on some kind of speed. His eyes alternate between eye contact with Anderson and leering at me, as if savoring thoughts of violating me, making me feel more exposed and vulnerable than ever.

Anderson walks over next to me and rolls me over again with his foot so I am now face down. He kneels next to me.

"Come here," he says to Umberto.

"Why?"

"Just do it." Though I can't see him, I get the sense that Anderson is wielding the gun, threatening Umberto as the two men now kneel next to me.

Anderson grabs two of the nearly numb fingers of my left hand. "Give me your arm," he commands Umberto. Before I know what's happening, Anderson takes my fingernails and digs them into Umberto's arm. The man curses and Anderson laughs. "Small price to pay for what you're about to enjoy," says Anderson.

He's planting DNA evidence.

I ball my hands into fists, causing a derisive snort from Anderson. "You want to do this the hard way?" He pries one of my fingers loose, then bends it back, nearly snapping the bone as a new pain shoots through my body. I moan and loosen my fists.

"That's better." Finger by finger, he scrapes my fingernails on Umberto's arm.

When Anderson's done, he turns me over again and the two men stand.

Though I should be petrified at what's to come, and am in fact trembling, I also find that I've discovered a strange but calm resolve. I am no longer afraid to die. But I beg God to spare me the unspeakable indecency of being raped. And to give me one final shot at taking Lawrence Anderson to the grave with me.

"I need a knife," says Umberto, his voice hoarse and gruff. I notice that his shirt is stained with sweat, both under his arms and in streaks on his chest. "I've got to cut her ankles free."

"So get one." Anderson motions toward the kitchen with his gun. Not a stun gun this time but a revolver. The stun gun is holstered on his belt.

"Put that thing down," says Umberto. "She's not going anywhere."

"I'm not worried about her," replies Anderson.

A few seconds later, Umberto is approaching me with a knife. I know this may be my final chance, and I pray for wisdom and courage. I am breathing rapidly through my nose, my chest heaving in and out. As he leans over to cut the tape binding my ankles, I smell the sweat of this man, this convicted rapist, this unfeeling felon with dark and evil eyes.

I will wait until my legs are free, then I will make a move. If nothing else, I will force them to kill me sooner than they planned.

As Umberto leans over to cut the tape, with Anderson hovering on the other side of the room, casually holding his gun, the police radio squawks again. Umberto takes advantage of the distraction to whisper something intended only for me.

"Trust me."

My eyes go wide, but Umberto acts as if he hasn't said a word. He slices through the duct tape on my ankles, but his words have paralyzed me with indecision. Before I can make a move, he flings me over his shoulder.

"Where are you going?" says Anderson.

"The bedroom."

That's when I freak. I start flailing my legs and ramming my chin again and again into Umberto's back. He squeezes me tighter around the legs, cursing me. Anderson smiles, enjoying the show, and follows closely behind as we walk toward the steps.

I am now fighting for my life, my adrenaline-laced body squirming and twisting. My breathing has all but stopped, and the chest pain is returning with a frenzy. I am screaming into the duct tape. "Mmm, mmm," and louder, "Mmmmmm!" all to no avail. The unbearable pressure is back in my chest, a pain as debilitating as the stun gun, yet still I struggle. I sense I'm at least making it difficult for Umberto, who stumbles toward the stairs.

Then, just before he starts climbing them, he spins around with astonishing speed, swinging my legs to kick the gun free from a startled Anderson's hands. In the same motion, Umberto tosses me to the side, sending me crashing into a wall and then to the floor. I look up to see Umberto take a swing at Anderson, even as Anderson is going for the stun gun on his belt. My head spins as I hear somebody come crashing through the front door. I try to stand, but the elephant is on my chest again and I gasp for breath. *Can't breathe! Unbearable pain!* The black box starts closing in on my vision. I hear the pop of a gun. I see Anderson's head jerk forward.

My last conscious thought is a prayer for Brad.

I regain consciousness surrounded by medical personnel. My duplex is now a beehive of activity, all confusing to me, as I struggle to clear the cobwebs from my thoughts. They are taking my blood pressure and checking my pulse. They are also shooting questions at me about how I feel.

Before my head can clear, they are carrying me to the ambulance on a stretcher. There are police everywhere, and the street outside my duplex feels like a dance floor with strobe lights. The paramedics keep peppering me with questions about chest pain and shortness of breath as they load me into the ambulance. They wipe the blood from my face and hook me up to oxygen and monitors. At some point it dawns on me that I am no longer bound by the duct tape. Nobody seems to be able to answer my mumbled questions about what happened in my duplex. "We've just got to focus on getting you better," they say. "We can worry about the other stuff later."

I am still having a hard time drawing a deep breath, but the chest pain is subsiding. They rush me to an emergency room where the bright lights disorient me again. They place me on an uncomfortable table in a trauma room and remove the oxygen mask. I feel like I am merely being swept along by events, like a stick riding the waves in the ocean. My brain is a thicket of cobwebs, my processing slowed like a computer with a bad virus. I am no longer experiencing the sharp chest pains, though I still feel a dull tightness in my chest.

Under questioning from the ER doc, I explain my heart history. He seems a little relieved by this and tells me that he doubts I'm experiencing a heart attack. "You're suffering from a diastolic dysfunction," he says. "This causes your ventricles to become stiff, and when you go through the kind of trauma you did tonight, the blood can back up in the lungs, causing shortness of breath, and even some abnormal functioning of the mitral or aortic valves.

"Still," he says, "you can never be sure. I'm going to give you some beta blockers, and we'll want to do an EKG and check your troponin I." He says this matter-of-factly, as if I spend my waking hours studying workups for heart conditions.

"Okay," I say.

He then hooks me up to an IV and has the nurses hustle me off for some blood work, an EKG, an x-ray of my lungs, and a sonogram of my heart. When I return, they place me in an ICU room. The doctors and nurses attach some electrodes to me, then talk in their secret medical code and write on their charts.

The chest pain is nearly gone now, and my breathing is getting back to normal. They wash my face more thoroughly, replace my clothes with a hospital gown, and start asking questions about my painful nose and cheekbones. When the doctor touches my nose in the wrong spot, I about jump out of my hospital bed. "I don't think it's broken," he says. "But we'll probably need to do another set of x-rays just to make sure."

A few minutes later, before they can whisk me off for more x-rays, I am both shocked and relieved to see Dr. Mason Reddick approach my bedside.

"So this is what you call avoiding stress?" he says. It's probably the only joke he's ever told, and he's just wasted it on a patient incapable of smiling.

"You're a lucky woman to be alive." He's looking at my chart, checking the monitors.

"It's a little hard to figure out exactly what's happened," he continues. "I've reviewed the EKG and lab work. I don't think you've damaged any heart muscle, but I do think the stress tonight, combined with your hypertrophic cardiomyopathy, may have caused a brief dysfunction of the mitral or aortic valves, or possibly even a dilated cardiomyopathy."

"In English please," I croak. I'm amazed at how weak my voice is.

"Not a heart attack, Leslie. But severe symptoms from the HCM. Sometimes this can lead to ventricular fibrillation—"

I give him the best dirty look I can manage.

"—a condition where the heart's lower chamber contracts in a rapid, unsynchronized way—it flutters. It usually pumps little or no blood when it does this, and it can be very dangerous, sometimes leading to sudden cardiac death."

That word I understand. Death. It seems to be stalking me.

"In other words, Leslie, we need to schedule your surgery as soon as possible. Tomorrow morning would not be too early."

I take all this in and then it dawns on my slow-motion brain that Reddick shouldn't even be here at this time of night. "How'd you find out I was here?" I ask.

Reddick smiles. "The hospital called your fiancé, and he insisted that I come immediately. The man is very persistent. I live a little closer than he does, but I'm sure he's on his way."

I want to see Brad so badly. Just thinking of him makes my eyes sting with tears.

I suddenly realize that I've got an incredible peace about the operation this time. Part of it is being sick and tired of struggling for breath. Part of it is not wanting to ever again experience what I went through tonight, knowing that I could have died. But part of it is knowing that this time I'm ready. Somehow, God delivered me from Anderson and Umberto. The operation ought to be a piece of cake.

"Keep that scar small," I say to Reddick. "I'm going to be a bride in a few weeks."

At that moment, Brad shoots through the door of my room. He

rushes to my bed and looks surprised to see me coherent. I feel the tears building in my eyes again as he gently takes my IV-sprouting hand.

"Careful," I say, "one of the fingers is a little sore."

"I love you," Brad says. There are tears in *his* eyes, too.

I'm so grateful he's here. His touch has a way of making everything better. I smile at him through the tears.

"I got here as fast as I could," Brad says.

"I know. Thanks." And just then it occurs to me—this is one of the few times in my life that I've ever seen Brad Carson show up anyplace right on time.

The rest of the night creeps by. Brad fills me in on what little he knows about the events at my home. Anderson is dead. The police are being incredibly tight-lipped. They would like to interview me, but Brad won't let that happen until after the operation.

My job, says Brad, is to sleep and gain some strength before my surgery at 8:00 a.m.

Like that's going to happen.

CHAPTER
NINETY-ONE

The fog is dense as the anesthesia begins to wear off. My mouth is like cotton, and I ought to ask for a drink. But then I think, nearly giddy, *Why bother?* My head feels the size of Texas, yet somehow it floats out there, unattached to my body, and all is well. *Real* well.

The third or fourth time I awake, things are not so good. There is less anesthesia, and this time I ask for a sip of water. Brad moves through the fog to help me. He puts a hand gently under my head and props me up like I'm made of porcelain.

"How're you feeling?" he asks.

I groan.

"Dr. Reddick says the operation went well. He said there was minimal damage to the heart and that he was able to surgically reduce the septal wall. He said you'll be as good as new. Better, really. Your breathing should be improved and—"

Brad stops as I squeeze his hand. All this talk is making my head swim. Exhausting me. "A little more?" I ask.

He gently gives me another drink. My breathing is easier. It's like the air is suddenly lighter, my lungs inflate effortlessly with every breath. But still, I'm so tired.

"The scar is actually smaller than I thought it would be," Brad says. "Dr. Reddick said—"

I squeeze his hand again. "Can we not talk right now?" I ask hoarsely.

"Sure. Sorry."

He bends down and kisses me on the forehead.

Just before I drift away, a thought jerks me back to the room. "Tara?" I ask.

"The judge declared a mistrial," Brad says. "Too much publicity about Anderson and you. He scheduled a new trial for September." He pauses.

"There's more?" I ask.

"Tara wanted me to tell you thanks," says Brad. "And that she's sorry."

I close my eyes and nod my head. At least I try to nod my head. Modern medication is wonderful.

I am in and out, in and out, for some undefined period of time that I will never remember. I finally open my eyes and come slowly back to reality. This time my chest is hurting from the surgery. In fact, my whole body feels like I went fifteen rounds with Mike Tyson. And like I didn't do a very good job of keeping my guard up to protect my nose.

I gaze around at the sterile, light green walls of my room, the television up in the corner. Brad is next to my bed, leaning back in the chair, his mouth open as he sleeps. He's wearing a pair of dress slacks with a light blue shirt, his suit coat and tie thrown over the back of the chair. There are some flowers and a note from Bella on the table next to my bed . The sun is trying to sneak through the blinds, meaning it must still be day.

I try to string the time together. The attack was just last night, Wednesday night, though it seems like forever ago. I had surgery this morning, so it must be late Thursday afternoon.

"Brad?" I say, but my voice is a fragile whisper. "Brad?"

He jerks up in his seat, smiles at me, and comes to my bedside. "Want some water?" he asks.

I nod. "And something for my headache," I whisper.

Brad takes care of me for a few minutes, and then a pleasant nurse enters the room and fusses over me some more. When she leaves, Brad tells me again how well the surgery went.

"I know. You already told me. Remember?"

He smiles sheepishly. "I didn't know if *you'd* remember. And, oh, your nose isn't broken either."

"Sure feels like it is."

Brad holds my hand and lovingly rubs my fingers, but it makes me wince. "Sorry," he says. "I forgot." He gently brushes some stray strands of hair away from my face. Just looking at him makes me want to cry. I'm still woozy, but I'm coherent enough to know that I'm going to be an emotional basket case for a while.

I glance toward the flowers. "Bella here?"

"Yeah. She's been in and out all day." Brad grins. "She's on a smoke break right now. She'll be mad that she wasn't here when you woke up."

We let a few minutes of silence pass, but I can tell Brad's got something more to tell me. I let him decide the timing.

"If you're up to it, you need to talk to the police," he says finally.

"Okay."

"And Mitchell Taylor is here as well. Says he'd like to talk to you first."

Mitchell Taylor? "Why?" I ask.

"Maybe we ought to let him tell you," says Brad.

Mitchell enters the room in a suit coat and tie. Why am I not surprised? He looks drawn, his eyes somber and sad. He walks to the edge of my bed while Brad stands on the other side.

"Thanks for seeing me," he says.

"Sure."

There is tension in the room, and I am determined to do nothing to relieve it. As far as I'm concerned, this man is responsible, at least in part, for what happened last night. There's a Mitchell Taylor mentality at Virginia Beach, a win-at-all-costs attitude that permeates law enforcement. It gives men like Anderson a God complex and drives them to take matters into their own hands.

"I want to start by saying how grateful I am that you're going to be okay," says Mitchell. "And by apologizing." He shifts his weight from one foot to the other. To his credit, he keeps looking me in the eye.

"This guy Umberto had been working with us...with me...on trying to nail Anderson. Even before you filed your complaint with Internal Affairs, we had suspicions. It's why we took Anderson off Tara's case. He was involved in several cases where someone mysteriously dropped the ball. One of those was the Barker pornography case"—Brad and I exchange a glance—"and another was a recent drug bust involving Umberto. We found Umberto, brought him in and squeezed him, offering a sweet deal for his cooperation against Anderson. Turns out Umberto didn't really want to live in Europe on one of Anderson's phony passports."

Mitchell takes a deep breath. The room is silent except for my machines, beeping out their steady rhythm. Brad has his arms folded. Mitchell is lucky that Bella isn't here.

"Umberto told us that Anderson was supposed to be calling him last night with an assignment. Nobody knew what it would be, but I had a suspicion it would relate to this case." Mitchell looks at Brad. "Your cross-examination yesterday pretty much doomed Anderson's career." Then Mitchell turns to me. "And he'd already threatened to arrest you on bogus charges if you didn't back off."

Mitchell pauses and sighs. "We thought Anderson might use

Umberto to plant some evidence or something, but we had no idea it would escalate to violence. We were just going to tape Anderson's phone call and then bust him. But by the time he called, he had already taken you as a hostage. We then made the decision to send Umberto in with a SWAT team backup. Umberto's job was to get you out of harm's way and away from Anderson as soon as possible so the SWAT team could do its job."

"Umberto needs a little practice," I say.

My comment seems to cut through some tension. Mitchell gives me a thin smile. "We should have had officers protecting both you and Brad from the moment we knew that Umberto would be getting an assignment last night," Mitchell continues. He looks at both Brad and me. "For that, I'm incredibly sorry."

Right now, in my depleted emotional state, I'm starting to feel sorry for Mitchell. Sure, he's been a hard-nosed prosecutor—make that a jerk—throughout this case. But he's only doing his job.

"I've sued people for less," says Brad.

"I'm sure you have," says Mitchell.

Then the corner of Brad's mouth curls into a small smile. "You did what you thought was right," he says. "And Leslie survived. And from the sound of things, we owe a huge debt to Umberto."

"I'll give him your thanks," says Mitchell.

"Now, about Tara's case," says Brad, always the negotiator, always looking to move in for the kill when he has the advantage. "After all this, can't we just plead her out as a juvenile?"

I turn my attention back to Mitchell. "Actually," he replies, "I did want to talk with you about Tara. Is this the right time?"

Mitchell looks at me, but Brad doesn't bother getting my approval. "Now's as good a time as any," says Brad.

Mitchell draws another deep breath. "Leslie's examination of Tara was masterful," Mitchell says. "And it got me thinking about a possibility I'd never considered before. What if she really *was* covering up for Jamie? It's certainly consistent with the scientific evidence."

I feel a sliver of excitement tingle up my spine. He did say "masterful," didn't he? For his part, Brad is smart enough to know when he doesn't need to say anything. So he just stands there, arms folded, putting on his best scowl.

"So on cross-examination, I decided to test something. As you know, I made it clear to Tara that if she got off on self-defense, I would prosecute her brother. It was really my own little test, like the way Solomon tested the mothers who were arguing over the baby." Mitchell is looking at Brad who lowers his eyebrows in confusion over the Solomon reference. "Never mind that," says Mitchell.

"My point was this: if Tara really wanted to protect her brother, she would realize that she could no longer argue self-defense. On the other hand, if Tara was the one who shot her stepdad, if she wasn't particularly concerned about protecting her brother, she'd keep arguing self-defense and let him fend for himself later. Sure enough, Tara very cleverly abandoned her self-defense argument. And she's quite a little actress."

Mitchell's strategy was brilliant. Though I would never tell him that. This is just so surreal, lying on my back in a hospital bed, the future of my first murder case being resolved by two men standing on either side of me, discussing the case as casually as two old ladies talking over tea.

"Sounds like an innocent defendant to me," says Brad. His arms are still crossed, but I'll bet he's got goose bumps on those arms. I do on mine. "No sense retrying her."

"Except," says Mitchell, "if we let her off completely, then I would be duty bound to prosecute Jamie."

I can't stand being the spectator any longer. After all, this is *my* case. "One year in a juvenile detention facility," I say. "Let her out during the day to attend school. Sentence her as a juvenile so she gets a clean record at age eighteen."

Mitchell thinks on this for a moment. "I could do that for Tara," he says. "And if she's determined to take her brother's punishment, I don't really have enough evidence to stop her and convict him. But if Jamie did this—even if he did it to protect his mother from being a punching bag—he's got to have some accountability. And this whole family needs help."

Brad frowns at this twist and kicks into argument mode. "You can't convict them both. And putting Jamie in juvenile detention is not the answer, Mitchell. Tara's right about that."

"I know," says Mitchell softly. "I wasn't done."

I give Brad my best "let him finish" look while Mitchell gathers his thoughts.

"The purpose of juvenile court is to rehabilitate, not punish," Mitchell says. "And that's especially true for the youngest defendants." He blows out a breath and looks Brad right in the eyes. "Tara gets her one year, as we discussed. Jamie pleads to accessory after the fact. He gets three years probation, reporting to one of our toughest probation officers every week. Conditions of probation would include family counseling, staying out of trouble at school, and some community service with one of our work release programs."

Brad raises an eyebrow at the last condition but Mitchell, not surprisingly, doesn't flinch. "I don't think a little manual labor would hurt this kid," he says.

Take the deal! I want to scream, thinking mostly of Tara. She keeps her brother out of jail, gets a clean record at age eighteen, and gets counseling in the meantime.

But Brad's rubbing his face. That's usually a good sign, but we don't need cute right now, or even brilliant. We just need the good sense to recognize a blue-light special when we see one.

"Brad," I say. He looks, and I motion for him to bend down so I can whisper in his ear. "If you want a wife waiting at the altar for you, then we're taking this deal."

He nods and stands back up. "My co-counsel's got a good point," he says to Mitchell. "Since we don't technically represent Jamie, we would have to get independent counsel for him to approve this deal."

"Of course," says Mitchell as I shoot Brad a dirty look. "We would also need court approval. I'm just saying that my willingness to plead out Tara would be conditioned on this type of help for Jamie."

"Then as long as we're talking package deals," says Brad, ignoring my exaggerated throat clearing, "let's talk Keisha McFadden."

Oh! I forgot about Keisha! I stop my throat clearing. Maybe Brad actually knows what he's doing. Though technically he shouldn't be conditioning one client's deal on another, I'm not sure those rules apply when it's the commonwealth who tied them together in the first place. In fact, I'm pretty sure that no rules apply when you're negotiating in a hospital room after recovering from the aftermath of an assault that the deputy commonwealth's attorney could have prevented.

"We had a deal on her, Mitchell," Brad continues. "It was a deal negotiated in good faith with Keri Massey, and we want it back."

Mitchell looks down at the floor and shuffles his feet.

"She's got two little boys," I add.

Brad and I wait in silence for a few moments, allowing the pressure to build. My machines *beep* and *swoosh,* hopefully reminding Mitchell of how I got here. How can he say no after everything *he* put us through?

I soon get my answer: he can't. "That's fair," he says, and I relax for the first time since Mitchell entered the room.

"Who's got the champagne?" I ask feebly.

There are a few minutes of small talk about details of the plea. Before Mitchell leaves, he lets me know that some detectives will need to take a statement from me. "I do have one question I wanted to ask you myself," he says.

"Okay."

"During the time Anderson held you hostage, did he ever say anything about Fowler being involved?"

I rewind the tape of last night, searching my brain for even a hint that Fowler might have been part of this. I realize immediately that I have complete power to implicate Fowler and that Anderson is not around to contradict it. But my new faith won't allow me to play the game that way. At least for today, sticking with the truth has been yielding some pretty incredible results.

"No," I say.

"Are you sure?" asks Brad.

"I'm sure."

After Mitchell leaves, Brad closes the door and walks somberly back to my bed. Then he throws his arms in the air. "Yessss!!!" he says. He follows with a pitiful version of an end-zone dance. It makes me laugh, which hurts like mad, so I tell him to stop.

At that moment Bella bursts through the doors, riding on a cloud of cigarette smoke. "You let Mitchell Taylor in here?" she says to Brad.

He spreads his palms: *guilty.*

"I can't believe that jerk had the audacity to show up," says Bella.

"He's just doing his job," I say. *And doing it pretty well.* Maybe I've misjudged Mitchell. Maybe underneath that suit coat, his white shirt isn't as stained and torn and bloodied as I thought. *For man looks at the outward appearance, but the Lord looks at the heart.*

I can tell Bella wants to argue with me, but even Bella is not willing to pick a fight with someone who just survived open-heart surgery.

"You look awful," she says, bending over to give me a kiss.

CHAPTER
NINETY-TWO

I love my mom, but it's impossible to get any rest with her around, even in a hospital room. I finally convince Brad to take Mom out to his house so she can rest a little there. I would have her stay in my duplex, but that place no longer feels safe. Where were my neighbors anyway?

I'm now a day and a half postsurgery and starting to feel human again. Not better, just human. My mom has helped me wash my hair and brush my teeth so that I no longer feel like there should be a guy at the door handing out gas masks. Dr. Reddick is pleased with the results of his slicing and sewing, and though he hasn't let me see the incision yet, he assures me that I'll have one of the smallest scars ever.

And it feels incredibly good to take deep breaths again.

After whisking my mom to his house, Brad returns on Friday afternoon. I had plenty of company this morning—Bella, Sarah, some friends from law school, a few other clients, even the pastor from First Baptist—so I am sleeping when Brad comes back in after lunch. He wakes me with his usual, "Good morning, beautiful." It's a nickname I know I don't deserve right now, but I'll answer to it anyway.

"Hey," I say.

"How're you feeling?"

"Like I just had open-heart surgery."

"Sooner or later," says Brad, "you'll have to quit using that lame excuse and get on with your life."

He's lucky I'm too sore to reach up and hit him.

"Tara's here," he says. "Trish and Jamie are meeting with D. J. Landers, who has already promised me that Jamie will take the plea."

"I don't like that guy," I say.

"That's okay," Brad says. "He doesn't care much for you either."

I'm too tired to smile, and Brad apparently notices. "You sure you're up to this?" he asks.

"You think I want to let you take credit for this deal without me?"

Brad leans in close and gives me a kiss on the cheek. We've figured out a way for him to sit on the side of the bed with me, and he takes his spot. He's holding my hand. As I look up at him, his face is framed by the window behind him, the sun giving him a halo effect.

"Can I ask you a question?" he says.

"Sure."

"When you...um...when you took your step of faith...when you prayed, did you get pretty emotional?"

I twist my head and knit my eyebrows a little. *What's he asking here?* "Brad, I was having heart surgery, getting ready for a controlled heart attack. Yeah, it was pretty emotional."

"But do you think it has to be?" he asks.

"Has to be emotional?"

"Yeah."

I squeeze his hand. *How do I know? Who made me the expert?* "I think different people come to Christ in different ways," I say. "I think the main thing is being sorry for your sins and knowing that Christ is the only way to obtain forgiveness."

He ponders this for a moment. My postsurgical heart is testing its new strength—beating faster with the implications of what he might be asking. Finally, I can stand it no longer. "Why are you asking?"

"Just wondering," he says.

Tara seems appreciative of the deal we've negotiated, though she isn't doing an end-zone dance like Brad did.

"You seem a little subdued," Brad suggests. He's standing in the corner while Tara stands next to my bed, careful not to touch me. "This is a great deal, Tara. And it protects Jamie."

"I know," Tara replies, "but it's still a year in jail."

The girl's got a point. Still, she did shoot her stepdad, even if he was already dead when she pulled the trigger.

"We don't have to take the deal," I say, ignoring the dirty look Brad is firing at me. "We can always try this case again. But even if we win, then they would try Jamie."

"It's a good deal," Tara says without conviction. "I've just got to get used to the thought of spending my senior year in prison."

As we talk through the particulars of the school-release program, Tara seems to warm to the idea. Yet I can tell that underneath her brave exterior, she's really pretty frightened.

"Will there be older women in with me?" she asks.

"No," Brad says. "This is a juvenile detention facility. Everybody will be under eighteen."

"But some of the girls are pretty hard, aren't they?" Tara asks. Her voice has become small as she morphs back into the little girl again.

Brad moves from his corner to the wall opposite Tara. He can now see the fear in her eyes. "You're a tough young lady," he says. "You'll be fine."

Tara looks up at him, and her eyes are moist. "I'm also pretty scared," she says.

I reach my hand up a little, and Tara takes it gingerly. "You're gonna do fine," I say. But the words seems hollow even to me.

"Tara," Brad says. "I don't know where you stand on this whole issue of faith in God. But it's pretty clear to me that somebody's been looking out for you and Leslie through this whole experience, and He's not going to stop now."

Those words, spoken so matter-of-factly, seem to be exactly what

Tara needs to hear. But I know they weren't just for Tara. The realization of what Brad's saying is pooling my own eyes with tears and causing my heart to drum with excitement.

And Brad is not even close to being done.

"The really cool thing, Tara, is that you helped me reach some conclusions about my own faith—or lack of it." Brad steals a quick glance at me, then looks back to her. "I could never buy into this whole Christianity thing—God requiring His Son to die in our place, even though Jesus never did anything wrong. I always thought—how could that be justice?"

Tara is eying Brad intently, working hard to hold the tears at bay.

"Then I watched what you did for Jamie." Brad lowers his voice, the trademark confidence replaced by an endearing humility. "It made me appreciate, for the first time really, the beauty of what Christ did on the cross. And the love that put Him there."

He shrugs, stepping closer. "Well, I didn't mean to preach." He pauses, and I witness the extraordinary sight of Brad Carson searching for words. "I'm your lawyer, Tara, not a priest. It's just that I watched Leslie turn to Christ to get through some pretty tough times. Now I understand why."

Tara purses her lips together but remains silent. She looks at me, then up at Brad. I squeeze her hand and she lets go.

As I watch Tara struggle to be brave, emotions flood over me. Concern for Tara, gratitude at what's happening with Brad. I try to hold it together and remain calm—for Tara's sake.

"Think about it," I say to Tara. "And if you want to talk about it, just let me know."

"I will," she promises.

"Tara," Brad says, his voice thick, as if something has lodged in his throat. "Jamie is lucky to have a sister like you."

CHAPTER NINETY-THREE

Saturday, August 13, six weeks later

We've fooled everyone. They all think we're honeymooning in Europe, but we're actually on the Outer Banks of North Carolina, less than a hundred miles from home. In typical over-the-top fashion, Brad has rented a huge beach house right on the ocean, with a pool and a beautiful back deck where we can watch the waves crash against the shore. It's now Saturday morning, and it's the first time all week that I've gotten out of bed earlier than Brad.

I wish we could stay on our honeymoon forever.

I rise silently from my side of the bed and pad into the bathroom. In a few minutes I'm ready for the day, dressed in shorts, sandals, and a tank top. It's still dark, just a few minutes before dawn. I am anxious to see the sun come up over the ocean.

My plan is to drive a few minutes down the road to the local grocery store and a bagel shop. I will grab two coffees and get Brad a bagel with cream cheese. I will get a yogurt and banana for me from the grocery store, together with a copy of the morning paper. Every morning, Brad has gotten up at dawn, gone for his morning run, then made the trip to the bagel shop and grocery store before I woke up. Today, with only two days left on our scheduled honeymoon, I decided it was my turn.

I arrive at the parking lot of the bagel shop just as the sun is peeking up over the ocean, casting a breathtaking mixture of reds and oranges and yellows across the ocean sky. I hop back in the Jeep and take the nearest route to the ocean, where I park and jump out with my digital camera in hand. Brad has got to see this!

I snap two pictures and admire my handiwork. I've seen post-cards look worse. Then I lean back on the hood of the Jeep and watch the sun paint its ever-changing picture on the eastern horizon. I say a prayer of thanks, realizing that life will never be better than it is right now.

Before I put the camera away, I scroll through the digital pictures that Bella took, reliving the events of last weekend for the hundred and tenth time. There's Brad, looking like a million bucks outside the doors of Bruton Parish. You can hardly tell from the photos that it rained on our wedding day. There's me in my Oleg Cassini dress and rhinestone tiara, ready to walk down the aisle and take my vows with the most handsome man in the civilized world. I notice how perfectly the dress covers my surgical scar, which by the way is healing quite nicely, despite the Outer Banks' sun. I'm beginning to think that Brad might be right—surgical scars are sexy.

I also notice that I'm smiling in the picture. And I'm pretty sure that I haven't stopped since.

There are pictures of some law school friends and my mom and Sarah and Trish. Nikki made an appearance, though Bella managed not to include her in any of the pictures. I wish Tara could have been there. Jamie behaved himself like a prince all day, though he didn't make any of the pictures either. There are no pictures of my dad, who was a no-show, just as I predicted he would be.

"At least," said my mom, "you invited him."

Another no-show was Brandon Matthews. Turns out that my first instincts about Brandon were right after all. About two weeks after the *Girl Next Door* trial concluded, a competitor of the *National Inquisitor* ran a cover story headlined "Jewel Bares All!" In it, Jewel claimed that the show failed to come through on some promises they made to her about future appearances, so she was blowing the whistle. She alleged that the entire first season of *Girl Next Door* was a scam designed to boost ratings for next year's show. Jewel claimed that everything was scripted—Brandon choosing her over the three remaining *Girl Next Door* candidates, Annie leaving brokenhearted, even the lawsuit resulting in Annie getting her own show and Brandon competing for her affections. Jewel claimed that everyone was in on the hoax from the beginning, including Brandon and Annie. To back up Jewel's claims, the tabloid ran several grainy pictures of Brandon and Annie, hand in hand on some out-of-the-way beach in the Bahamas.

Since Brandon was under investigation for perjury at the time of our wedding, I guess he decided to keep a low profile. Besides, if he had shown his face, I'm pretty sure that Brad would have killed him.

I press the Camera button again, and it displays my favorite picture of all. It's a shot of Brad and me leaving the reception in the Hummer limo he rented, with both of us peering out the window. You can see the balloons and streamers all over the inside of the limo, put there by the wedding party because it was too wet to decorate the outside. And Brad has this wonderfully sly smile on his face, like he must be the smartest lawyer in the world to have talked me into marrying him.

But in truth, I know that I'm the lucky one.

I put the camera away and climb back into the Jeep, pick up the coffees and bagel, and then head to the grocery store. I grab my yogurt and banana, all the while sipping on my coffee, then head for the newspapers, prepared to face one of the few actual decisions I will make all day. Each day of the week, Brad would either bring back a copy of *USA Today* or the local paper, the *Virginian-Pilot*. His choice would depend on whether or not the store had received that day's edition of the various papers. One of the things we love about the Outer Banks is that it runs on its own laid-back schedule, oblivious to the rest of the world. It's not unusual for a morning edition of any given paper to hit the stands at about nine or ten o'clock.

Knowing that we already have the weekend edition of *USA Today*, published on Friday, I reach down with my free hand and grab a copy of the *Virginian-Pilot*. It has today's date, so one of my biggest decisions of the day has just been made. Another monumental decision—where we will eat lunch—looms on the horizon.

Honeymoons are awesome.

Waiting in line, I glance down at the front-page headline and almost spit my coffee on the guy in front of me. Stunned, I begin skimming the article and feel like I need to pinch myself to see if I'm dreaming. "Unbelievable," I mumble. "Oh my gosh!"

"Excuse me," says the lady behind me. The checkout clerk is now waiting on me. "Sorry," I say. "You can go ahead." Then I put my nose back in the article.

The article is giving me goose bumps and bringing back a torrent of emotions from the Bannister case. I suddenly feel the need to get out of the checkout line, alone with this article, and focus on every word. I pay for my items and, in a blur of emotion, head toward the Jeep.

I'm reading like mad even as I walk across the parking lot. There are a lot of confidential and unnamed sources cited in the article, and I begin to wonder if the reporter's got his facts straight. But this isn't the *National Inquisitor!* For something this important, the *Virginian-Pilot* would check and double-check, or the defamation lawsuits would begin flying. Besides, there's one sentence that I'm sure is correct. *Attempts to reach Leslie Connors, lead attorney for Tara Bannister, have been unsuccessful.* Brad and I have been operating on strict honeymoon rules. No cell phones and no computers. No communication with the outside world. We even banned watching television, except for DVDs that we check out from the local Blockbuster.

But now the outside world has found us.

CHAPTER NINETY-FOUR

The newspaper is trembling in my hand as I sit in the Jeep staring at the huge headline on the front page, above the fold: "Top Beach Prosecutor Indicted."

In my excitement, I find myself holding my breath. Breathe, Leslie. Relax! I force myself to slow down and go back to the first few paragraphs, carefully devouring every word.

> Virginia Beach, Va.—In a dramatic turn of events Friday afternoon, a special Virginia Beach grand jury issued an indictment for attempted insurance fraud against Commonwealth's Attorney Harlan Fowler. According to sources close to the investigation, the indictment was the culmination of a months-long investigation into the activities of Fowler, who has served as commonwealth's attorney for Virginia Beach for nearly eighteen years.
>
> The indictment was made public in a brief press conference called by Fowler's chief deputy, attorney Mitchell Taylor. Taylor answered only a few questions from the media, then pledged to continue "following the facts wherever they might lead." In a terse press release issued approximately one hour later, Fowler called the indictment a "tragic and misguided power grab from within my office." He vowed to prove his innocence and defend his reputation as a "dedicated and fair prosecutor." Fowler did not return calls from reporters seeking further comment.

The article proceeds to detail the "months-long investigation" of Fowler, which originally focused on his conduct in the prosecution of the child pornography ring swirling around Coach Freddie Barker. Turns out that Mack Strobel, who is quoted liberally in the article, discovered that his law partner, Melvin Phillips, had embezzled more than three hundred thousand dollars from the firm's trust fund. Phillips admitted to Strobel that he had used the money as a bribe to keep from being prosecuted in connection with the Barker pornography ring. Strobel approached Mitchell Taylor with this information and negotiated a secret plea agreement for Phillips to get a light sentence on the embezzlement charge in exchange for his cooperation and grand jury testimony.

The primary target of the grand jury was apparently Fowler, and a secondary target was Detective Anderson, the lead investigator on the Barker case. But the grand jury refused to indict when Phillips could not directly implicate either of the men. Phillips gave his money to Barker, who allegedly said that he was dealing directly with Fowler. But by the time this information came to light nearly a year after the original pornography charges, Barker had already served his time and vanished. Attempts by Mitchell Taylor to obtain information from Barker's lawyer, D. J. Landers, were blocked by the attorney-client privilege. As a result, the special grand jury disbanded without issuing an indictment.

But the man who told me that "justice is a patient suitor" apparently decided that she sometimes needs a little help in wooing an elusive man. As I continue to read about Strobel's elaborate plot, I feel both used and grateful. I fold back the newspaper to page A-11, where the story is continued from the front page. Wow! Strobel stopped at nothing to implicate Fowler, the man who bought and sold justice at the Beach, costing Strobel's firm nearly three hundred thousand.

In his interview with this paper, Strobel said that he always believed part of the bribe paid from the firm's trust fund made it into the hands of Fowler and possibly the hands of Detective Anderson as well. "We couldn't prove it to the special grand jury," said Strobel, "because we couldn't find Barker. But there's no doubt in my mind that Barker was not acting alone. And that's not all. I also believe that Fowler conspired with James Bannister in an attempt to defraud Benefit Financial Insurance Company out of millions of dollars by faking Bannister's death. That scheme was foiled by Bannister's premature and very real death at the hands of his sixteen-year-old stepdaughter."

Ironically, it was Bannister's death that gave Strobel a new opportunity to implicate Fowler. Seizing the opportunity, Strobel ended up representing Bannister's life insurance company, Benefit Financial, and convinced them not to pay Fowler until a thorough investigation could be completed. As part of that investigation, Strobel fed enough information to the defense attorneys for Tara Bannister to convince them that Fowler was somehow implicated in James Bannister's death.

Attempts to reach Leslie Connors, lead attorney for Tara Bannister, have been unsuccessful. Firm spokeswoman Bella Harper said that Connors is out of the country and "definitely not available for comment."

Firm spokeswoman. I smile at the title Bella gave to herself while Brad and I are "out of the country." As I read on, I'm also pretty sure that the "firm spokeswoman" is one of the "confidential sources" who helped the paper piece together this story.

Court records reflect that Connors did try to have Fowler and the attorneys in his office removed from prosecuting the Bannister case based on an alleged conflict of interest. Though the legal brief that accompanied that motion was filed under seal, confidential sources claim that it contained allegations that Fowler was somehow involved in Bannister's death.

This triggered a week of intense pressure on Fowler that threatened his career. After the defense attorneys filed the motion, Strobel met secretly with Fowler and told Fowler that he was prepared to aggravate the situation by going public with allegations that Fowler and Anderson indirectly accepted a bribe in the child pornography case. According to Strobel, Fowler denied any wrongdoing but did seem intrigued by a possible solution suggested by Strobel.

"I told him that I could alleviate all this pressure on him, both in court and out, by having Benefit Financial close its investigation and pay him the full amount of the benefits under the life insurance policy. Harlan could then use that result to demonstrate to the court that there was no basis for saying he was involved in the death of James Bannister."

Strobel said he offered to convince his client to cut this deal so long as Harlan Fowler fulfilled one critical condition. Fowler would be required to pay $200,000 of the insurance proceeds under the table to Strobel as a kickback. Fowler allegedly agreed to this secret deal, and Strobel then convinced Benefit Financial to settle Fowler's insurance claim by paying the full amount under the policy.

According to sources, Strobel secretly alerted Mitchell Taylor to the kickback he had negotiated with Fowler, and Taylor reconvened the special grand jury. On Friday morning, after obtaining court approval for the settlement and receiving the kickback money from Fowler, Strobel walked into the grand jury room and testified about Fowler's complicity in the insurance fraud scheme.

By early afternoon the grand jury had returned an indictment against Fowler for attempted insurance fraud. Later in
the day, Strobel filed a petition for declaratory judgment to
relieve his client, Benefit Financial, from its obligation to pay
Fowler anything under the insurance policy because of the
attempted fraud. Following that court filing, Strobel agreed to
an interview with the *Virginian-Pilot,* supplying the details of
the sting operation that triggered Fowler's indictment.

"It's a page out of the history books," said Strobel. "The
feds never had enough evidence to convict Al Capone for his
organized crime activities, so they got him for tax evasion. I
knew the grand jury didn't have enough evidence to link
Fowler to the bribery, so I helped put his fingerprints on an
insurance fraud scheme."

The unprecedented nature of the case raises several complex ethical issues. Taylor has said he will petition the Virginia
Beach circuit court to appoint a special prosecutor to handle
the case from this point forward, avoiding any alleged conflict
of interest on his part. Fowler has not yet indicated whether he
will voluntarily step down as commonwealth's attorney pending the trial or fight to keep his position.

When informed that legal experts are not aware of any
other cases where a sitting commonwealth's attorney had been
indicted by a grand jury impaneled by a member of his own
staff, Strobel was philosophical. "Harlan loves history and
always wanted to make a little of his own," Strobel said. "But I
don't think this is what he had in mind."

I glance from the main article to a sidebar about Detective Anderson that recites facts from prior stories about his assault on me and
resulting death at the hands of the SWAT team. When I finish I place

the newspaper down and try to process my conflicting emotions. My coffee has gone cold, untouched while I consumed the article with the same intensity I felt during the Bannister trial.

I now fully understand why Anderson and Fowler were so anxious to get Tara's case resolved. They knew Fowler was a beneficiary of Bannister's life insurance. They knew Tara would eventually tell us about the assault in Vegas and show us Barker's video. They knew we would try to link the two cases together, snooping around and asking questions about the Barker case, perhaps uncovering Fowler's gambling debts and Melvin Phillips's bribe. Like cockroaches scampering from the light, Anderson and Fowler wanted a quick plea bargain on Tara's case to keep their illegal activities in the Barker case hidden from scrutiny. From the day Tara walked into my office, they started pulling out all the stops to achieve that result.

But I had no idea that Mitchell Taylor and Mack Strobel were also busy behind the scenes seeking justice. Was anything in this case the way it seemed? My mind races again to Pastor Eric's object lesson. You can't tell a lawyer by his suit, I decide. Mitchell Taylor, true to his word, pursued justice even at the cost of indicting a mentor. Maybe I *will* try his Sunday-school class. And Mack Strobel. I still don't trust him, but at least I'm not the only one he's been double-crossing. I may even need to call my nemesis and, after swallowing hard, thank him for being so cunning. Is the enemy of my enemy my friend?

But there's one lawyer I can trust. Brad Carson. I can't wait to see his reaction to this article, but then I immediately have second thoughts. Our remaining two days of honeymoon oblivion will be shattered. Brad will want to jump right into the middle of it, making phone calls, holding a press conference of his own. The law, that jealous mistress, will strike again and woo away my husband.

Unless...

I go back into the store, grab a shopping cart, and throw every copy of the *Virginian-Pilot* into it. I grab one copy of today's edition of the *Charlotte Observer*, make sure it doesn't cover this same story, and return to my original checkout line. The clerk looks at the stacks of papers and raises an eyebrow.

"Must be something pretty interesting in there," she says.

"You have no idea."

I find an out-of-the-way dumpster and discard all but one copy of the *Virginian-Pilot*, which I slide under the front passenger seat. Brad doesn't need this distraction for the next two days. And I will keep him away from stores and newspaper stands for the rest of the weekend. On the way home from the Outer Banks on Monday, I will pull out the paper and hand it to him as one final present from our honeymoon. But in the meantime, even a hard-charging legal eagle like Brad is entitled to relax a little, spend some time by the ocean, windsurf, and read a good novel. Nope, with all the activities we have scheduled, there's simply no time during the day to deal with a high-profile legal case that will take his focus away from his new bride and relaxation.

And we've already got plans for the nights.

ACKNOWLEDGMENTS

No male author in his right mind would attempt to write a book entirely from the first-person perspective of his female protagonist. So naturally I jumped right in. I never would've tried this without an awesome team of advance readers who helped me understand the elusive subtleties of the female persona and who gleefully pointed out those numerous instances where my male bias snuck in. Many thanks to Rhonda and Rosalyn Singer, Robin Pawling, Lyla Curtis, Cheryl Reccord, Karen Singer, and Helen Spitler for keeping me straight in this regard. In addition, thanks to Michael Garnier and Virginia VanValkenburg for bringing sharp legal minds to the story that kept my fictional lawyers grounded in reality, and to Mary Hartman, the consummate detail person and my cultural guru for all things Tidewater.

And all these folks were just round one. The second round consisted of the best editing team in the business. I am so grateful God has granted me the privilege of working with Dudley Delffs, Laura Wright, and others. To them, and to my advance readers, I am indebted for the good things in this book. The mistakes are evidence that I can slide a few errors past even the most sophisticated efforts of those who try to catch and correct them.

I know you're supposed to say a few nice things about your publisher on this page, but mine is so good I'd do it even if they didn't pay me (don't tell). Thanks to Don Pape for being a relentless champion and enlightened sounding board for my writing. And thanks to Steve Cobb, Brian McGinley, Ginia Hairston, and the rest of the Water-Brook Press team for believing in my stories from the very start.

I've treaded on some pretty sensitive issues in this one—abuse, Tourette's, heart conditions, and representing guilty clients. Thanks to those who opened their own hurts and shared their own challenges to help me navigate these issues with (hopefully) the authenticity and insight they deserve. You know who you are.

And in the last but certainly not least category, praise be to God who has called me to "speak the wisdom of God in a mystery" (1 Corinthians 2:7). What could be more fun?